the Padre Puppets

A JIMMY REDSTONE / ANGELLA MARTINEZ THRILLER

DAVID HARRY

Union Beach LP Publishing

Disclaimer

Everything in this book, except for the establishments frequented by Jimmy and Angella on South Padre Island, are fictional. The words spoken by Steve Hathcock and Griff Mangun (who are real people) are, of course, fictional. South Padre Island has been, and continues to be, a gem, a wonderful place to live, work, and vacation. A true island in the sun with something for everyone.

Copyright

ISBN: 978-09963650-7-9 Trade Paperback
Library of Congress Control Number (LCCN) 2020908241

Published by Union Beach, LP
at Ft. Myers, Florida, USA
Printed in the United States

SOUTH PADRE ISLAND ESTABLISHMENTS FREQUENTED BY JIMMY REDSTONE AND ANGELLA MARTINEZ

Almost Always Available Locksmith
Coastal Current
Hilton Garden Inn
Island Adventure Park

Jack In The Box
Rudy's Bar-B-Q (Pharr)
South Shore Automotive
Ted's

Please stop by and tell them Jimmy and Angella sent you

FROM THE EPIC OF GILGAMESH MYSTICAL KING OF MESOPOTAMIA

To Gilgamesh's beauty Great Ishtar lifted her eyes. "Come, Gilgamesh, be my lover! Give me the taste of your body. Would that you were my husband, and I were your wife! I'd order harnessed for you a chariot of lapis, its wheels of gold and its horns of precious amber. You will drive storm demons--powerful mules! As you enter our House, the Purification Priests will kiss your feet the way they do in Aratta. Kings, rulers, princes will bend down before you. Mountains and lands will bring their yield to you. Your goats will drop triplets, your ewes twins. Even loaded down, your donkey will overtake the mule. Your horses will win fame for their running. Your ox under its yoke will have no rival"

Circa 2000 BCE

ONE

Griff was seated at a back-corner table when we walked into Ted's for our weekly pecan pancake fix. Well, well, well," he called from lips hidden behind a bushy beard. "Angella Martinez! Jimmy Redstone! As I live and breathe! Come here and join me." His normally friendly voice working overtime. Griff, who with his wife, Joni, owned *Paragraphs On Padre,* a wonderful bookstore, about to permanently close, has the height to play Santa in the local Christmas celebrations and the personality to read stories to children during children's hour. "I was hoping you two'd make an appearance. Rumor has it you've been back on island a week."

"A week and a day," Jimmy corrected, as we made our way over to where he was seated, "but who's keeping track?"

Griff stood for a moment as we took our seats. "Just about everyone here on the island. There's a rumor…"

I extended my left hand across the table. "Rumor of our engagement is not overexaggerated. See for yourself." Actually, there were several rumors making the rounds. We were, of course, prepared to talk about our engagement, which was fun. We were not prepared to talk about Jimmy's arrest, or the money missing from an up-island hidden treasure site. And we certainly were not about to discuss any bonus we might have received from our employer, Great Southern Insurance, for locating long missing artwork. Suffice it to say, neither Jimmy nor I needed to work another day in our lives if that is what we decided.

My hand lay dwarfed in Griff's while he examined my finger. "I see an engagement ring that's eye-popping. But what I don't see, I don't see a wedding band. Would I be right to assume you haven't yet tied the knot?"

"I don't prefer to think of being married and knots in the same sentence. But if you're asking whether we eloped, we didn't." What I didn't confess is that elope is exactly what Jimmy had suggested. 'Go to Vegas and make it all legal', is how he put it. But I wanted a more traditional wedding, with my brothers, his mother, maybe his son, and as many friends as we could rustle up. After being together for a decade we could wait a few more months and get it right. When I mentioned putting Tiny, our former Homeland Security handler, on the invite list, Jimmy's eyes rolled backward.

"Angella wants a wedding," Jimmy broke in, "with all the trappings; the family, the friends, the gorgeous dress, bridesmaids, the whole nine yards. Can't say as I blame her. So, that's what we'll do, even though I'd prefer a small quiet affair."

"How about not using *affair* in the same breath as marriage?" I teased.

"Point well taken," Jimmy good-naturedly answered.

"Jimmy, you're sounding very domestic," Griff quipped. "Not exactly your image."

"Images can be scrubbed. I'm working on it." Jimmy glanced in my direction, his lower face displaying the beginnings of a grimace. "With her encouragement, I should add."

Not picking up on Jimmy's discomfort, Griff winked at me. "Any time frame in mind? Or is that an Angella question?"

"That *is* an Angella question. But my thought, for what it's worth," Jimmy volunteered, his face again masked, "I'd say three, four, months."

"You both continuing to work?"

The question, of course, was directed to our rumored bonus. It wasn't in Griff's nature to pry, but nothing passes unnoticed—and undiscussed—on this island. He was simply gathering information to be in a position to answer the myriad of questions store customers were bound to have. Even before the ten o'clock bookstore opening word that we met for breakfast would have reached not only the remote corners of the Island, but also the fishing fleet captains and crews out on the Gulf. Griff was bound to have a steady stream of *browsers* all day.

"Steve!" Griff called, pushing his chair back and standing. "Over here."

I turned to see our mutual friend, Steve Hathcock, coming toward us. Had word of our presence already spread, or was his arrival just plain coincidence? Whichever it was, Steve was most welcome. In fact, we planned on stopping by *Almost Always Available Locksmith,* his place of business, after breakfast. Yesterday, Steve sent us a note after reading an article in the local paper detailing the results of the Federal Court hearing where Jimmy was supposedly caught with millions of dollars. The article quoted the court filings in which Jimmy was charged with illegally digging up a treasure trove of cash from an unspecified location far north on the island. Steve is an acclaimed expert on lost treasures.

"When I first heard about your arrest," Steve's note read, "I thought you found the Pride's treasure. We need to talk—and soon."

"I was just leaving," Griff announced. "Promises to be a busy day and I have a few chores to finish before opening time. I'll leave you three to your business."

"Don't leave on my account," Steve, ever the gentleman, said. "Anything we talk about is open to the public—well at least to friends."

That didn't stop Griff from walking over to pay his bill, and as we found out later, picking up ours as well. On his way out, Griff stopped back at our table. "Either of you want to chew the fat about your plans, wedding or otherwise, you know where to find me."

"So, the rumor's true," Steve commented, his bushy face breaking into a large smile. "I'm pleased for the both of you. So much of what passes as fact on this sand bar is nothing but…but…sand. Slips right through your fingers easy as water."

"But not before it does damage," I replied, mostly to myself.

"Steve," an agitated Jimmy jumped in, "what the hell'd you mean by your note? What in God's name is the Pride treasure anyway? And why would I know where it's located anyway?"

"Those pancakes sure look good, "Steve said as he signaled Karen that he would have the same. "Oh, and a cup of coffee too…" His voice trailed off as a steaming cup was set in front of him. "By the way," he said, blowing across the rim of the cup, "can we get together later? Someplace more private," he added, taking a tentative sip. I am in need of your expertise on a rather delicate situation."

And that's precisely what we did. Our conversation over breakfast was limited to his two businesses, the lock shop and the rare books store. Not that I knew much about old books, but Steve's a natural born storyteller. As he spoke, several of his lost-treasure stories came alive, especially the one where he was on a reality TV show leading an expedition up island to hunt for buried treasure—metal detectors and all. According to him, they would have dug up something valuable if only daylight had lasted a few more hours. But that's the nature of buried treasure stories; if only this would have been, then we would have found the gold.

"Jonah and I have plans to mount an expedition and do it right this time," Steve continued. "We have the coordinates all mapped out and we are in the process of working out the details of our agreement with the landowner. Lucky for us the site is on private property. Either of you interested?"

"I've had enough digging adventures to fill a lifetime," Jimmy calmly replied. "I'll pass if you don't mind."

"Likewise," I added. "I'm going to pass on this one. Wish you luck."

"Understand completely," Steve said, falling silent as he finished the last of his pancakes. He slipped a pencil from his right pocket and a notepad from somewhere under his butt and scribbled something, taking care to block it from view. There wasn't anybody around who could see what he wrote, but still he took precautions. Ripping the sheet from the pad, he carefully folded it once and handed it to Jimmy. "Open this outside. Don't discuss the location, especially not in your car."

On more than one occasion we learned that Steve's advice was always excellent. Problem was, if he was counting on fooling hidden cameras and microphones, not voicing the location was bound to fail. Our car's GPS could easily be tracked, as could our cell phones. Steve knew this full well.

Stepping outside, and squinting in the bright sunshine, Jimmy read the instructions. His face lit up, which was not the response I was prepared for. I was dying to know what the note said, but he quickly refolded it and shoved it in his pocket, nodding toward our car.

Without another word we were off, heading north, up island. A pang of concern formed. In the ten or so years we've been working together, mostly bad things have happened to us up island. That's a bit of an exaggeration, but not by much.

When we drove out of *Ted's* parking lot, Jimmy said, "Turn off your phone. Keep the car GPS off as well."

"Unless you're prepared to break the GPS, I mean physically break it, I think our government has hot-wired the thing."

"Humor me."

"I've already turned my cell off, for all the good that'll do. Don't know how to disable the GPS other than not use it."

"That'll have to do," Jimmy mumbled. He fell silent. We drove north until the road ended just beyond *Island Adventure Park,* where horseback riding on the beach is featured along with zip line rides. The only human in sight was an attractive brunette shepherding a cute little white dog toward a fire-red Prius. The dog's name, according to his harness, was Franco.

Jimmy stepped from the car and proceeded to walk up the sand dune on the west side of the road. I followed behind, taking a moment to remove my shoes and nod a hello to the woman.

Despite my bad memories from this part of the island, this remained my favorite place on earth. The terrain up here, at least in my imagination, makes me believe I'm on the moon. Except for drones and spy satellites, it's secluded, yet close to civilization.

I stood beside Jimmy, our fingers interlocked, lost in my own thoughts. Several minutes went by before I said, "Can we speak now? I assume we're not being monitored out here. What did Steve's note say?"

Jimmy squeezed my hand, but didn't answer. Something was troubling him.

It took another ten minutes or so before he pulled me close and kissed me for a delightfully long time. Pulling away, he said, "You know, Angella, paranoia can eat you alive. I'm very much aware of that, yet…yet…I can't get it out of my head our government's hell bent on putting me, and possibly you, away. I don't know who we pissed off or why, but somebody's got us in the crosshairs and I'm at a loss to get us out."

Jimmy's not a downer kind of guy, nor is he prone to wild conspiracy theories. "What brought this on?" I asked.

"Your mention of Tiny got me thinking. They trapped me digging in that old water well. We were lucky it ended as it did. They knew every move I made even before I made it. We were set up."

"But we came out of it…well, far better than we could have hoped. Returning the Kings Cup to Santiago was a major achievement." Mention of the Kings Cup brought to mind that gorgeous peace of pottery from the tomb of Lord

Aratta, a legendary figure from the Jiroft culture. The Jiroft, as I learned, were centuries before Mesopotamia and the cup proved the Bronze Age began far earlier than previously known.

"Had a lot of help from our Israeli friends. Not so much from our side."

"Is that what triggered your eye roll when I suggested inviting Tiny to the wedding? If that troubles you, then let's not."

"No. Tiny's okay."

"And then what about Ben-Yuval?" Levi Ben-Yuval is a general in the Israel Defense Force and a high official of the Mossad. "You know, Jimmy, he's saved our bacon more than once."

"Keep your friends close, and your enemies closer, seems a good thing to remember. I don't believe Tiny was behind my arrest, need to be cautious is all."

"You think it's not over?"

"Hope so, but afraid not."

Retirement is a touchy subject for Jimmy and when I bring it up, he manages to change the subject. I took a deep breath. "You do know, Jimmy," I began, more tentative than I had planned, "we have the money, and well…you're approaching retirement age. So why don't…"

"Since when's sixty-four over the hill?"

"I didn't say anything about being over the hill…or anything like that. I'm just saying time's right to plan." He remained silent, so I raced on. "I mean, I'd like a life away from getting shot at, arrested, that sort of thing."

"Who's shooting at us?"

"Hopefully, no one. That's my point, let's travel, get away from…from investigations."

"You talking about Steve and his note?"

Jimmy clearly wasn't ready for this discussion, so I changed the subject. "Speaking of Steve, where is he? I thought we drove up here to meet him?"

"He's much too cautious—or should I say suspicious—to meet out in the open like this."

"So why are we here?"

"Enjoying the scenery. Spending time together." Jimmy again pulled me close and whispered in my ear, "I love you."

I don't know why he whispered, but I loved the message. "I love you, as well," I whispered back, pulling him tighter against my body.

TWO

The hour drive from South Padre Island to Harlingen passed more quickly than usual, I guess mainly because we were discussing wedding plans. Angella made plans with her friend Abby to go wedding dress shopping. Abigail Johnson, former chief Pentagon reporter for the *Washington Post* and now the country's most respected national security blogger, lives in Virginia, meaning, we, or at least Angella, would be going east in the near future. Wedding logistics were just beginning, and I resolved to follow Angella's lead.

I pulled off the Interstate, drove along the access road for about a mile, and turned into the theater parking lot.

"We're going to the movies!" Angella shouted, throwing me one of her I-don't-understand-you glances. "I thought we were to meet Steve. Don't get me wrong. This is a nice surprise. But where'd I go wrong?"

"Can't we do both?"

"Three of us sitting in a movie talking over a big bucket of popcorn doesn't make sense. Jimmy, sometimes I don't understand..."

"You can have your own popcorn. Promise."

"Don't you find this a bit...well, strange. Even for Steve."

"Pirates Of The Caribbean," I said, as we approached the entrance. "Dead Men Tell No Tales."

"He trying to tell us something? I mean with the subtitle."

"We'll find out soon enough," I replied. "He just pulled into the lot."

We waited by the ticket booth for Steve to join us. When he did, his first words were, "Glad you both could make it. Movie doesn't begin for fifteen minutes yet, so we can talk in the lobby."

"And just who are you trying to avoid?" I asked. "Movie lobbies may be a new first for exchanging secrets."

"I thought the movie would be appropriate after what I have to tell you. We can sit over there," Steve said, pointing to a cluster of chairs arranged in a semi-circle. "There's no chance of them planting microphones here ahead of time."

Talk about paranoia. This guy's got it in spades.

The moment we were seated Steve leaned in. "Let me give you a little background on what and why I have asked you to meet with me in such a secretive way. Alonzo Alvarez de Pineda was on a mapping expedition when he discovered the Brazos Pass in 1519. He wrote about finding spars and pieces of tattered sails from ships that had wrecked along these shores many years in the past. The reason for so many wrecks is due to shifting sandbars found just offshore. What people don't understand about a barrier island such as SPI is that it is constantly moving. The wind marches sand dunes along at a rate of less than a foot most years, then along comes a storm and frog marches the sand uncovering hidden treasures." Steve paused, lowered his voice even more, then continued. "There's treasure and then there's treasure. It's been said there's a lost treasure ship for every mile of Padre Island beach."

Steve stood, dug his hand deep into a baggy side pocket and extracted a leather pouch. He untied the drawstring and produced a coin of some sort. Thrusting it in my direction, he said, "Here, take it."

"This is odd shaped for a coin," I said. "Is that copper or what?"

"Silver, mostly," Steve quickly replied. "Needs a bit of a polish."

"Never saw a coin so…so ragged looking. Anything but smooth around the edges."

"Short version is in 1794 Congress authorized minting of silver dollar coins. However, Congress didn't authorize the purchase of silver for the coins. The Mint Director, a man by the name of David Rittenhouse, supplied silver from his own personal holdings. Rittenhouse received 1,758 of the coins in payment for his silver. The coins were poorly struck because they only had hand operated coining presses designed for coins half this size."

"That would definitely explain the wavy circumference and lack of uniformity," Angella said. "Is that an eagle? And how many stars?"

"It sure is, Angella. And there are fifteen stars. That face on the other side is an allegorical liberty with long flowing hair. Hence the name, Flowing Hair Dollar."

"So, what's the story?" I asked. "How much can a silver dollar be worth?"

"Another long one. I'll make it short. The Treasury, in an attempt to unify our currency away from each state minting its own money, distributed these silver dollars to foreign governments to spark their interest. At least that's what one source says anyway. This is one of the first ones ever struck and it's believed that several of the same vintage were intercepted by pirates from the Pride and hidden in wine barrels to avoid customs detection."

"The Pride?" Angella asked, handing the coin back to me. "Never heard of it. Bet you're about to tell us it's a sunken ship."

"Nineteenth century sailing ship. Perhaps. Perhaps not. I mean about the sunken part. May still be out there for all I know." His smile was mischievous. "However, two hundred years is a bit long in the tooth, even for a rogue sailing ship." Steve paused for dramatic effect, then added, "But that silver piece you have in your hand is real enough. There are others where that came from."

"You have them?" I asked.

"Depends on the meaning of 'have'."

"Value?"

"Each one, I'd say a million, maybe even more."

"Not so sure, "Angella said, "you should be walking around with even one in your pocket."

"That's why you're here. I need a few things. One is insurance. The other…the other is protection."

"Lock it up."

"Where?"

"Bank vault is one place," I responded. My thought went immediately to the problems I encountered when I put sixty million in a bank vault on the island and the bank was robbed. "I understand why you need insurance."

Angella leaned in close, her voice low. "If you want, I'll call our boss, see if he'll go for a policy. Premium won't be cheap."

"Therein lies the problem."

Now it was my turn. "You said there's more of these. Do we need to insure the others?"

"They're safe for now."

"I have an idea. Are there more than ten of them?"

"At least ten."

"Assuming this coin passes muster, maybe our boss, Jack Silver, will allow you to put this one up to insure ten of the others. You willing to do that?"

"Is there another way? That's a ten percent premium!"

"It's a big risk. I don't even know if Silver will go for it."

"I'm not comfortable. I'd like to explore other ways."

"You can work it out with him. Under my plan it makes no difference what the value really turns out to be. You're putting up like kind. If this coin turns out to be worth a billion dollars, Silver still has ten percent, or whatever his take typically is."

Steve's eyes showed concern. "He'll go for that you think?" he asked, apparently changing his mind. "If he doesn't, I'm screwed big time."

"Can't hurt for trying. Angella, why don't you call Jack, take his temperature?"

"Listen, you two," Steve interrupted, "I'm being followed. They're aware I have this coin and will stop at nothing to get the others. My life's…"

I glanced around and saw no one I considered dangerous. "If they know you have it, " I said, going along for the moment, "why haven't they come for it?"

"They're waiting for me to lead them to the others."

"I don't see anyone lurking about. Do you Angella?"

Before she answered, Steve said, "I gave them the slip. Pulled into the *Jack In The Box* a few blocks up the road and went out the back door. Left my car there. They didn't see me leave so we're safe for now. Phone's off, so they can't track."

Angella stood, pulled out her phone and started for an empty corner of the lobby. Halfway across the wide expanse she turned back to face us. "Why don't the two of you go see the movie. No sense wasting three perfectly good movie tickets. I'll join you when I get it all arranged with Silver."

"Hold up a minute," Steve responded. "There's also several barrels of wine that…that are part of the find. Over two hundred years old. Could still be good."

"The value of old wine," I said, "could be…I really don't know what it could be."

"This wine's from old Persia, Jimmy. Shiraz region to be exact. Said to have been grown and bottled, in this case, put in barrels, on a royal estate. The wine is special."

"Persian wine?" I questioned, having expected its origin to have been French, or possibly Spanish.

"Matter of fact, wine was first made in that part of the world as early as six-thousand years before the birth of Christ

"I assume you don't have any of the wine on your person."

"Heavens no!"

"Okay, then. Let's just concentrate on the coins. We'll do the wine when you produce a…a barrel."

"Wine value could be substantial," Steve answered, tugging at his beard. "In some circles, could even be more valuable than the coins."

"Can't deal with what I can't see. For now, we'll focus on the coins."

THREE

"Over here," I called to Jimmy two hours later as he turned the corner coming back into the lobby area. "Where's Steve?"

"Men's room. You never did join us. What gives?"

"Been on the line with Silver. Trading pictures with him and several of his experts. Even rousted a Lloyds underwriter from a hot game of darts to get this done. That coin, well to say the least, that coin has set off a fire storm. If it's the real thing, and all the experts agree that it has a high probability of being authentic, it's worth over a hundred million. And the Lloyds' guy believes that's low. Took him almost an hour to round up enough Coverholders to form a syndicate with sufficient muscle to handle coverage."

"So, the coins, all nine of them, are insured?"

"Actually ten. Silver insisted they cover his *fee* coin. Didn't try to deal with the wine. The coin didn't take them by surprise. He's been hearing rumors for a while and was waiting for something tangible to surface. Problem is, the insurance folks aren't the only ones who've heard the rumors. Trust me, Steve's not being paranoid about this. This coin and wine story is big in the Mexican cartel world. Silver says the turf war between three of the cartels, the Gulfs who Santiago heads, the Zetas, and the Sinaloas, has never been this bad. The stakes are really high."

"So, tell me what's new down there. They been killing each other for as far back as I recall."

"The Sinaloas are taking advantage of the turmoil and moving east, grabbing territory as they consolidate from the Pacific to the Gulf. Zetas are fighting back. Word is the intruders are gaining momentum."

"That must be why Santiago is backing away from drug trafficking and moving into stolen treasures. He's aligned the Gulfs with the Zetas."

"Who the hell ever knows about Santiago and who he's pals with this month? But it does seem he's losing his grip on the Zetas. The head Zeta, a guy known as Z Forty-Three, went missing a month ago. Z Forty-Four has taken over and intends to make a quick name for himself. He's planning to do so by showing he can run U.S. based operations. What better way of doing that than by capturing a load of highly valuable coins?"

"So, Silver believes the coins are in play?"

"That he does. He's certain the folks following Steve belong to the Zeta cartel."

"What's the plan? If Steve's being followed, we just can't be driving around with this coin."

"We're to remain right here. Silver's sending an armored pickup service."

"Not taking any chances."

"Who's not taking chances?" Steve asked from halfway across the lobby, his ears working better than I would have guessed.

"Our boss," I said, filling him in on the conversations I had with Silver.

"What about the wine?"

"He checked with a wine historian friend of his and according to the expert, depending on the condition, we're maybe talking hundreds of millions. But, for now, until you, or somebody produces a sample, we can't do anything."

"Not good!" Steve replied, his hands opening and closing in agitation.

"What's not good?" Jimmy asked, clearly puzzled at Steve's response.

"There are only three of us who know anything about that wine. Rumors have been floating for over a year and the speculation has become...heated. If Silver spoke to the wrong guy, then I'm in real trouble! Oh, hell, I better warn Kay to get out of our place! If my name's linked to the wine, then the first place they'll look is my house!"

Steve called his wife and I called Lieutenant Carrie Malone of the SPI police department. She wasn't at her desk and I hesitated to leave a message. Rather, I asked her to call me when she could.

"Good news," Steve said a moment later. "Kay's off island visiting her sister and agreed to spend the night. I'll go directly over there from here. How about alerting your cop friends? These people move fast. A lot faster than you might think."

"In process," I said, not elaborating further. If I hadn't known Steve for such a long time, I'd put him down as a paranoid fanatic. But that's not his nature, so this was the time for an ounce of prevention.

"I assume the wine's not there. In your house, I mean."

"Your assumption's positive," Steve said, his mind elsewhere.

"In case something happens, mind telling us where..."

"Case something happens, that wine will be gone for another hundred years," Steve snapped, totally unlike him.

"Sorry, you can tell I'm agitated. I've memorized the coordinates and they stay up here." He touched his head.

"How'd you get them?"

"A lot of research in some old books. And…and a bit of luck. An old article I found buried in a pile of papers I was about to throw out gave me the key. Taken from an interview back during prohibition. That's all I'm going to say about it."

Waiting for the coin pickup, I probed Steve's story about his finding the coordinates. It was obvious he wasn't about to give away anything more of value. But he did say, "As a historian, I naturally went back to see what the witnesses wrote or told people over the years. In the twenties they were dredging the ship channel and found a portion of the *Pride's* hull. Been down there a while. That's what formed the basis of an article I wrote for the *Coastal Current* discussing the demise of the *Pride* and of other sailing ships, such as *La Reine Des Mers*."

"Queen of the Seas," I said, remembering that article. "But…hey…didn't that article point out that the wine barrels they found were blown up?"

"Good memory, Angella. You're right. That's what the history books say. But what I never could find was anything reported about the men who planted those explosives."

"That's important because…?" Jimmy asked.

"Because what if they were under water and separated one or more of the barrels before blowing up the ship?"

"But," I pressed, "the article is careful to point out that observers smelled the wine after the explosion."

"Maybe they blew up a barrel or two. Maybe the observers smelled what they wanted to smell. And just maybe the story's a plant. The original fake news, if you will. That's all lost now."

"If, as you surmise, they *saved* the wine, wouldn't they have brought it to the surface? Someone would have seen it." I was clearly fascinated with Steve's story.

"Angella, that's, of course, what everyone has thought over the years. But…but what if they simply buried it all in the sand?"

"Certainly, a possibility," I said, "but that would do them no good unless they…"

"Unless they came back after prohibition," Steve added.

"Bet you're about to tell us that's what happened," Jimmy interrupted, playing off the large smile now on Steve's face.

"That's what I found in the paper I almost threw out. Names were Harrison Gillis and Tinker Fitch. The paper I found was a page from the 1936 *PI Hotel* ledger. They stayed there twelve days in March. The ledger page contained a note that the men went missing on the twelfth day without paying their bill or cleaning out their room. Police blotter confirms their disappearance, but the case was never solved."

"Your guess," I asked, "as to what happened?"

"Supposition only. They located the wine and were asking around about dredging it up. Perhaps they found someone who did just that. Then that person, or persons, decided not to split it with ole Tinker and Harrison. Sadly, we'll never know."

"But you believe the wine's still down there?"

"Maybe not every barrel, but enough to be worth a lot of money. A whole lot of money."

"And you're positive you know the coordinates?" Jimmy probed, not one to get caught off base.

"I do."

"And you got them how?"

"Can't tell you that. Sorry."

"I'm guessing we wouldn't be having this discussion if you didn't think the coordinates were real," Jimmy said, clearly upset that Steve wouldn't reveal his source.

"Oh, crap! I screwed up!" Steve began pacing frantically until he was almost running in circles.

"What now?" I asked.

"I called Kay! They're monitoring my phone! That's why I had turned it off. Forgot!" He pulled his phone out of his pocket and quickly turned it off. "Too little, too late, I'm afraid."

"Who's *they*?" I asked Steve. "Government?"

"Don't righty know. But my guess is cartel. They don't need no stink'n court orders. Just do it."

FBI doesn't usually need warrants to follow people, so I didn't exactly follow Steve's logic. I swiveled my body to get a better view of the door to the outside. Nothing unusual was happening. No one was watching us and all the people who had come in over the past fifteen or so minutes had proceeded directly to the candy counter and then into the hallways leading to the theaters.

"Oh," Steve said, apparently observing me scan the front doors, "they won't come inside. Not if it's who I think they are. At least not in daylight when it's occupied. These are night crawlers."

I changed my mind about leaving a message for Lt. Malone and redialed her number. I was just starting to provide the details when she came on the line. I filled her in on what little I knew, then handed Steve the phone to bring her up to speed on the rest. The call ended without me speaking to Malone further.

A few minutes later I received a one-word text from her. "Gracias." That was her way of acknowledging we were dealing with a cartel.

"So how was the movie?" I asked while we waited for the messenger service.

"Not the best in the series, I'm afraid," Steve answered from across the lobby, his head down, apparently lost in his own world. I had been certain he wouldn't even hear the question, let alone bother to answer. Agitation, at least on the surface, was uncharacteristic of him. Yet, here he was, acting as if the apocalypse had begun.

Before I could ask him to explain, two uniformed women came through the front doors. One paused by the door and the other continued toward us. They both carried weapons, and from their chunky appearances they both were wearing Kevlar vests.

"You Angella?" the woman closest to me asked, her voice soft, her mouth and eyes set hard.

"I am," I replied.

"You have a package for us?"

"Not exactly a package," I said, as I retrieved the pouch with the flowing hair coin. "There's a valuable coin in there."

"Take it out."

I did so and held it in my hand. The woman produced her cell phone, snapped a photo of each side, studied her work, then forwarded the images onto someone at the other end of the line. "Be a moment. If the coin passes muster, I'll take it off your hands. Sure is an unusual shape for a coin. That from our country?"

"One of the very first ever minted," Hathcock replied, seeming reluctant to part with it.

We waited in silence for less than a minute. "Okay, I can take that coin now. I suggest you remain in here for a while. There is…is always the possibility of trouble outside. There's a car out there with two men inside watching the building. Police were notified, so they should be gone by now. But don't chance it."

"And if they're not?" Jimmy asked, joining the conversation. Steve remained across the lobby, head still down. But, if previous experience is any guide, he was listening to every word.

"If they're not," the guard assured us, "we'll deal with them. Driver's armed, and we have a fourth in the back."

"Shouldn't you wait in here until the locals arrive?" Jimmy asked. "Less chance for…"

"Can't. Schedule to keep," the woman answered, her eyes hard set again. "This is what we're trained for. Marines taught me to be prepared. Got this covered."

Jimmy threw a salute. A cross between something official and mockery. "Been working the valley most of my life. If the locals are not out there by now, they've been bought," he told the guard. "Means the watchers are serious—deadly serious. They've been following that coin and…"

Before Jimmy could finish, the guard turned and retreated toward the door. Turning to me, Jimmy said, "Once that coin goes inside that armored truck it's essentially lost to the bad guys. If the coin's the target, they'll make their move quickly."

"So?" I asked, pulling out my phone in anticipation of what Jimmy wanted me to do. I waited for his instructions to alert either the feds or the state. I didn't know which he was more comfortable with.

"Alert Contentus. State can get on scene fastest. If the locals aren't already here, we have a problem."

Contentus was Jimmy's old boss at the Texas Rangers. He was still in my Favorites.

A moment later I said to Jimmy, "Rangers are seven minutes out. Locals went to the wrong shopping center. They're five out."

"That's a lifetime," Jimmy said, propelling himself toward the front door, his instinct honed over years of training to run toward danger having taken control. I was directly behind him.

The bright sun light blinded me and all I could see were blurs. I almost bumped into a post and stopped to let my eyes adjust. An unmistakable gunshot rang out. Then, a second followed closely by a third. It sounded like at least two guns, and possibly a third.

"Get down!" Jimmy said from somewhere in front and below me.

Below me? Oh, my God, Jimmy's been hit and he's down!

I forgot we walked up several steps from the parking area before buying our tickets. My concern eased slightly. Another shot was fired.

Slowly, my vision returned, and with it I saw Jimmy on the bottom step. Sitting or lying was yet unclear. The armored truck was directly in front of him, casting a shadow in our direction. Two guards lay face down on the ground within that shadow. As my vision improved, I could make out that they were the two woman who came inside the theatre for the coin. They had both been shot before they even made it to the van.

Jimmy motioned me to get down, just as two men came around the side of the van heading toward the fallen bodies. The guard we spoke to earlier rolled onto her side and reached for her gun. Before she could draw her weapon, the man closest to her fired a bullet into her face. The second man put a bullet into the back of the other guard's head. Both of the assailants looked directly at Jimmy and me. The second guy raised his gun and pointed it straight at my face.

"*Déjalos!*" the first man yelled, reaching down and pulling the leather pouch from the lifeless fingers of the dead messenger. "*Lo tengo, ven!*"

Both men then quickly disappeared around the truck. Jimmy was instantly up and racing toward the closest messenger. He slid the woman's weapon from her now open holster and ran after the shooters. I was just behind Jimmy as we came out from behind the truck.

The shooters climbed into a black Mercedes SUV at the same instant the driver's side window of the armored truck rolled down. A man's voice from inside the truck shouted, "Stop!"

The second robber turned and pointed his gun toward the open truck window.

A shot sounded.

Jimmy was down on the ground directly in front of me.

The SUV, its tires screeching, quickly gathered speed and tore out of the lot.

My heart was pumping hard and my body shook uncontrollably as I bent down over Jimmy's prone body.

FOUR

"Three dead bodies is big news, even for South Texas," Lt. Contentus said, stepping out of a state-owned helicopter. "Do we have identification of the two messengers?"

"We do, sir," I said, moving forward to shake hands with the man who runs the Texas Rangers; the man who has always treated Jimmy fairly.

"Knock off the formality, Angella. You and Jimmy are civilians now. Miller will do nicely. Another six months and I'll be joining you in retirement. Speaking of Jimmy, how's he doing?"

"As well as can be expected. The messenger service is calling him a hero for saving the life of their guard. I think Jimmy's reliving the Bad Man Tex shooting and all the trauma that came with that…that incident."

"More than a mere incident, Angella. Ballistics were against him on that one. Jimmy shot the man in cold blood. I can't imagine him having any problem with this one."

"Maybe not legal problems, but certainly internal. He hasn't said much since the shooting. Not even to me."

Contentus looked concerned. "It's not every day one shoots and kills the head hombre of a major cartel. Forty-Four was scheduled to take over the Zetas next month. That'll cause a ripple down there for sure. Far's I know, Jimmy wasn't hit. That's the good news."

"Thank goodness for that! His training took over. He fired and dove for the ground. May have hit his chin, but he didn't say. They could'a shot both of us when they shot the two messengers, but he told the other one, one of the two who got away, not to. Told him to leave us."

"I heard about that. You'll have to identify the two you saw. I understand the dead guy killed one of the messengers."

"Shot her right in front of us. Name's Maria Guterella, former Marine and…and just engaged last week to be married. That's her fiancé over there," I said, pointing to a man sitting with his head bent forward staring absently at the ground. "He's a mechanic. Works not far from here."

"You have any idea why they spared you? Have anything to do with that…that insurance deal with the Pirate?"

Recovering the long-lost Pirate for the Great American Insurance Company is what our bonus was based on. "Don't see any connection."

"Didn't you have some involvement with Santiago in that deal?"

This guy gets around. "Not for the Pirate, but…"

"But what?" Contentus pressed hard, sensing a thread to follow.

"Just that we did recover the Kings Cup. I think he may have sold it to some Iranian for a huge profit. Not sure of that part, though."

Contentus studied me a moment, obviously deciding I had nothing further of value for him at this point. "So, where's Jimmy?" he asked.

"Don't know. Your folks isolated him immediately. State police gave chase, but the SUV had a good four, five-minute lead."

"For those guys that's an eternity. They're dug in somewhere close, be in Mexico by morning. We've closed the border crossings, but that means nothing."

"Harlingen police never did arrive. What's up with that?"

"My unofficial take, and this is only me speaking, I'd put my money on the dispatcher being on the payroll. Sent them to the wrong place. Been happening up and down the river. So, tell me about that coin. Must be something special."

I filled Contentus in on what Steve told us and what little I was able to gather from the Internet while waiting for Jimmy to be released.

Contentus listened to what I said, but his eyes were busy taking in the crime scene as the coroner's truck slowly made its way across the parking lot, coming to a stop midway between the three bodies, placing it nose-to-nose with the armored truck. He looked up; his eyes narrowed as if something was troubling him. "Listen, Angella. Do me a big favor. Don't mention the coin to the press. I don't want to start a beach stampede for hidden treasure. And for God's sake don't breathe a word about the wine. We'll have our hands full with this mess as it is. Governor is about to land and there'll be a news conference. Fox and CNN are already in a battle to get exclusives." The lieutenant glanced down at his cell phone, then continued, "Car's been found about fifteen miles from here. Place called the *Valley Outlet Mall.* No idea where the perps disappeared to from there. Doubt if they stole a car. That would make it too easy for us to track them. My money's on someone picking them up. We'll check surveillance, but my guess it'll show nothing. You ready to give a statement?"

"Whenever," I replied, trying to keep up with moving targets.

"Guillimo'll be here in a few minutes. I'll ask him to interview you first, let you get out of here."

Johnny Guillimo is the Texas Ranger who replaced Jimmy as Contentus' go-to guy. Not an easy guy to get close to, but over the years he's picked Jimmy's brain enough times that he owes us. I didn't expect a hard time from him. "Appreciate that."

"He's down here working the Zetas fentanyl trade. They're setting up labs to convert the pure chemical for street use. Many of those labs are on our side of the river. Costs them about three thousand a kilo. Street value's over a million. Supports a lot of infrastructure."

"Still coming from China?" I asked, wondering if I was missing something.

"China is the main supplier of the synthetic opioid base chemical. Cartels love it because there's no growing season, no land to cultivate, no crops for the government to burn. All they require is cash, vast amounts of cash, and that's where that coin comes in. Zetas are in a war with the Sinaloas, and cash is king." Contentus' phone buzzed again. This time he said, "Gotta go. Mayor wants me at his side while he explains to the press why his officers were directed to the wrong shopping center."

"What will you say?"

"I have no speaking part. Simply creating a veneer of credibility along with the police chief and Highway Patrol Captain. The heat'll shift to the governor when he arrives in…" Contentus checked his watch. "…in twenty minutes."

"Any chance of catching dinner?" I ventured, anticipating Jimmy would appreciate a little time with his former boss—and long-time mentor. "Or at least a quick beer? I know Jimmy would love to catch up."

"Depends."

"On what?"

"On his report. On what his role is in all this."

"He has no role."

"He shot and killed a man. That's a role."

"Saved the guard's life, that's what he did."

"That's your story, Angella. We'll see if that's the way ballistics lines up." Contentus' sudden shift away from Jimmy made me believe he had heard something. He moved past me and hurried over to the makeshift tent the police set up as a base of operations. From the looks of things, they planned to be here a while.

Contentus' doubts puzzled me. My phone sounded before I could wrestle that thought to earth. It was my friend Abigail Johnson, owner of an Internet newsletter appropriately called, *Abby's World*, specializing in terrorist activities around the world. Abby won several Pulitzer Prizes while at the Washington Post. "Angella," she began immediately, "what the hell'd you get yourself into now? Your name just popped up. And Jimmy! He shot the Zetas' next in command! I was doing an in-depth on Forty-Four and I can vouch for him being one bad hombre. Among a lot of bad hombres, I should add. What the hell happened?"

I can't talk about the coins or the wine, so what can I tell her? I asked myself. "A client gave us a valuable asset to insure and Silver called an armored messenger service to pick it up. Zetas killed two of the guards and was about to shoot a third when Jimmy shot the guy you're calling Forty-Four. I don't know if it's really Forty-Four, or some other guy. In fact, that's all I know."

Abby was silent a long moment, apparently digesting what I just told her. "Angella," she finally said, her tone friendly, but firm, "don't play me. What the hell kind of valuable asset you lugging around requires an armored car? And why at a theatre and not at the client's house? "

"I'm not at liberty...off the record?"

"Off the record. Now what the hell's going on?"

"I wish I knew."

"Who's gagging you?"

"Lieutenant Contentus of the Texas..."

"I know Miller well. Tell you what, give me all you know, and I won't publish without his consent."

"He'll not give it."

"You'd be surprised what information I can trade. Now what do you have?"

"Can I trust you? Sorry, but...but I don't want to be burnt in this."

"I'm probably the only person you *can* trust. Jimmy aside."

I proceeded to tell Abby about Hathcock and his stories of treasures, lost and found. When I finished, she said, "I don't know much about the coin and I'm thinking it doesn't factor in with the Zetas, not yet anyway. But that wine's another story altogether. Rumor's been circulating at high levels about ceramic wine casks, not barrels, but casks, holding the key to regime change in Iran. My sources tell me the wine casks are, or soon will be, in the possession of the heir to the Persian Kingdom. At the right time he will produce the casks and reclaim Persia from the revolution. I've also heard stories about that wine being lost under the ocean."

"Under the Gulf," I corrected.

"What's the difference? Anyway, let's focus on that coin for a moment. The name of the game in Mexico right now is territory. Territory's held with money flowing from street-ready fentanyl. But before you have fentanyl to sell you need to buy the base chemical from China. That takes big money. Real big money. That coin, and ones like it, infuses big money quick. The coins are exponential in relation to building territory. You get in their way, they cut your head off. No questions asked."

"I don't have any more coins."

"You and I know that. The Zetas don't. And beside that—"

"What?"

"I've said enough."

"No, what?"

"Jimmy killed one of their leaders. It's now personal."

"You're saying?"

"I'm only saying be careful. No one is immune to their violence. Those folks have no regard for human life."

Unfortunately, I just witnessed the gruesome reality of that statement. How easy it had been for the two men, neither with their faces covered, to fire bullets into the heads of two women. Their facial expressions hadn't changed, nor had their eyes. Sociopaths to the core. "Thanks for the warning, Abby," I managed.

"Hey, on a lighter note, how're the wedding plans coming?"

"Working on it. Jimmy's excited. He's pretending not to be, but he is. That reminds me, I have to schedule time with you. Check your calendar and we'll get it done."

"I'm thinking of visiting you two. A little time on that gorgeous beach of yours will do wonders. How about week after next?"

"Works for me."

"Call me if you want to talk," Abby said before hanging up.

I went back to the theater and was about to go inside when I spotted a familiar person walking briskly toward me. "Merry!" I called. "Merry Ayers! What the…what're you doing here?" Merry was our SPI lawyer and was the last person I would have expected to see in Harlingen.

"See those cameras over there?" She answered, pointing in the direction of several TV trucks, their antenna bridges fully extended, people moving in all directions.

I nodded.

"Well, Angella, your picture's been all over the news for the last two hours. One channel has you shooting two guards. Another has Jimmy doing the shooting. They can't even agree on who you work for. Great Southern Insurance or Homeland Security. One, believe this or not, even has Jimmy still being a Texas Ranger. Makes a better story. Cartel meets Texas Ranger. Texas Ranger wins. Shootout at the O. K. Corral kind of thing. Thought I'd better get myself on out here just in case."

"In case of what? Hey, don't get me wrong, I appreciate you coming, but it's…it's not like I've been arrested, don't exactly need a lawyer. Not yet anyway."

"Everybody can use a friend. Forget the friend stuff. I'm your lawyer. That way, anything you tell me is in confidence."

"I have nothing…"

"You never know what you know…or have. Just say nothing to anyone without me present. Okay?"

"If you say so."

"I say so. And no press interviews. None! Not even off the record with that Abby friend of yours." Merry paused, studied my face a moment then said, "Say it's not true. Tell me you didn't…"

"I did. Just hung up. Don't worry, it's off the record. I trust her."

"I hope it's off the record. What's rung can't be unrung. But no more. Now, where's Jimmy. According to several of the more reliable reporters he shot at least one person. I need to be there with him. He has a way of..." She looked around as if hoping to see Jimmy. "...of getting himself in more trouble than he needs to be in."

I pointed to the tent where I last saw him. "He only shot..."

"Stop! What you tell me about what you saw may not be privileged. Better to get it from him directly." She threw me her car keys. "Car's around the corner. Blue Honda. You can sit in there and stay cooler than out here. I'll be back soon as I can. Talk to no one."

I paced back and forth in front of the theater for several minutes before deciding to take Ayers up on her generous, and very welcome offer. I turned the corner and then it dawned on me why I headed for the theater in the first place. It was to find Steve. The last I saw him was when we rushed out of the theater in pursuit of the messengers. I thought he remained inside. I trotted up the steps, opened the door and walked in. The lobby was empty and most of the lights were off. A janitor sweeping in the corner, called out, "We're closed. Police closed us down. Lady, you need to leave now."

"Sorry," I called back. "Is there anyone left in here?"

"Only person here is myself. Be leaving soon's I finish up here."

"No one in the bathrooms?"

"Listen, lady, I said no one's here. That means, no one's here. Now please leave."

"Sorry," I called again and turned to leave. That's when I spotted a piece of white paper on the leather chair we were sitting in. It was a locksmith business card bearing Steve's name. I turned it over and found a number written on the back. I slipped the card in my pocket and headed toward the blue Honda.

FIVE

"FBI's taken over the investigation." Ayers informed me seventy-five minutes later. I had just dozed off when she tapped on the window of her car before opening the door and sliding in behind the wheel.

"You keep Jimmy from incriminating himself?" I asked, struggling to wake up quickly. I thought back over recent events and recalled dialing the number Steve had written on his card. An electronic rendition of his wife Kay's voice encouraged me to leave a message, which I did. So far, no call back.

"Did what I could," lawyer Ayers answered. "But truth is, I was all but tossed out. Some big guy said Jimmy wasn't a subject of any criminal wrongdoing, at least not for his actions in the parking lot. They maintain he's simply a fact witness, and my services wouldn't be required."

"Did you see him? Is he injured?"

"Hate to say this, Angella, but I was refused access. There's not much I can do at this point. Truth is, I believe they know *exactly* what happened in that parking lot. If not, they'd have you in custody as well. Hey, what's that on your lap?"

I must have fallen asleep before putting my wedding planning book back in my bag. I had been passing the time by working on the invite list. *Sister Jamie, My Mom, My Dad, Brother Mikael, Brother Juan, Abby, Ayers, Lt. Carrie Malone?,*

Jimmy's son Lester, Jimmy's Mother, Lt. Contentus, Tiny???, Ben-Yuval??

"I see my name there. How nice of you to include me."

I quickly glanced down to see if I had put a question mark beside her name as I had intended to do. Thankfully, I had not. "Big guy, you say? How big?"

"Big. Seven foot. Or very close to it. Short, military style haircut."

"Hear a name?"

"Did not."

"From around here, or did he fly in?"

"Said something about being in Houston when he heard the news. Only…only he arrived in the same van as the FBI Director. And I know for certain the director came from DC. He said as much."

That Tiny would lie about where he had come from didn't surprise me. It was his nature to lie, to tell half-truths, to misdirect. That's what high-ranking spooks do. He was our handler, but I often think Jimmy and I are still alive despite him, not because of him. But, then again, in the world in which he operates, lying keeps him alive. And hopefully that extends to all the agents he runs.

"You know who it is?"

"Good guess."

"Said to tell you to wait in your car, they would be finished soon."

So, he knows I'm here and exactly where to find me. Why am I surprised?

"Oh. One more thought. It may not be Jimmy's fault, but he did kill a man. And that takes a toll on anyone, Jimmy included."

Except a sociopath.

I grunted something in the affirmative, but knowing Jimmy as I do, killing a man who had just put a bullet in a young woman's brain would not have a lasting effect on him—if it had any effect at all. After all, my partner, I guess I have to now think of him as my fiancé, was a trained Army Ranger. While I can outperform him on a pistol range, I can't hold a candle to his ability to nail a target over two-thousand feet away. His personal best is right at a mile. And from all indications, he hasn't lost that ability. Judging from today, he hasn't lost it at short range either.

Merry put the car in gear. "I'll drop you off at your car if you wish."

"That won't be necessary, but thanks. Just assure me again they're not holding Jimmy for the shooting."

"If they were, I wouldn't be here with you, now would I?"

"You certain?"

"As certain as one can be under these conditions."

"What conditions?

"DEA, FBI, Texas Rangers, the Governor. You name it. This is high profile. Even the President's weighed in. Three dead in a Texas border town, nothing's going to be easy. The cable networks are badgering for interviews. Time to lay low. It's a dark night. Please allow me to drive you to your car."

"With all the police activity and those lights they set up I can't imagine getting into any…any unusual activity."

"Just the same, I'll feel better if I drop you."

"If you insist," I reluctantly agreed. The walk was what I needed to clear my head. I decided to take that walk after she dropped me. "Car's around front. In the middle."

"I know. It's the only car on that side of the lot."

"How long you think they'll keep that tent city out there?"

"Can't imagine much longer. Those two poor women were both just released to funeral homes. The male appears to be a foreign national, Guxmán, a Zeta, Z Forty-Four to be exact, with all that entails. Mexico's in the mix and given what's been going on between our countries, I'm guessing Mr. Forty-Four, or whatever the hell his name is, will be spending a few days on ice over at the local morgue. Should be thankful we don't treat him as he treats his victims. Feed him to the alligators in the Rio Grande. Even that's too good for him. Just say'n. Well here we are, Angella. Call me if you need anything. Do me a favor and keep your car door locked until Jimmy gets here."

"I will," I replied. "And thanks for coming all the way out to help. Much appreciated. I'll call if we need anything further."

"I'll be visiting my sister in Brownsville. Don't hesitate to call if you need anything."

I transferred from Merry's car to mine, getting in on the driver's side and immediately starting the engine.

"You'd better learn to be more careful," a voice I didn't immediately recognize said from the back seat. "Look *before* you leap. Otherwise your life expectancy is nil."

I still didn't know who was in the car. But I took a modicum of comfort from the fact that had his intention been bad, I would already be a victim. Actually, maybe I was and didn't yet know it. I assessed my chances of pushing the door open and rolling out. Slim to none. He was too close behind me. His hands would be around my neck long before the door was open wide enough to slide through. If he had a knife it would be even worse.

"Put the car in gear and drive forward naturally, just as if you were going home."

"What the hell..."

"Just drive. We'll talk later. Need this to look like you got in and simply drove off, all on your own. That lawyer of yours is lurking over to the side. So, stop talking and concentrate. Cameras are recording your every move. I'm not one of the bad guys." He paused, then added, "Of course that's all in the way you choose to look at it."

"Where'm I going?"

"Head south on seventy-seven. I'll let you know when to get off."

Onto the Interstate I went, fully expecting to exit at Highway one hundred, the road running east to SPI. But instead, we continued south toward Brownsville and Mexico. After what had happened today, crossing the Rio Grande for me would be a death sentence. Not even the Mexican government could protect me from the cartels. Visions of people hanging from bridges, their stomachs cut open, filled my head. I fought to keep my hands from shaking, but I was losing that battle.

The closer we came to Mexico, the worse it was getting. I determined to turn off the limited access highway and take my chances on the city streets. I had no chance once we crossed into Mexico.

There were now only three exits remaining in Texas. I slowly started drifting into the right lane only to find I was blocked by a car in my blind spot moving at the same speed as I was.

I sped up and the car to my right did the same.

Okay then, I'll slow down.

To no avail. The black SUV matched my speed exactly. I glanced to my left and found an identical black SUV keeping pace on that side as well. I was being escorted. How long they had been there I didn't know, but they showed no signs of leaving any time soon. Short of stopping dead in my tracks on the freeway, I had no alternative but to continue south.

My captor, realizing I now knew I was being escorted, said, "Consider them protection. Keep harm away if you will."

"Protection from what? Who the hell are you?"

"All in due course. We've not been followed and that's a positive. Although I didn't think we would be. They know where you live, so there's no need to expose themselves with a tail. Now do exactly as I say."

"Why?"

"Because my job is to keep you alive. And I'm going to do that job whether you make it easy or hard. I prefer easy, but hard will work as well. Your choice."

"You have my attention," I said, playing along for time. This had all the markings of a Tiny run operation, only without the real Tiny. Problem was, I'm a private citizen no longer working for Homeland Security. In theory, Tiny didn't have jurisdiction over my movements. But using Tiny and theory in the same thought was a stretch. I'd been kidnapped. And by whom I had no idea.

"Stay in the center lane until the road bends to the left. The right lane will then disappear." The voice waited for the road to bend, then said, "Okay, make the next right."

I checked the side mirror and noted the SUV was far enough back for me to turn right. As soon as I did, both SUVs fell into line behind me. We were definitely headed toward the border. Ahead, overhead lights were flashing red and the only movement came from cars creeping closer together. It didn't appear as if anyone was going across the bridge anytime soon.

"Now move over to the far-left lane," the guy in the back seat commanded. "When you get to that driveway up there, turn in."

It was slow getting to the driveway and when we finally inched our way through the jam, he said, "Okay. Now drive to the far edge of this parking lot over toward that building, the one marked U.S. Customs and Border Protection." A moment later, he said, "Go slow now. Continue along the side of the building. At the ramp go down."

The two SUVs were no longer in sight.

Halfway down the ramp an overhead door went up. Two armed uniformed Border Protection agents appeared, one on either side of the car. The backseat window rolled down, the agent on the near side bent down, words were exchanged, the agent stood and said, "Very well, Sir. We've been expecting you. Miss, you can park right over there and take the elevator to the third floor."

Nothing further was spoken until we were in the elevator and the door closed. "Sorry for the mystery, Angella, but we believe your car's being monitored. My name's D. William Pickale, Special Agent with the DEA. We have a mess on our hands. Not the mess you might think by the way. Your partner's fast action earlier today might just be the big break we need. Remains to be seen. I hear he's gone from partner to fiancé. Congratulations are in order."

I didn't know whether to thank him or kick him in the leg. I was still upset from that unnecessarily stressful drive down seventy-seven, and angry with all of this. The doors opened before I could fully gather coherent thoughts.

I followed Pickale down a long hallway with windowless doors on either side. The only distinguishing characteristic from one door to the next was a small number glued on at eye level. They were ascending, each by ten.

"I thought this was all Border Patrol," I commented, hoping to get Pickale talking. His deadpan silence was maddening.

"Three floors. Ground being Border Patrol. Second for ICE and third for DEA. And never the three shall twine."

Remembering what it was like when Jimmy and I worked for DHS, I said, "Sounds like nothing has changed. You folks don't play well together."

"Enough said. Especially in here."

He pulled open the door marked 390S and in we went, seemingly joining a party already in progress. The room was dark, and it took a moment for my eyes to adjust. I assumed the S on the door indicated this was a Sensitive Compartmented Information Facility, otherwise referred to as a SCIF, and pronounced 'SKIFF'. The government seems to be using more and more of these rooms lately, probably because of the increasing use of highly sensitive hidden digital transmitters.

I took two steps into the room and a woman came forward holding open a lead bag. Reluctantly, I dropped my cell inside, and she proceeded to run a wand up and down my body, paying particular attention to my breasts and between my legs. The woman whispered, "Sorry, Angella, but bras and panties have become a favorite target for the little buggers. Particularly with the folks we are most concerned about." She asked me to sit and hand her my shoes. A moment later she pronounced me clear and passed them back.

I felt better when I realized Pickale was subjected to the same routine and also cleared. Both screening folks then left the SCIF, closing and locking the door behind them.

"Dill," a dark-complexioned man who I vaguely recognized, said, "please do the honors."

Pickale responded. "Angella, as I told you, my name's D. William Pickale. The D stands for Dillard. My parents had a sense of humor, hence Dill." He laughed, but the room remained silent. "The man who just spoke is Head DEA Administrator, Vincent Lambert. I believe the two of you met a few years back. Sitting next to Mr. Lambert is Virginia Neues. She's the DEA Sector Head for the lower Rio Grande. And the man next…"

"Oh, I know him," I blurted out, startled that Captain Ernest Boyle, the top guy at the SPI Coast Guard Station, was in the room. "Captain Boyle."

"Rear Admiral Boyle," Dill corrected. "He's responsible for the Gulf of Mexico and is based in Key West. What's important for our purposes today, is the Rio Grande."

"Congratulations on your promotion, Admiral," I said, hoping like hell Jimmy and he wouldn't get into it as they had in the past. There had never been any love between the two of them and I couldn't imagine how they could work together going forward.

"Thank you, Angella," Boyle answered, his face revealing nothing. "Look forward to working with you."

"And next to the Admiral we have FBI Counterterrorism Division Head Newton Fairwell."

Fairwell, a hard-faced, no nonsense type, nodded in my direction.

"And finally, Deputy Homeland Secretary Diane Sweet."

"Nice finally meeting you, Angella," Sweet said. "Our time at DHS overlapped a bit. I came on about three months before you resigned. I was sorry to see you go. You and your partner were a real asset. I'm thinking of the Jamaica Phony Pony case where you did the Service a big favor by exposing a deep plant. We owe you a big one for that alone."

"Thank you. Team effort," was all I could manage. This was a good time to follow Jimmy's rules of the road; namely, gather as many facts as possible while saying as little as you can get away with. Thinking of Jimmy, I checked the dark corners of the room hoping he was tucked away in one of them.

No such luck.

Sweet said, "You've had yourself one hell of a day. And it's funny how somethings just seem to workout. As you'll soon learn, we've been working on a major situation for years now. And finally, we're ready to pull the trigger, so to speak, and we still had one piece to get into place. That's where we hit a roadblock." She glanced around. "Some might say we were sabotaged from within. But…but that's a major problem for another day." She again looked around, this time her eyes stopping on Boyle who glared back at her. "Okay, let me go over the background now and we'll drill down later. We have a few videos for you to see." She reached for a small remote and touched a button. "Oh, before we begin, I know you haven't eaten anything for hours. Must be starved. Sorry for that. While we're filling in the background, please help yourself to a sandwich. The chicken salad is excellent."

Until the Deputy Homeland Secretary said anything about food, I had been okay. Immediately, I felt famished and took her up on the offer. When I returned to the table with a plate of chicken salad and a slice of rye bread, a large screen at the front of the room came alive. Immediately, I recognized the outside of the theater, cars filling the spaces and overflowing to the side lot. A moment later a dark SUV pulls into the lot, circles twice, then stops along the far perimeter. Time stamp, 14:57.

If I had access to my phone, I could verify my memory that suggested this was shortly after the time I called Lt. Malone. It was also about the time Steve called Kay.

The tape fast-forwarded to 15:38. The armored messenger truck rolled to a stop directly in front of the theater. Two guards came from the passenger door and proceeded up the steps. My stomach knotted knowing they were both now lying in the morgue.

Fast forward again. This time to 15:51. The guards go back down the steps heading toward their truck. Jimmy appears in the doorway and walks outside with me directly behind him. I don't need to see the remainder; it's seared into my brain. The video only runs for another minute, but it seems a lifetime.

"Is that how you remember it?" Sweet gently asked. "Is there anything you wish to add?"

"I can't believe all that shooting occurred in a minute."

"Less than a minute, actually," DEA Sector Head Neues, said.

It was now a little after eight, less than four hours since this went down and yet the DHS Deputy Secretary had already flown in from DC. *What am I missing here?* "How did you obtain those videos?" I asked, trying to come up to speed. "Don't look like satellite images. At least not the type we used when I was…was with DHS."

Sweet's eyes swept the table before she answered. "Drone images. We…"

Boyle leaned forward, cutting Sweet off. "Normally I'd maintain a need to know. But in this case, in light of what we will be asking you to do as a private citizen, I think it only proper you be read into the full scope of what we have on our plates. Anybody wish to challenge me on this?" Hearing no objections, Boyle continued, "What you are about to hear, and the mission we are about to ask you to perform, is top secret. Your clearance has been renewed, as has your partner's. So, everything you hear, do or say, from this point until I instruct you the mission is over, is top secret. You understand me?"

"And if I refuse the mission?"

"Not an option. Next question?"

"Where's Jimmy?"

"Next question," Boyle said, resorting to his old unlikable self.

Sweet broke the tension. "What the admiral is saying is that what we are about to ask you to do has been vetted at the highest level and is in the nation's best interest. Lives, many lives, are dependent upon what happens in the next forty-eight hours. When you know the scope of the problem, we're certain you'll agree. Fair enough?"

It didn't appear as though I had much of an option in any event, so moving forward seemed the best plan. I nodded in agreement.

"You must voice your agreement, Angella," Boyle said, "to keep all mission details top secret. Once you agree, failure to do so is, as you know, is a crime. Do you agree?"

"Yes, I agree," I answered, knowing I had no real choice.

"Good. Now look at this. You might know this, but the man Jimmy shot was slated to be the next Zeta chief. Man named Carlos Guxmán. Locally known as *Viudo.* Widow-maker. Known by the cartel as Z Forty-Four."

Time stamp 17:11. At first, I didn't realize what I was seeing. The video was dark and bumpy. A street with no sidewalks. A house. One car parked on the street. Steve Hathcock's house. I recognized his lock shop business and the workbench out front.

A car drove down the street. From east to west.

A moment later that same car came back heading east, slowly passing Steve's house.

Time stamp 17:14. Same car slowly going west.

Time stamp 17:31. A fire truck rolls up. Lights and siren active. Two firemen push open the front door and run inside. A third fireman follows them inside. The first two firemen came out ten minutes later, but the third fireman doesn't. The truck leaves.

"What's that about?" I asked, knowing there was a point to the video, but failing to find it.

"SPI put a car on the street for surveillance," Boyle said. "Actually, as a result of your call to Malone. The drive-by knew it. Maybe just a lucky guess. maybe someone inside the department? The bad guys called the fire department and reported a woman trapped in a bedroom with smoke pouring in. You saw the rest. That third party, whoever it was, went in disguised as a firefighter and searched the place when the real firefighters left. We've asked Hathcock to remain where he is, but our folks did a video tour with him and it doesn't appear anything of importance was taken."

"Looking for the wine?" I inquired. "Or the coins?"

"Too early to be certain." Boyle turned to my escort. "Dill, the floor's yours. Lay out the plan.

SIX

"Are you people crazy—or what!" I shouted from across the room. "Let me get this straight! You want Angella to travel into Mexico to see Santiago by herself? No FBI, no DEA, no nothing! In what universe does that make sense?" I faced my old boss Contentus, but my wrath was directed at Tiny. He was speaking for the feds who just informed me of the dumbest operational idea I'd heard in years. And I've heard more than my fair share of dumb ideas.

"Hey, pal," Tiny calmly replied, "I'm only the messenger. Capisci? But here's how I see it. That family massacre over in Sonora has our government working overtime. POTUS sent his top people down here with instructions to, and I quote, 'clean up the frigg'n mess or don't come back!' If that doesn't motivate them, nothing will. Your friend Santiago claims he knows who's behind the ambush and why. And more important, where to find the perps. According to him, his communication channels are monitored and if word gets out he' a snitch then he, his wife—maybe I should say wives—and daughter are as good as dead. He'll only speak to you or Angella. And only in person. This shooting makes it impossible for you to cross the border. You step one foot south of the Rio Grande and you're a dead man."

If I wasn't safe down there neither was Angella. "Where Angella goes, I go! Not negotiable."

"As I said, that's not possible. Your picture is on every cell phone in Mexico. The Zetas want you hanging from a bridge overpass, your private parts stuffed in your mouth. And what the Zetas want, the Zetas get. The man who nails you will be an instant hero."

"So, drop me behind enemy lines. Won't be the first time. A little practice and I'm ready to go."

"Even if you land without killing yourself, we can't risk it."

"Why?" I demanded.

It was Contentus' time to respond. "That's simple. Any covert operation, like flying you over the border, parachuting you in, or even landing you on a beach, requires communication between our governments. And that's not…"

"So. Communicate. Been doing it for years. Those channels are well oiled."

"Too oiled, I'm afraid. The cartels are well dug in. They've infiltrated both sides. Witness what happened earlier. How they even have the police dispatcher in their pocket. That's why I'm involved in this. The cartels routinely know where and what we're doing. They know our every move. Recently, we ran an operation without telling our Mexican counterparts. The Zetas knew our plans down to the minute—and they knew them within minutes of formulation. Corruption runs deep on both sides of the border, funded primarily by opioids."

"So why go for the coins if money's no object?"

Now it was Contentus' turn to fall silent. Tiny leaned back in his chair and watched the Texas Ranger chief walk across the room, apparently content to be off the firing line.

Contentus stopped pacing, turned and said, "Money's always an object. These folks are insatiable. There's always one more politician, one more police department, one more military unit, one more something or other to bribe. There's a war going on, and not just with the government. They're fighting each other for control. Control of the opioid business, as well as for control of the people." He paused, turning away for a moment. When he turned back his face was less flushed, and his tone was back to normal. "Jimmy, you of all people can well appreciate that getting their hands on Hathcock's coins would dramatically move up their time frame. And time is the one commodity no leader can expand—or waste. Someone is always coming for them, so they optimize around the present. Obtaining those coins is their immediate top priority. The future is someone else's problem."

"I don't see what Angella visiting Santiago has to do with the coins. I thought her visit was to help find the killers."

"I misspoke. You're their top priority. Revenge. Second priority is the coins. Because of your proximity to the coins, those priorities have now merged."

Something was off here. It had taken me a while to process what had been troubling me for several minutes. "What you just told me isn't just speculation, is it? We've infiltrated their operations."

Contentus turned to face me. "I'll level with you, Jimmy. Owe you that much. Let's just say, we're well connected. Not to the level Santiago is, but well enough. That's how we knew where and when to place the drones."

"You anticipated that theater robbery?"

"Not exactly as it went down, no. But…but we knew they were on to the coins. Thought they'd follow the armored truck and we'd pick them off at the next stop." Contentus looked down, his jaw clenched, and his fingers rolled into a tight fist, he continued. "This operation got away from us. It simply did. And for that I'm terribly sorry."

Being sorry didn't bring back two young people who had their entire lives ahead of them. They were now lying on undertaker slabs; their bodies being prepared for burial. Being sorry didn't bring back the Zeta I killed. I didn't have to say it. Contentus knew it all too well.

I looked over at Tiny who's nature was not to say anything more than what the recipient could plainly see for him or herself. This time he made an exception. "Let's just say we're heavily embedded and leave it at that."

"Let's get back to Angella," I suggested, still trying to wrap my head around what these two wanted from me. "You're both saying, based on inside knowledge, that she'll be safe visiting Santiago. Why the hell would they allow that?"

This time it was Tiny who took the lead. "For starters, Santiago is a Drug Lord and one of them. They have no idea he's about to turn. Also, they haven't connected Angella to the shooting."

"Surely they know Angella made the call to Silver. They also know she and I are…are a team."

"In their world not a lot of woman team with men. They work like the old American Mafia, keeping their women at home and out of it. They believe Angella was just ordering insurance for Steve. They didn't kill her—or you—because at the time you presented no threat."

"There's been articles recently where women have been involved with…"

"Mostly to sell newspapers," Contentus interrupted. "Sex sells, north and south. Sure, some of the cartels have women. And one or two have risen to the top. But mostly they use women for…for just that, the sex trade. Women beget women for sex slavery. Don't understand it, but it's there. That's not what we're dealing with here."

"You still don't have my permission for Angella to travel in Mexico unescorted."

From across the room, Tiny said, "Sorry to break it to you, my friend, but Angella's not your property and your permission isn't at all required. We're talking to you as a courtesy heads-up."

"Bullshit! You'd not give a heads up to your own mother if it could even remotely compromise an operation! What the hell's this charade about? And where the hell's Angella anyhow?"

They were double teaming me. Now it was Contentus' turn in the cage. "Can't answer that last question. But as to the first, we're planning to divert their attention from Angella by…by having them chase you. Classic distraction."

"Bait!"

"You can look at it that way."

"What other way should I look at it?"

"As protecting your fiancée."

"How does that work?"

"You're up, Tiny," Contentus said, his voice not entirely concealing his skepticism "Way above my pay grade."

The naturally reluctant Tiny, born of a lifetime running covert CIA operations around the world, took his time formulating exactly what he was prepared to say. He was trained to focus on what he wanted me to know and guess at, and on what he didn't want me to stumble upon. It was this latter category that I was most interested in. When he finally spoke, he began with background. "As I said, earlier, capturing you is uppermost on the Zetas' minds. The only thing that trumps that, and barely so, is protecting their delivery channels from the south to the north. There are three main aspects of the channels, namely: transport people, actual supply and buyers."

My patience, what little I have for this sort of briefing, was wearing thin. "Tell me something I don't know," I demanded. I was concerned they were also using her as bait in some half-baked scheme. "This background is a waste of time. Tell me where Angella is and what your real plans are."

"Patience, my boy, patience. Just being certain we're all on the same page. As I was about to say, the transport people are expendable. That source is unlimited. The supply follows the money, so it's not as vulnerable as you might imagine. But if delivery is thrown off, then the buyers get uneasy and go to their backup sources. This has a snowball effect in that if money dries up, the opioid supply dwindles and trouble brews. So...so it behooves each cartel to keep their buyers happy."

Even Contentus was getting antsy with this basic supply chain discussion, and waved his hand in a hurry up motion.

"I'm getting there. So, here's the plan. It's multi-faceted. First, DEA applies pressure to the Zetas' supply line here in Texas. That forces them to move their protection west, which subsequently turns up heat they'll take from the Sinaloas operating in the west. But...but that alone isn't enough because it's baked into their operations already."

"So why bother?"

"Every little bit helps. Given the coin robbery and their shooting of the two guards, if we didn't pressure them, they'd think something was up. And second, we're going to provide close protection for Angella."

"What's that mean?"

"Don't say I never do anything for you. I heard you before and I managed to have the game plan modified. A DEA agent will accompany Angella down to the prison. He can't go inside, but that's not where a problem will occur. Feel better?"

"Should I?"

"Best I can do."

"Not much. But better than her going alone. They know about the wine?"

"They do now. Angella's call to Silver. Actually, not her call, but Silver's follow up calls."

"So, the wine's now in play?"

"I can't imagine it's not."

And I can't imagine what Tiny was doing all the way down here in South Texas talking to me about Angella's drive into Mexico to see Santiago. Even using New Math, it didn't add up. What these two did not say was far more important than what they did say.

SEVEN

Admiral Boyle finished his summary of the operation by saying, "Agent Pickale will be heading up the ground operation on both sides of the border. You two can work out exactly how you prefer that to be scripted." He paused to see if I had any comment. When I remained silent, he went around the table, "Secretary Sweet, anything to add?"

"Angella, I'm sure you're aware we don't need an incident over this. Relations are already strained. Three people dead in Texas captured the President's attention. Coming on top of the slaughter last week of American's down there, his temperature's hot. Won't take much for him to blow. So, at all costs don't add to the problem."

What the hell that meant with respect to what I was supposed to do I had no idea. I've painfully learned over the years that with bureaucrats the less said the better. So, I followed Jimmy's tutelage and said nothing.

"Mr. Lambert, Ms. Neues, any words of wisdom from DEA?"

Lambert glanced to his Sector Head, who said, "We'll communicate through Agent Pickale, thank you."

"And Special Agent Fairwell? FBI have anything to add?"

"To my knowledge, State has not obtained permission for DEA to work in country on this operation. So, agent Pickale will be traveling incognito."

"Nor will they," Deputy Homeland Secretary Sweet answered. "Way too many…shall we say…ears for that. And for that reason, we'll not be flying drones or surveillance of any kind. The communications at the prison is sophisticated and they'd pick us up in an instant."

I was curious. "Then how do the cartels monitor Santiago?"

Boyle responded, "How does Santiago run his cartel from solitary? How does he know everything that's going on? Bribes up and down the government. You either take their money and give them what they want or…or they hang you from a bridge and move on to the next guy." He glanced around. "I see no more questions. We're adjourned here. Good luck, Ms. Martinez and give my best to your…your partner."

"What the hell was that about?" I asked Dill when the room emptied. "I mean you don't need the Homeland Secretary and all that other brass to tell me to go visit Santiago in prison. Overkill."

"Obviously, there's more going on than just this."

"And what would that be, may I ask?"

"If I knew I probably couldn't tell you anyway. But truth is, I don't know."

I didn't for a moment believe Dill. But confronting him wouldn't advance my cause. "Your takeaway?"

"No lethal force—at least on our part. Our government clearly wants no dead bodies left on their soil. It would take away the President's talking points. How we going to do this?"

"Don't understand what you're asking."

"I've been tasked to protect you. To do that I need to be close. Given your engagement, I assume sleeping in the same room is out."

At first, I thought he was joking about sleeping together, but when I realized he wasn't, I stipulated, "You wouldn't be sleeping in my room whether I was engaged or not. Another comment like that and I'll…hey, just keep this on a professional level. Understand?"

"Message received. For the record, I wasn't coming on to you. Just doing my job."

"See that you don't!"

"Do my job?"

"No. Come on to me."

"We'll be traveling in the same car. That's a given. So, can we be brother and sister? You have two brothers. You comfortable with me taking the identity of one of them?"

He made it sound as if he had just thought of the idea, but I knew from experience he hadn't. "Works for me if you can make it work," I conceded.

"Already worked out. These folks work fast." Dill opened the only file folder remaining on the table and brought out a brown sealed envelope. He proceeded to break the seal and extract a blue U.S. Passport and handed it to me. I expected to see the name, Mikael Martinez, my oldest brother who was roughly the same age as Dill. But instead, it was in the name of my middle brother, the McAllen car salesman. "Why Juan and not Mikael? You certainly don't look like a Juan to me."

"Mikael's traveling in Europe."

"He must be celebrating. Just sold his electrical business. Made a few bucks, I understand. But why does that matter? You're going into Mexico. They don't have access to our immigration data base."

"There's evidence someone on our side's on their payroll. Can't take the chance. Me passing as Juan is less problematic than them realizing my travel history data shows I'm in Germany or some such place. One I can argue over. The other's deadly. Just need you to handle one loose end."

"And that is?"

"Call your brother and make certain he's not planning to leave the country."

"Trust me, he's not. I doubt if he even has a passport."

"Can't leave it to chance."

"We never talk. He'll know something's up if I call."

"He know about your engagement?"

"Is there anything you folks don't know about me?"

"Hope not. I assume you haven't told him."

"I haven't. Not yet."

"Do it now. Perfect excuse."

"No date's set."

"Just tell him."

"How about we wait 'till morning? He's either sleeping, or…"

"Or?"

"Stoned."

"Morning it'll be then. Where'd you like to stay tonight?"

"In my own bed."

"That can be arranged, but only if there's an accommodation for me in your apartment. Penthouse I understand."

"For the record, it's not our apartment. It belongs to Great Southern Insurance. We're tenants."

"Call it what you will. I understand it's plush, to say the least."

"Perks of the job. Silver treats us well. Speaking of us, I assume Jimmy'll be there."

"Not a good assumption."

"How in the hell long does it take to obtain a statement?"

"Not my operation. Only thing I know is he won't be on SPI tonight."

"So where will he be?"

"Above my pay grade."

"Tell me he's safe and not…not being held for shooting that…that murderer!"

"He's safe and not being held for any shooting."

"Let me talk to him."

"That I can't do. If we're staying at your place it's time we made our way to the island." Dill turned and started toward the door. I held my ground. "What now?" Dill asked when he realized I wasn't following him.

"I'm still digesting this. You and I are traveling as brother and sister to visit a drug lord in a maximum-security prison in Coahuila, Mexico and you don't think that will raise suspicion?"

"Look, I'm only your escort. From what little I do know, Jimmy insisted on an escort. I drew the short straw, so don't take it out on me. As I understand the situation, you and Jimmy delivered a valuable piece of artwork, actually two pieces, to Santiago not long ago. IRS, in the person of someone named Carmella Schenley Hampton, got her feathers ruffled big time. DEA, doing her bidding, paid a visit on Santiago and one thing led to another. Santiago trusts you and Jimmy. Why I don't know, but he does. And that works for us. Santiago will call you tonight at eleven." He checked his watch. "That's fifteen minutes from now so we need to be out of this building to receive the call. Need I say more?"

One thing I knew from years of working with these folks is that if I had to take a call at eleven, one way or another, I would take that call at eleven. "Okay, let's go." I decided to save the unpleasantness, which was certain to come, for later. Working with Jimmy and his fabulous instincts all these years has spoiled me. I was curious to find out how Dill would respond under pressure

Nothing more was said as he led the way back through the barren halls and proceeded down several flights of steps to the garage. Dill signaled for me to hold up while he opened the passenger door, rummaged through the glove compartment and removed what appeared to be a small iPod which he examined before saying, "Okay to enter."

"What the hell's that thing?" I asked. "Never saw it before."

"Your car was swept for bugs. I understand one was removed. This little puppy lets us know the car is still free of surveillance." He again checked his watch. "Gotta move and get on outside. Prison calls need to be well timed, even for a guy like Santiago who essentially has free rein. We don't want to miss it."

Once outside, Dill instructed, "Just head to the island the way you normally would. We still have four minutes."

"You seem pretty certain Santiago'll call. From my experience I've not known him to be predictable for anything. Stays alive that way."

"This time he's driving the narrative. Our government has something he wants—most likely needs—and he's willing to give up something big."

"And he'll only do that by speaking directly to me?"

"That art you delivered, especially the Kings Cup, was worth a fortune to him. The man has an exaggerated sense of gratitude, maybe trust, for people who deliver as you and Jimmy have. Oh, that reminds me. He demanded both of you visit. You'll have to explain what happened to Jimmy."

My cell rang before I could explore what Dill just told me. But this I did know. He timed that last piece of news so I wouldn't be able to develop it further. Dill was the new Tiny.

"Hello," I said, being as neutral as I could to not tip off Santiago, or, more importantly, the call monitors, that I was expecting the call. "This is Angella."

"Hello, Angella. I was hoping you would answer my call. Are you alone or is your fiancé with you?"

"My, my. News travels fast."

"Joy keeps me up to date. But you know all that."

Santiago was referring to his *local wife*, Joy Malcom, who runs his state-side operations from her condo on South Padre Island. "I haven't seen Joy since…" I was going to say, since I delivered the Kings Cup to her, but thought better of it. IRS could very easily be on the line and there was no percentage in making their job any easier. "…since Jimmy and I left for our vacation."

"You had a nice cruise I understand."

Is there anything this man doesn't know?

"You asked about Jimmy. As a matter of fact, Jimmy's off visiting…family. He drove up to Austin to visit his mother. He wanted to tell her the good news in person. I took the opportunity to drive over to McAllen to tell my brother." Lying to Santiago is always dangerous. Outside of Jimmy, he's perhaps the most perceptive man I've ever known. "As it turns out," I quickly added, "my brother and I are driving back to SPI right now as we speak."

"If this is not a good time to speak, then…"

"He's taking a nap. Long day for him. We can talk."

"What's his name?"

"Juan Martinez."

"You say McAllen. What's he do there?"

"Car sales."

"What dealer? My friends are always in need of good reliable cars."

I glanced over at Dill who gave no indication that he was monitoring the call. "I don't know the name of the place he works. I was at his house."

"When you find out, please let me know so I can send business his way. In fact, Joy's in the market for a new car. How about calling her in the morning with the name?"

"I'll do that, but Juan will be with me for several days on the island."

"No worries. Joy can go look and I'll see your brother gets the credit."

"Okay," I agreed. "I'll call Joy in the morning."

"Call her when your brother wakes up. Joy's a night owl."

"I'll do that."

"That will be nice of you. It's always good doing business with people you can trust. Not much of that going on these days. Hey, my time's almost up and I wanted to personally thank you for the nice work you did for us."

"No need to…"

"There's every need to. Only I must do it in person. That's important to me. Very important."

"When do you have in mind? Jimmy's in Austin and I have my brother…"

"Tomorrow. Bring your brother along if you wish."

"Tomorrow? I'm not…"

"Cross over at around ten and drive to my ranch. You'll have lunch with my wife. You remember my daughter, Patricia May? She'll be there as well. Then you'll be escorted to my quarters. Be back on your island by nightfall. Well, maybe a bit later than that. Long day, but I'm certain you're up to it. I very much look forward to visiting with you and thanking you in person."

"But..."

"There can be no buts. My wife is looking forward to seeing you again, as am I. Good night, Angella. And pleasant dreams."

When the line went dead, Dill said, "Good job, Angella. Like the way you handled Santiago's questions."

"You're not wearing a com. How the hell do you know what he was asking?"

"New imbedded technology. Just out a few months back. Still working out the kinks."

"Imbedded? What? In your chest or something?"

"Ear. Against the tympanic membrane I'm told. Held in there by something the techies call ear glue. But it's more like ear wax. Battery good for a week or so."

"Is it still on? Live?"

"I turned it off."

"How? I didn't see you do anything."

"That's the beauty of this beast. I simply tapped my right ear. It's a natural movement that no one associates with electronics—at least not yet."

"As you heard, he was gathering info on my brother so his folks can check him—you—out."

"That's not really going to be your problem."

"Whose problem is it then?" I asked, working out in my mind the best way to alert Juan. It was hard to do much while driving seventy-five miles an hour down Route Forty-Eight.

"If you're thinking of calling your brother, don't bother."

"I have to warn him. Give him a heads up."

"Bit late for that."

"What the hell's going on?"

"FBI has him in custody. He'll be safely under their control for a few days."

"You folks stop at nothing! Ruin people's lives at will! The hell with this!"

"As I said, it's a bit late for the drama. Get your game face on. It's business from here on out. And, just so you know, your brother's life won't be ruined. He'll be well compensated, and all charges will disappear. Think of it as a forced vacation—with benefits."

"What did they ostensibly arrest him for?"

"Drug possession. What else?"

EIGHT

It took me almost a day to realize I had played right into their hands. Perhaps I knew it from the beginning. Perhaps I was blinded by being separated from Angella and knowing she had been put in great danger. And just perhaps…perhaps it was jealousy that she was on an operation with another man—presumably a younger man closer to her age. Whatever the cause, I was deep in Mexico when it hit me. I was flying naked, no backup, and no way for extraction. Should I be fortunate enough to survive an attack by the Zetas, the American embassy would decline to recognize the fake passport I was traveling under. Tiny had made that clear when he handed me the passport. "You need to know this is an unsanctioned operation. This passport will get you in and out of Mexico, but it's not worth much more than that," were his exact words.

I slipped out of the motel at three-thirty in the morning intending to conceal myself until daylight when I could catch a Lyft to McAllen, rent a car and cross into Mexico. Logistics baffled me for the longest time. The car Tiny assigned to me was in the parking lot and I had the keys. My problem with that car was it most certainly would have been equipped with a tracking device. The last thing I wanted was for our government to track where I was going. Crossing the border in a stolen car can become a major headache, so stealing a car was not a good option.

Luck, or so I thought, was with me when I crossed the motel parking lot heading toward the wooded area just beyond. A cab pulled into the circular drive in front of the door and out tumbled a tipsy couple who managed, to make it inside without doing serious damage to themselves in the process. "McAllen Airport," I said to the driver, having not yet figured out I was doing exactly as Tiny anticipated.

"You go'n to Houston? First flight outta there's five-twenty. Nothing after that for a while."

"Ya. Houston."

"Have to charge you extra. No chance of getting a return fare."

It was only a thirty-minute ride from where we were, so he had no need to charge extra. And it wasn't that business was booming. "Just go, son. I'll make it worth your while."

The airport was not as dead as I thought it would be when we arrived at four-ten. People were already arriving for the Houston flight. The cabbie was wrong. People were waiting for incoming flights as well. Rentals didn't open until six, so I found a seat off in a corner where I could watch the doors to see if I had been followed.

Nothing I could discern. Clean escape.

Sitting there, my thoughts turned to border crossing possibilities. My first inclination was to drive up the river to the Los Ebanos crossing, taking the hand drawn ferry across to Gustavo Diaz Ordaz, Tamaulipas. Two problems with that. First, it didn't open until nine. But DHS has been periodically closing the ferry, so I didn't know how long the wait would be. At three cars for each crossing, it could take all day. Second, I would be a sitting duck going across the river. I decided on the Anzalduas International Bridge up in

Mission. Usually, but not always, faster than the Hidalgo Reynosa crossing.

Negotiating for a car authorized to travel in Mexico proved more time consuming than I remembered it to be. The insurance coverage was mandatory and expensive. Not being on an expense account made it difficult to accept. By seven-ten I was finally on my way, heading west toward the crossing.

I thought about removing the com from my ear. But all things considered, I decided to allow it to remain in place. I was told its battery lasted well over a week, longer, depending on usage which was strictly, at least that's what I was led to believe, under my control. There were four modes; incoming only, outgoing only, two-way, and off. The instructions were to pulse my ear using a thumb or finger with the number of pulses corresponding to the desired mode. It took almost an hour for me to master it.

Four pulses for off was the most difficult. There were two modes for dialing. The easiest was to simply pulse twice for outgoing. At the beep, voice dial the number. In situations where it was unsafe to speak, I could tap out the numbers. Even though I hadn't mastered that feature. I was informed that using the outgoing only mode and not immediately saying or tapping out numbers would connect me to a handler.

"Oh, and one more fact," Tiny added, leaning close as if exchanging top secret information with an informant, "communications are highly encoded and not traceable, even by us."

What could possibly go wrong?

I tapped my right ear three times and heard three beeps. In theory I now had two-way communication. I spoke Angella's cell number, not knowing what to expect.

Within fifteen seconds Tiny came on the line. "What the hell you think you're doing? Where the hell are you?"

"Out and about. I want to speak to Angella."

"Not a chance, my friend. And if you get close to her you'll not only prevent Santiago from providing critical information, you'll be putting Angella's life in great danger. Capisci?"

"The question is, do you understand me? I'm not playing your stupid games. I'm not your puppet!"

"Jimmy, you're wrong on this. I assure you. Go west. Stay away from the Reclusorio Prison. The Zetas are on the lookout!"

"How the hell you know where I am? I thought this thing's not trackable."

"It's not, my friend. But you're in Nuevo León, almost to the town of China."

"If you're not tracking me, then how the hell…"

"They are! A low-rung Sinaloa runner going by the name José picked you up at the bridge. White Ford Escort. Rental. They haven't kidnapped you yet because José was told to follow. Not sure they trust him to get the job done. Others have been dispatched."

"And you didn't bother to let me know?"

"You want to be on your own? Then be on your frigg'n own! You interfere with our operation then we'll act." Tiny paused, then added, "Truth is, Jimmy, as I told you last night, there's very little we can do south of the border. Our hands are tied." The com went silent for several seconds. When Tiny came back he was less abrasive. "Listen, pal. You want to protect Angella, do exactly as I tell you. Head west. Give Monterey and the prison a wide birth and hope the Sinaloas have patience. They want you for ransom. Zetas' want revenge. Classic bargaining chip."

I tapped my right ear four times and the sound went dead. A few miles down the road I turned off the highway just before entering the town of China. I parked beside a small warehouse and watched cars go by. Ten minutes passed and I hadn't seen anything suspicious. But I was famished. I recalled a great pastry shop by the name of *Pastelería Arcoiris* not far ahead. I pulled back onto the road and a few minutes later the bright pink one-story building came into view. I pulled over, taking note of any car that pulled over with me. Again, nothing.

Wouldn't put it past Tiny to manipulate me with a phony 'you're being followed' tactic.

While I was inside a gray Camaro drove slowly down the street, turned the corner just past the bakery and stopped. I couldn't see the car's front doors, so I didn't know if anyone got out. I hadn't carried my Beretta for years, but I naturally patted my side and its empty space sent a shiver down my spine.

First things first. I ordered *huevos revueltos y choizo salchichas* and a large *café.* For good measure, I added a half dozen chocolate *conchas.* If this was going to be my last meal, I wanted to do it right. Taking an empty table in the far back corner, I sipped my coffee and downed two of the wonderful pastries while I waited for the eggs to arrive.

An hour went by and not one suspicious person entered the shop. And no one canvassed the shop from the outside. Whoever was following me was good—and patient. I considered leaving the car and trying to escape on foot, but quickly abandoned the thought. Foot travel in a hostile country made little sense. Public highway was my best avenue for escape. If they wanted me dead, my hiding in this shop wouldn't slow them down even for a moment.

Depending upon timing, Angella wouldn't be nearing Monterey for at least three more hours, assuming she was going directly to the prison. If she wasn't going directly, I couldn't imagine where she would stop. Or why?

If I'm being followed the last thing I want, and I have to agree with Tiny on this, is to lead them to Angella. That's assuming they don't already have Angella in their crosshairs. The original plan was for me to drive northwest, skirting Monterey as far as possible. A decoy leading the predator away from the nest.

What ever happened to free will?

They were playing me, and I was helpless to change the script.

I ate the last of the *conchas,* bought a bottle of water and three rainbow cupcakes for the road. I walked to my car maintaining a carefree attitude. At least that's what I hoped my followers thought. The gray Camaro wasn't beside the building, or anywhere in sight.

I was a good mile out of town before I saw the Camaro. It was in my rearview mirror and coming on fast. Camaros were dominant down here, so I couldn't be certain it was the same one. But for planning purposes I assumed it was.

I sped up.

The Camaro kept pace.

I slowed down.

The Camaro slowed as well.

With no place to pull off the road, I accelerated to eight-five KMH which is slightly over the speed limit. The gray car maintained its distance. I considered speeding to encourage the cops to stop me but thought better of it. Who the hell knew which side *they* were on? And if arrested I would be an even easier target.

When my gas tank fell to a quarter, I began looking for a petrol station which are not as prevalent in Mexico as in the States. I had an hour to find one that was open. Headed west on State Road Four Hundred, intending to swing north on State Road Five and drive toward Los Herrero. By my calculation, I was less than fifteen minutes away.

The State Five road sign came into view and I waited until the last possible moment before twisting the wheel sharply to the right, sending the car's left wheels up off the gravel roadbed. The right wheels struggled for purchase. The rear slipped sideways several feet as I skidded onto the intersecting roadway. Halfway through the maneuver the left side of the car went airborne while the right side skidded even further. I lost control and the car was on its own, teetering first to the right and then back to the left and then back to the right again. I threw my weight against my driver side door trying to persuade the car back to the left. I braced for a rollover and airbag deployment, knowing I'd be lucky to get out alive. Broken bones were a given. Talk about easy pickin's for the Sinaloas—or the Zetas.

I hung on to the steering wheel as the left side of the car continued upward, aware that when it passed the apex there would be no going back. The car continued skidding, balanced as it was on two wheels. I was helpless to control which way it would land, on its wheels or on its roof. The road in front of me that was slowly rotating upside down became stationary and remained that way for what seemed like an eternity. Then the road began turning itself right side up as the engine weight took over, pulling the car down hard onto all four wheels.

The immediate battle was won, but the war was about to be lost. I was in the left lane with an eighteen-wheeler quickly bearing down, horn blaring. There was no possible time to maneuver back into the right lane to avoid a head-on collision.

The truck's horn was deafening as instinct took over and I swerved left in time for my right front bumper to just barely scrape the truck's right fender. My rear fender was not so lucky. The impact lifted the small car and rotated it back toward the truck so that its hood was aiming to pass under the truck's body midway between the wheels.

I must have had the brake pedal mashed to the floor the whole time because the instant the car hit the ground the wheels dug in and slid to a stop. The truck's rear wheels hit the Escort's right headlight and the car bounced away from the truck avoiding full impact, coming to rest on the narrow berm.

My heart was racing, and my fingers were numb. I was in no condition to drive but sitting alone out here wasn't a good option.

The gray car that had been following me was ahead of me on Highway Five. The chased was now the chaser. Similar to the cartoon cat who chases the dog until the dog turns and chases the cat. If I learned anything from those shows, it was that the roles would inevitably reverse.

NINE

Dill was driving my car when we crossed the Gateway International Bridge into Matamoros. We purposely left the apartment late so as to avoid the Brownsville rush hour traffic. Our plan mostly succeeded, and except for the natural slowness of border crossings, all went well. Dill vetoed my suggestion that we use one of the McAllen crossings, arguing that the longer we were in Mexico the more time Santiago's enemies had to monitor us and become comfortable that we were who we claimed to be. I didn't subscribe to that theory and held my thoughts.

Caught up in surprisingly heavy traffic, we slowed down on Highway Twenty and were about a third of the way to Reynosa. At this rate we wouldn't arrive at the ranch until well into the afternoon. Apparently, that was the plan all along because when I mentioned it to Dill he responded, "They're not expecting us until after three. Not a problem." That's not how I interpreted my conversation with Santiago, but Dill, as mission chief, was in control of everything we did, including the clock.

The traffic came to a standstill. "Now what's the problem?" I asked.

"It could be anything from a kidnapping to a guy run out of gas."

"Or just police harassment," I added, not realizing how perceptive that statement would turn out to be.

We inched forward car length by car length. Dill tapped his ear and a moment later asked, his question seemingly directed to the windshield, "What's the holdup along Twenty, east of Reynosa?" A moment later, he told me, "Nothing they know about." After a moment, he added, "Here's a piece of information I'm not supposed to share with you. But what they don't know..." he winked, "Your partner's gone rogue. He was told to act as a decoy and drive west away from where we are going. Instead, he skipped out in the middle of the night and is in Mexico, coming in this direction."

"Where exactly is he?"

"Town called China. Know it?"

"There's a fabulous bakery and breakfast place there. Jimmy loves that little place. Best pastry anywhere."

"Doubt if he rented a car and drove over for a quick breakfast. You have to admit that's extreme, even for him."

Jimmy wasn't on a joy ride. He's on his way to intercept me, but he doesn't know the timeline has changed. "Does that change our plans?" I asked, struggling to keep my voice calm despite the turmoil building inside. "Should we turn back?"

"Right now, we can't turn in any direction. Until instructed otherwise, we press on." We rounded a bend and Dill exclaimed, "Oh, hell!" He tapped his ear. "Here's the problem."

About twenty cars ahead of us the road was blocked by a portable gate with an arm that went up and down. Whether the arm was controlled by friend or foe was impossible to discern. "They're wearing gray-blue uniforms, making them Federal Police," I said after studying the situation a few minutes. "That's marginally better than highway robbers."

"Perhaps," Dill responded, not committing one way or the other. "That our people don't know about it is troubling. I have to assume this is an ad-hoc operation of some sort. Uniforms can be stolen."

"At least they're letting cars through. That's positive."

"We'll see."

"U.S. plates," the uniformed man announced in heavily accented English when it was Dill's turn to roll down his window. Several other uniformed men stood around. No guns were drawn, but hands were at the ready. I was right; these were the uniforms of the National Police. Whether these men belonged in those uniforms or not was another story. *"Pasaportes."*

Dill produced his but signaled for me to wait until asked.

I didn't have to wait very long. *"Su Señora."*

I handed him mine.

"Tu destino?"

"Vamos al rancho de Santiago."

I played my only real card telling him we were visiting Santiago's ranch. May have been wishful thinking, but the shoulders of the man holding our passports went back and his head came up. He stepped over to a much smaller man and the two of them studied the passports a long time. The leader then again approached the car, this time his hand was on the top of his weapon. *"Fuera del carro. Vosotros dos!"* he barked.

I don't know if the name Santiago is a positive or a negative with these guys. The vibes pointed toward the downside. "He wants us both out of the car," I translated, not knowing if Dill understood Spanish.

"Okay. Let's do just as he asks."

I assume headquarters is listening to this exchange, but I really don't know for sure. As soon as we were both standing on the uneven pavement, the shorter one of the officers reached in for the keys. He proceeded to the trunk and threw it open, taking a quick step back as he did so. It appeared as if he expected something to explode in his face. Jimmy often told me stories of dealers' trunks being wired. The endings were never pretty.

I mentally inventoried what I remembered being in the trunk, but I had no idea of what Jimmy might have stashed away. We often drove over to the shooting range in my car and could very easily have forgotten to remove a weapon. Or, more likely, ammunition. It wouldn't have been Jimmy who forgot to remove the ammunition. That would have been more my thing. "The last thing you want, Angella," he cautioned more than once, "is to be rear-ended and have one of those rounds go off. Not likely, but if it happens it won't make for a good day." Sound advice, but sometimes distractions happen. Items fall from duffle bags. Duffle bags are forgotten. And, not to be overlooked, cops plant stuff when it suits their purpose. I wasn't aware of anyone planting anything, but truth is I didn't have any idea what purpose these *cops* had with us.

"Abre esa bolsa!" The short guy barked, continuing to keep his distance from the trunk. He wanted me to open the bag.

As far as I remembered, the only thing in there was a change of clothes for me and Jimmy in case we were caught away from our apartment without warning. In our business, that happened often enough to warrant being prepared. My only hope was that Jimmy didn't have his spare weapon in there. Not likely, but not entirely to be ruled out.

I reached into the trunk with trepidation. First glance indicated that the bag in question, along with Dill's small travel bag, were the only items of possible interest. I opened my bag. One by one I took out items of clothing. A tan blouse, a pair of shorts, two pairs of panties, a bra and a pair of woman's slacks, followed by a man's pair of pants. I looked up and the officer nodded for me to continue. I then produced a man's tee shirt, a man's sport shirt, two pair of men's underwear and two pairs of men's socks, followed by two pairs of women's socks. These items now filled the entire front end of the trunk.

"Quitar la bolsa!"

I lifted the bag as instructed and was surprised to find it was heavy. Something I hadn't seen remained inside, seemingly tucked into a corner.

Jimmy's spare pistol?

The weight was about right. My guess was about two pounds. Maybe a bit more or a bit less.

Or some sort of special ammunition carrier, perhaps lined with lead to prevent an accident?

All kinds of questions flooded my mind. I couldn't imagine how something that large would have escaped my notice and I fought the urge to swing the bag into the face of the guy standing over me.

"Abre la bolsa!"

I carefully reached into the bag and my fingers touched what I guessed to be a leather pouch. Slowly, I lifted the heavy pouch from the box. It was tied closed with a leather thong similar to the one that held Hathcock's bag closed, only much longer.

"Abrelo!" the short guy shouted, clearly impatient with my slow progress.

I continued weighing options, but none of them were promising.

"Do as he says, Angella," Dill advised. "We're on borrowed time here." Dill might have heard something from high command. Or he picked up a vibe from the air. "Give them what they want."

My fingers fumbled with the tight knot and I had to concentrate to work it open.

The tall officer who first spoke to us was standing over me, his weapon now mostly out of his holster. *"Date prisa, no tenemos todo el día!"*

Telling me to hurry up meant they were running out of time. A horn blasted from somewhere back in the traffic line and immediately several others sounded. The officers standing around the car were clearly agitated and jumpy. If this was a rogue operation, which it appeared to be, their superiors would have been informed by now. Their patience was at an end.

The knot finally gave way and the top of the pouch opened revealing what appeared to be a gold bar. I slipped it out, noting that '1 Kg' was stamped in the center. To say I was puzzled is the understatement of the year. Shocked is more accurate. And confused. "What the hell's…"

"Gold bar," Dill said. "One kilo."

I struggled to do the conversion into ounces so I could calculate the value and failed miserably.

"Fue esto declarado?"

How could I have declared this if I hadn't even known it was in the trunk?

"No. *Lo hice…"*

"Say nothing further," Dill broke in. "The hole's deep enough."

"Debes dármelo por falta de declaración."

"Do as he says. We can argue later. They have every right to confiscate the bar. One kilo is a little over $50K, far above the $10K that you're allowed without declaring. Just pray they don't decide to arrest us on money laundering charges."

I slipped the gold bar back into the bag and held it out to the officer.

He took the bag, then said, *"Ahora sal de aquí. Si eres inteligente, te olvidarás de esto."*

The gate went up and Dill sped away down an empty road. "We have our passports and they told us to forget about it means they're rogue. They hit the mother lode with you. They'll pack up and get out of there while the getting's good."

That answered my question as to whether or not Dill speaks the language. "I have no idea how that gold got in the bag, or even who put it there. Or, why?"

"Some mysteries are often better left unsolved," he replied. "No harm, no foul."

"Easy to say. Not your money."

"May not be yours either, if I'm to believe your story."

"Believe what you want," I snapped, remembering he's DEA.

We drove in silence for several minutes when Dill exclaimed, "Oh, hell. Here they come!" He tapped his ear and spoke quickly, telling whoever was listening that two police vehicles were now closing in fast from behind, their blue and red lights flashing.

"Stay calm," Dill said to me, as the first of the two cars pulled out to pass. "Just might be those guys back there closing up shop."

The first car sped past and I expected it to slow and pull us over. Instead, it continued down the road. The second car was now alongside. I again braced myself, expecting to be bumped from the side and run off the road. Or, equally as bad, shot at.

Neither happened. The second car pulled into our lane directly in front of us. Dill put his foot on the brake in preparation for an emergency stop. I crossed my arms over my chest expecting the airbag to explode in my face.

But instead of slowing down, the second car increased its speed in pursuit of the first. It also soon disappeared from sight.

"As I thought," Dill said. "They're getting the hell outta Dodge."

"Except we're fifty thousand lighter. Maybe it's Jimmy's."

"Could have been much worse."

Dill had a point. We could both be lying dead back there, the vultures circling overhead.

We drove in silence for the next several hours. The Santiago ranch was now less than three miles ahead. I had been to his spread many years ago and somehow this felt wrong. On our previous visit I recalled turning off the main road in the center of a small town with several gas stations, two restaurants and even a Burger King. This time, the turn off was several miles beyond a cluster of brightly painted wooden houses, several with boards across their windows. Homes I have no memory of seeing before today. Also, I distinctly recalled turning right, north. This time we turned southwest. Perhaps Santiago moved. Perhaps we are approaching from a different road. Perhaps my agitation is a remnant of our being robbed by the police.

I shared my concern with Dill, who listened quietly. When I finished, he tapped his ear and repeated my words as if reciting a passage from memory for a class play. A few minutes later, he said, "Here's the scoop. When Santiago went to jail, he bought this place so his wife could be closer for visitation purposes. The ranch you remember is one of six spreads he owns, two of them in Texas I might add, is north of here about fifty miles. Your memory's spot on."

"So, it's not my imagination."

"As I said, you're spot on." Dill studied the odometer before announcing, "We're about a mile out." A few minutes later he swung onto a tree-lined dirt road. "My instructions are to follow this road to the house and park in the circular drive. We're to go around back. Lunch is being set out. I don't know about you, Angella, but I'm hungry."

Dill drove slowly, allowing us to absorb our surroundings. I searched for security cameras as we approached the house but saw nothing of interest. Yet it was a certainty we were being observed from several angles.

Unstrapping his seatbelt, Dill commented, "I can't help but think this is an interview, a screening interview, prior to our meeting with Santiago. Is that something his wife would do?"

"From what I know about Santiago's wife, she's not involved in the operations in anyway. He's been very consistent in that over the years. Why change now?"

"Maybe I'm wrong. Maybe lunch is exactly what it appears to be. Simply lunch."

"And I'm the Queen of England," I said, stepping out of the car into the shockingly hot air. Full sun. No wind. Low humidity was the saving factor. But not low enough to prevent sweat from forming on my forehead as we walked to the back of the house. I paused to wipe it dry which meant that Dill turned the corner into the rear yard before me.

"You must be, *Señora* Santiago," I heard him say. "My name's Juan Martinez, Angella's brother."

"Please call me Joy," came the response. "I'm your hostess for today."

There was no mistaking the voice. It clearly belonged to Joy Malcom, the American *wife* of Gulf Cartel Lord Roberto Alterez Santiago, now a life resident of the maximum security Reclusorio Saltillo Prison

TEN

A sign, the only one I had seen for fifteen minutes, proclaimed a Pemex station two kilometers ahead. That gave me a mile to plan how I wanted to handle the fill-up. If I were in their shoes, that's exactly where I'd be waiting. I'd know how far my car had driven and how much fuel the tank holds. I'd also know I couldn't chance passing up this one. From their prospective, I either hit that truck or I would pull in at the Pemex.

The mouse comes to the cat.

Timing is always key in these situations. Throwing off the timing becomes the first order of business. I started that process by continuing past the station. No sign of the gray car. But, then again, there were many places the car could have been concealed.

A quarter mile past the station I slowed in anticipation of turning back and pulled onto the grass shoulder beside the roadbed. I waited for a car to pass; one I hadn't seen behind me a moment earlier. I couldn't determine if that was the gray car, but it also pulled onto the shoulder.

I immediately pressed the accelerator as hard as I could and my rental shot forward, its tires throwing stones and twigs into the windshield of the car behind me. That car also sped up and was no more than twenty feet to my rear when I spun the wheel to the left aiming for a narrow dirt road. The pursuit car continued down the road.

I waited a few minutes and when the car didn't reappear, I turned around and proceeded back to the station. I tapped my ear and said, "Stopping for gas at a Pemex station. Wish me luck."

Silence was returned.

"Lleno de magna, por favor," I said to the attendant who bent down to the driver's side window. I had been in Mexico enough to know the important phrases. And living with Angella for all these years had dramatically improved my vocabulary and pronunciation. *"Tarjetas de crédito?"*

"Solamente efectivo."

Cash was best. The instant my credit card went through Tiny would know exactly where I was. That is, assuming he didn't already know. Problem was, Mexican gas stations didn't accept dollars as a general rule. *"Dólares?"* I asked, holding up a wad of U.S. cash.

"Sí. No Hay Problema."

Now we were getting somewhere.

The equally good news is that no car came into the station while I was filling up. I paid the attendant and added five as a tip.

"Gracias."

We were both happy.

But not for long.

Within thirty seconds of my pulling back onto the highway, the gray Camaro fell in behind me. Again I floored it and was soon doing 135 KPH. The Camaro failed to keep up. Searching the road ahead for a place to turn off and hide proved useless. There simply weren't any decent places to go except straight ahead. I maxed the car out at 150 KPH, about 90 MPH, if my math—and memory—were anywhere near accurate.

The plan was working—until it wasn't.

The first sign that the cat would have the last laugh came when my car misfired, shaking the steering column so violently that my fingers lost contact with the wheel. I quickly reduced speed, but the situation was already out of control. The car slowed on its own and began backfiring without stopping. I glanced in the rear-view mirror and couldn't see the road due to all the blue smoke billowing behind me.

The very polite gas station attendant, the one who had so graciously accepted my dollars—and my tip—had put something other than pure petrol in the tank. Judging by the smell of the fumes, it was most likely diesel. I didn't know if this car would ever run again, but I did know enough to realize it wouldn't be running any time soon.

Adrenalin rush. Flight or fight? Neither was possible, so I resorted to my Air Force Ranger training. Funny how certain things pop into your mind. Such as name, rank, and serial number. Totally useless in this situation, but at least my mind hadn't shut down. Enemy combatant analysis: Number seen? Physical size? Possible number not seen? Weapons: Mine? Theirs? Environmental analysis: Terrain? Weather? Concealment? Communications: Electronics? Smoke or fire signals? Voice? On and on the list went, but any positives eluded me.

Are they waiting for reinforcements?

And how many *theys* are there? Instinct screamed for me to take action sooner rather than later. But to what avail? My terrain evaluation ruled out effective hiding places in this barren stretch of flat, arid land. I continued to remind myself they were the ones who orchestrated the car stoppage at this location, and I was now positioned exactly where they wanted me.

My gut tightened, as if in anticipation of being kicked. They were toying with me, perhaps allowing my adrenalin rush to subside. Their tactics seemingly were working. Out of nowhere a face appeared beside my window; the type of face that communicated trouble long before any words were even spoken. Three tattooed tears streamed downward from the right eye, possibly signifying this man has lost three good friends. Perhaps signifying he murdered three people. In any event, the tears, along with a large red and black scorpion on the left side of his neck, captured my full attention.

Needless to say I was surprised when, in perfect Southern Texas English, he demanded, "Get your hands up where I can see them!"

I did as instructed.

"Have any weapons?"

"No," I answered, forcing my voice to remain as normal as possible.

"Slowly open the door and step out. You're a dead hombre, you make one wrong move."

Again, I did as instructed. The man was built on the squat side, but he commanded the scene and wasn't anybody I was overly inclined to take on.

"Mister Jimmy Redstone," Scorpion Man drawled, "you're a wanted man in these parts. Wanted for the murder of *Viudo*. The Zetas have a big price on your head. I kill you, I become a hero. King around here. You understand me?"

"How could I not?" What I didn't understand was why I was still alive. The scorpion was a strong indication that my captor was a member of the Sinaloa cartel as Tiny had suggested. And the Sinaloas were not known for their leniency. Killing me would, indeed, make Scorpion Man king—in both worlds.

His eyes flared in sudden anger and a knife appeared in his left hand. Judging from his speed and dexterity I had little chance of defending myself if he wanted me dead. "Here's the drill, Redstone. Left to my own, I'd cut your throat. Hang you in town, your balls stuffed in your mouth. But…" He paused for effect. "But…a mutual friend has requested your life be spared. I will honor that request, but only if you behave. One false step and I'll fillet you like a fish."

"What friend?" I asked, hoping to get him talking.

"I've told you enough! Now walk to that car and get in back. The men in there don't speak English and are not disciplined. They want you dead. The one in the front seat with the Z on his neck is a Zeta. He's known as *Manosrápidas.* You killed his cousin. The slightest provocation and…"

"What's stopping him from coming after me?"

"I am."

"Zetas don't take orders from Sinaloas. I'm not…"

"His mother and sister live in Sinaloa territory. He'll follow orders—but only to a point. It won't take much for him to go off. Right now he's calm. Can't promise what tomorrow'll bring. So, do what you wish. Frankly, I win either way." He paused a moment, then added, "I can promise you this with absolute certainty. You will not leave Mexico alive without my help. And that promise you can take to the bank."

From the way he spat out the words, I didn't see much hope of leaving Mexico outside a body bag regardless of what I did. "You have a name? Something you go by." Before the question was fully out of my mouth, I realized I already knew the answer. It had been years, back when I was still with the Texas Rangers, when I saw his face in an operational briefing. This man was University of Texas educated and the last I heard he was the top man in the South West Region cocaine distribution network. His main specialty, however, was enforcement. I hadn't immediately recognized *el Carnicero,* The Butcher, because a recently added scorpion now covered the scar that ran down the side of his neck.

"Some call me *el Carnicero.*"

Not a very funny joke, *el Carnicero* posing as my protector. With him in charge there wouldn't be enough of me remaining to bother with a body bag. And escaping his deadly network of sociopathic killers was wishful thinking.

I studied him a long beat. "I thought you were…"

"Dead." A slight smile, more in the nature of a lip twitch, momentarily appeared on his gruesome face. "As they say, rumors of my demise have been greatly exaggerated."

ELEVEN

"Angella, my dear, you look as though you've seen a ghost." Joy's sweet drawl broke through my shock. "Don't just stand there. Come on, give me a hug."

I dutifully forced myself to walk fully around the corner of the main house and into the gorgeously planted yard. A winding pathway led to a magnificent circular gazebo, framed by blazing yellow azaleas. Joy had shed the nylon warm-up suit she usually wore around the island for a flattering light blue cotton dress. Her hug was less than enthusiastic. Even though her arms were around me, her eyes never left Dill. "So, Angella, I understand this handsome gentleman is your brother?"

"It is," I responded. "Juan Martinez this is Joy Malcom. Joy is..."

"Let's just say I'm Morris' business partner. Hey, any relative of Angella is a friend of mine." She threw her arms open wide. "Don't be shy, Juan. Get over here and give me a big one."

Morris Malcom is the name Santiago goes by, used to go by, when he visited in the States. Joy holds herself out as being married to Morris. As best as Jimmy and I can figure, they have never been married despite their *marriage* being registered in Brownsville. FBI believes Joy heads up Santiago's state side operations, financial as well as logistical. For all the dumb-blonde smoke and good cheer she blows, she's good at what she does. FBI's been trying for years to nail her. So far to no avail.

The hug lasted several beats too long, and when it finally broke Dill's face was flushed. Could have been from the weather, but my money was elsewhere. Joy may have found a live one.

"Come along you two," Joy purred, "must be starving. Lunch is served. Have the best Sangria in the world. Special recipe, concocted by Morris, embellished by me."

Joy was right about the Sangria. It was perfect with the broiled fish and roasted potatoes served by two men, dressed all in black, except for a white pattern woven into their sombreros. I knew the pattern but couldn't place it. Then, while they served dessert in the form of *tres leches,* I finally placed the pattern. Three stylized letters. CDG. Standing for *Cártel del Gulfo.* Santiago was, and still is, lord of CDG.

Dill sat quietly while Joy and I bantered back and forth about this and that. She was careful to avoid the hot button topics, such as missing artwork and dead bodies on the beach that comprised most of our conversations over the past few years. Now she was my new best friend, exchanging tips on travel destinations, as if she and Santiago were about to depart on a world tour. Santiago, serving a life sentence, wasn't about to be traveling any time soon. The topic turned to food and I complimented her on the lightness of the pastry.

"An old Santiago family recipe," she replied. "I'll email you a copy."

How she acquired the Santiago family files I had no idea.

And where was his real wife?

"And you, Juan, what is it exactly you do?"

It took Dill a moment before he realized he was being addressed. Clearly, he wasn't accustomed to being an impersonator. "Oh, sorry. I was lost in thought there for a moment. I sell cars. Up in McAllen."

"What kind?"

"Cars? You mean, what company?"

"Dealership. Which one?"

"Used cars. Private lot."

"What's the best-selling car on your lot?"

Dill studied Joy's face for an instant before answering. "Depends," he said.

"On what?" Joy pressed.

"Depends upon the buyer. Women like Hondas. Men, Fords."

How he knew that tidbit I don't know. But he sounded authoritative. Authoritative enough for her to move on. "How's the market?"

"Credit's easy. That favors new cars. But we're holding our own."

"You say women like Hondas. What year's most popular?"

Malcom's interest in used car sales sent a warning fluttering through my body. She's probing Dill, not the market. "Joy," I began, trying to deflect the conversation. "I can't get over how wonderful this *tres leches* really is. Did you make it yourself? I mean, using the Santiago recipe, or what?"

Drawing her lips tight for an instant to show her annoyance with my interruption, she replied, "Cooking and baking down here is a joint effort. I am, after all, domesticated."

"I didn't mean to imply you're not. I just want to…well, I'd love to make this for Jimmy."

"I'll see to it you receive the recipe, Angella. Now, where were we? Oh, I remember. What's the most popular year for those Honda used car sales?"

"Last year. It's always the previous year."

I didn't know if Dill was being fed information via his earpiece or if he was winging it. I suspected the former.

"You said you live in McAllen. How long you been there?"

Slight pause. "Twelve years."

"And where before that?"

No pretense now. This was an interrogation. Joy was on to Dill not being my brother.

"Edinburg," Dill promptly answered. "And before that, San Antonio."

"You have a Facebook page?"

Oh, shit! My brother's page contains his picture. This isn't going to end well.

"I do," Dill answered as if he had anticipated the question.

Joy stood and glanced around the gazebo. "Oh, now where did my cell go? That little devil is always getting away. Oh, there it is!"

She retrieved it from the serving table, glided back to where we were sitting, fumbled with the screen until she found what she was looking for, and then handed the phone to Dill. "Please, dear sir, bring up your page if you will."

I was tempted to intervene, but the two black clad *servers* were positioned directly behind me. I had to allow this to play itself out.

Dill took the phone, entered a string of numbers, which I assume, he was receiving from his handlers, and a moment later his Facebook page appeared. And to my surprise Dill's picture appeared opposite the name Juan Martinez. My faith in my master's thoroughness was restored.

Joy seemed satisfied that Juan was who he said he was and turned back into the Joy Malcom I knew from the island.

"How's that gorgeous hunk of a man you're living with Angella? I'm so jealous of you, you know. I was really looking forward to, you know, the three of us out here alone. Just good friends doing what good friends do."

With Joy I never knew when she was playing or serious. Either way, I was uncomfortable, but I felt it wise to play along, rather than taking the chance the conversation would refocus on Dill. "I'm certain Jimmy is upset he can't be here. But you do know we're engaged and that..."

"Engaged. Married. Living together. All the same to me. Relationships need not be exclusive. Now do they dear? Juan, what's your take on that?"

"On what?"

"On whether relationships need be exclusive."

"I haven't given it much thought, but I'd vote for exclusive."

"You, Angella. How do you come out?"

"Same as D...my brother."

"Shame," she winked, "you two don't know what you're missing." Joy nodded and the servers moved forward. I braced myself for whatever was coming, not willing to give in without a fight. The man closest to me reached over my shoulder and began clearing the table. As he did so, the knife sheath he wore beneath his black tunic rubbed against my arm. "Silent, but deadly," I heard Jimmy remind me. I remained seated; my hands folded on the table in front of me, ready to move quickly if necessary.

"Let's take a walk. The heat won't be so bad out among the trees. And if it gets too unbearable we can always take a dip."

With Joy in the lead we stepped out of the screened gazebo heading toward a stand of trees that formed the backdrop to a magnificent garden. Bringing up the rear was one of the black-clad servers. Or perhaps a third CDG member, I couldn't be certain.

The *walk* was much longer than I anticipated. We covered a good two miles or more, along what began as a stream and ended with a dam forming a waterfall perfect for rafting. We came upon a rack holding several rafts. Life preservers hung from a line strung between two cypress trees.

"Anyone for a ride?" Joy enquired. "It's not exactly white-water, but it's not a bathtub either."

"No, thanks," I said.

"What about you, Juan? Challenge you to a race. First one down to the bend wins."

"I'm with my sister on this," Dill replied, reluctance in his voice. I had the impression he'd welcome a float down a lazy river in a raft with the seductive Joy Malcom.

Trying to appear cooperative, I made a suggestion. "If you two like, I can go back to the house while you have your race or take a float or whatever. I'm sure your…your server…would be happy to escort me back."

"Oh, don't be silly, Angella. If Juan wants to go rafting, there's no reason for you to leave. How about it, Juan? What's your pleasure?"

"Some other time, perhaps." Dill was now well into his role and playing it well.

"Have it your way. Couple a kill joys. But you two are missing out on a fun experience. Don't say I didn't try. Just being hospitable."

We slowly made our way back to the main house. I walked alone behind Joy and Dill who were lost in conversation. From the looks of it, Joy found a new male interest.

Back at the house, we sat inside a screened in porch and entertained each other with stories from our respective pasts, nothing serious or revealing. Around nine o'clock one of the servers appeared with a large tray holding several cheeses and what appeared to be homemade flat crackers. I recognized the typical *queso blanco*, or white cheese, as well as the Monterey Jack. The third one eluded me.

"That's Manchego," Malcom explained. "Sheep's milk from Spain. Morris' favorite."

"And these…these crackers," Dill asked, having already eaten two of them. "They're so…buttery."

"Another family recipe. Homemade."

"They're excellent!" Dill exclaimed after polishing off a third one. "And that sheep cheese is excellent as well."

"Glad you enjoy," Malcom said, handing me a freshly cut slice.

"I agree. That is good."

"More wine, either of you?" Malcom asked. "I'm ready to call it a night. You folks need an early start in the morning."

Around ten fifteen we were shown to our rooms. Dill's was next to mine on the second floor. I wanted to open the windows and enjoy the scented air that was so wonderful in the garden, but I was told it was prudent to keep the windows closed when the air conditioner was on.

Slightly after three in the morning I woke to a sound from outside. Thinking it only a dream, I adjusted my pillow and closed my eyes, but I heard it again. This time the sound of footsteps was clearly coming from the adjoining room. Dill's room.

Heavy breathing? Joy getting it on with Dill?

That's not what I'd expect from a DEA agent who's here to protect me. But, hey, men will be men.

And Joy will be Joy.

Footsteps moving faster now.

Why's Joy in such a hurry to leave Dill's room?

Off in the distance I heard the pulsating sound of a helicopter engine. The sound quickly grew louder, followed almost at once by the unmistakable pulsing of rotating blades. The copter passed directly over the house, circled once, and then seemingly settled down not far away.

I saw nothing from the window, but I could now clearly hear the pulsating engine and figured it to be on the lawn on the opposite side of the house.

I ran to the door only to find it locked from the outside. Pounding brought no response. I pulled with all the force I could muster, but to no avail. I pounded again. Still nothing.

The engine noise increased in pitch and the whoosh of the blades sped up. I raced back to the window in time to catch a glimpse of the tail rotor at roof level just as it tipped to the right and disappeared. In less than thirty seconds all was calm again, as if nothing had happened.

But it had. I heard it and I saw it. And worse, I did nothing about it.

Back at the door, I alternately shook and pounded it.

"Oh, Angella," Joy's voice broke through the noise I was making, "your door's stuck. Hold a moment and I'll summon help."

I stopped pounding and listened. For what, I don't know.

Within a minute, footsteps approached. "One moment, Angella," Malcom called through the door, "And we'll have this stubborn door open."

I stepped well back, half expecting it to be smashed inward.

I heard a lock turn and saw the doorknob turn. The door opened and in stepped Malcom. She wore her familiar warm-up pants and beach walking shirt. "Oh, my dear woman!" she cried, rushing over to me. "I'm so sorry you got stuck in here. These locks are sometime fussy. Is everything okay?"

"Yes. That…" I was going to say helicopter but decided the less I said the better, "….noise I heard in the next room. What…"

"Oh, goodness, Angella. Your brother…Juan…got so sick we had to send him to the hospital. Must have eaten something bad."

"Hospital? I must go. Be with him."

"You have an appointment with Morris in…" she consulted her phone. "…in four hours. You can't be late. You can go to the hospital after."

"How did you transport him?"

"The only way safe. By medical helicopter. I'm sure you heard it."

The problem was the helicopter I heard, and saw, was a personal one. Two seats at best. Not one that would be used to transport the sick or injured.

"Now try and grab a few more hours sleep, my dear. Morris needs you to be fresh and alert for his meeting. I'll come get you at six-thirty."

Joy closed the door behind her. I suspect I was again locked inside. I didn't check to see, partly because I didn't want to know. But mostly because there was nothing I could do about it anyway.

TWELVE

Needless to say, after my brief encounter with Malcom, I didn't get back to sleep as she suggested. Didn't even try. I hadn't heard from Jimmy and that was more than troubling. Active minds in the middle of the night can be as troubling as they are helpful. Mine was working overtime, one topic to the other and back again. Central to it all was not hearing from my partner—and lover.

And what about Dill? I didn't for a moment believe he took sick in the middle of the night. At least, not without some assistance from Joy and her crew. But what did Malcom have to gain from Dill being carted off?

They know he's an agent. Nothing else makes sense. Home office took care of my brother's Facebook page, but with social media, pictures now pop up everywhere. Maybe on Instagram? Snapchat? What about his dealer's web site? That's the problem with last minute improvisation. There's always a loose end that nails you.

Even assuming they knew Dill was DEA or FBI, they could have just detained him along the way. It was a simple matter to prevent him from entering the prison if that's what their intention was. Helicoptering him out in the middle of the night was overkill.

Unless he's dead!

Alarmed at the thought, I strained my memory trying to recall what I heard just before fully awakening.

Some sound, some voice, anything shedding light on what really had happened in the adjoining bedroom. Other than a few groans I initially thought to be evidence of sexual activity, I conjured up nothing.

Maybe under hypnosis I would remember more?

I shuddered at the thought of the FBI subjecting me to that type of therapy in their never-ending quest to gather information.

A far-off engine broke the silence.

Another helicopter?

Was that good or bad? The engine sound slowly increased in volume and the louder it became, the more car-like it was. Some people can differentiate vehicle makes and even models by the sound, or more technically, the timbre, of its engine. I'm not one of them. But I'm not hearing a truck, I'll take credit for that much.

I showered before falling into bed, but I felt…well, contaminated. I needed hot water flowing over my body. Instead, I quickly finished dressing, and hastily packed my small bag in preparation for whatever awaited on the other side of the door. I was as ready as I was ever going to be.

Pulling the blinds open, I violated my instructions by opening the window. The soft beginnings of daylight coupled with the wonderful fragrance were calming. Colors were barely perceptible, and the hills in the distance were just coming out of the shadows. A Range Rover drove slowly up to the house and stopped almost directly below my window. I leaned forward as far as possible, but I couldn't see who was in the vehicle.

I was startled by a loud knock on the door behind me. "Angella," Malcom's overly friendly voice called, "time to go. Ride's here."

When I yanked my door open, I half expected it to be locked. But this time the door was so smooth I grabbed the wall to prevent myself from falling backward.

"Good morning again, Angella," Malcom cooed, as if nothing had happened in the middle of the night. "I've asked the staff to whip up pecan pancakes. I know how much you enjoy them at *Ted's*. These are almost, but not quite, as good as theirs."

"No thanks. Not hungry."

"I suggest you reconsider. It'll be hours, maybe six or seven, before you'll have the opportunity to get anything to eat after you leave here."

I wanted to get away from her and this place as soon as possible, but Joy's offer made sense since I'd been awake for several hours. "Any word on my brother?"

"I'm afraid I've heard nothing from the hospital. Let's hope no news is good news," she replied. But the look on her face, whether she intended it or not, made it clear Dill was either dead, or she expected him to be dead in the not too distant future. That same look also revealed she knew Dill was not my brother. "Now, how about those pancakes? I'll join you. We can eat in the morning room. That's my favorite place. We have another gorgeous day to enjoy."

I reluctantly follow her down the hall past the room I saw Dill enter. The door was closed, and I forced myself to continue walking. Either it was locked or there was nothing out of the ordinary to see. These folks were professionals.

The morning room was, indeed, delightful, positioned as it was on the east side of the house. A garden outside the full-length glass windows was alive with color. A clearwater fishpond, bisected by a wooden foot bridge, sat in the center of the tranquil tree-lined space. Thankfully, we ate in silence, not something I thought Joy capable of doing.

The pancakes, contrary to Joy's advertisement, were at least as good as *Teds*.

I took my last bite and suddenly became aware of one of the black-clad servers from the night before standing just inside the room. He nodded to Joy. "Afraid it's time for you to go, Angella. Luis will show you to the car." As we stood, she opened her arms for a goodbye hug.

I tried not to betray my agitation when I embraced her and thanked her for her hospitality. In response, she sounded sincere when she told me she looked forward to seeing me back on the Island soon.

"Tell Morris hello for me," she called as I followed Luis from the sunroom. "And please know you're welcome to stay here anytime you're passing through."

I hope Santiago doesn't expect me to visit him more than once?

Luis interrupted before I had time to dwell on that thought. *"Por favor, sígame señorita."* Carrying my bag, he walked briskly through the front corridor and out the front door.

"Oh, wait one more second, Angella," Joy called just before I got to the door, "I need you for one more moment." She pointed to a chair in the hallway. "Please sit over there and take your shoes off."

I hesitated and her eyes took on the hardness I last saw when we negotiated over the Kings Cup a few months back.

Reluctantly, I sat down while she retrieved a large canvas bag from a sideboard. She extracted two foot-looking objects, each with openings on top. They were foot molds of some sort. "Here, slip these on your feet."

"What the..."

"Just do it, Angella. No time for twenty questions!"

"How do you know what size my feet are?"

"Think about it. You've been our guest since yesterday afternoon. Now put them on, stand up and let's see you walk in them. It's like trying on a new pair of shoes."

Indeed, they felt like shoes, but looked like feet, toes and all. The left fit perfectly, but the right one wobbled a little as I walked.

"How do they fit?"

"Right one's slipping."

"Sit. Luis, please fix the problem."

Luis pulled over a small bench and sat in front of me just as a shoe salesman would have. I extended my leg onto his lap and he pulled out leather tabs near the heel causing the mold to contract around my foot.

"Try it now," Joy said, her voice back to being nearly pleasant.

"Feels much better."

"Ok. Luis, give her the shoes."

Luis dutifully went over to the sideboard and this time produced two sneakers, at least size ten, maybe even twelve, and a pair of tan socks to match my slacks. He handed me the socks. I put them on and then he held out the sneakers. I looked at Malcom expectantly.

"Put them on, Angella," she said, her voice still hardened, but a slight smile appeared. "We have a tight schedule to keep. Really tight. Prison time waits for no person." She stood and waited impatiently for me to comply. "Now, again walk around the room to be sure the shoes are okay.

The shoes were heavy, like they were made out of ceramic instead of canvas or cloth. I forced my legs to move properly to keep from toppling over.

"You've got the hang of it, now," Malcom announced a few minutes later. "Luis'll be stopping for fuel along the way. Be sure to practice. Don't want you tripping when you enter the prison."

"Won't they detect..."

"Designed not to. Never have in the past. They only scan down to the calves."

"There's always a first time," I said.

"You better hope that's not your luck. Now get going. Safe travels."

"If Luis is driving," I protested, "what about my car?"

"I'll be driving it back to the island for you. No extra charge.

THIRTEEN

The drive to the prison with Luis was uneventful. He refused to answer any questions and the only time he spoke was when we stopped for fuel and he instructed me to practice walking. *"Practica caminar,"* he repeated several times, as if I hadn't heard, or understood, him the first time.

I walked the perimeter of the station, being careful to avoid the animal droppings that seemed to be the rule rather than the exception. As I walked, Luis kept an eye on his watch. Thinking I was holding him up from his time-oriented appointed rounds I hurried as fast as the heavy shoes would allow over to where he stood in the shade of the only tree in sight. He waved me away, his arm circumscribing a circle. I did another lap around the property.

Halfway around I began to believe this wasn't about me learning to walk in men's large size sneakers. It was about me getting kidnapped—or worse. The area behind the small service building was hidden from view from anyone in the store as well as from anyone driving along the small road in front. The land behind and to the sides of the station was relatively flat with tall grassy weeds extending off into the distance as far as I could see. A sniper using a Remington 700 XCR with a single .308 round could easily fire a kill shot from a mile or more away. For all I knew, there was a crosshair focused on my forehead. Foolishly, I ducked.

The lead-heavy shoes, twice the size of the ones I normally wear, didn't make the trek easy. On my second circuit of the building I stumbled as much, or maybe even more, than initially. My legs were beyond tired and my feet throbbed. The only redeeming detail being that my cadence was unpredictable. A small comfort at best, but I hadn't yet been shot.

Luis was still under the tree when I emerged the third time. He again studied his watch for what seemed an excessively long time. Finally, he looked up and motioned me toward the car.

The dashboard clock read 8:56. But that wasn't the clock controlling our activities. The Apple watch on his wrist, presumably tethered to his cell phone, was the one he had been consulting, almost on a continuous basis, for the past fifteen minutes. The massive lights defining the corners of the prison yard came into view, but the actual prison walls remained out of sight behind what appeared to be a forested area. We turned off the main road about a mile back and were bumping along a hard-packed dirt road with more than its share of holes and ruts. A rock-strewn muddy stream ran, actually trickled, beside the road on our left. A field of what appeared to be beans stretched out to the right. The only thing moving out there was a lone tractor inching its way across the field a few hundred yards away. I made a mental note to never eat Mexican produce again on the assumption that this polluted excuse for a stream irrigated those fields.

Slowly what at first appeared on the horizon as a blur began to take shape as concrete walls that morphed into stone as we came closer. Luis slowed way down, keeping an eye on his watch. Directly in front of us I could see the arched entrance to a massive stone structure.

Nine o'clock seemed to be the magic time. I didn't know if he had to be at the gate at precisely nine, or just before nine or right after nine. I had no doubt this was a timed operation, meaning the guard most likely only knew someone was to do something at a precise time.

Suddenly, Luis turned to me saying, *"Fuera. Camina por esa puerta. Solo di Santiago."* I was to walk through the gate and ask for Santiago.

"Prisa. Prisa!"

That I had to hurry meant I was right in thinking this was a timed maneuver. I stepped out of the Land Rover and turned to ask about my travel bag. But Luis was already accelerating back down the pocked dusty remnant of a road.

Careful not to stumble, I made my way up the weed-covered dirt path to what appeared to be a pedestrian entrance. Tentatively pulling the door open I was met by an armed guard who stood off to the right. A metal detector was positioned directly in front of a long hallway which I presumed I had to traverse to gain entrance to the prison.

"Santiago," I said as instructed, then adding, "I'm here to see him." I had considered using Spanish, but there's no question I'm an American and Spanish would be unexpected.

"Over here," the guard said in surprisingly good English. "Do you have anything on you dangerous or sharp? Ammunition, explosives, knives, blades?"

"No."

"Read that sign." He pointed to a list on the wall behind him titled: ITEMS NOT PERMITTED.

I read the list and looked up at him.

"Anything for you to declare?"

I didn't know what was in my shoes, but there was no doubt that whatever it was violated at least one or more of the prohibited items. "Nothing," I answered, hoping to sound convincing.

Now for the real test. What would the scanner detect? I could almost hear bells going off and visualized uniforms rushing at me from all directions, safeties being clicked off as they ran.

The guard took his time looking me up and down.

"Por aquí por favor."

He pointed to a passage off to his right that seemed to bypass the scanner. I headed in that direction.

"Detener. Te escanearé a mano."

He was going to hand scan me. *But why the switch to Spanish?*

With my arms up over my head, he and his scanner didn't miss an inch of my torso, back or front.

"Piernas aparte."

I dutifully spread my legs, not knowing what to expect. The wand moved slowly down the back of my right leg, stopping at mid-calf as promised. Then the left leg. Then the right front followed by the left front, each time stopping just below my calf.

The guard pulled a two-way radio from his back pocket, pushed a button, began to say something, then stopped.

He's staring at my feet!

The radio still in his hands, he said, "Lady, those are the biggest feet I've ever seen on a woman your size." He again brought the radio up to his mouth.

Before he said anything, I smiled as big a smile as I could muster given everything going through my brain. "Everyone says that. My father…my father was a basketball player. Six foot nine and a half. Size seventeen shoes. I'm grateful mine are only...twelve."

"Play pro?"

"Unfortunately, no. Blew out his knee at Kansas."

"Sorry about that," the guard said. Keying the radio, he mumbled a few words, then turned to me. "You're to meet Santiago in the yard at exactly nine fifteen. Ten minutes is what you get. Not a second longer. You come right back out this way. No detours. Got that?"

Ten minutes? I thought we'd have more time. "I do," I managed to respond, keeping concern from my tone.

"Yard's third door on the left. Woman's toilet is second door. You have four minutes to spare."

I was inside a Mexican maximum-security prison and unescorted. That meant I was being monitored. I walked to the bathroom doing my best not to stumble. That weed walking at the petrol station was now paying dividends. Once inside I started to relax, but thankfully remembered before I did anything stupid that in a prison you only disappear from their sight when they want it that way.

At precisely nine-fifteen I stepped through the third door on the left. The yard was empty. But only for several seconds. A door on the far end opened and in walked a much slimmer version of the man I last saw at his trial nine years or so ago. Roberto Alterez Santiago. The *husband* Joy Malcom calls Morris.

I met Santiago halfway and he threw his arms around me much as Joy did. Only his was not a hug of affection, it was a hug so he could whisper instructions. "There's been an incident," he immediately began. "Had to pull strings to get even ten minutes. Make it count. Follow me. The cameras don't capture that spot by the window. We'll exchange shoes over there. Everything else I say will be okay if they hear it." He released the hug and when we stepped apart, said, "Angella, it is indeed nice of you to come visit me. How have you been?"

"Great," I answered, keeping it short. "And you?"

"As well as can be expected in a place such as this. Come on, let's walk as we talk. I need the exercise." He took my hand and led me in the direction of the window. "I asked you to stop by so I could personally thank you for delivering my art. I trust you received everything you wanted as well."

"You are welcome," I answered, being careful not to mention by name any of the art pieces we dealt in. "And I'm pleased with how it all turned out."

We took a few more steps in silence as he approached the window. Santiago leaned against the wall and his head nod told me to do the same. He slipped off his right shoe, which I noted was identical to the one I was wearing. He handed it to me and waited with his foot off the ground for me to hand him my right shoe. He then proceeded to remove his left shoe and the drill was repeated. When our shoes were exchanged, our yard walk resumed.

Back in the center of the yard, Santiago said, "We're going to say goodbye in a moment. Time's almost up. Give me another hug."

"Oh, I almost forgot. Joy said to say hello."

"I trust you had a pleasant stay."

"I did."

Santiago pulled me close, his voice low. "The name the FBI wants is Scorpion. He's a Sinoloa. But, Angella, be very careful. There's a problem. They have Jimmy and Scorpion is keeping him alive in exchange for me not giving him up. Hold that name until Jimmy's clear."

"Jimmy?" I exclaimed louder than I had intended. "What..."

Santiago's arms pulled me even closer. "Say no more," he said into my ear. "I assure you he's safe for now. There's a new development. Has to do with lost wine. No time now. Joy'll be in touch. The fentanyl supplier from China is Jin Sung. Give that to your FBI friends."

The far door opened, and a guard stepped into the yard. Santiago released me. "I can keep Jimmy alive no more than four days," he called as we moved apart. "Work fast."

"Silencio!" The guard shouted.

I started to wave goodbye, but the gesture was useless. Santiago walked briskly toward the far end, not troubled in the least by the weight of his new shoes. For my part, the shoes I now wore, while still much too heavy for pure leather, were significantly lighter than the ones I walked in with. Now I had to work to keep my feet from lifting too high off the ground. Getting it right was difficult and I stumbled several times trying. Video surveillance was certain to spot my erratic movements. While my entrance may have been smoothed by money, I doubted very much if my exit was so protected.

The front of my right sneaker caught the door ledge and I stumbled forward from the yard to the hallway. I hadn't realized how bright the sunlight was until the hallway appeared pitch black.

I paused to allow my eyes to adjust. "Keep moving," a voice in the hall commanded.

"Can't see."

"Just walk. It's clear."

His hand on my left shoulder could have been meant as reassurance. But I took it as a hostile act. My body shuddered in rebellion.

"Keep moving. Your time's up."

I carefully put one foot in front of the other trying to make my way back to the entrance without falling. At least that's the direction I believed I was walking.

Shadows began to form into walls. I saw a door and pulled it open. Directly in front of me was the X-ray machine.

Shit! *Do they scan on the way out?*

The same man who interrogated me on the way in was waiting for me to leave. Either they didn't care what anyone smuggled out, or the fix was in, because he again motioned me around the scanner. However, he studied my shoes again a few seconds too long. He flipped through several images on his cell phone, finally finding the one he wanted. He held it out in front of him and with one eye on the cell image and one on my shoes, said, "Have a good visit?"

"I did," I answered, grinning with what must have been the most lopsided smile he had ever seen.

Silence.

I took a deep breath. God only knew what he would find if he examined the shoes.

After what seemed an eternity, but was closer to ten seconds, he announced, "Good to go."

The temptation to run for my life was overwhelming. Under the circumstances, if I moved much faster than I had been walking, I'd likely fall on my face. Who knows what would be in store for me then.

Moments later, I was back outside breathing fresh air. I hadn't seen any cabs on the way in and there weren't any out here now. Asking the guard was my only real option and that had its own pitfalls.

A Range Rover turned the corner and I could only hope it was Luis, giving a new meaning to any port in a storm.

Indeed, it was Luis. I energetically flung myself into the passenger's seat, silently wishing he would floor it and get us the hell out of here. Only he didn't floor it, but rather slowly accelerated past the front gate, seemingly taking forever to pass the guard station.

"What the hell you doing?" he demanded, glaring at me.

"Getting these god-awful shoes off my feet! Something inside hurts like hell!"

"Not now. You're on camera. They catch you, you're a dead woman."

"Shit!" I exclaimed. "This wasn't about Santiago passing me a private message. It was about...about smuggling."

"Consider two purposes." For a guy who hadn't said a dozen words on the ride over, Luis was now positively chatty.

"So, there *is* something in this shoe?"

"I have no idea what's in that shoe. Honestly, don't care. We're outside camera range now. Take them off if you wish."

I brought my right leg up over my left knee in preparation of removing the shoe that hurt the most. The shoe slid off taking the foot mold with it. My stocking was damp and covered in blood. A small inmate-made knife concealed within the shoe had penetrated the mold, coming to rest with its point imbedded in the flesh of my foot. "What the hell!" I exclaimed.

Luis, seeing the knife, barked, "Get that back inside and put that shoe back on!"

"Not on your life. I'm lucky it didn't cut a nerve or something! Enough of this!"

"Then you best wipe it clean and toss it out. Chances are there's a roadblock up ahead. If you're caught, you'll be facing murder charges. Your government can't protect you."

There was no chance of my removing all of my DNA without chemicals. Even a few cells would be enough, so my only real hope was for that knife never to be found. I cleaned it the best I could and had Luis pull to the side of the narrow roadway. I waited for the one car behind us to pass and then heaved the knife as far as I could into the thick underbrush.

Luck was with me. No other cars came along, and the knife settled to a level where I couldn't see it. I grudgingly climbed back in the car and Luis resumed our journey to wherever.

FOURTEEN

Other than my being worried about Angella, the first twenty-four hours of my captivity went surprisingly well considering who my captors were. In addition to *el Carnicero,* the Scorpion, there was the Zeta cousin, *Manosrápidas,* which loosely translates to Fasthands, and a rather large hombre who at times was called *el Asesino,* Killer. To some folks Killer was also known as *Encarnizado,* Cutthroat. The pecking order was established early on. When the car I was riding in came to a stop high up on a mountain at what appeared to be an abandoned shack, *Señor el Carnicero,* ordered me to open the back door and get out. The moment the door was unlatched, Cutthroat shoved me out through the door opening. My left knee landed hard on the razor-sharp, stone-embedded dirt, slicing it open, blood gushing down my torn pants leg.

Before I could stand, *el Carnicero,* dragged the big guy from the car and had his knife firmly against the side of Cutthroat's neck. He yelled something in Spanish, the words coming faster than I could interpret. Fasthands, the Zeta cousin, ran over to me, knife ready and instead of plunging the blade into my neck, he bent, placed its point into the ragged opening of my slacks and with a flick of his wrist the left pant leg fell away. A nasty-looking, dirt and stone infested laceration ran across my kneecap and extended down the outside of my leg about two inches.

Another quick slash of the wrist and the pant fabric hung from the point of his knife. His head nod indicating he expected me to use the material to stop the flow of blood. Fasthands certainly was an accurate name for this guy.

el Carnicero continued speaking Spanish so fast I couldn't follow. But what I think he said was something along the lines of get him inside and clean him up, because in the next instant the big guy shoved his arms under my back while the cousin picked up my legs and carried me into the shack. The interior was clean. But other than two large wooden boxes positioned along a far wall and a small table with two chairs sitting under a tiny window along the opposite wall, the place was devoid of furniture. No plumbing fixtures or water lines were visible in this hovel.

el Carnicero dug into one of the boxes and produced a heating plate and a small propane tank typically used by plumbers. Pulling out a pot, he motioned to the big guy. *"Agua." El Asesino* and the pot left. I assume in pursuit of water.

Fasthands waved me into a chair. He kneeled in front of me and untied the make-shift tourniquet. Dampening the material in the still oozing blood, he cleaned as much of the dirt and stones as he could from the wound. Using his ever-present knife, he dislodged the remaining stones. When he was satisfied, he flashed an angry glance in the direction of *el Carnicero* to see what his archrival now expected of him. Fasthands was clearly biding his time, waiting for the opportunity to put an end to me—and possibly to *el Carnicero* as well.

The door flew open, the big guy walked in splashing water everywhere and putting the pot on the burner to boil. What they expected to do with such a large pot of boiling water I had no idea, but it was not my place to give instructions. I already had my hands full trying to handle the sharp pain that shot through my leg and up my spine every time *Manosrápidas* moved it. It felt as if a sliver of stone was pressing against a nerve.

As it turned out, the boiling water was not for my wound. It was the beginning of dinner, which would be a stew made from vegetables growing a few hundred yards up the mountain. Meat would be whatever they could kill.

Fasthands was instructed to sanitize his knife in the propane flame. He did so and then proceeded to dig out a few remaining stones. His surgical dexterity was remarkable, almost as if he really cared. When he was satisfied the wound as clean as he could get it, he wrapped it with my pant leg, cutting the end of the material lengthwise, allowing him to tie it around my leg.

When Fasthands was finished, *el Carnicero* strolled over to inspect my knee. "That'll hold you for four days. After that you're on your own."

"What's that mean?" I asked.

"Santiago asked for four days. Four days he gets."

"What happens then?"

"I either take you back to the border, or I leave you up here with him." He nodded in the direction of the Zeta cousin.

"Who determines which?"

"Santiago."

Angella was meeting with Santiago, and based on what I just heard, I assume he'll ask her to do something for him in exchange for the information she was to obtain from him. Presumably something only she, or I, could accomplish. Also, presumably, this *favor* would take less than four days to complete. I had no idea what Santiago would be requesting, or whether it would be possible for Angella to deliver, especially within this time frame. Breaking free of these guys, and getting down off this mountain, as difficult as that might be, now seemed to be my only real option.

"Redstone," *el Carnicero* said, apparently reading my mind, "given your little accident, I don't anticipate you'll try to escape. Don't make me regret not binding you. You step one foot outside without my permission you're a *hombre muerto.*"

And if I remain here, I'll be just as dead.

FIFTEEN

Maybe it was the way Luis looked at me every few minutes after I threw the shank away that caused my heart to race and my skin to feel clammy. His face was neutral and there was a concerned look in his eyes. Three roadblocks didn't help my stomach spasms, the third stoppage coming several minutes after the music program on the car radio was interrupted with the news that a prisoner named Manuel Ramirez, a man serving a life sentence at Reclusorio Saltillo Prison, had just died of stab wounds received earlier in the day. This wasn't going to end well no matter how I spun the facts. Not hearing from Jimmy in two days compounded the situation. And to make matters even worse, Luis refused to provide an update on Pickale's condition despite my asking several times.

We'd been driving northeast for several hours when it finally became clear we were most likely headed to Matamoros. On the outskirts of town Luis insisted I change back into the shoes I had worn out of the prison.

"Not on your life!" I snapped back at him.

"Have it your way. But don't say I didn't warn you."

"Of what? What's the warning?"

"When these things happen, the prison officials interview everyone who came out of that prison after the stabbing. Your name's on that list. Border guards might or might not stop you, but because you'll be walking across the bridge, they'll capture video of you. Won't look good coming out of the prison wearing size twelves and crossing the border wearing sixes."

"I'll take my chances," I snapped back.

Luis drove in silence several minutes. "As I said, have it your way. You'll be crossing over at Matamoros. I'm told you're familiar with their operation."

"Done it many times."

"Okay, then you know it's three blocks up that way." Luis pointed generally off to his right. "This is the closest I go. Good luck."

I approached the immigration official at the Mexican side of the bridge fully expecting to be taken aside and forced to endure the indignity of a strip search. I slowly walked the last hundred yards, preferring to wait for a group of young folks who were clustered in front of the immigration pavilion saying their goodbyes, nice-seeing-yous, don't-wait-so-long-next-times; more goodbyes, keep-in-touches, and promises to post updates. Stalling was awkward, but it was far better to cross with a group than by myself. As I killed time, I felt someone shadowing me. I used every trick I knew but failed to locate anyone suspicious. Nevertheless, the feeling I was under surveillance continued.

Nothing much changed with the group ahead of me. They were still hugging, kissing and promising. I was about to give up and go it alone when a young man, who appeared to be in his early twenties, broke free. A woman his age followed. Then two more women and another man began walking toward the immigration agent. They were all waved through without incident.

I fell in behind them, still trying, but failing, to improvise a plausible story as to the discrepancy in my shoe size. Jimmy was good at these things, but I wasn't. To my pleasant surprise, I also was waved onto the bridge. Given my druthers I'd rather be in front of that group than behind. More protection that way. The thought of unknown folks coming up behind me halfway across the Rio Grande sent chills up my spine.

"Keep walking, Angella," a voice said from directly behind me. "Don't look around. I'm not talking to you."

I concentrated so hard on getting my timing right with the group ahead of me that I hadn't been aware of anyone approaching from behind.

Classic rookie mistake.

It took me several steps before I realized it was Dill's voice.

"You okay?" I excitedly asked, forcing my eyes to remain on the group ahead of me. "Had me worried."

"No time for that now. U.S. immigration's been alerted. When you pass though, grab a cab or Uber and go directly to the island. Hilton Garden Inn. Room's reserved in your own name."

"Where's Jimmy? Is he okay?"

I received no answer. I asked a second time and was again greeted with silence. I glanced behind me to find Dill more than ten feet back and walking back into Matamoros. Training told me to continue walking. My heart screamed to break protocol and go back.

I stopped walking and turned back. "Breaking protocol, Angella," Jimmy's voice boomed in my head, "is hardly ever a good idea. It could cost you your life."

I took several steps in pursuit of Dill before Jimmy's voice took command. Nothing I could learn from Pickale would change anything. I turned and hurried to catch up to the group.

The U.S. Customs and Immigration agent barely glanced at my passport before waving me through. I brought up the Uber App on my cell but noticed an Island Taxi drifting by. I flagged it down. Once in the cab, I called Jimmy. The call went immediately to his voice mail. The sound of his recorded voice briefly calmed me, but that was short lived. My sense of foreboding returned with a vengeance.

I tried putting the past two days behind me and concentrating on the future while checking into the *Hilton Garden Inn.* Our immediate plan, now that we have the money, is to buy a house of our own. We've been discussing leaving Great Southern Insurance, but no decision has been made. Jimmy, as it turns out, is more of an adrenalin junkie than I had realized. And, while I hate to admit it, I'm becoming one myself. So, our future endeavors are unclear.

Key in hand, I took the elevator up to the fourth floor and opened the door to the suite that had been assigned to me.

Speaking of adrenalin rushes, I opened the connecting door to our apartment and my heart missed a beat—possibly several. There Jimmy was, sitting in a chair in front of the window, the same crooked smile on his face that I had come to love. Relief washed away the over-bearing gloom and I was half-way across the room when I sensed, rather than knew, something was wrong. Jimmy had remained seated, his arms loose in his lap instead of opening to welcome me. I stopped just short of jumping into his now seemingly unwelcoming lap.

An awkward moment followed in which I studied my lover. Something was off and I couldn't immediately pinpoint what it was.

His hair's wrong!

Jimmy's hair is soft brown, straight, and beginning to thin in front. This guy had a full head of dark hair tending toward curling. Mouth is spot on, but the eyes are narrower. Nose and cheeks are identical. Skin lighter in color but tougher in texture.

This guy's much younger than Jimmy!

Brother? Jimmy doesn't have a brother. At least not one I know about. Suddenly, it hit me. "Oh, my God!" I exclaimed, "Lester! What the hell?"

Les was Jimmy's estranged son who lived in Alaska, fishing and doing odd jobs around. Les generally kept to himself. Jimmy stopped sending him money a few years back, and to my knowledge hadn't heard from him since.

"Took you long enough," he said standing, his arms open for a hug.

Too young, even for Les!

I held back, conflicted—and confused. I studied this guy and took a step back. "Now, what the hell's going on? You're not Les!"

The door to the bathroom opened and out stepped Tiny, our seven-foot former handler. His government ID proclaims he's employed by the Secret Service. In reality he's full CIA. "You made good time, Angella. Didn't know if we still had juice on the Mexican side."

"What the hell's going on? Who's this guy?"

"Slow down. Loved your reaction to our new Jimmy. You validated the operation."

"What operation?" I shot back, "And where the hell's Jimmy?"

"One question at a time. Angella, this is Agent Deyton. Deyton, this is Jimmy Redstone's fiancée, Angella Martinez."

"Nice to finally meet you," Deyton said, stepping forward to shake hands.

Same height as Jimmy.

Confused and angry, I shot back, "I don't know the game you're playing, but…"

"Now's not the time for getting into all that's happened. We're on a tight schedule."

Tiny's always on a tight schedule and he's an expert at redirecting the conversation. I wasn't buying into his diversion. I needed time to get my bearings. "Give me a moment here. I know this man here as Lester Redstone, Jimmy's son. Who the hell's Deyton? And why's he here anyway?"

"Slow down Angella!" Tiny's face tightened into his don't-push-me-any-further mode. "All in due course. As I said, we're on a tight schedule, so let's work while we talk. Deyton is right now, and has been for a period of time, impersonating Lester for reasons not important to this operation. He's about to be made up to impersonate Jimmy. To do that we require a change of Jimmy's clothes, including shoes, socks and underwear. "We'll also need a recent picture. As recent as possible."

I hesitated, causing Tiny to bark, "Now, Angella! Move! I need that picture and I need you to go to your apartment, get what we need and bring it back to us ASAP. Time's not our friend."

A soft knock sounded at the door. Tiny opened it a crack, then seeing who was there, opened it the full way. An Asian woman, pulling a large suitcase, came into the room and marched directly to the desk next to the window. She immediately began unloading the contents onto the desk. Only it wasn't clothes she was unpacking, but rather jars and cans and tubes of various colors, along with every type and size of brush and applicator imaginable. Out came hair clippers, combs, brushes, spray bottles and a myriad of scissors along with several gowns. One or more of us was about to be transformed.

"Angella, this is Hue Duc," Tiny said. "She works for the Company."

Deyton slipped the gown over his head and settled back in the chair. This obviously was not a new routine for him. "Ready," he said, his voice surprisingly similar to Jimmy's. "Let's get this show on the road."

"Angella, before you go, show me that picture of Jimmy," Tiny said, holding his hand out for my cell phone. He studied it a moment. "When was this taken?"

"About an hour before...before we went into the theater."

"Good. Then the hair will be cut right. That's critical. Send it to me. And then go get those items we need."

Jimmy and I had been briefed years ago about the CIA using disguises, as well as magic, to obtain their objectives. If this wasn't so serious, I'd be having fun. They were about to turn this Jimmy look-a-like into Jimmy. But why? What's the end game here?

Tiny's phone beeped when the forwarded photo arrived, and he busied himself forwarding it on to Hue Duc. I was out of the suite before he finished.

Ten minutes to my apartment; ten minutes rounding up what I was tasked to procure; ten minutes back to the hotel. In the half hour I had been gone, Deyton, alias Lester Redstone, was now Jimmy Redstone. It's a good thing Hue

Duc hadn't transformed him earlier or I would have embarrassed myself by leaping into his arms.

Satisfied that the clothes were right, Tiny motioned me to follow him into the bathroom. Pulling the door closed behind him, his voice low, he said, "I won't pull any punches here, Angella. Zetas got Jimmy up in the mountains and want him dead. Santiago's holding them off, but that's sketchy at best. We only have a slim window to free him and we need to work fast."

Santiago's last words to me now flooded back. "Santiago told me four days. Now you're saying…" My stomach knotted and I felt sick. "Did something change?"

The big guy looked away. In all the time he'd been our handler he may not always have told us the full truth, but he never hid his face. Slowly, the big guy turned back. "Listen to me, Angella. This operation has way too many moving parts, even for me. Parts I have no control over. I wish I did, but I don't. And, at this point, no one really does."

"CIA can do anything it wants," I replied, fighting the horrible sinking feeling deep within me. "I've seen it often enough."

"There's always a political price to pay. This is not a good time to be getting the cartels wound up against us. And even if we could control the outcome up there with Jimmy, he's a small fish in a large ocean, I'm afraid."

"Jimmy's expendable is what you're saying! His life's not worth the political cost to save him! How dare you! After all we've…"

"Don't go there, Angella. And that's not what I said. Of course, we'll do what we can to save him. That's what we're doing out there. But…but please understand, the margin's slim. We can't control the Zetas. I know Santiago thinks he can, but…"

"He guaranteed me we have four days."

"There's a contingency on those four days."

"What contingency?"

"He's been working with the CIA on…on let's just say for now a top-level operation. He needs your cooperation and was going to ask you."

"Something happened and our time was cut. I'm to obtain the info from Malcom. That's all I know."

"That squares with what we know as well. The pieces are falling into place. Need to hope they fall fast enough."

"You gotta save Jimmy. That's what I know!"

"Listen, Angella, I don't have time to debate this with you, but he went into Mexico on his own. He's naked as far as our government's concerned. Jimmy's caught in a crossfire. In the wrong place at the wrong time. I can't change that."

His words cut to my core. I felt as if he had slammed me against the wall. "How the hell you live with yourself?"

"I said I won't debate this. But truth is I'm on your side. You and Jimmy have done good work for the government, and we owe you both. That's why we're taking the *only* option we have. It's a challenge, and in the end will only work if every single failure point, and there are many, falls in Jimmy's favor."

"And that plan is?"

"I'm calling it Operation Delay. Agent Deyton will impersonate Jimmy. Call him Jimmy2 if you wish."

"Jimmy2?"

"Best for you to think of him as Jimmy. One slip and you could be signing both their death warrants."

When I didn't respond, Tiny continued. "Jimmy2 will…" Tiny checked his watch. "…in ten hours and fifteen minutes, at exactly zero three-thirty, be inserted into the cabin where Jimmy's being detained. Concurrently, Jimmy will be extracted."

"One life for another. How's that work?"

"Jimmy2 is close to forty years younger than Redstone. Odds aren't good, but higher. In this business, odds are critical."

"What happens in four days?"

Tiny again looked away. Only this time his eyes returned almost immediately. "The mission is top secret and I'm not authorized to discuss it. Even if I was, this isn't the place." He glanced at the light fixture. "I have your back on this. Have faith."

"I have four days to accomplish my mission for Santiago," I replied. "Will I be briefed before then?"

"If not, all this is for naught."

"Will Santiago be able to hold the Zetas off that long?"

"Truthfully, I have my doubts. I know that's not what you wanted to hear. But you asked."

Tiny nailed it. Something had been nagging me all day. The only honorable thing I've ever attributed to the cartels is their determination to get revenge for killing one of theirs. Jimmy wasn't coming home without Tiny's help.

While I was thinking, Tiny was texting. Moments later, he said, "Angella, how about you and me taking a walk on the beach."

The water slowly rolled in and out over the soft sand just above the high-water line. We headed north several minutes before Tiny spoke. "What I'm about to tell you is, as I said, top secret. I've permission to read you in now. You understand your responsibilities in this?"

"I do," I said, recalling all the rules and regulations surrounding top secret material.

"Good. We know far more than you might think about Santiago and his plans. Having you go in for the name of a drug lord who killed those Americans was a…a pretext. For over three years the Company's been setting up a regime change in Iran. We…"

"Iran! What's Iran to do with…"

"Hold your questions. I'll tell you what I can. You'll have to guess at the rest."

I nodded, and he continued, "Sayyid Ali Hosseini Khamenei is now the supreme religious leader. He's Shia, eighty and going strong. But for how long no one really can predict. Hassan Rouhani is about ten years his junior and is the political leader of Iran. As you know, there's unrest in that country."

I recalled something I heard on TV a week or so back. "There's talk of General Bijan Mazdani taking over, is there not?"

"Yes, and well, no. Not so simple. As brutal as Mazdani's been, and he's as bad as they come, he has a…a what I'll call a compassionate heart. CIA's backing him, but it' not a straightforward situation."

"Why would I ever think otherwise?"

Tiny picked up on my sarcasm. "I hear you, Angella. As I said, we've been working this for over three years. In order to defeat the Islamic Revolution that threw out the Shah, we need the people of Iran behind this rebellion. And to achieve that we need a great majority of the people to believe in a new person."

"I thought you said that'll be Mazdani. But he's one of them."

"As I said, maybe yes, maybe no. Follow me here. Two operations are going forward simultaneously. First, the people of Iran are being educated to accept that the Saracens were the original rulers of Persia. The Saracens were neither Sunni nor Shia, so that works for our purposes. Covers the religious divide if you will."

"Saracens? Never heard of them?"

"Lost in time. In fact, they may have been the original rulers of Persia. Very highly advanced civilization. Keep following me here. The groundwork has been laid for a person who can trace his ancestral heritage back to a Saracen, and even better, back to a Saracen King, to come forward and rule Iran."

"You're about to tell me you found that person."

"Created that person is more accurate. That's where Mazdani fits in."

"Mazdani?"

"Mazdani," Tiny confirmed.

"May I ask how?"

"I'll tell you what I know. I don't promise I have all this right, but I'm close. King Frederic II was a thirteenth century king of several countries, including the Holy Roman Empire. Some scholars trace his ancestry back to the Saracens, who were Muslim. In a perfect world, that would blend Christians and Islamists under one ruler—a new King of Prussia, an extension of the House of Hohenstaufen. That dynasty lasted almost two centuries. Their coat of arms shows three lions on a yellow background."

Visualizing the lions brought to mind our recent art transaction with Santiago. "Like the panthers on the Kings Cup? That piece came from Iran-Persia."

"Kings Cup is much earlier in time. But, yes, that's why you and Jimmy are involved. Historical lore ties the dynasty back to that Cup. As crazy as this whole operation sounds, it's made possible by the folklore surrounding the Kings Cup."

"Why would the people of Iran ever believe a European family ruled Iran—or Persia?"

"People believe what they want to believe. Called suspended disbelief. I'm told the real selling point is that King Frederick II was King of Jerusalem at one point also. And here's a fascinating piece of history. The Epic of King Gilgamesh is about four thousand years old. Gilgamesh was handsome and beloved by his people. The story is believed to be the earliest surviving great work of fiction and perhaps the second oldest religious text. It was, of course, originally passed down by word of mouth. The mythical story is believed to have come from Mesopotamia and around 1800 BCE it was captured on stone tablets."

Going along with the CIA's grand plan, I said, "That certainly supports their desire to run the Jews out of the Holy Land. I see why they're willing to suspend judgment. I'm guessing the plan then is to tie Mazdani back to an earlier dynasty."

"You got it."

"Tying Mazdani to ancient mythology, however, seems far out. Even for the CIA."

"Best chance we have for a regime change that doesn't blow up in our faces."

"And I assume that's where Jimmy and I come into the picture. Am I getting warm?"

"Burning. Before that…that unfortunate shooting at the theater in Harlingen it would have been straight forward. But…but now we're in improv mode."

Improvisation and covert operations are not a good mix. The knots in my stomach returned with a vengeance. "In what respect is the plan compromised?"

"Trust. Mazdani believing he's a true descendent of the Hohenstaufen Dynasty is key to everything. Before the shooting, he trusted you and Jimmy because you delivered the Kings Cup. Now…well, now he's not so certain."

"Trust what?" I asked, now more puzzled than ever. "So, he doesn't trust us. What's that to do with him becoming King?"

"Logically, nothing. But the plan was for him to find wine casks, ceramic casks with the three-lion coat of arms baked into the surface. The legend that's been circulating is that the casks contain wine from the town of Shiraz where Mazdani's ancestors owned property. The casks bear the family coat of arms. Those casks have never been located and are said to be in the possession of the heir to the Hohenstaufen Dynasty."

The conversation Jimmy and I had with Steve in the theater lobby played in my head. Sunken sailing ships, hidden treasures, silver coins, and…and wine! Tiny was staring at the horizon when I said, "You can't be serious! You're really suggesting the wine Steve claims is buried off the beach at Boca Chica is the Shiraz from some King's Iranian orchard?"

"Hey Angella," Tiny replied, slowly turning back to face me, "I'm just the messenger in all this. I'm giving you the straight story from the operation. Truth is not my domain."

"But it's the truth you want me to sell Mazdani!"

"Not me, Angella. The Company."

"Steve said the wine on the ship is French—and in barrels. Not Shiraz from Iran and in casks."

"Details. Details. Your job—at least it was your job before the shooting—is to convince Mazdani the wine's genuine. And when he's in possession of the casks, the coat of arms will prove he's the heir to the dynasty. Gilgamesh if you will."

"Far-fetched at best. Stupid if you ask me."

Ignoring my comment, Tiny continued, "King of Persia. Mazdani's been dreaming of that for a long while now. A little suppression of disbelief goes a long way."

"Big suppression if you ask me. Mind telling me what Santiago has to do with all this?"

"You spoke to your boss Silver about insuring the wine. Silver made some calls and lo and behold word got back to Santiago. Not so much because of the dynasty part of it. More like the money part of it. Billions are at stake here. He put two and two together. Nobody ever said Santiago's stupid."

I wasn't buying what Tiny or his bosses were selling. "It's only money to Santiago," I replied. "Why would he get in the middle of...of an Iranian revolution? He has more money than he can ever possibly use."

"What if Mazdani promised Santiago his freedom?"

"Is that even possible?"

"Mazdani's well connected. Imagine his power when he's King."

"I thought alcohol was banned in Iran. So, why's Mazdani..."

"That's Islamic. Don't believe all the people feel the same way. Remember, wine was invented over there. The wine here in question comes from the royal grape. But, hey, as I said, I'm only the messenger."

Sometimes you just need to get knocked in the stomach to understand. This was one of those times. "You want Jimmy and I to negotiate directly with Mazdani. Convince him he's the next King."

"Yes and no. Convince him the wine's real. He'll convince himself he's the new King."

"And that's why you're springing Jimmy from that cabin? Nothing to do with paying us back for great work. That was just more CIA bull shit!"

"Not BS. Not on my part anyway. I meant it. Only my feelings alone won't be enough to activate Operation Delay."

"And why in the world would you even think Mazdani would trust us?"

"Because Santiago's vouching for you. That's why."

"That'll be enough?"

"That, and a hell of a lot of work going on in the background."

"What type of work?"

"Better off not knowing. Capisci?"

"Got it," I mumbled, the sinking feeling now all consuming.

SIXTEEN

My knee was throbbing when I woke from a frightening dream of two men sawing off my leg. Someone in the background was calling out the cadence. Heave, and the big saw went from right to left. Ho, and the saw moved back across the bone. The heave-ho's were steady, but my leg never fell to the ground. The pain was unbearable, but no noise escaped when I screamed.

I woke, struggling to free my arms so I could shove the men away. The room's darkness receded into shadows. Two of my captors were on the floor, wrapped in sheets, snoring softly. The third guy, the cousin, was in the chair, his chin down against his chest. I couldn't tell if his eyes were open.

The time was three-twenty.

Startled by my movement, Cousin's head popped up and his eyes opened wide. He stumbled trying to jump to his feet, his ever-present knife in his hand. From the look on his face it wouldn't take much for him to use it on me.

"Dreaming," I whispered, trying not to disturb the others. As if that would make a difference.

Cousin took a step in my direction and froze, his attention diverted to a sound coming from behind the shack: the sound of an engine or perhaps a motorcycle. Sound, dependent on many factors; distance from the listener, moisture content of the air, altitude, and terrain, is often deceiving. My best guess: it's coming from somewhere down the mountain.

Then, as suddenly as it started, the sound disappeared, leaving a void in its wake. A puzzled look appeared on Cousin's tattooed-ravaged face. He was clearly debating with himself as to whether he heard anything. In his macho world crying wolf was a sign of weakness. His life depended on his believability under fire and raising the alarm when an alarm wasn't warranted showed weakness. He said nothing.

Cousin studied me a moment, determined I was no threat, at least not at this moment, and turned back to his chair. He was clearly sleepy, so I decided to lie still until I was certain he was out.

When I woke, the filthy shack was white with no window where one had existed before. I was in a real room, with a real bed, with real lights, real walls, a real door, and a real TV. The sheets were clean, and I was covered with a soft blanket.

I don't recall visiting with St Peter, but this was surely heaven.

I tensed when a man wearing a blue gown with a name stitched on its left side walked through that real door.

"Where am I?" I asked, trying not to show how disoriented I was.

"McAllen Medical Center. I'm Nurse Phillips."

"What time is it?"

"Six-thirty-two. Now lie still. Need to get your vitals."

Three hours had elapsed in an instant. Or had it been twenty-seven hours?

A horrible thought crossed my mind and I cautiously reached down to make sure there still was a leg below my knee, but quickly withdrew my hand. I wasn't ready to deal with the reality of a lost leg.

"You're finally awake," Tiny's voice called from somewhere behind me. I turned my head but couldn't see him. "Case you're wondering, you still have your leg. Thanks to Dr. Patel. You just missed him. Can't be far." Tiny stepped forward and addressed the nurse. "Phillips, how about getting Doc back in here?"

The nurse returned a few minutes later with a tall, slender, gray-haired Indian man, a stethoscope draped around his neck. Without introduction, he began, "The tissue around that knee was in pretty bad shape when you arrived. You're not completely home free just yet, but we removed the debris and cleaned up what we could. Antibiotics should do the rest. Another day without treatment and you would have lost the leg—and most-likely your life. Whoever tried to clean it didn't do you any favors."

"Why's that?

"Judging from the bacteria count, whatever they used has a sordid history."

What a surprise!

"Mind telling me how long I'll be here?"

"Oh, you're free to go. The nurse will give you instructions on how to change the dressing. That cream's critical for a few days. You want to keep your leg, apply it as directed. It's that simple."

"He's sure a ray of sunshine," I said to Tiny when Patel left. "Learned bedside manner in a morgue."

"They got you out just in time. I'm told it was touch and go there for a while. Patel may not be much at the bedside, but I understand he's a genius with trauma wounds."

"What the hell's going on? How'd I get here? Last I remember I was up in some filthy shack somewhere on top of a mountain. Heard an engine far off. Then..."

"Special ops used a form of sevoflurane gas to knock everyone out, you included. We substituted a look-alike. There'll be no memory of anything that happened. They think you're still up there with them. We've done this once or twice. Trust me, it works."

I had heard of such operations but never witnessed one. The clothes I came into the hospital with were folded neatly in a plastic bag which was sitting on a table in the corner. The shoes were on top. They were from my closet on SPI. "Did Angella select those for me, or did one of your minions break into my place?"

"Wouldn't even dream of it," Tiny said, his face as straight as ever. "Yes, Angella selected everything."

"She's okay then? Back from Mexico, I assume."

"She's fine. Told me to say hello for her."

Thinking about the shoes, I realized Angella had sent a message. She called this particular pair my happy shoes because I only wear them when we're going someplace fun. I interpreted her message as saying she's okay but wants to be with me.

"Who's the look-alike? Anyone I know?"

"Not here."

"Is Angella..."

"Not here," Tiny repeated, this time with an edge that told me he'd not answer another operational question in this environment. Knowing Tiny, he had no intention of ever filling me in.

"So, where do I go from here?"

"Certainly not back to your place. For all we know, the Zetas have it under watch."

"Where then?"

"Motel over near the outlet mall in Mercedes. Your pal Contentus has kindly agreed to keep a vigilant eye on the two of you."

"Angella?"

"Wouldn't dream of anyone else. Unless…"

"There's no, *unless*! Get me out of here."

"Not until the doc issues the discharge. Maybe an hour or two. They want the knockout drugs gone before they set you free."

- - - -

Angella was indeed at the motel. Only the motel wasn't near the outlet mall in Mercedes. It was in Edinburg, not far from the UTRGV campus. She hadn't been briefed on my knee injury and her distress was evident. She insisted I relate every moment of my time in Mexico before telling me her story. She wanted every detail, as if she was gathering a mosaic to save for posterity. She pulled me close several times, putting her head on my chest, and holding me tight.

I confessed I knew nothing after hearing that engine in the middle of the night.

She replied with, "I think I know what happened from there. Just hold me."

We lay together that way, neither of us talking, until I finally said, "Now it's your turn. Tell me what you've been up to."

"What makes you think I've anything to tell?"

"You now keeping secrets from me? You sent a message with those shoes. I know you're involved in something. I just don't know what it is."

"After."

"After what?" I innocently responded, totally misreading my partner and lover.

"Doctors restrict you from anything?"

"Nothing."

"Your knee hurt?"

"Actually, feel nothing at all. Numb."

"Hope nothing else's numb," she teased, all the while unbuttoning my shirt.

We made love and thankfully only my knee was numb. Afterwards, I slept for what I thought was an hour, maybe two at most, but when my eyes opened it was dark out. Angella, sitting in the only chair in the room, hurried over and joined me in bed. "Feeling better?" she asked.

"I felt great when I fell asleep. Can't say as I feel any better now."

"Oh, Jimmy! I do love you! I hate it when we're apart and I don't know what's happening to you." She kissed me and then rolled into bed beside me. "What I don't understand about your story is why you were in Mexico in the first place."

"I knew you were on your way to visit Santiago and I was down there to help. The plan they devised had me driving west as a diversion. It was dumb, at best. But, you know, I've been thinking they knew all along I'd go on my own to protect you. In fact, they counted on it. We're nothing but puppets on an invisible string."

"You think they wanted you captured?"

"You think they just happen to have a Jimmy look-alike standing by? Perhaps tucked away in central casting? Speaking of look-alikes, you get to meet the guy?"

"I did," Angella responded, her eyes avoiding mine.

"What's that funny look for?"

"Oh, nothing. I...I was just thinking how much he looked like you. Hair a bit fuller, eyes off somewhat. But enough to have fooled me for a moment when I first saw him."

"Wonder where they found this guy? You know his name?"

"Tiny called him Agent Deyton."

"FBI? Homeland? DEA? What?"

"Wasn't told. Didn't ask."

"Your turn to tell all," I said to Angella. "We need to figure out why they made a substitution and not a simple extraction. This so-called Agent Deyton, whoever he is, has a mission and I very much doubt it's to play Jimmy Redstone for any long period of time."

Angella rolled close. "I love you, Jimmy Redstone," she said, kissing me lightly. She then began to relate all that had happened to her.

SEVENTEEN

It was a subdued Joy Malcom who now sat across from me at *Rudy's Country Store & Bar-B-Q* in Pharr. I knew *Rudy's* well. Jimmy and I frequented the place as often as we could. It was a favorite with law enforcement, from local police, to sheriffs, to state police, Texas Rangers, Border Protection, you name it. Some in uniforms, many not. They all received a discount for their meals. And they had one thing in common; they all carried loaded weapons—and were willing to use them. I often noted that one discharge could lead to a massacre.

Joy's carefree persona was replaced by stooped shoulders, her over-sized smile nonexistent, her eyes quiet. I half expected Joy to announce Morris had been killed in prison. I couldn't help but think that the man deserved to be publicly hanged at high noon. I have to admit that his promise to keep Jimmy alive did color my attitude toward the man's demise. "Slight change in plans," Malcom began, finally looking directly at me. "Seems Morris has been accused of murder."

"He's serving a life sentence for murder now. I don't understand."

"That's the problem! The murder he's now being accused of occurred about an hour before you arrived at the prison." Silence fell around us as Joy studied me a long moment. Realizing I wouldn't impart any information, she continued. "They found a knife in the brush a few miles away. Knife, they say, has his fingerprints all over it. Blood on the knife matches the dead prisoner."

I lost the poker-face battle. Joy instantly pounced. "So, you know about the knife?"

"What makes you…?"

"Should have snapped a picture of your face," she said, fishing her phone out of her pocket. "Bet you don't play cards. No matter, my dear, Luis has you on candid camera." She turned her phone so I could see the image of myself, the knife clearly in my hands, my arm raised in a throwing motion. "There's more where that came from. Want to see?"

My face flushed as all semblance of polite conversation ended. "What is it you want from me?" I demanded.

She glanced around at the many tables of law enforcement officers, causing me to wonder why she chose this place to meet. Any one of these folks could be recording us right now. Leaning close, she said, "We're relying on you to play this straight. The wine. Morris is brokering the wine, you know the sunken treasure wine, to an Iranian. Name's Mazdani. Guy believes it's from his ancestral estate. Worth a lot of money. Know what wine I'm talking about?"

"If it's the lost wine I discussed with Great Insurance then I know what wine you're referring to." She knows I know, so there's no advantage in denying it.

"Good. Then there should be no misunderstanding."

"What, exactly, do you want from me?"

"Simple. Convince this Mazdani guy the wine's genuine and you can deliver it to him."

"That assumes the wine can be found. That's a big assumption."

"Morris assures me it will be found. If he says so, then it is true."

"Not sure what it is I can do. Sorry."

Her eyes set hard, but then relaxed when she realized her bargaining position wasn't as strong as she'd like it to be. "Here's the deal. Since Morris can no longer meet with Mazdani, or with anyone really, he needs you to deal directly."

"And if I agree?"

"Morris will continue to protect Jimmy."

"What assurances do I have?"

"Morris' word."

"Need more than that."

"Ten percent of the value."

"Twenty-five."

"Fifteen. And final."

"I'll do my best," I told Malcom, knowing all the while this is the operation Tiny outlined for me.

"Morris will agree to extending protection on your lover until next Wednesday. That gives you a full week to produce the wine."

"Wait! I thought I only had to convince Mazdani the wine's genuine. Now you want…"

"Operation's changed. You, in person, are to deliver one unopened barrel of that wine to Mazdani. And you are to assure both him and me the remaining barrels are safely secured."

"You expect me to do all that—in a week?"

"You will if you desire to remain out of prison and see Jimmy alive again."

I leaned across the table and in a harsh whisper, said, "Go to hell, Joy. And take Santiago with you!"

"My, my," Malcom said, standing to face me. "I offer you freedom, as well as your fiancè back, and all I get is hostility. Such gratitude."

Two men and three women, all but one wearing police uniforms, turned to face us. One woman not wearing a uniform moved her hand so that it now rested on her shoulder bag.

I disengaged from Malcom and turned my back on her. From behind me she said, "I'll be in touch. And sooner than you might suppose. Think hard about my proposition."

I took Joy's advice and thought hard about what she said—and had not said. She gave no hint she was aware of Jimmy's extraction. In fact, just the opposite. That was good news. I also knew that if the CIA, or whatever organization is running this operation, could get Jimmy out they could also go in to remove his double if they so choose. What Joy didn't know was that everything she had said had been monitored in real time, captured both with audio and video. How much longer our government would allow Malcom to run free was a question I couldn't answer. I'm certain the time's not far off when she'll no longer be valuable to them and they'll roll her up faster than a spring-loaded clothesline.

- - - - -

I drove to McAllen, then further west to the town of Mission and then on to the Laurel Hill Cemetery, where Tiny and Jimmy were waiting. I pulled to a stop and both stepped out of a black car with dark tinted windows.

"I have to hand it to you, Tiny," I said, "for selecting isolated spots. Unless the dead have ears, you've outdone yourself."

"Not my idea."

"Whose then?"

Tiny pointed to a car that just parked in front of mine. "He suggested this cemetery. Said something about doing research and killing two birds."

The familiar figure of Steve Hathcock eased himself onto the roadway, taking a moment to adjust his hat and scan the surroundings. Taking a tentative step toward the cemetery entrance, he saw us ahead of him and quickened his pace. Together we walked through the cemetery, passing vases of red and white flowers seemingly on every grave site. If any place could be safe to meet and talk, surely this would be it. Nothing was moving as far as I could see. Nonetheless, Tiny wasn't satisfied until we were all positioned behind a massive above-ground burial vault sporting the well-weathered name of Garza arched across the top.

"Here's the deal, Mr. Hathcock," Tiny began without preamble, "the time has come to provide the coordinates of where the wine barrels are located."

"I'm fully prepared to do so," Steve calmly said, "But first, what guarantee do I have that I'll be adequately compensated?"

"Actually, none."

"So, why…"

"I assume telling you it would be in service to your government won't cut it," Tiny replied, a slight flicker of a smile in his eye.

"You got that darn right."

"Then here's the deal. We have a fast approaching deadline to make a deal with a very motivated buyer. Perhaps the most motivated buyer in the world. I highly doubt if this opportunity will remain open much longer. So, here's what's on the table. Ten percent finder fee to you."

"Must I produce the barrels for that, or will the coordinates be enough?"

"Coordinates. But only if they're accurate."

"Even if extracting the wine is a major challenge."

"Even so."

"Make it fifteen percent and the coordinates are yours. Hey, any silver dollar coins in those barrels are mine and mine alone."

"Fair enough," Tiny acknowledged, not apparently surprised that the barrels contain silver dollars. Or perhaps he knows they don't. With Tiny, there's no way to guess.

"To be clear, you agree any coins found are mine. Every last one of them."

"Agreed. And you get twelve percent of the wine value as well," Tiny said, enjoying whatever game he was running on Steve.

"Fourteen," Steve said.

"Thirteen," Tiny said, reaching his hand out in a congratulatory gesture.

"Thirteen," Steve said, taking Tiny's hand. "But I doubt if you can reach the site by Tuesday."

"Try us. You have the coordinates written down somewhere?"

"Memorized. Only I know them."

"How'd you get them," I asked, curious how Steve knew where the wine was buried when all the folks who have been looking for it over many years couldn't find the site.

"Read a lot of books. Studied tons of maps. Talked to a lot of the old timers."

"So did everyone else before you," Jimmy added. "That's how treasures are found. You can't be the first to track this down."

"You passed the Garcia family back there. Grandson dug up an old safe a year or so back. Sold it for scrap iron. A friend of mine bought it and found a diary. That diary led me to Matamoros and an heir of one of the pirates from the Pride. A delightful young woman who has in her possession several other diaries of men from that ship. She even suggested that one of those diaries belonged to Lafitte himself. According to her, the records she has refer to the Pride as the Arro-Gance. I think to avoid any of them being linked directly to the Pride."

"Why would that be," I asked.

"To avoid being hanged for piracy would be my guess. But, here's the important thing I found. One of those diaries had coordinate references to an old map centered around a town called Bagdad which, at the time, was on the south bank of the Rio Grande. The coordinates to the Arro-Gance are measured from that town."

"Seems straightforward enough," Jimmy said, becoming impatient with Steve's wondering story.

"Except for the shifting sands. Bagdad's not where it once was."

"Cut to the chase," Tiny chimed in, "what's the bottom line here?"

"Bottom line is it just so happens I bought that map ten years ago from a fellow over in Reynosa. Only copy in existence far's I can tell. I plotted the coordinates from that old diary onto my Bagdad map and corrected for sand shift. So, bottom line, I have the exact modern-day coordinates."

"I'm waiting," Tiny said. "Time's not on our side. Spit them out!"

"When you plot these, you may find you have more than time to contend with," Steve said, closing his eyes as if conjuring up the numbers.

I knew Steve better than that. He was savoring the moment.

When Steve conjured long enough, he began spouting numbers. "25.3043N, 90.0559W."

The instant Steve closed his eyes Tiny, anticipating what was coming, opened a coordinate converter on his cell phone. Tiny was now entering the numbers as fast as Steve said them. When Steve revealed the last number, Tiny turned his screen to face us. The site appeared to be the Gulf of Mexico just off Boca Chica Beach. That was right where someone, I don't recall whom, had projected it to be. Steve was dealing in old news.

"That's where the Rio Grande flows into the Gulf," Jimmy said. "Right where I would expect a treasure to be hidden. Big mud flat now." Jimmy thought a moment then said, "Oh shit!"

I had no idea what Jimmy's 'Oh, shit' meant, but it certainly didn't bode well. My heart sank.

"That could be in Mexican waters," Jimmy tentatively announced. "We'd never be able to pull this off. Not without starting a border fight."

"We can approach from the north, can't we?" I countered. "Stay out of Mexico."

Jimmy thought for a moment before responding. "Only if the wine's north of the border. But, if it's north that's exactly where the SpaceX launch pad is located. We can't be mounting an expedition under Elon Musk's Starship rocket. That'll never work."

"It's not under the beach," Steve said, a satisfied look spreading across his normally serious face. "It's buried in a natural depression exactly fifty-three feet down. That's just below the thermocline and into the discontinuity layer. That means the temperature should have been constant at around fifty degrees. The wine may be well reserved. Perfect, I would expect."

I waited for him to finish his thought before I challenged him. "Steve," I began, "people have been talking for…for a while now about wine being found off Boca Chica Beach. What really makes your coordinates better than theirs?"

"What coordinates do they have? 'Off the beach' is not a coordinate. There are countless miles to search. And at what depth? All that talk is speculation. Mine're accurate. Take to the bank accurate."

"Assuming you're right, Steve," Jimmy said, "how the hell do we haul the barrels out without getting into Mexican territory?"

"I did my part. You have the coordinates. Go for it."

I didn't hold out much hope. "Even if we can get onto SpaceX property, which I doubt we can, we can't be setting up digging equipment around the launch pad."

Tiny, who had been studying his phone, said "To make matters worse, there's a test launch set next week. Target date for the launch is Wednesday."

"That translates into increased activity on the beach—and scrutiny," Jimmy said. "Exactly what we can't tolerate."

"Been thinking hard about this for a while," Steve injected. "Launch preparation plays in our favor. They're working twenty-four seven to get ready for the test. People coming and going at all hours, doing all manner of stuff. This launch site is new, so there're lots of amateurs posting all kinds of crap. Some of it's right on, some wonky. We could use social media to distract folks. Equipment can be coming and going, and we claim it's part of the launch."

"Cut to the chase, Hathcock!" Tiny's patience was at an end. "What's your plan?"

"Dig a water well north of the access road. Only instead of going all the way down for water, we go down vertically to the fifty-three-foot depth. Then we drill southeast horizontally. Nobody'd be the wiser."

"How the hell do we get the wine out with a water pipe?" I asked, troubled by what I had heard so far. "Suck it out?"

"The water well concept is for public consumption, Angella. The actual hole will be thirty inches or so in diameter."

"That's all sand down there," Tiny said. "We can't be drilling a thirty-inch tunnel on the shoreline. It'll collapse before we go three feet."

"Not if it's lined. This is oil drilling country, my friend. These guys can drill for miles and hit a pin. With the electronics they use these days, once the shaft gets within fifty feet of the barrels it'll adjust both horizontally and vertically perfectly."

Tiny thought a moment, then responded, "Could work, I would think. Have a name in mind for the drilling since you've thought it all out?"

"That, partner," Steve said, doffing his hat in mock tribute, "is where you come in. I'm a locksmith and historian, not a frigg'n engineer."

"Then excuse me while I get things underway." Tiny moved off by himself, his cell phone to his ear.

When Tiny was out of hearing range, Steve asked, "Why do I get the feeling I've just stepped into something won't come off my shoe?"

"What's that supposed to mean?" I asked.

"Got the feeling Tiny already knew those coordinates. I'm in over my head here. Time to stop digging."

Steve excused himself, telling us he was going off in search of a grave marker he claimed could prove some point or another with respect to Texas/Mexican history. He refused to elaborate further, saying only that we'd have to read his next book to find out what he was researching. He seemed more excited about his research than he did about retrieving the wine.

Jimmy and I spent the next several minutes enjoying quiet time together, letting the warm, windless day, perform its magic, while taking in the fragrance of the freshly cut flowers all around us. I thought about how nice it would be to live somewhere with Jimmy, a place where the two of us could walk arm in arm enjoying life together, instead of constantly wondering what nasty things were waiting for us around the next bend. After the last few days I needed to hold and touch his solid body more than ever. How wonderful it would be, if only…

"Jimmy," Tiny's voice brought me back to the present, "how about you and Angella meeting me at the McAllen Crossing, Room 103, at seventeen hundred hours?"

"Is that necessary?" Jimmy foolishly asked.

"Unquestionably. That'll give the team time to gather and we'll go over plans at that point." Checking his watch, he added with an uncharacteristic smile, "That gives you a little over four hours of private time. Use it wisely. Capisci?"

"What was that about?" I asked Jimmy after Tiny exited the cemetery. "Sometimes that man gives you more information than you can possibly use, and other times not enough to keep you alive. I never know which we've received."

"More important," Jimmy responded, a playful grin on his face, and his arm around my waist, "let's take his advice and use our time wisely."

"Your knee up to it?"

"There's only one way to find out."

"You driving, or am I?"

"You. I'm saving my knee."

EIGHTEEN

Room 103 turned out to be a sound proofed sensitive information conference room, a SCIF if you will, with the usual display of flat screened TVs mounted on the front wall. Two conference tables flanked them with chairs on the near side all facing the monitors.

Angella's eyes lit up when she came through the door. Her focus was on a DEA agent I met only moments before. She ran over and hugged him. "Oh, it's good to see you again. I take it you're okay. Thanks for helping me get out of Mexico without incident." She turned to me. "Jimmy, come over here and meet Dill. Dill Pickale. He's the guy I was telling you about. The one who escorted me in Mexico."

"We met a few minutes ago," I said. "Thanks for taking care of Angella. Appreciate it."

"I wasn't sick," Dill confessed. "Drugged is more accurate. Sorry to have left you, Angella. But it seems to have turned out well anyway."

Coast Guard Captain Ernest Boyle came through the door and I tuned Dill out. Over the years Boyle and I have barely been civil to one another. I don't know what it is about him, but he grates on me like few others ever have. My body heaved when I realized he was now wearing two stars. Angella often cautioned me that the brig was in my future if I continued to bait him. If she was right then, now I'd be lucky not to face a firing squad. I held out my hand in greeting. As polite as I could manage, I said, "Hello, Rear Admiral Boyle. You're looking well. Appears congratulations are in order."

"Thanks, Redstone," Boyle briskly replied. "So, how's your knee? Heard it was touch and go there for a while."

"Swelling's down, the pain's minimal. Thanks for asking."

Never one for small talk, Boyle cut the banter short. "I see you met Dill. He's with DEA. And this," Boyle nodded in the direction of a woman who entered the room behind him, "is Deputy Homeland Secretary Diane Sweet."

Sweet's handshake was stronger than Boyle's and caught me by surprise. *Overcompensation?*

"And this gentleman is with the FBI. Heads their Counterterrorism Division. Name's Newton Fairwell. Assume for the purposes of this meeting that both he and Dill hold the proxy of their boss, the Attorney General." Boyle glanced around, motioned for the armed escort to leave and close the door behind him. He took a seat at the far table. Secretary Sweet sat beside him and Tiny eased his large frame into a chair at the far end. That left the worker bees, Angella, Fairwell, Pickale and me at the near table.

Boyle picked up a remote and a moment later a blow-up of the Gulf of Mexico, just off the Boca Chica Beach appeared in front of us. It was the same one we saw earlier on Tiny's phone. Only this time the footprint of SpaceX was superimposed over the terrain. Then a second screen came alive displaying an aerial view taken from directly overhead the launch site. This snapshot clearly showed a squat-looking rocket on the launch pad, its nose pointing toward the sky. "As I understand the plan," Boyle began, "a tunnel will be dug starting here." A white X appeared on the image a distance up the beach from where the rocket was positioned. "Plan is for the tunnel to go vertically downward some fifty-three feet, then, correct me if I'm wrong here, turn horizontal and proceed at that depth straight out under the Gulf until it intersects with our target, which is here." A second white X appeared out in the Gulf of Mexico almost directly east from the Rio Grande River mouth. "I have this right?"

No one corrected him.

"I asked, is this right?" Boyle glared at the room. "The answer is a yes or a no!" He focused on the big guy across from him. "Tiny, this is a CIA operation. You represent the CIA, so do we have your blessing?"

"Not exactly, sir," Tiny answered, clearly uncomfortable. "I'm of the belief the horizontal tunnel portion will run south under the beach area and pass just in front, that is, to the east of, the launch pad. It won't turn east toward the target until here." Using another laser pointer, Tiny positioned the red dot on the beach just north of the mouth of the Rio Grande. "Here's where the tunnel will turn east and intersect the target site here." The red dot now focused on an area in the Gulf of Mexico. "At all times the tunnel will remain north of the border."

"Why the hell not just dig it directly as I showed it? Save time."

"I can shed light on this," Secretary Sweet chimed in. "Department of Energy voiced a concern with the tunnel casings being positioned off-shore. Claims it's their jurisdiction and they can't give permission without an environmental impact statement—and public hearings. They raised questions as to who owns the mineral rights. And frankly, they believe we're operating too close to the Mexican border."

Boyle was having none of this. "What's wrong with you people? This is a military operation! Got no time for bullshit studies and permits! I'll get the White House on the line and have this resolved in minutes!" He grabbed his phone, realized that he had no signal, and stood to leave.

"Hold on a moment will you Admiral," Sweet calmly responded, "I believe the route we have laid out here works just fine. Better even than direct."

"Why's that?" Boyle shot back, his neck showing red lines up to his ears.

"Hand me that pointer, will you Tiny." Sweet took the offered pointer and moved the red dot to highlight the first white X. "Here's your starting point for the tunnel." She then dragged the dot north along the beach a good distance and moved it several feet west. "We plan to start here. Far enough away from the launch pad and fortuitously on a property deeded to an individual some years ago and long since abandoned. It's private land and makes drilling for water a plausible cover. Since it's private, the Texas Land Office doesn't care and if they don't care there's no one to inform Energy. Staying under the beach and not tunneling under water until way down here." Sweet moved the red dot so it again appeared on the beach just north of the river. "This route gives us less under water exposure. A collapse under sand is far easier to deal with than one under water. And...and our environmental exposure is significantly less as well. Furthermore, we can fight over who owns the treasure later."

"If it can be completed in time," Boyle conceded, "I'm on board. Anyone have any thoughts?" Boyle looked from one to the other of us, then said, "I hear no objections. Now that we have the route, let's move on to the actual drilling. Two different drillers will be involved." Boyle's X danced all over the beach, finally settling about a half-mile north of the launch site on the property Sweet identified. "The vertical part over here," he said, "will be drilled by a traditional water drilling company." He paused to be certain all eyes were focused on the screen. "Now this horizontal part under the beach and out to the target site will be handled by the military."

Dill frowned but said nothing.

"Speak up, Pickale. You troubled or what?"

"I know a bit about drilling," Dill reluctantly answered. "Father worked over in East Texas. Owned a supply company before he retired. And they won't share their equipment. Whoever puts in the casings for the vertical portion will insist on going all the way."

"Leave that to me," Boyle barked. "Just get someone in here who can drill straight down. I'll handle the rest."

"*Waterwell Riggers* out of Pharr is about the best in the business," Dill volunteered. "I assume the shaft will be much larger than a normal water well. They can go all the way up to five feet in diameter. I saw several of their derricks over in the Brownsville Channel being worked on. They won't be need'n them for drilling on land, but I bet they have a few crews hanging loose."

Secretary Sweet leaned forward. "I suggest we go with three-foot diameter casing. Who the hell knows what size those barrels are?"

Boyle frowned. "That's assuming there are even barrels to extract—and assuming they're worth extracting."

Sweet's face tightened and her eyes narrowed. "Admiral let's just trust that wine's where we believe it to be. And the barrels are intact. This promises to change the Middle East dynamics for a lifetime to come. I'll have my folks contact *Waterwell Riggers.* Dill, you coordinate with Elon Musk about our activities on the beach. Tell him no launch before next Thursday. Friday would be better. I say we set Tuesday for tunnel completion. Leaving wine extraction for Wednesday."

"What if he insists on launching sooner?"

"Mention my name. He needs more from us than we need from him. He won't be a problem. Promise." Sweet looked down the table at Boyle. "You, sir, I assume will arrange for the military portion of the tunnel."

"Positive on that, Madam Secretary," Boyle snapped.

Sweet looked around the room to see if anyone had anything further to say. When everyone remained silent, she said, "Vertical drilling needs to begin by tomorrow morning and horizontal by…by…help me here."

"I'll have my folks work it. One way or another the tunnel will be operational come sunup Wednesday." Boyle checked the room. No one said anything. He then announced, "Meeting's over. Redstone. Martinez. Fairwell. Remain. Secretary Sweet, you're optional if you wish."

Sweet, who was his boss, glared at the Admiral, started to respond, thought better of it and made her way out to the corridor. I couldn't help but think she hadn't risen to her position by not carefully picking her fights.

Tiny walked out with the rest of them, leaving Angella, FBI Agent Fairwell and me alone with Boyle. As soon as the door closed, Boyle turned to me. "Listen, Redstone. You and I have had our differences over the years. I don't mind telling you I'm not your biggest fan. If I had my way, you wouldn't be anywhere near this operation. But that ship has sailed. Fact is, you're a frigg'n cowboy, a wild card, and everyone knows it. Going forward, you get your ass off script…and well, just keep in mind all rescue operations are under my command. If you're told to sit in a room until a certain trigger event, then by God you sit in that room until the trigger occurs. And I don't care what the hell reason you have for violating that order. You sit in that room! You understand me?"

"Yes, sir," I said, forcing myself not to mock salute. Angella tensed while Boyle was talking. Now that I hadn't taken the bait, she relaxed, even smiled slightly.

"I'll leave these two to you, Fairwell. Be sure they both understand their respective roles, but nothing beyond what they need to hear. You never know if one or both will manage to get themselves left behind."

"Yes, sir," the agent said following my lead and keeping his thoughts to himself.

"What the hell you two ever do to rile him up?" Fairwell asked after Boyle slammed the door behind him.

"I've worked with a ton of flag officers over the years and never one so…so blatantly hostile."

"He may be an officer," I offered, "but he's certainly no gentleman."

Angella added, "Jimmy and Boyle are like two dogs who hate each other at first sight. Who knows why? Maybe their tails weren't wagging energetically enough."

"Not a good guy to piss off. He's the one arranged to have you extracted from the mountain. From what I just heard I'm surprised he didn't abort the plan. Anyway, let's get on with the briefing. Angella, you spoke with the woman Joy Malcom. I need to know everything she said. What she knows. What you believe she didn't say. Everything. Hold back nothing."

Angella glanced at me and I nodded my consent. Knowing the FBI, they most likely had it all on tape anyway. They were now just doing what they do best, checking Angella's reliability—and honesty.

When Angella finished relating her most recent conversation with Malcom, Fairwell said, "Now tell me everything that happened from the instant you entered Mexico, until you were on the bridge home. I assume Santiago gave you the name of the top fentanyl supplier. Let's start with that and go from there. Again, leave out nothing."

Fairwell only interrupted her narrative when Angella related the part about the prison guard commenting on her shoe size. He had her go over that portion several times, before asking, "Did they take pictures?"

"Not that I was aware. Check that. The guard was using his cell for something. Might have taken pictures."

"Were there surveillance cameras?"

"I have to assume so, but I wasn't aware of any."

"Did you happen to glance up to check the ceiling?"

"Never thought to."

"The shoes you wore out, were they identical to the ones you wore in?"

"As far as I could tell. Yes."

"And you exchanged shoes with Santiago in the yard?"

"Against the wall, near a door. He said we were out of camera range there."

"And the shank, the one you threw away. That, you say, was in the right shoe when you walked out?"

"Yes. Hey, am I in trouble?"

"Not with us you're not. But with our friends to the south, who knows. We can assume they have footage of you going in and coming out wearing those oversized shoes. They also know Santiago wears those exact same shoes. I wouldn't think they believe in coincidences any more than we do."

"So," Angella said, following up on her concerns, "without that picture of me throwing the shank in the bushes they have only speculation. With it, they got me dead to rights."

"They may also have footage of you at the border wearing your normal size shoes. That footage will provide evidence that you acted improperly, perhaps smuggling something into or out of the prison. They've put people in prison for far less. Hate to tell you, but you need to know what cards they're holding." Fairwell turned to me. "Anything to add?"

"Angella's covered it."

"Okay, then. Jimmy, now talk to me about the men who kidnapped you. What were they driving? Who approached you? What was said? Again, I want everything you know. Descriptions of the men, the cabin, the road leading up there. As I told Angella, start from your crossing into Mexico until you woke up in the hospital"

I assumed everything I said was being recorded. Martha Stewart, as well as everybody who pays any attention to these things, well knows lying or making false statements to the FBI can, and often does, result in prison time. I was wearing an earpiece at that time so, in theory anyway, they already knew more than I did. That just meant that I had to play it straight and give Fairwell everything I did, saw and heard.

When I finally finished, he simply asked, "Anything you want to add, correct or elaborate on?"

"Can't think of anything."

"Okay, then. Let's move on to the wine extraction part of this operation. As you know, everything depends on Mazdani believing the wine is genuine and not an American trick. I don't know if he knows this or not, but wine can be tested for heritage."

"This is what's bothering me," Angella said, her face twisted into a frown, "the wine Steve's talking about, according to his sources, is French wine. He told us about the manifest that lists French wine in barrels. To be authentic, the wine under the Gulf needs to come from a Persian vineyard. If he has it tested this whole operation is in jeopardy."

"Great observation, Angella. I'm told the manifest is in error. Wine was listed as French to avoid certain duties." Fairwell winked. "And tests...well, they depend on the lab doing the testing. Get my drift. Not to worry."

I got his drift and I'm certain Angella did as well. A lot of time and money had been pumped into this operation and we'd better get with the program. But I also had concerns. "I always thought wine turned to vinegar if exposed to air for any period of time. This wine's in wood barrels. Wood is porous. Air had to get to it. So, what makes anyone think they can test anything?"

"Good question," Fairwell acknowledged. "Truth is I don't know the answer. Perhaps the experts believe the barrels are sealed in some way. But for our purposes we're going with the plan."

"And that is?" Angella asked.

"When the first barrel comes out of the ground, the plan is to video record you placing it in a sealed, protective environment to maintain its temperature and humidity. Experts are thinking it's been at fifty-three degrees with sixty percent humidity. We'll see."

I chimed in, "Steve said there could be as many as twenty barrels. What about the others?"

“Our folks are saying ten at most and likely six.”

Angella thought a moment, then asked, “If I’m only taking one, what about the others?”

“They’ve been down there all these years, another few days—or weeks—is not an issue. What we need is buy-off by Mazdani that he accepts at least one of them as genuine. Part of that buy-off is being certain he sees the actual barrels coming out of the ground and…and that the barrels have the coat of arms on them.”

“The three lions?”

“Three lions,” Fairwell responded, nodding in appreciation that I already knew that.

I was confused. “But I thought the coat-of-arms was in ceramic, on casks, not on barrels?”

“Beyond my pay grade, I’m afraid,” Fairwell reluctantly confessed.

“What does buy-off look like?” I asked, preferring to know when Angella’s mission would be complete.

“Couple of parts. First, Mazdani must accept Angella and her story. And…”

“Which is?” I inquired. “What is Angella’s story?”

“Coming to it. As I was saying, Angella will produce the barrel, protective shell and all. Mazdani will open it, but not before he satisfies himself that the barrel is genuine. If he’s so satisfied, then he’ll sample the contents. I suspect he’ll test it first.”

“To determine if it’s spoiled or…or poisoned?”

Angella was ahead of me with her question.

"Spoilage mostly. There are far easier ways to poison him than to go to this much effort. This guy's betting his life on the wine being genuine Shiraz from a royal estate. Selective disbelief or some such thing. He desperately wants to believe the wine on that ship was produced by his family. So that's what he'll believe. We must do nothing to change that belief."

"And this lineage thing?" Angella asked. "Can he pull it off?"

"Ever since he first heard the rumors, about three years ago, he's been planning. We've been planting clues and stories in various places around the world. And it's working. He's already been approached from numerous governments expressing their support. We've been...augmenting so to speak, his narrative. The negative stuff we've uncovered has been...shall we say...eliminated. If he believes the wine is genuine, Mazdani will—with a little help from his friends—become King of Persia."

"If the wine is spoiled, which it most likely will be," I asked, "will all bets be off?"

"Not necessarily. The massive profits may go away. But he'll still be king. A king owned by us."

Fairwell was finished with his briefing, such as it was. He stood to leave.

"Now that we know what Angella's mission is, how's she going to pull it off?"

"Need to know, Redstone. Need to know."

NINETEEN

I was contemplating my response to effectively having been read out of the operation, when Admiral Boyle reentered the room. "Good news to report. Mazdani's been discussing the wine with several experts and he's excited to the extreme. Seems there's massive support for a new leader with direct ties back to the Staufer Dynasty."

Puzzled, I said, "Staufer Dynasty? I thought…"

"I know, Redstone, you were told Hohenstaufen. They're one in the same. Mazdani prefers Staufer. He's tying the Staufer Dynasty to the Qajars who ruled when Persia was split about evenly between Armenian and Muslim. Better for our purposes."

"And the bad news?" I asked. "There's always bad news."

"Hold your horses, Redstone. I never knew you to be a pessimist." Boyle had a way of issuing a challenge without saying anything. In this case, his eyes did the work.

Angella's hand on my side was enough of a warning to silence me—for now.

"If you'll allow me to continue, I'll..."

I bowed my head in mock subservience, keeping my mouth shut.

"...tell you. All the experts he's consulted, and he's consulted many, have assured him the original manifest of the sailing ship Pride, not the manifest in the French Customs Ministry, listed ten barrels of wine made from grapes grown in Shiraz, Persia. He's also convinced the Sailing Ship Pride sank off South Padre Island with the Shiraz wine still on board. He's skeptical the wine would have survived this long or, if it did survive, that it would still be identifiable as having come from the royal vineyard."

"That's a lot to overcome. What will it take to convince him?"

"That's really the money question. And that's where you come in. You're to meet and convince him the wine's genuine."

"You just said his own experts haven't been able to accomplish that task. I have no background in wine to speak of. So, what do I bring to the table they don't?"

"In Mazdani's eyes you come highly accredited as an honest person. Santiago and his network have seen to that. You delivered something called the Kings Cup. Here's my thought for what it's worth. Slight change of plans. We bring Mazdani to the site and let him be the first to see the wine before it's even dug out of the ground. He'll see the barrels as they're uncovered and supervise them being placed in protective jackets."

"How in the hell are we going to accomplish that?" I asked, no longer able to hold my silence. "That shaft is three feet in diameter. We can't be taking Mazdani, or anyone else, in there."

"Been thinking of this all wrong. We're not drilling for oil. We're tunneling for solid minerals. Think copper. Coal. Military says piece of cake. Instead of making the bore three foot, we're making it ten, possibly twelve. For this short a distance they'll use an auger and follow behind with preformed tunnel-like supports. The borehole will need minimal support since it only need remain in position a week or two at most. Military has just the system."

"That's a lot of equipment to muster in a day," I said, skeptical about logistics.

"Nothing a C-5 Galaxy can't handle. It'll take a full day to gather the material and a crew, so we won't start the tunnel until Sunday at the earliest. That pushes our time frame out a few days. With the larger bore size there's no possibility of finishing before early Wednesday morning. Even that will be tight."

Something was troubling Boyle, but I couldn't determine what it was. "Even with the increased size," I said, "aren't we still on track with our original time frame?"

"Biggest problem," Boyle replied, "is Tuesday's the latest Santiago can guarantee to keep you alive up on the mountain."

"Should I assume we somehow have an extra day?" I asked, wondering where Boyle was going.

"Santiago, if you can trust him, claims he managed to somehow convince Mazdani to intercede. According to Santiago, Mazdani bought one more day. Until Wednesday sunup."

"That seems to have fixed the problem," I said.

"Only if you trust Santiago," Boyle shot back, making me believe he knew something I didn't about Santiago.

"Second biggest problem?" Angella, who had been sitting quietly, asked.

"Maybe not a real problem. But a concern. Musk insists they must launch Wednesday. Something to do with the location of a tracking satellite. They need it in order to capture both the launch rocket, as well as the payload. Wednesday has several small windows and if they miss those it'll be a while before the next launch possibility."

"Consider this," I said. "Use the launch as a reason for Mazdani to visit the island. Special VIP treatment. That'll cover his reason to be in the vicinity and play well back in Iran."

"I'll run it up the flagpole, Redstone. See who salutes," Boyle said and exited the room.

Fairwell rejoined us. I turned to him. "What I don't understand is this. You extracted me from the mountain. Why not just go up and get my look-alike? Woof, he's out of there."

"For the same reason we didn't just extract you and leave them with nothing. You, in the form of your look-alike—let's call him Jimmy2—are being interrogated. In essence you're up there talking to your captors, convincing Mazdani, who's been watching you on a monitor, that you're with Santiago and no longer an American agent."

"Good luck with that."

"It's the best we can do. Improvising because of the shooting. Rehabilitating you in his eyes. Best laid plans and all that. Look, shit happens. But, truth is, the Company still feels good about this operation."

They felt good about the Bay of Pigs. Until they didn't.

"Don't know if I can really trust the CIA's assessment on operational integrity."

"Hate to break it to you, Redstone, but this operation's much bigger than you. We need someone Mazdani can trust with his life."

"I thought that was Angella."

"She's the initial piece in this. Her job is to make Mazdani comfortable with American support; secure believing the wine is genuine. As was just decided, she's also now tasked with getting him to see the wine being extracted from under the Gulf."

"My mission then is?"

"To persuade Mazdani to enter the tunnel with you—and Angella. That it's not a trap. You do that by convincing him you're with Santiago—and him.

"I thought that's what I was doing?" Angella said, with a puzzled expression.

"Sorry, Angella. Truth is, in his world women can only do so much. You're the key to getting Mazdani with us. But, as he sees life, men must only rely on men. I wish it weren't so, but I can't change his culture."

"But he hates America," Angella shot back. "Does he not?"

"That's the tricky part. He hates America, but…but here's where he's going to get the massive amount of money and support it takes to overthrow the Revolution. He's teetering on the fence over this aspect. You two need to push him over."

Angella remained quiet several minutes, obviously troubled, then calmly asked, "You do realize, he's spent his entire life hating us. And we're supposed to change a lifetime in a few hours? That doesn't add up."

"All I can say, Angella, is he's a political animal at heart. In that arena, the old axiom, the enemy of my enemy is my friend, is very much true. Couple that with his burning desire to become King and unite all of Iran, and our assessment is we have a better than even chance to pull this off."

"If everything goes in our favor," Angella quipped.

"Then, let's hope everything goes as planned. Take a seat and we'll go over the plans."

Sitting where Fairwell pointed, the screen came again. Only this time we were inside the mountain cabin and there I was wearing the same clothes I had been wearing when they extracted me, only filthy now. My beard was several days old and whoever this Jimmy2 character was, he was younger than me and his beard is darker. In all other aspects, even I would have been fooled. "What exactly am I listening for?"

"Background first. One of the guys that captured you, the big one, goes by *Encarnizado*, he's…"

"Cutthroat. Quick with the knife."

"They're all quick with the knife. Least that's my experience. Anyway, this...this Cutthroat has a sideline going. In addition to the fentanyl, he's branched into human trafficking. Women, mostly young girls, are his specialty. His women come from the Middle East and his supplier goes by the name of *el Bandito*. As luck would have it, we turned this guy Cutthroat about six weeks ago. He's wired as we speak."

Human trafficking, especially young girls, is a raw topic for Angella. To her, freeing those women was of far more importance than toppling the Iranian government. "This *el Bandito*?" she questioned, "You have a real name for him?"

Fairwell sucked in his breath and tossed his head back, as if he just opened a refrigerator door and was hit with a foul odor. Tight lipped, he worked through what he was about to say.

"Just say it," I instructed. "It can't be as bad as that face you just pulled. You want our cooperation; we want yours in return."

"Not to leave this room?"

Angella and I both nodded.

"Nothing official, but street rumors are that General Mazdani and *el Bandito* are one in the same."

"And we're going to make this guy King!" Angella was furious. She jumped to her feet and began pacing the room. "What the hell!"

"Calm down, Angella. First of all, we're not certain we have that right. Cutthroat hasn't met the top man. We're working on it."

"But if he's King, then…"

"Let's focus on our mission. Secretary Sweet's down here working the *el Bandito* issue. She'll roll him up the instant she gets anything resembling reliable. You might have picked up tension between her and the Admiral. That's what is at the heart of it. We know there's a major movement of women planned very soon, but we don't know in what sector. Every night there's a few, but intelligence suggests a big push is coming. But…but that's not on our plate. For our purposes, Cutthroat is up in that shack trying to get you, Jimmy, to talk about your involvement with Santiago. Jimmy2's been scripted to talk as though he supports Santiago, and by extension, human trafficking. Idea being to increase Mazdani's trust in you, especially after you shot one of theirs."

"That's disgusting to even think about," Angella snapped, as agitated as I had ever seen her. "If my involvement helps him enslave women, I'm out!"

"I hear you, Angella. Loud and clear. Truth is, I'm with you on this. But…" Fairwell took a moment to compose his thoughts. Unlike Tiny, I sensed he was sorting through what he could tell us and what he couldn't. Tiny mostly told us nothing beyond what was required for the immediate operation. "Here's the thing. The intelligence is unclear. We have Zetas ratting out Sinaloas, who rat on Gulfs. The Mexican government is in the middle. Usually we can trust their military to play it straight—but not always."

A light went off in my head. "Is that why Boyle's running the show? Military to military?"

"Bingo! But only half the story. Coast Guard belongs to Homeland Security. Sweet is Boyle's boss so to speak."

Angella broke in. "Yet, Boyle's in charge?"

"Complicated, at best," Fairwell patiently said. "CIA reports to the Director of National Intelligence who reports essentially to the President. The...let's just call it the Wine To King, WTK, operation because you're not cleared for the actual operational name...The WTK operation was assigned to the Joint Chiefs because of the close working ties our military has with Mexico. Military *borrowed* Boyle from the Coast Guard because of his extensive connections along the Texas/Mexico border. Following me?"

"So far," I said. "But where does Deputy Homeland Secretary Sweet fit in here?"

"As I said, she's directly coordinating the crackdown on trafficking. That operation is separate from the WTK operation. In fact, Sweet didn't even know of the WTK existence until the shooting. Everyone's been scrambling since then. Angella, Sweet's as outraged as you about us making a king out of...of a war criminal and woman trafficker."

"What's she doing about it?" Angella demanded.

"That remains to be seen," Fairwell sympathetically answered. "Way above my pay grade. And frankly, above yours as well. Let's get on with the Wine-To-King operation and leave the trafficking to Sweet—and her superiors. I care that your lives hinge on getting this right."

Never mind that I don't have a pay grade.

"You serious?"

"As serious as a bullet to the brain, Angella. As you well know, these folks don't play nice. They kill first and never ask questions."

The video of what was going on in the cabin was extremely poor. I assume this was a bandwidth issue. Images of people remained on screen for long periods of time and at times the audio was garbled. But for the most part, I could clearly hear the verbal exchanges. There was no question they had been edited over a course of time and I began to think the video was intentionally grainy to hide the editing.

I tuned out of the rest of what Jimmy2 was saying and focused on what I knew, thought I knew, and what I didn't know. And the more I concentrated, the less certain I was that I knew the truth about anything relevant to this operation.

"Jimmy," Angella exclaimed several minutes later, "Jimmy2 has me convinced he'd fight against the U.S. should it come to that. He also's convinced me he'd support a Jihad. He's doing such a good job I could see Boyle sending a drone after him—you."

"Get it right, Angella," Agent Fairwell called from across the room. "Iranian's are Shia. Jihad refers to Sunni."

"So's Mazdani Shia?"

"Shia, with a strong Armenian influence. At least that's how he sees himself and that's all we need be concerned with. If you want to tag him, call him militia. He'll respond positively to that."

"How about, King?" I quipped. "King Mazdani."

"That'll be soon enough," Fairwell said with conviction.

He actually believes this messed up operation still has legs.

Angella digested what she just learned, started to ask a question, but instead asked, "How's his English?"

"Flawless. Brown educated with dual degrees in petroleum engineering and business management. Spent time at Oxford as well."

"I see why bringing him out to the tunnel in person makes sense."

"It does, Angella. He's a hands-on guy. Doesn't trust much of what he's told. In his current culture deception is the rule. He remains alive by verification—and cross-checking. We know he's desperate to get his hands on the wine barrels but…but he won't go anywhere near them until he's fully satisfied he can do so safely, and…and, of course, without exposure to the Ayatollah."

Something Fairwell just said stirred a thought. "The barrels. He wants to get to the barrels. At first, I translated that to mean the wine in the barrels, but I'm not so positive it's the wine."

"What then?" Angella asked.

"The barrels themselves. This guy's claiming a heritage back to a former dynasty. I bet he's mostly interested in the family crest."

Fairwell's face came alive for the first time. "Family crest is important. If Jimmy's right, and he very well might be, then I do believe your job just got easier—at least in one aspect."

Fairwell's changed tone sent a warning. "What other aspects are there?" I asked.

"For one," Fairwell quickly responded as if he had rehearsed this part, "his reluctance to believe anyone he hasn't known all his life."

"And two?"

"He's rumored to be somewhat of a lady's man."

The way Fairwell tried to casually slip this in triggered my antenna. "I call bullshit on this operation! I'm not allowing Angella to..."

"I can take care of myself." Angella's mouth went tight, as it does when she's angry with me for being overprotective.

"Aren't you the one who wants out of this life?" I snapped. "You're walking right into it"

"It is what it is, Jimmy. Aren't you the one who preaches to go with the flow when it's inevitable? Take your own advice."

"Not in this context!" Jimmy shot back.

I didn't really know what being a *lady's man* meant in the Muslim terrorist culture. But from the images on TV it wasn't a good thing. I couldn't remain idle and not try to mitigate the situation. "Is this briefing over?" I asked. "I need space to think. And answers to questions!"

"Questions such as?" Fairwell responded, looking as if he was genuinely concerned.

"Such as what's the book on him with women? Mutilation? Domination? What?"

"How about good old-fashioned gallantry? Guy believes women find him irresistible."

"It's not easy to resist with a knife at your throat."

"Nothing in the file suggests nonconsensual sex, if that's what you're asking."

"Because women don't report it, doesn't mean it didn't happen. Unfortunately, we now have plenty of evidence to support that fact."

"Jimmy!" Angella hissed. "Back off! I can handle myself."

"How about we modify the operation?" I suggested. "I'll go with Angella to convince the Iranian to claim his wine."

"As the good Admiral might say, 'That ship has sailed, and you weren't on board'. As I will say, Mazdani almost never allows another man in a room with him without his bodyguard."

"And Angella's going in alone?"

"Look, Jimmy," Fairwell said, his voice sympathetic as well as commanding, "this operation's gone off the rails in several respects, not the least of which was you shooting the Zeta leader and then getting yourself captured. For better or worse, you're supposed to be up on that mountain. How in the hell can you visit him in Mexico City? Logistics don't work."

Fairwell's face was tight with tension for a moment. Then something seemed to ease his concern. "Tell you what. Let me see if it's safe to fit Angella with a camera, or even a mic. We'll then be able to monitor the operation. That work for you?"

"Monitoring from hours away. Useless! She's not going in alone! Period!"

Angella's eyes turned to fire. "Jimmy! Enough! Let it be! I told you I can take care of myself! And I mean it!"

Fairwell stepped between us. "Let's take a break. Food service is available next floor up. Be back here in fifteen."

I followed Angella out of the room, having no intention of showing up in fifteen minutes—or ever.

TWENTY

There was no talking to Jimmy as he paced the hallway outside the small cafeteria. From experience I knew to keep my distance when he was working through issues. I was busy also working on the mess we were in. I've often thought about how our government coordinates itself to keep from tripping over its own feet, especially when running covert operations. Now I was painfully aware that they don't. And trip they do. And it's the low folks in the pecking order, like Jimmy and me, whose lives are on the line when disparate operations collide.

I don't know what conclusions Jimmy reached, but I was now playing with the premise that the whole sunken ship with vintage wine and old coins was a fabrication assembled from actual facts.

Fact 1: Wine was pressed in Shiraz in about 1877.

Fact 2: Some or all that wine was put into wooden barrels.

Fact 3: Some or all those wooden wine barrels were shipped from Persia, via a sailing ship, to some foreign country. My guess is from the port city of Bushehr, which, if my memory is correct, is not far from Shiraz.

Fact 4: The wine barrels had on them the three-lion Staufer Dynasty crest.

Fact 5: Mazdani can show clear family linkage to that three-lion crest.

Fact 6: A ship carrying the Shiraz wine sank off the coast of South Padre Island. Question: Was the wine from Persia or France as the manifest claims?

Fact 7: Wine barrels from the sunken ship were moved to a location just east of the mouth of the Rio Grande River.

My take on all these facts: Facts 1, 2 and 3 are most likely actual facts, except the manifest says Cherbourg, France and not Bushehr. Fact 4 can be made up. However, if those lions are not on the barrels when they are dug up this whole charade fails, which the operational masterminds must have taken into account. Planting evidence and creating urban myths is not exactly a new undertaking for them, but it's now infinitely easier with social media.

It's a simple matter for the CIA and the FBI to fabricate entire lives. So, if they want Mazdani and his followers to believe he descends from the Staufer Dynasty, then the records will show exactly that. For my purposes then I must assume Fact 5 to be true.

Ships have been sinking off the SPI coast for centuries and rumors of have always existed of buried treasures filled with gold bullion and coins. But Steve's *evidence* of wine being uncovered during the depression and being blown up at the government's request appears plausible. Was it French or Persian wine? Subject of debate. My take, at least for now, assume Facts 6 and 7 to be true.

Now what?

Before I could work any further through this web my cell phone, which had been blocked while we were in the SCIF, downloaded several messages. The one from Attorney Merry Ayers caught my eye. Apparently, Joy was trying to reach me. When that failed, Joy called Ayers. Seems she wants assurance I'm cooperating with Morris. "You're to meet with someone she would only identify as a general on Monday at 19:00. Place to be set. Must confirm."

I sent Ayers a one-word response: Confirmed.

Jimmy's pacing had apparently aggravated his wound because he was resting against the wall. "Let's get something to eat," I gently suggested. "Do us both some good."

He answered with a question. "Could that imposter be Lester? I spoke to Les a few days ago about the wedding. He was up in Alaska about to get on a fishing boat for a month. I assume that's where he is."

Fact 8: People may not be who you believe they are, whether in person or on the phone. I didn't think Jimmy2 was Les. The imposter was younger than Les. But…but makeup in the right hands does wonders. "I met the guy. He's younger than your son. But…"

"You have doubts?"

"I do. Sorry." I pulled Jimmy close and hugged him, told him I loved him and not to worry so much about me. Then I said, "I think it's now clear, we're in the middle of a…a hot mess. CIAs been stirring this witch's brew a lot longer than we've been told. It goes all the way to the White House and who the hell knows how many countries are in on it. We jump out now, we're in the proverbial fire. Your advice for these situations, has always been suck it up and do your best. That was good advice then—and it's good now."

"It's just not right they're putting your life at risk without..."

"Jimmy, honey, that's the life we've both selected. When I became a cop I knew someday I could easily be looking down the wrong side of a discharging gun. It goes with the territory."

"That was then. This is now. No need to seek out that hot gun. I can't be without you."

"That's a topic for another day. A walk on the beach type of day. Today's a workday. Come on, get a sandwich, we have work to do. You always say the best way to come out the other end in one piece is preparation. So, let's go prepare."

To my surprise—and delight—Jimmy pulled me close and kissed me.

"Hey, you two," Fairwell called from inside the small eating area. "In other circumstances I'd tell you to get a room. But there's no time for that now. Grab a quick bite. In a few minutes, Jimmy, you're scheduled to meet with...I'll give you his name in private. And Angella you're about to learn more than you ever wanted to learn about the General and his culture. You do know, I believe, you're having dinner with him Tuesday night?"

"My message said Monday. One of us has it wrong."

"I'll have to check. But I'm pretty confident it's Tuesday. Monday's too soon. I'll go clear this up and be back for you both in a moment. Now get something to eat. May be your last chance for a while." He disappeared down the hall. Clearly the date change caught him off guard. Agent Fairwell, in my assessment, never wanted to be caught off guard. Whether this was a major glitch or something minor I couldn't assess.

We finished our lunch in silence and Jimmy out of the blue said, "I do love you, Angella. Perhaps more than you know. What you heard earlier is my concern. I know you can take care of yourself, but…you know I've spent so much of my life taking care of those around me I sometimes forget I could step back and it'll work out fine."

"I know Jimmy. I love you as well. Let's get through this, get ourselves married and…and live happily ever after."

"Define living happily ever after."

"Retire. Travel."

"I'm not sure I'm built for retirement."

"It's time, Jimmy. It's time. Maybe not full retirement, but no more field work. How about teaching? That's something you have a positive gift for. And you'll enjoy the challenge. Please think about it."

"Right now, I have all I can do to think about what's directly ahead for us. Next week is the far future. Planning horizon is not that far off."

"Speaking of planning for the future, you just triggered something I've been meaning to ask. Dill and I were stopped by rogue cops on our way to see Santiago. On the first leg, when we were using my car, they found a leather pouch similar to the one Steve gave us in the trunk with a one kilo gold bar inside."

"A kilo? Let's see, worth about fifty K or so. Where was it?"

"In our travel bag. I assume from your reaction it wasn't yours."

"Of course, it wasn't mine. You think it was?"

"With all that's going on, I don't know what to think anymore."

"Sounds like we need to…"

"Hate to break this up," Fairwell called, "but it's show time."

"Hold the thought," I said to Jimmy, somewhat confused by the situation.

Fairwell escorted me down the hall to a smallish classroom and locked the door behind us. DEA agent Dill appeared alongside Fairwell, and the last I saw, he and Jimmy were heading for the steps leading down to the SCIF. We were again being separated. Perhaps that was a good thing. Only time would tell.

"Angella," Fairwell began when we were back in our room, "you're right. Meeting's on for Monday. Everything's being sped up. We'll begin by prepping you for your time with Mazdani. As I said earlier, he grew up in a world where nothing is what it seems. Friends are not always friends. Even relatives are not always relatives. Even when they are, they often can't be trusted. It's no wonder he has trust issues. We have problems, however, other than trust. Three other major factors are at play here." Fairwell paused, making certain I was following, then continued. "The first is Trump's take out of Qassem Soleimani. That destabilized the conventional Iranian thinking about American behavior and how far we're prepared to go. Ramifications are yet to be fully known. The second is the age of the Ayatollah. There will be a change at the top not long from now. Put this together with the unrest of the people themselves and…and shall we say, self-doubts as to the political future of the country arise."

"Why the doubts?"

"Goes with the territory. Oppressive leadership, religious conflicts, you name it. It all works to our advantage."

"And you think a couple of barrels of old wine will convince Mazdani he's king?"

"Just one piece of a very big puzzle."

"And if it fails?"

"Don't consider failure, Angella."

"It's certainly a possibility."

"Then the puzzle will have a hole in it. Hopefully, the picture will still be recognizable."

The next several days were a blur. More details of Iranian life, culture, and religion, were thrown at me faster than I could possibly absorb in a lifetime. Jimmy, for his part, was reluctant to discuss what he was being subjected to. My sense of it was that he didn't want me worrying about him. That made me even more anxious. I worked hard to conceal my concern.

Things on the tunnel front were moving surprisingly fast. They were ahead of Boyle's aggressive schedule. Our government might not be adept at getting out of its own way for most things, but where the military is concerned, they're logistical masters. Video clips of the operation were routinely displayed during the course of our tutoring sessions. The first images were of large tubes cut in half along their longitudinal axis and loaded onto semi-trailers. Fairwell explained that each pipe section was fifty feet long and designed to nest inside each other for transportation. Each trailer carried four sections. At the job site two sections would be banded together to form a tube fifty feet long. So, if my math was any good, I rounded a mile of tunnel up to six thousand feet, which meant it would require sixty truckloads, plus all the banding material, the sealant, and the tools required to put it all together. And that didn't take into account the drilling augers and shafts. A long shot of the site revealed a caravan of tractor trailers stretching for miles. How they planned to get everything transported from the staging area, which was an unnamed island somewhere warm, and then flown down to Brownsville, Texas and ultimately delivered to Boca Chica Beach in less than two days strained my imagination.

"Piece of cake for those folks," Fairwell said, tossing a nod to the female supply sergeant now on-screen barking orders we could not hear to a beat-looking grunt with mud or grease streaks across the front of his work blouse. "I don't fancy myself much with logistics, but trust me, that's all been calculated and there won't be any whoopsies."

"How can you be certain?"

"With Admiral Boyle, or even with that supply sergeant you just saw, on your case, would you be prone to a whoops?"

"You telling me something?"

"Nothing you don't already know. We'll pull this operation off as planned. Period. End of sentence." Fairwell smiled slightly when I shook my head in affirmation. "Now, back to work. Time to talk about wine."

At least we weren't talking about what I had to wear or how to style my hair, or what lipstick and perfume was permissible. That session had sent chills down my spine and was why Jimmy and I had been separated.

If I was freaked out, Jimmy would have been more than furious imagining me alone with a womanizing Would-be King.

TWENTY-ONE

The first several days of our "training" went better than I could have expected. Angella and I were separated during the day but allowed to have dinner and sleep together at night. In exchange, we each reaffirmed at the end of every day that we would not discuss with the other what we had "learned". Our wedding planning continued, and our mutual invite lists expanded as the days progressed.

On Sunday we drove over to Boca Chica Beach and watched fascinated as last minute preparations were frantically underway on the SpaceX launch pad. It was hard to accept that the squat rocket, called Starship, sitting on the launch pad right here in front of us would soon be lifting a payload into space. Plans called for this site to be used for sending people to Mars. The stuff dreams are made from.

Tractor trailer trucks were lined up on the street beside the launch area waiting for large tunnel sections to be lifted from them onto large-wheeled flat wagons. Tractors pulled the wagons a short distance to the sand and then turned north, disappearing up the beach. Empty wagons waited on the side to be loaded.

Dill, who stopped to chat with the man directing the operation, walked over to us. "Well," he said, "some operation they got going here."

"The launch or the tunnel construction?" Angella asked. "They're both impressive."

"I was thinking of Starship and blasting that sucker to Mars. But what's going on below the earth is just as impressive. That's the last of the sections for today. New load arrives late tonight. Come on, we're going up to the entrance. Fairwell said to go ahead without him. He'll catch up."

Jimmy and I jumped into Dill's four-wheel drive Jeep which he drove straight north on the hard-packed sand a half mile or so. He rolled to a stop behind a wagon holding the tunnel section that just came up the beach, and announced, "All out."

A massive derrick stood above a five-foot hole in the sand with a large slowly rotating rod hanging from the center and extending down into the hole. We watched as a section of the split tunnel was hoisted into a vertical orientation and moved into position partially surrounding the rod with its lower end poised over the hole. The section then disappeared into the earth. The next tunnel section was hoisted into place and it also was lowered into the hole.

Noise coming from the drilling rig towering above us made it hard to hear. I leaned close to Dill. "I thought this hole only goes vertically for about fifty feet and then turns south down the beach."

"It does. You seem troubled."

"How then do those tunnel sections turn the corner down there?"

"Good question," he replied. "Let's ask the expert." He motioned to a small man with a shaved head and a neatly trimmed mustache. The man continued talking into his hand-held radio for a moment and then snapped the device onto his waist and strolled over. "Jackson," Dill said to the little man, "this is Jimmy and Angella. They're working with us on this...project. Jimmy and Angella, Jackson's operations manager. Anything happening on or under the sand belongs to him."

I held out my hand in greeting and judging from his grip I wouldn't want to tangle with this guy. Case hardened to the core.

"Jimmy was asking about those pipes that just went down the hole. If the drill shaft bends how do these sections bend to follow? They look rigid."

"Elementary, my dear Watson," the bald guy replied. "Follow me. You'll need hard hats. Anyone going down is required to wear them. Angella, that your name?"

"It is," Angella responded.

"Okay, Angella, join us if you wish. Just be careful where you step. Dill, you coming?"

"Have work to do. Check on a few things. Have them back here in an hour."

"Will do," Jackson responded. He didn't salute or snap his feet, but it was clear he was military and carrying out an order.

We followed Jackson over to a temporary outhouse positioned far up in the dunes. *Rent-A-Potty* was stenciled over the door and a lock hung open in the hasp. Inside, a ladder extending down into a hole replaced the expected potty seat. Three feet of the ladder was exposed above the sand. Several hard hats hung on the inside wall.

"Anyone of these will do," Jackson noted. "They adjust in size by a strap."

Angella took the one closest to her and I did the same. Jackson then said, "Be sure and keep your eyes open. This is a work in progress and the time frame doesn't allow full compliance with standards. Things move and shake, and shit happens. I'm sure you know, it flows downhill. Pardon my French, young lady, but you can't be any further downhill than this." He nodded toward the ladder. "Jimmy, you first. The lady will follow. And I'll follow her. Wait for us at the bottom."

Throwing a salute, I sat on the floor, dropped my legs and rolled over into the hole grabbing both rails of the wobbly ladder. This hole had to be more than fifty feet, or five stories if we were going all the way to the bottom. That's one hell of a long ladder and I was thankful I couldn't see the bottom. About twenty steps down I couldn't hear anything below me. In fact, I heard nothing at all. Surprising, because Angella was supposedly on the ladder just above me.

I stopped to listen and feel for movement.

No sound and no movement.

Continuing downward without Angella made no sense. The questions flooded in. Should I retreat? What about air? Water seepage? Gases?

"Angella," I called out, "You up there?"

Nothing.

I called again, only louder this time.

Still nothing.

The goal-oriented portion of my brain screamed, 'continue downward,' fighting all the while with the self-preservation portion which demanded I go to the surface. The result being I froze in place. Long ago, in Army Ranger training, those who found themselves in this very situation either quickly broke free or were flushed out. I never really understood the problem before now. This was the first time in my life I felt the torment those trainees had experienced. I also grasped something even more fundamental. I was afraid for Angella. No, that wasn't it exactly. I was afraid of not having more time with her, of not being able to spend our life together. I needed her more than I needed to force myself into yet any more dangerous situations.

I quickly began moving back up the ladder all the while focusing on the absolute void below me. My right hand hit something on the next rung up and I flinched, causing my left foot to slip off the rung. My body swung outward and hit the cold hard-packed sand on the other side of the hole. A large chunk broke off and fell away into dead silence.

Struggling to regain my grip on the ladder, I missed twice before I finally managed to grasp the side rail. Once my upper body was stabilized, I was able to secure my foot on a rung.

"Jimmy!" I heard a faint voice from somewhere above. "Something just hit my foot! Is that you down there? I can't see!"

"It's me, Angella," I yelled back up at her. "I can barely hear you."

"Jimmy? Is that…"

She was standing on the rung just above me, yet her voice was muffled, as if it traveled a long distance.

"Angella, I'm just below you."

"Jimmy?"

"Yes," I yelled, trying to project upward.

"I can't hear you."

Her movement signaled she was about to take a step down, so I quickly resumed my descent.

Rung by rung I slowly continued down, not certain if Angella was following, but knowing going back up was not an option. It took another five minutes before my feet hit a solid surface.

I moved away from the ladder into a hollowed-out chamber that lit up when I entered. The light was triggered by a battery powered light that hung from the dome and illuminated the space. Angella appeared from above and I ran toward her intending to pull her close, but I barely touched her hand before Jackson appeared.

"Okay, folks," he announced. "That took longer than expected. We need to get moving if we're to meet the hour deadline. Follow me and duck your head."

He moved off to his left and entered a low, perhaps five feet tall, tunnel that didn't seem to be supported by much of anything. The tunnel was no more than ten feet long and led us into a massive cave with a circular hole in the ceiling, as well as a matching circular hole in the wall opposite from where we entered. Large metal jacks extending in every direction held plywood sheets against the walls and ceiling.

The rotating shaft we saw from above extended down through the ceiling, disappearing into what appeared to be a large metal box positioned on the floor in the center of the cave. A slightly larger shaft ran out from a side of the box into a massive circular hole in the opposite wall. Parallel tracks disappeared into the hole beneath the rotating shaft. A large, flat work vehicle straddled the shaft, its wheels resting on the tracks.

The tunnel sections we watched being lowered into the hole were now lying on the ground and two workmen were guiding them onto a forklift in preparation for loading them onto the work vehicle.

Jackson, who had gone over to speak with the two men, returned and said, "Those sections are about to be installed at the end of the tunnel. The two sections will then be snapped together. Then the structure will be interlocked with the previous sections to form a continuous tunnel." Jackson's voice had taken on the tone of a bored docent.

"Pardon me for asking a dumb question," Angella said, "but those pipe sections seem to be...well, frankly, much too thin to hold up much of anything."

Jackson, glared at her, his attitude projecting he was tired of playing nice to visitors. He muttered, "Trust me, it'll hold just fine."

"Look, buddy," I said, "we're no happier being down here than you are having us here. We've got full clearances. Check with Admiral Boyle if you want. So, knock off the attitude and make this worthwhile."

Jackson took a step back and looked up at me. His eyes hardened and in other circumstances I'm certain he would have thrown a punch. Seeming to realize that it wouldn't end well for him if he took that route, he said, "Look, I have work to do, a schedule to keep. This is a distraction." He said something into his radio, listened, then turned back to us. "I'll do my best to brief you. It's all in the geometry—and composition. Those tunnel sections, we call them shells, are made of titanium, with titanium inner ribs. About half the weight of steel and much stronger because of the ribs. Believe me, when the shells are assembled and properly locked together not much will dislodge them. Will take a direct explosion to do that. In addition, and I wouldn't say this to anyone without clearance, each shell has special built-in features."

"Such as?" I asked.

"Such as air ducts. Such as electrical and communications. Such as cameras, that sort of thing."

"Cameras," Angella repeated, looking around for a lens.

"Let's just say nothing down here goes unrecorded. You scratch your...nose, they got it on tape."

One thing was clear. These tunnel sections were never intended for use in coal mines. These suckers were designed for tunnels into and out of places that did not particularly welcome American troops within their borders, such as Mexico, North Korea, China, or Iran. That explained the speed with which this operation was mounted and carried out. It also explains why sound didn't travel in the tunnel. It wasn't entirely the sand. These folks either had a special coating they pumped into the dirt, or…or they're using electronics to block sound movement. My vote is the latter. "This is pretty expensive equipment for a coal mine, I would say."

"Let's just say coal mines are probably not the highest or best use for these tunnel sections. Come on, I'll show you how they're interconnected. Neat system. And the beauty is we can install them fast enough to keep pace with the bore."

We followed Jackson across the main cave and into the tunnel, the numbers 1 and 2 showing on the insides of the mated shells. I observed the numbers 40 and 41 on the two shells just being delivered. If each shell is fifty feet long, then the tunnel would now extend two thousand feet, about a half mile. Not a very comforting thought when six thousand feet is required.

We caught a ride on the flat truck transporting the shells and rode along in silence as Jackson barked orders into his radio. When he finished talking, I asked a question that I believed I knew the answer to. "How do you get radio reception this far out?"

"One of the features built into the shells," Jackson said with pride, "is a built-in antenna." After my little *talk* with him, this guy became a regular encyclopedia and making the most of his permission to talk about his work.

The flat truck we rode on was essentially over the top of the drill shaft which, in turn, was held at waist level by a series of bearings atop metal posts. I visualized a giant auger at the end of the rotating shaft cutting into the earth at the far end of the tunnel. What I couldn't visualize was how the auger moved forward without the appearance of the shaft moving as well. I posed that question to our guide.

"Jimmy, that shaft you see there is moving horizontally as well as turning. It's just that you can't see the forward progress. If I put a mark on the shaft near a bearing support, you'd see the mark move forward faster than you might imagine."

Hearing was difficult, putting a damper on the questions. The silence was unlike anything I ever experienced. Unnerving.

"Okay, here we are," Jackson announced loudly as our ride slowed and came to a stop. "End of the line, as it were. All off."

We followed Jackson's lead and stepped onto the titanium tube marked 38 that was already in place.

"Step back a few feet and stay away from the edge there." Jackson pointed to where the tunnel lining ended and the ragged dirt-rock wall began. The side walls were dry, but the dirt floor ahead was dotted with puddles of what appeared to be water. "This is a tricky operation the way we have it engineered. Typically, we'd have brought in a more sophisticated rig to position the shells in place. But...but, unfortunately, it's halfway around the world and time doesn't permit. Anyway, we've kluged together an assembly system that worked well until a few hours ago when it started giving us problems. Engineers made adjustments, but it's touch and go for now until the kinks are worked out."

Angella, usually not one to concern herself with the inner workings of mechanical things, asked, "What exactly is the problem? Tie bands around them and connect the joints. Seems straightforward."

"If we had access to the outside of the shells, you'd be right on. But in here we can't do that. When the shells are mated there's no room between the outside of the structure and the raw walls. The machine we don't have is designed to slide the bands around the outside. Without that machine, we need to use inside expansion bands. Problem is, both shells must be held in place from the inside while the bands are positioned and locked in place. Slight movement and the structure collapses. Unfortunately, this close to shore the earth's not stable. Had a shift a few times already. Not pretty."

"You think they've solved the problem?" I asked, my attention focused on the right shell which was now being lifted into place."

"We'll know in a moment, won't we? See that latch?" Jackson asked, pointing to a hook-like piece extending out from the end of the shell now being raised. "That latch mates up with the notch in this shell, the shell we're now standing in."

I had to admit that before Jackson pointed to the notch just above my head, I hadn't noticed it. "I see the notch. Yes."

"That's critical. They must interlock or…or we get instability. That could prove fatal."

"What's that cord for?" Angella asked. "The one coming out from just behind the notch."

"Emergency use."

"Emergency?" Angella's curiosity had been piqued. "What kind of emergency? Medical or what?"

"It triggers explosive devices imbedded in the raw walls upstream from the trigger."

"Explosive devices?" Angella's eyes went wide.

"Nobody ever said this was a safe environment. Lot of bad stuff happens down here. The raw tunnel wall could collapse. A fire could ignite. Gas leak explode. Shit happens. You pull that cord, a section of the upstream tunnel collapses and seals off the problem. The last thing in the world you want is for the problem to propagate down the tunnel. These titanium sections are enormously strong around the circumference. But...but unfortunately they'll collapse like an accordion if pressured longitudinally."

While Jackson was explaining the emergency operation procedure, the second shell, the one marked 40, was being lifted into place. Its hook was brought into contact with the notch from shell 38, the shell we were standing in. A light came on inside the new tunnel section allowing us to see mechanical arms being extended from the work vehicle that hold the shells in place.

Jackson, his guide mode now on full display, said, "Now that the arms have the shells positioned, the interior bands, think of them as barrel hoops, will be expanded and locked. Once that step is completed, the new section will be as strong as this one. That's the step that's been giving us nightmares."

As we watched, pieces of metal, each about two feet in length were snapped together by ingenious looking mechanical hands to form a band. As the band grew in length, it moved outward toward the shell. Upon contact with the inner side of the shell the band bent and slowly encircled the shell. The growing band continued around the shell until the front end made a complete circle, at which point the two ends of the band were locked together.

"First band complete," Jackson announced, relief in his voice. "That's the far end and the most critical. That's the end we've been having trouble with. Now the machine will come back this way and do this end. Once that's in place, I'll rest easier."

"I see four bands in the section we're standing in," Angella observed. "Do they all get four?"

"Three at minimum. Depends on the raw tunnel structure, moisture content, a lot of things. Could be five or even six."

While all of this was taking place, the drill rod never stopped turning and the hole under the Gulf of Mexico continued to grow in length. That meant that as soon as this new section was in place, the automated truck would return to the entrance and bring back two more half shell fifty-foot sections. This operation reminded me of the Dirty Jobs TV program.

A loud screech suddenly pierced the silence. It was a thousand time louder than chalk on a blackboard and sent a bolt of pain throughout my body. Angella's face contorted as she slammed her hands over her ears.

The noise seemed to come from directly above our heads, and with silence all around, the screech was deafening even though I saw nothing unusual. A second, even louder screech erupted from the other side of the tunnel. Now *my* face knotted in pain and I thought my ear drums would burst. Angella appeared momentarily disoriented.

The entire structure began to shake. I recalled what Jackson said about the longitudinal weakness of the titanium. I watched the edge of the tunnel curl away from the dirt wall and bend inward. The floor we stood on started to lift and I fell backward, catching myself before I was thrown to the ground.

Abruptly, a pulsating siren broke the silence, and lights began to flash in unison.

Jackson, who was thrown backward against the side wall, regained his balance and moved gingerly forward toward the curling end of the tunnel, his arm grasping for the emergency cord. He missed it as it curled upward away from his outstretched fingers. "Angella," he yelled, "pull that cord over your head! Now!"

Angella stared at him in disbelief, not yet accepting that to save the entire tunnel it was necessary to blow up part of it. She lifted her arm but was thrown backward when the ground heaved again.

The tunnel continued to shutter when Jackson finally managed to reach and pull the cord on his side of the tunnel. An explosion shook the earth ahead of us and dirt tumbled down onto the collapsing shell. "Angella! For the love of God, pull yours!" Jackson shouted.

"Reach a little higher, Angella," I yelled encouraging her. "Jump if you have to!"

She jumped and grabbed the cord, but nothing happened.

"Hang on it!" Jackson yelled across to her. "Yank it as hard as you possibly can!"

It took her full body weight before the explosives finally actuated causing the walls and floor to shake violently. It seemed as though the entire tunnel was about to collapse on us. "Down!" Jackson shouted. "Get down! And crawl back to the next section! This thing may still roll up!"

The vibrations grew stronger and were now perfectly in rhythm. Something about harmonics leaped into mind and I visualized the entire tunnel rolling up with us on the inside. I crawled toward Angella. If we were going to die, it should be together.

She must have had the same idea because when I turned to look for her, she was right beside me. I threw my arms around her pulling her closer. The instant we touched the tunnel vibrations stopped and quiet returned.

Jackson's voice broke through my thoughts and I was about to tell him to back off when I realized he wasn't scolding us. "All's well," he said. "We can begin walking out. Won't have far to go, they've sent the truck back for us. Be here in a few. Got a mess to clean up and not much time to do it. Let's go."

"But you just blew the tunnel up!" Angella exclaimed, brushing herself off as she stood. "Won't that delay…?"

"That's the beauty of this system. Those explosives are positioned to collapse only one section at a time. That protects the rest of the tunnel. Take them no time to get it back. The hardest part is extracting the collapsed tunnel shells and bringing in replacements."

"Engineers need to go back to the drawing boards," I said. "This is not the way to run the railroad."

"We've come over a half-mile. We'll get the other half. And we'll do it on time. And that, my friend, is a promise. Now let's get out of their way. They have work to do."

I observed that for the first time since we've been on the site the drill rod had stopped turning.

TWENTY-TWO

"Angella," the note just inside the door to our penthouse office began, "be careful! You're on the PFM wanted list. Do NOT travel in Mexico. Call me ASAP. Merry." Coming on the heels of our close call in the tunnel, I should be numb to the news that the Federal Ministerial Police had issued an arrest citation for me. But I wasn't. I was troubled, mainly because our current operation had me visiting General Mazdani in Mexico City.

I was also troubled by Jimmy's insistence he hadn't reinjured his knee. In fact, his slacks had been soaked in blood. Dill, despite Jimmy's protests, had ordered him to the hospital. Jimmy had turned his back and walked away. Jackson had planted his feet in the sand directly in front of Jimmy. Looking up, the little man, his mustached lip twitching, had said, "Take one more step, buddy, and I'll have the guards arrest you. And from what I understand of your relationship with the Admiral, you'll find yourself in the brig by nightfall! Now what will it be?"

Three uniformed Marines appeared seemingly out of nowhere and stood close to the dunes, their eyes scrutinizing Jimmy.

Jimmy started to take that step, but before I could warn him, he relented. Turning to me, a resolved look across his face, said, "Seems I'm going over to the hospital. How about you going to the island and getting me a change of clothes?" His eyes went to my ripped blouse and his face softened. "You okay? Looks like..."

"Just a few scrapes," I replied, eyeing a three-inch tear down the left arm of my blouse and the oil stains on both legs of my slacks. "Nothing serious."

The *nothing serious* part was true. Despite the tunnel floor containing debris of all types, from crushed rock to metal clippings, to oil pools, to sharp cutting tools, my skin was only slightly scraped. I sported a superficial red line down my arm, but nothing more serious. The blouse, of course, was ruined. In addition to a neat slice, it had now become imbedded with oily stones and dirt. "You go to the hospital with Dill, and I'll round up Fairwell and have him take me to the island. Let these guys earn their keep."

Agent Fairwell apparently returned to the Border Protection building in Brownsville because that's where he was waiting when Dill dropped me off twenty minutes later.

Fairwell at first was reluctant to allow me back into the apartment, fearing Santiago's folks had the place bugged. But he relented and warned me to say nothing from the time I entered the building until I was back in the parking lot. "Who the hell knows who's monitoring what?" he asked. "We're too deep into this now to be compromised."

Before entering our office/apartment, I read Ayers' note several times, trying to decide how to play it. Fairwell remained in the elevator lobby, not wanting to risk his image appearing on a surveillance monitor.

I folded the note, careful not to put it down while I gathered what I needed for myself and Jimmy, and I added one of Jimmy's new white shirts for Dill. Oil from my blouse had transferred to his shirt when he lifted me out of the hole onto the sandy beach. It was my way of thanking him.

Back in the car I suggested we stop by Merry Ayers' office and I handed him the note.

"Good plan. It would be good to find out how Ayers knew about the PFM," Fairwell responded, a puzzled expression on his face. "But it's Sunday."

"That woman's a workhorse. She uses Sunday as a catch-up day. Let's just stop by and see if she's in." I thought about the PFM, which is the Mexican equivalent of the FBI, and not an organization to take lightly. They had agents everywhere and were well connected with their U.S. counterparts. "You don't seem surprised. I take it you knew about the PFM wanting me?" I said.

"As a matter of fact, Angella, I did. Came out late yesterday. Need to change our plans a bit."

"A bit! You can't be serious about me still going into Mexico to see Mazdani!"

"Operational detail," Fairwell said, waving his arm in dismissal. "Just have to avoid you being caught's all."

Ayers' car was the only one in the lot and Fairwell parked next to it. He was standing next to me before I could protest further.

"Oh, Angella!" Ayers exclaimed a moment later when we stepped into her office. She was studying a document on her computer screen. "Did you get my note?"

"That's why we're here. This is Agent Fairwell."

"We've met," Ayers' said. "I trust you're keeping my client safe."

"Doing my best, counselor."

"Well, Angella, I'm afraid I can't say much in his presence. No privilege with him here." She turned her computer screen in my direction. Across the top was a single word: INTERPOL. "You've been Red Noticed! That's not good."

Not addressing the Interpol notice, Fairwell impatiently demanded, "How did you know about the PFM? That was private."

"That I can tell you. A client of mine, Joy Malcom, told me. She asked that I pass that info along to Angella. I tried, but Angella's phone seems to be off-line, or disconnected, or something. I couldn't get through. Joy's been trying and couldn't get through either."

"I didn't know you and Joy…they were on the other side of our lawsuit. Isn't that a conflict?" I said, surprised that she now represented Joy Malcom.

"That suit is settled, as you know. You and Jimmy now have…"

I was certain Merry was about to mention the ten million Jimmy and I cleared in our recent transaction with Santiago. But Merry must have read the warnings in my eyes.

"…now have much in common and are not adverse in any way that I know. I don't expect any more transactions with them. Am I mistaken?"

"That depends," I said, giving myself time to sort it all out. If Ayers was representing Malcom, there was more behind this than I knew. And certainly, sharing such information with the FBI was not in my best interest. "Depends upon how everything works out, I suppose."

"How did Malcom come to know about the PFM?" Fairwell demanded again.

"You will just have to direct that question to my client. As for me, I don't intend to answer another anything further for the FBI. And I will instruct my clients likewise. Do I make myself clear?"

"Loud and clear," Agent Fairwell acknowledged, apparently accustomed to lawyers playing hardball. "Next time we speak, I'll have a subpoena in my hand."

"Good luck with that." Ayers turned to me, her infectious smile back in place. "Joy asked me to pass on something to you. It has to do with protecting Jimmy." She glanced at Fairwell. "Can I…?"

"It's okay," I assured her. "That's what he's here for."

"Three pieces of info. The Mexican interest in you was sparked by something to do with your shoes. The size maybe?" She studied my feet a moment, then continued. "I don't see anything abnormal about your feet, but I believe she said they have pictures of you entering and leaving the prison with size eleven or twelve shoes. But later that day you crossed the border wearing size five. I don't understand why that's important but…but Joy says there may be a murder charge involved. I hope none of that's true, but…but they may try to have you extradited. The Red Notice supports that thought. Understand, Angella, there's really nothing I can do until you're arrested over here and then…then it may be too late."

"Let's not worry ourselves about extradition," Fairwell quickly pointed out. A bit too quick for my liking, I thought. "That's been wired around already. Not going to happen, at least any time soon."

"Wired on what side of the border," Ayers asked.

"Need to know. Sorry. Please continue with what Malcom said."

Ayers consulted a yellow pad on her desk. "Here's her exact quote. 'Because of the PFM, Morris' ability to protect Jimmy is gone. Not possible to go beyond Tuesday.' Does any of that make sense?"

Fairwell's expression didn't change, as if he already knew everything Ayers reported. "And the second piece from Malcom?" he asked, his tone softer.

Ayers looked at me before responding.

I nodded, and she continued, "You're to deal with the General directly. Anything he wants. No money is to pass through Morris' hands, nothing."

"How does Santiago—Morris—plan to get compensated?" I was thinking out loud and hadn't intended it as a question to Ayers.

"That's why I was hired by Malcom. You're to deliver one unopened barrel to me."

"One barrel of what?" I was testing to see if Malcom, or rather Santiago, really trusted her *lawyer* with business information.

"Of whatever you're selling the General."

"And what if delivery is impossible?"

"Then you must provide the coordinates." Ayers looked from me to Agent Fairwell, and then back to me. "Listen, Angella. I don't have a clue what you're selling some general. And quite frankly, I don't want to know. I was informed that whatever it is it's legal. If it's not, then count me out. You understand me?"

"I understand. And, if it makes you feel better, the commodity is not illegal. But…but it is highly valuable."

We turned to leave when I realized we weren't finished. "And the third item?"

Ayers looked at me quizzically before consulting her pad. "Gold bar my note says. Do you know anything about a missing gold bar? Joy claims you owe her a gold bar."

"Good luck with that!"

- - - - -

We drove in silence back to the Brownsville Border Protection building, the School, as I now thought of it. The field trip to see the tunnel construction generated more questions than it answered. Questions I was not comfortable contemplating. Strictly speaking, it wasn't the questions that were uncomfortable, but rather the answers. The amount of money and effort being thrown at this project was beyond anything I could imagine. Clearly the powers that be smelled regime change. And regime change required the blessing of not only the White House and the military, but a good segment of Congress as well. The troubling part was that regime changes are inherently messy, fraught with internal, as well as external, horrors. People, many people, are always killed. Mine and Jimmy's lives are easily lost in the noise if you're looking at the big picture.

Fairwell slowed the car, flashed his shield, and the guard waved him into the garage. If we were going to have a private conversation, now would be the time. "Let's be honest with each other," I began, trying hard to erase the futility of it all from my voice. "If I had free will here, I'd not go into Mexico to meet Mazdani. I take it there's no chance of him coming up here?"

"I ran that idea up the pole a while ago to be honest with you."

"Shot it down, I assume."

"Hole right through the center. DOA."

"Same with me not going down there?"

"Blew that flag right off the pole. Sorry."

"What then?"

"You're going in as Janet Talliger."

"Who the hell..."

"PR person assigned to the embassy. She had a *sudden family emergency* this morning. Flew home to Houston to see her *ailing* mother."

"I take it she and I share attributes."

"You're both female. In this situation, that's all that matters. Diplomatic courtesy will cover it at the airport. After that, you're on your own."

"Details?"

"We fly up to Houston tonight. You're on the first flight to Mexico City in the morning."

"I need to see Jimmy."

"They're keeping him in hospital for the night."

"How bad is it?"

"Don't have details. Precautionary is what I've been told. Judging from your blouse, that floor down there was none too clean."

"Take me to see him. We have all night to get to Houston."

Fairwell parked the car and we both got out.

"Well?"

"Tell you what. While you're getting your stuff, I'll check with Dill. See what I can do. I'm going over there to drop off his new clothes anyway."

I nodded in agreement but held out little hope. But why not? How would it harm the operational plans if I spent an hour at Jimmy's bedside? As I understood the mission, he played no role going forward. Jimmy's double was up in the mountains convincing his captors that he was one of them at heart. I was tasked with convincing Mazdani to believe the wine is real and that the barrels will prove he's the successor to the Staufer Dynasty. To that end I was authorized to invite him to go into the tunnel to see for himself that the barrels were being dug out of the earth from the shipwreck. Jimmy wasn't involved in this phase, so what the hell was he being trained to do? What couldn't he tell me?

By the time we regrouped, I was ready to take Fairwell's head off. "So?" I demanded, "what's the verdict?"

"If you're asking can you spend time with Jimmy, the answer's yes. There's a small visiting room on his floor and it's been reserved for you two. Dill suggested you bring dinner. Jimmy got there too late to order, so this'll work out well."

The drive from the border to the hospital took twelve minutes, including a quick visit to a drive-through rib place. Pulling to a stop in front of the hospital, Fairwell said, "I have things to do. He's on the third floor, south wing. Here, take his stuff." He pulled the bag I had taken from the apartment from the back seat and handed it to me. "We're booked on a ten-fifteen flight. Pick you up at nine."

"Isn't that cutting it close?"

"I think they'll accommodate us. Just be outside on time. And that's an order."

"Aye, aye, sir," I responded, stopping short of throwing him one of Jimmy's patented mock salutes.

TWENTY-THREE

Compartmentalization is what the CIA calls only knowing your part of an operation and not informing your partner, or anyone else, what exactly is going on. Concern for security is the justification. I'm not buying any of it. Angella is certainly not a security concern, and her knowing exactly what my role is in getting Mazdani to trust us would not impact her performance in any way. Yet, I had to abide by the *rules of engagement* as Agent Pickale called them.

But it's one thing to passively not talk about briefings, keeping the information to yourself. It's certainly another thing to actively mislead your partner. That's what just happened. A big fat charade put on for the sole purpose of setting up a smoke screen around Angella. The collapse of the tunnel section was—at least I believe it was—an accident. Convenient, perhaps, but an accident nonetheless. Had the tunnel collapse not occurred, the script called for me to fall and pretend to reinjure my healing knee. I had been with supplied fake blood and all.

When Angella insisted on visiting me in the hospital they scrambled to pull strings and set it up for us to dine in a visiting room at a hospital I hadn't been in for years. The charade included a room with my name on it, a gown, and an IV needle taped to my left arm with a tube extending from a hanging bottle.

Angella arrived with two large bags. One held a change of clothes for me and a fresh shirt for Dill. The other was filled with ribs, mashed potatoes and two beers. We dug in.

Had she studied the setup she would have noticed there was nothing dripping from the bottle. My guilt level reached its limit. Never again, I vowed. Never again!

I learned she was about to catch a flight and couldn't tell me where she was going, or when she'd be back. I couldn't tell her that as soon as she went out the front door, I was going out the back. Dill was driving me to Mexico.

One thing was perfectly clear. We were about to be married and this was not a good way to start that journey. In fact, I couldn't think of a worse beginning. I tried to comfort myself with a motto Drill Sergeant Boyd continually drilled into us. "It's not how you begin; it's how you end that counts." I think he was referring to not coming home in a body bag.

Pickale drove us south from the border. My destination was the mountain shack where I had been held captive. The plan was for him to drop me along the road where I was to walk for a distance until a clandestine operation team picked me up for insertion back into the cabin. I assume they would be using the same method as they used to extract me. The reason I was going back up there was simple. Intelligence picked up signals that *el Bandito* was running an operation Tuesday night which required his presence on the mountain. If he was going up there that meant I had to be there and not my double. This plan made no sense and had more holes than a sieve. Also making no sense was Pickale's reasoning as to why he had to drop me off. According to him, it was so he could deny he ever knew the U.S. was operating illegally in Mexico. As if anyone would believe him. I chalked it up to squirrels will be squirrels. I also chalked it up to me having no idea what the real plan was. I was on strings; my arms and legs controlled from afar. A human puppet if you will.

This part of Mexico is patrolled heavily by the drug cartels, making anyone out walking a target. Shoot first and ask no questions is their motto. And the area Pickale was talking about was dead center in Zeta territory. He dismissed my concern with a wave of his hand.

Around midnight we stopped to refuel. Pickale, in one of his rare talkative moments, advised, "If you're hungry, grab something to eat, this promises to be a long night."

"How far we going?"

"In miles, not very far. Time-wise, all night."

I bought two protein bars and a bottle of water. Pickale picked up two waters. Seems he thought his night would be shorter than mine.

"Almost there," Pickale announced sometime later.

His voice interrupted a dream in which I was being pecked at by two large white birds. Leaden legs prevented me from running from them. Blood, streaming down the side of my face, drew more birds. "Where are we?" I asked, blinking myself awake and gingerly touching my face to see if the dream was real.

"Route Fifty-Four, south of Cerralvo."

The first rays of the sun were on the horizon, meaning I must have slept for several hours. "You been driving all this time, or…or did you stop?"

"Took a break a while back. Didn't want to disturb you. There's a station coming up soon. I suggest you use the facilities. Not much after that."

It was almost eight when we stopped at the pump. A gray Chevrolet was parked off to the side. No one appeared to be in it. I walked inside the small building while Pickale pumped petrol into the tank.

The Chevy was gone when I came out and Pickale moved our car to a spot directly in front of the door. I ducked inside. The car moved forward even before I could pull the door closed, which caused me to focus on the door and not on the driver. A stupid move on my part.

The driver's fragrant scent reached my senses before her words registered. "Good morning, darl'n," she purred. "You'll just have to forgive me for not hugging you. Shame that'll have to wait for later."

"Joy! What the hell! You're about the last person in the world I'd expect out here!"

"You didn't come see me, my dear, so I came to see you. I thought you'd be thrilled to see me."

"How did you…"

"No time for the long version, my dear man. When that DEA agent came to my house impersonating Angella's brother, I figured he was FBI, or some such thing. Then, when you showed up in Brownsville leaving an exact double up on the mountain Morris got worried. And when Morris is worried, I'm worried. Couldn't reach Angella, or you. So, I left a message with your lawyer. I'm told Angella got…"

"How the hell'd you know I was in Brownsville?"

"Jimmy, my love, there's a hell of a lot you don't know. I'm willing to wager I'm better connected than you are." Joy laughed. "You must know Morris has people on both sides. How else you think he moves stuff as freely as he does?"

"That still doesn't explain why you're involved…I mean with me right now."

"I'm what the FBI calls a Confidential Informant."

"On Santiago?"

"Oh, Jimmy, heavens no! I'd never…not on Morris! Heavens no! On the border people. Both sides. In exchange for names, I get immunity from anything I might have done. And, as I said, there's a hell of a lot you don't know."

"Immunity from what, exactly?"

"Hate to break it to you, but that's none of your business." She laughed again, this time a little deeper. "I won't hold that against you. Once a lawman, always a lawman. But let's move on from that."

"You're driving. It's your conversation."

"So, you're making an honest woman out of Angella. I owe you a congratulations."

"Isn't that a sexist remark? There's nothing dishonest about our relationship now."

"My, my, Jimmy. Hit a nerve, did I? Okay, I'll change the subject. I'm talking to you now because of the wine. That site you have out in the water, that site has wine and coins as I understand it. The wine's our concern. Not the coins. Hathcock, or whomever, can do whatever with those. We'll even help if that works out better."

"You seem to know more about what's going on than I do.

Joy's face came fully alive. "Jimmy, darling, sometimes you're so naïve. Hate to break it to you, but they're playing you and Angella. Exploiting your relationship with Morris to get what they need."

"Seems to me it's the opposite. You folks, Santiago and you, are exploiting our relationship with the government."

"Business is always a two-way street, my dear. What's that they say about backs and scratching?" Joy went silent for a long moment. When she spoke again her tone was modulated and reserved. We were finally coming to the purpose for this bizarre car ride up into the Mexican hill country. "Here's the thing. Morris got himself in a spot of trouble. There's evidence he knifed a competitor. He might get himself off because no one saw him do it. But...but the cartels take care of their own, as you certainly know. He'll escape being electrocuted, but unless he's out of there, they'll finish him off."

"So how do I...?

"Money. And protection. Protection mainly."

"What does that mean?"

"Means that Mazdani has promised him safe harbor in Iran, in exchange for..."

"The wine."

"The wine's only the starting point to his becoming King. The wine with his family crest is the real key."

As usual, Joy confused me. Nothing's ever straight forward with her. "You know we're working on the wine and getting Mazdani's buy-in. What else do you want?"

"Talk is cheap, Jimmy. That wine's worth...worth hundreds of millions. Maybe even several billion. It's the money, and what it buys, that seals the deal—for everyone. I told the lawyer we need one barrel." She paused; her smile faded. "New plan. Mazdani gets it all."

"And if that doesn't happen?" I asked, anxious to force all her cards onto the table.

"Open the glove compartment."

I did as instructed.

"Open it," Joy said as I pulled out a white sealed envelope.

A picture of Angella throwing a knife into the bushes was on top of several other pictures, including one showing her extracting the knife from an oversized shoe. I don't know enough about Mexican law, but I could see a scenario in which these pictures could be used to hang Angella for the murder. "What exactly do you want?"

"My deal with the Feds is to assist getting you back inside that cabin and to keep you there without having you killed by the Zetas. Morris had it arranged through Tuesday. That Zeta cousin's proving antsy, but I managed 'till Wednesday. Gives you two days, for what I don't know. But why the hell you're going back up there's beyond me."

"Where's the money figure in?"

"Yes, the money. In the form of the wine barrels. Mazdani gets all the barrels. He needs the money to support becoming King. Grease a lot of skids type of thing."

"Not my wine to be bargaining away," I said, being as honest as I could be. "What exactly do you want from us?"

"For starters, don't mess up the operation. And when the wine's uncovered, don't stop Mazdani from claiming all of it."

"That's a government matter. Nothing I can..."

"I have about as much trust in our government as...as I do in the Mexican government. And that's not saying much. Just promise you won't help them screw Mazdani out of that wine."

"That I can do," I quickly responded, having no idea if I could fulfill that promise or not.

"Keep this in mind, Jimmy. For the operation to have any chance of success, Mazdani must buy into Angella. Morris holds that key. One word from him and she's...well, she's history."

"That a threat?"

"A fact's all it is. A fact."

"Government's cut a deal with Hathcock. I can't get in the middle of..."

"Leave Hathcock to me."

"You want us to sell him out?"

"He's not exactly being sold out. I understand he used one of the coins to insure the other nine coins."

"Right or wrong?"

"Assume you're right."

"When you find the wine barrels, the coins are inside."

"You know that how?"

"Mazdani knows more about that wine than you think. Anyway, once the barrels are found and you verify the coins, that's all Hathcock needs."

I must be dense, but I wasn't following. "Run that by me again."

"Once the coins are verified and if they should disappear before getting to Hathcock, that triggers an insurance payout."

"Sounds like insurance fraud to me."

"Sticks and stones, Jimmy. Call it what you will. Coins go missing, Hathcock files a claim. Courts will straighten it out." Joy drove in silence a few miles allowing her comments to simmer. Then she said, "Think of it, Jimmy dear, as keeping you—and Angella—alive. A small price to pay."

Something Malcom mentioned earlier was playing at the back of my mind. "You said something about why I was going up there. I think it was a question."

"Just thinking out loud. Look'n out for a dear friend's all. Mazdani thinks you're up there. Leave well enough alone. Unless I'm mistaken, that body double is an FBI guy well equipped to handle himself. Why put yourself in harm's way?"

Good question. "Intelligence suggests Mazdani is talking about going up there in person to talk to me directly. Body double won't do for that."

Malcom again drove in silence for several minutes leading me to believe the subject was now closed. She surprised me by saying, "They're playing you. Mazdani's booked on a flight to Matamoros, late Monday night. If anyone's going up there, it'll be his chief of staff, guy by the name of Major Caveh Shirvani. Goes by Cav."

"You positive?" This didn't make sense. If Joy knew about the flight plans certainly the CIA knew about them as well.

"Listen, Jimmy. In this business nothing's as it seems. And nothing's positive. This guy Cav, he's known to be…well, to be blunt, running women across the border. Morris stays out of that stuff, but…but there's talk about a major operation going down very soon. I wouldn't be surprised if Cav's planning to be close just in case he's needed."

"By close, you mean up on that mountain?

"That place they held you. That's operations headquarters for the women. All around up there are…are places where the best of the women are kept for the pleasure of certain men."

"Maybe Mazdani's going up there for…for the pleasure?"

"Doubt it. He has all the women he ever needs right there with him. Least that's what I'm told." Malcom again fell silent. When she next spoke, it was to ask if I was okay seeing to it Mazdani received all the wine.

"I'll think about it," I said, having no intention of doing any such thing.

"Take all the time you want, darl'n. Problem is, see that car down there?" She pointed to a dark sedan parked just to the side of the road about a half mile ahead. "That's your ride up the mountain. Need your answer by the time we get there or..."

Or it would be a one-way ride up to the cabin. She didn't have to finish her sentence.

Joy slowed and moved off the road, coming to a stop ten feet from the sedan. "Jimmy," she said, her eyes set as hard as I had ever seen them, her mouth tense, "Morris' sons are gone and he's treating you like one of his own. You're under his wing now. That comes with obligations. Don't think of going rogue, the organization is much too large—and powerful—for that." Joy's smile was now back in place. Getting out of the car, she motioned me to join her. "Your answer, Jimmy dear?"

"I seem to have no choice. I'm in. To the best of my ability, that is."

"That certainly deserves a big hug. If not for me, then make it for the cameras." She threw her arms open. "Come on, don't hold back. Show your love."

I hugged her as a brother would hug a sister.

"Jimmy, darling, I'm choosing to believe your promise of supporting Morris is more sincere than that hug. I really hope our trust is not misplaced."

TWENTY-FOUR

My flight from Houston to Mexico City was on time and, in fact, we landed twenty-minutes early. But early is only relative. Agent Fairwell's rationale for not allowing me to spend more time in the hospital with Jimmy was because of our early Monday morning flight to Mexico. That was an outright lie. On the trip up to Houston he casually let it be known we'd be sleeping late because our flight south didn't leave until two-fifteen. "Good news, Angella." Fairwell added before I could challenge him, "Mazdani invited you to dinner at seven at the *Las Alcobas* Hotel where he's staying."

"*Las Alcobas*? Isn't that..."

"It's a luxury collection of hotels. This is one of their finest."

"Over a grand a night from what I recall."

"He has ten rooms on the floor," Fairwell added.

"Ten? For what?"

"Bodyguards. Staff. Meetings. And...wives."

"By wives do you mean..."

"Women friends. Goes with the territory." Fairwell, seeing my reaction, tried to soothe me by saying, "You don't have to condone it, but let it be. We have bigger fish."

So, women are now akin to fish!

I was pissed, but I guessed this was only the first of many revelations about Fairwell, and most likely not the worst. "Is our government springing for my room? Isn't that a tad over budget?"

"Budget's not the issue, Angella." Fairwell turned his back to me and from the slump of his shoulders I expected him to deliver bad news.

"So, what *is* the issue? What aren't you telling me?"

He took his time in answering. I think trying to get his words just right. "You are, as we discussed, entering Mexico under the name of Janet Talliger."

"So?" I still didn't understand the problem and my patience was wearing thin.

"You can't register at the *Alcobas* under the name of Talliger because..."

Finally, it hit home. "Because Mazdani knows me as Martinez! So, what's the plan?"

"*Galeria Plaza*."

"Never heard of it."

"Mid-range. Clean. Quiet."

I hadn't expected Fairwell to accompany me on the flight, but he had, informing me he would remain at the *Galeria*. What he didn't tell me was that we were sharing a room.

"Not on your life!" I hissed when the clerk went into the office to take the room agreement off the printer.

"Discuss it in the room." His voice was in full command mode. "Don't make a scene."

"Now tell me this instant what the hell's going on," I demanded the moment the door closed behind us. I've no intention of..."

"Need I remind you, Angella, that I'm running this operation and not you? For this purpose, I report directly to Admiral Boyle who reports to..."

"I'm duly impressed!" I shot back. "But I'm not sleeping..."

"Just listen!" Fairwell snapped, "You're not staying here at all."

"Where then? If I can't register as Martinez because I'm wanted for questioning, and I can't register as Talliger because...because why?"

"Because that's not the plan. The plan is..."

"Thanks for sharing earlier! You expect me to trust you, but yet...yet..." I choked off what I was going to say. "Trust runs in both directions. You want mine, so return the favor! So, what the hell *is* the plan?"

"You'll be staying in one of those ten rooms at the *Alcobas.* No need to register. You're a guest of an Iranian official. No questions asked."

Speaking of going from the frying pan to the fire. I preferred the frying pan. Once I was in a room controlled by Mazdani I was, for all practical purposes, on foreign soil, under rules of engagement I didn't understand. "This is insane! You mean I'm going over to that hotel, having dinner with Mazdani and then...then moving into his...his compound?"

"You make it sound like...like we've asked you to jump off the Empire State Building."

"At least if you'd done that I'd know what the outcome would be! This plan...this plan leaves me..."

"Alive! Listen, Angella, nothing bad will happen."

"Define bad! Rape may not be your primary concern but pardon me if it's mine! I'm essentially a hostage and he can... he can...You said yourself he keeps women!"

"Angella! He has no known history of rape—or any such thing."

"History is only what people write down. You have no idea what he'll do or not do!" The situation was now out of my control and smelling worse with every revelation. I railed at the thought.

Jimmy was right all along!

Fairwell clenched his fists and walked toward the window, his back again to me. He stood stone still for several minutes. When he turned back his face was mostly calm. The red streaks that spread up his neck were gone. "You're right. We don't know what the General will do. But the bottom line, there's no turning back. We have every reason to believe you'll be perfectly safe. But…but in our business risks do come with the job. I can't control that."

"But I can! I'm out of here!" I grabbed my bag and reached for the door.

"Not advisable, Angella. Not at all. Open that door and I'll have no option but to report that fact."

"Report it to whom? Boyle? Just what're you threatening?"

"What'll you think Boyle'll do when his operation's in danger of compromise?"

Fairwell didn't have to spell it out. He knew I was perfectly capable of working through my options without his help. "Just a guess, but you won't make Talliger's passport available to me, will you?" Thinking of the Mexican warrant for my arrest made my heart stop.

"Correct," he answered, slumping into the only chair in the room.

"And I can't imagine you'd be willing to leave the car for me." Even if he had, the Interpol Red Notice prevented me from escaping, even if I drove south.

"Correct, again."

"And if I don't go to dinner with Mazdani and stay in his custody, there won't be further reason for Santiago to keep Jimmy, actually Jimmy's double, alive."

"Three for three. You're batting a thousand."

Refuse to meet with Mazdani. Meet with Mazdani and sleep here at the Plaza with Fairwell. Meet with Mazdani and sleep in one of his bedrooms. Three bad options. "Compromise," I suggested. "I'll meet with Mazdani and…and will come back here for the night."

"Not one of your choices, I'm afraid."

"And just why not?"

"Above my pay grade. Possibly the powers that be believe spending the night under his roof, so to speak, will cement the deal. Get him to trust you kind of thing."

"Since when did sleeping with a target become part of the FBI's operational procedures?"

"That's uncalled for, Angella! We're not asking you to sleep with the guy. Besides, technically speaking, this is a CIA operation."

"Don't be cute! You know better than that! That's not what Mazdani wants from me."

"With all due respect, Angella, how the hell you know what he wants?" Fairwell shot back, one of the few times he raised his voice to me. "He has a stable of women at his disposal anytime he wants. Or maybe he's celibate. You don't know a damn thing about his sex life! It's not in your nature to be making assumptions based on assumptions. Don't begin now." Fairwell took a deep breath before continuing. "Look, Angella, we've both been under a lot of pressure. Take a step back. FBI has no reason to believe Mazdani has any tendencies to abuse women—in any manner. You wouldn't be going in if we did. That I can promise. As you well know, people aren't perfect. People go off script all the time. So, can I promise Mazdani won't make advances? Of course, I can't."

"Don't give me that crap! He runs women for prostitution for God sake! You think he cares about morality?"

"I'm sorry, Angella. All I can say is that our intelligence suggests..."

"And if they're wrong?"

"All bets are off. Do what you need to do."

"So, you're telling me to comply?"

"Hell, no! I'm telling you just what I said. Do what you need to do. That's all."

Kill him is what I heard. Is that what this is about? Setting me up as an assassin?

Puppets, all dancing at the end of strings. How far up do the strings extend? To the President? Most likely not directly. Perhaps, not even to Deputy Homeland Secretary Diane Sweet. Tiny? Speculation doesn't help. How to best protect myself does and I had no intention of sharing answers to that problem with Fairwell.

Unexpectedly, my cell buzzed. "Joy," I answered, "Got your message if that's what you're calling about."

"I know," she replied. "Just spoke to Jimmy. Give you the short version. He's agreed to deliver all the barrels to Morris."

"And just why would he do that? That's not our deal."

"He'll fill you in. It boils down to a matter of life or death."

"Whose life or death?"

"Angella, use your imagination. Jimmy's life is in Morris' hands. That's a big burden. Catch my drift?"

I caught her drift the instant she raised the ante.

"You're suddenly so quiet," Malcom said. "You in or out?"

"I'm with Jimmy, whatever he said."

"I take it then you're in."

"If that's what Jimmy said."

"Okay, then. Enjoy your dinner with Mazdani. Bye."

"You win," I said to Fairwell.

This round.

I calmed myself enough to call out, "Hey, Fairwell, don't wait up for me."

Asshole!

Never take the first cab in line, nor the second for that matter, was what I'd been taught. When you have a suitcase and there's only one cab in sight the best choice is to begin walking. I was still seething from my latest encounter with my supposed handler. Walking the streets of Mexico City or any major city, in a sketchy area is always dangerous. Pulling a bag puts a target on you.

To hell with it.

I opened the cab door, tossed my bag on the seat, and announced, "*Las Alcobas Hotel.*"

The driver's eyes lit up, no doubt expecting a generous tip. "*No hay problema, señora.*" And off we sped, hopefully going where I had directed.

The brick and curved glass façade of the *Las Alcobas Hotel* is gorgeous and totally unexpected. I was grateful the driver hadn't peppered me with questions along the way. I was reaching for my purse to fish out the fare, fully intending to double it, when the street-side door flew open. A hand reached in for my bag. Almost at the same instant, the door beside me opened and a tall slender bearded

Semitic-looking man said, "Welcome, *Senóra* Martinez." His English was Oxford perfect.

I remained in my seat, not willing to surrender myself to the self-assured man towering over the cab.

"I'm your host," the tall man said, bending down so his head was even with mine. "Name's Caveh Shirvani. Cav will work. I work for General Mazdani. You can think of me as his chief of staff."

I took his offered hand and gingerly stepped from the cab, my eye following my bag as it went up the few steps and disappeared into the hotel.

Taking my elbow, he said, "I'll show you into the hotel. I understand you are scheduled to remain with us overnight. You'll be in Room 2112."

By the time I came through the door into the well-appointed front lobby my suitcase was nowhere in sight. "My bag," I said to my host, "Where…"

"Your bag, *Senóra,* has been taken to your quarters. Rajif here will escort you. Rajif has very little English and has been instructed not to speak with you. Please direct all questions to me. You and the General shall be having dinner at seven in his private room. Rajif will come round for you fifteen minutes to the hour. Dress code is casual, so wear something comfortable. Here is my number." Handing me an engraved card, he added, "If you require anything, anything at all, at any time of the day or night, please do not hesitate to ring me up. I trust your stay with us will prove fruitful."

I wanted to ask who all had keys to Room 2112, but the likelihood of obtaining accurate information was null. I sucked it up, and simply said, "Pleased to meet you, Cav. I look forward to dinner with the General."

"Please do remember, I'm here for your every need. Don't hesitate. Time of day or night should be of no concern. Anything you might require, at any time."

Rajif indeed remained silent as we rode the elevator to the twenty-first floor. He opened the door, bowing his head slightly as I stepped inside. *"Gracias Señor,"* I said, before realizing I was speaking Spanish to an Iranian.

What have I gotten myself into?

"Hable Español?" came the surprising reply.

"Si." I responded, wondering why he wanted to know if I spoke Spanish. His Spanish was high bred, leading me to assume he was assigned to the Iranian Consulate in Mexico City by the Mexican government. A diplomatic spy if you will. But he had violated his instructions. Why?

"Americana?"

"Si."

"Cuidado con el Sr. Shirvani. El no es tu amigo," he stage whispered. Then asked, *"Costo de asilo?"*

Before I could respond, he abruptly turned and left.

"Gracias," I called to his disappearing back, leaving me to wonder what he meant by Shirvani not being my friend.

And what was that about the cost of asylum?

Another something to file away while I readied myself for my command performance with Iranian's number two man, General Bijan Mazdani, the wannabe King of Persia.

Room 2112 was a mini suite, complete with a king size bed, dresser and several chairs, two of them spanning a small table which held two glasses and a champagne bucket, complete with an unopened bottle of Louis Roederer, Cristal Brut 2008, on ice.

The knock on my door came several minutes early. "*Un Minuto*!" I called out to Rajif, giving myself a moment to apply lipstick and do a last touch up of my hair.

But instead of waiting, the door swung open and in stepped Shirvani. "Why did you speak Spanish to an Iranian?" he demanded. The voice was pleasant enough; his mouth almost in a smile, but his eyes told another story entirely.

Without looking away from the mirror, I replied, "This is Mexico. Down here I naturally speak Spanish. Wasn't thinking beyond that."

His face registered skepticism. "Not important. Rajif has been…reassigned," Shirvani explained, continuing into the bathroom and standing directly behind me. "Go easy, the General prefers his women without makeup. And, may I add, you're one of those women who doesn't require makeup to be…be attractive."

His women! I'm not one of his women!

We were minutes from meeting Mazdani, or I would have reacted even more negatively than I did. But I had to establish boundaries. "Is it your custom to invade people's space?" I asked, forcing myself to continue what I was doing. "In our country, you would be considered rude."

"Let me remind you, Ms. Martinez," he shot back, placing emphasis on my name, "we are not in your country." His facial expression hadn't changed, but he did take a step backward. A small victory in my favor.

"Neither are we in yours," I countered, pressing what I took to be a slight advantage.

"I am your host. And quite frankly, the only person standing between you and..."

"And what?"

"Let's just say, failure of your mission."

"And my mission, as you put it, is?"

"Convince the General you and your partner are trustworthy friends."

Judging from his belligerent stance, I assumed this guy Cav was not convinced Jimmy and I were acting solely for the benefit of his boss. "What's your take? Are we his friends?"

"In my world, I'm not entitled to an opinion. I believe what the General believes. Nothing more, nothing less."

"And what does the General believe?"

"That's for him to tell you—if he sees fit. And from what I understand, it's for you to convince him of whatever it is you came here to convince him of." He let that statement sink in before continuing. "Now we must be going. The general does not trust people who are late."

"What else does the General not trust?"

"People who don't look him in the eye when they speak to him, and...and people who don't honor his requests."

"What type of requests?

"Comes in all varieties. You will know what his intentions are by what room you are returned to. This room, Twelve, and the night is over for you. Room Ten, and...and let's just say it will be a longer night."

This last was said with what I took to be a knowing smirk. But because Mazdani's chief of staff already turned toward the door, I wasn't really sure. However, I was certain my time with the General would be challenging.

TWENTY-FIVE

Cav waited for me to catch up to him at the end of the hall and then he disappeared around a corner I didn't know existed. Two uniformed men were positioned on either side of the hallway forming a narrow passage between them. I didn't immediately recognize the uniforms and saw no markings, in English, Spanish—or Farsi.

Cav walked past the guards, nodding his head in my direction. Neither man moved to make more room. Cav knocked softly on a large double door and without waiting for a response he pushed it open and ushered me ahead of him. "Make yourself comfortable, Angella. The General will be with you promptly at seven. In case you are interested, everything in this room originated in Iran."

It was as if I had been transported back in time and space to a fantasy world centered around two massive Persian carpets; one defining a living room and the other a dining area. The table was glass with eight curved wood-outlined leather chairs around it and two place settings positioned across from each other. The center of the dining room carpet was primarily blue with patterns of tan radiating outward. In the living room the carpet center was red, again with tan extending outward. The pink window curtains appeared to be silk, trimmed with a light tan material. Two sofas faced each other in the living room with an elegant glass-topped coffee table between them. The glass was supported by curved wooden legs with lions' faces hand-carved into the wood. Two silk covered chairs were between the sofas on one side of the grouping, while a white leather chaise faced the grouping from the other side.

I felt as if I had taken a magic carpet ride into another world, a world in which I was a sightseeing visitor. Standing felt awkward, but sitting on these magnificent pieces seemed just as uncomfortable. I circled the living room once, finally selecting one of the silk chairs. I eased myself down and was reaching for my cell phone when a soft baritone voice from behind said, "Welcome, Mademoiselle Martinez. I am so very pleased you were able to come visit me. Go ahead, stay seated if you wish."

I quickly stood, turning to face the man who I had been schooled on for the past several days. My first impression was that the man across the room was someone other than Mazdani. He appeared many pounds lighter and several inches taller than I imaged from the photos and videos I studied. But the voice matched perfectly, and so did his eyes; deep set, dark brown, with a hint of passion. It had been that passion that set me on edge when I first saw his picture back in Brownsville. A man so alive, I remember thinking. "Pleased to meet you, General Mazdani," I managed. "It is certainly my pleasure being here."

I expected him to extend his hand in greeting, but instead he bowed. Lifting his head, he gently took my hand in his and moved it upwards toward his lips. This guy seemed more French than Iranian. I thought back over what I learned about his schooling and recalled only that he spent two years at Oxford after attending Brown University. I knew of nothing in France.

"Tonight, Mademoiselle, there are no generals here. Call me Bijan. In America, people pronounce it Bryan. I would be very pleased if you will call me Bryan."

"Call me, Angella," I replied, trying to gain my footing. "Works both ways."

"As you wish, Mademoiselle. Angella it shall be."

The door opened and in marched several men, all dressed identically in tan waiter's jackets and white pants. One of the men pushed a loaded cart.

"I trust you won't mind having a private dinner here in the suite. I've asked my chef to prepare something special for a special woman." His eyes sparkled. "And I understand Chef decided upon *khoresh-e fesenjan*, the Iranian wedding dinner. He's made it tonight with lamb. Will that be a problem?"

Wedding dinner!

"Lamb will be just fine." I lied with a smile. Truth is, lamb is not my favorite, but I can manage it.

"Excuse me, General." A rotund man wearing the same uniform as the others, but with a chef's hat, called from across the room. "We've had a slight change of menu. Tonight, the *khoresh* will be duck."

Before Mazdani could react, I announced, "Duck's even better."

"Duck with walnuts," the chef explained. "Simmered for hours with my family's own spice recipe. I believe you will enjoy." He bowed, stepping back at the same time.

My immediate thought was that the chef, or someone else, had researched me and found that I prefer duck over lamb.

Maybe I'm overthinking this?

"Come, my lady," Mazdani said, his hand on my elbow, gently guiding me to my place at the table. "*Khoresht* is best consumed hot." He waited for me to be seated, then took his place opposite me. "I know in America the people begin their meals with a salad. I find I most enjoy my salad dish after the main meal. It keeps me from overindulging in sweets. Better for my health. I trust you will humor me."

"By all means, Gen…Bryan." After thinking about this man as Mazdani, the man who coordinated terrorism throughout the Middle East and sold women into sexual slavery, it was hard to change gears and think of him in other terms. But if my mission was to have any hope of success, I'd have to relax and let it play out. "It smells so good. What is that heavenly flavor?"

"That is a question most definitely for the chef. His family has been in the food preparation business for generations. Almost every ingredient comes from his family farm."

My exposure to Middle Eastern food before this was limited, so I was pleasantly surprised by the flavors in the soup-like *khoresh*. The duck was tender and cooked to perfection. Mazdani explained the difference between the four breads on the table: barbari, sangak, taftoon, and lavash.

He spoke at length about the regions they each came from and the cultural differences between them. In keeping with my lessons, he referred to the country as Persia, and not Iran, and from his obvious passion it was clear he loved his country. I hadn't expected this terrorist leader to be so…so domestic. Mazdani in person was much more nuanced than the Mazdani of the classroom.

I didn't wait long to have my French theory confirmed. Mazdani spoke about his life in Paris for six years when he was assigned to the Iranian embassy as a military attaché. He made no secret he was there as a spy and enjoyed learning along with the culture. "I had the honor of dining with President Chirac many times. He was a very shrewd man and taught me to cross my t's and dot my i's as American's like to say."

After the salad course, he proposed adjourning back to the living room where dessert would be served. Mazdani explained that Persians are tea drinkers by nature, Armenian tea to be exact. He went on to explain that *ghahveh Turk,* Turkish coffee, is gaining popularity across his country. "Your preference?" he asked when one of the servers appeared in the room. "*Ghahveh* or tea? If it helps, we are having *shole-zard*. That's a form of rice pudding made with saffron."

"Tea, if you please. The…how do you pronounce it, gava...sounds good."

"Close. *Ghahveh.* A little more V sound, but you did well for trying."

Our conversation was light, with him telling me how he spent his childhood under the Shah, and me describing how it was to grow up along the Texas/Mexican border. He was particularly interested in what drew me to law enforcement. He asked how Jimmy and I met and why we left Homeland Security. Mazdani listened to every word and I visualized the wheels turning as he processed the information.

"I owe you no end of gratitude, Angella, for finding and returning to Persia that wondrously grand Kings Cup. What a magnificent piece of art that is. And to think it dates back to the Jiroft era. And those lions' heads on the cup are magnificent."

They're panthers, but who's going to tell him?

"My friend, Alterez, assures me you were adequately compensated. Am I correct?"

Our compensation came from our boss, Jack Silver, for locating another piece of lost artwork. But it was all part of the same series of transactions. "You are, indeed, correct. I'm happy to learn you're enjoying the Cup."

"Would you mind sharing your future plans with me?"

"If you're asking whether Jimmy and I plan to remain with Great Southern the answer is we haven't decided."

"I'm certain you have some idea," he pressed. "Retirement?"

"Thinking about it," I confessed. "No real decision yet."

"Perhaps when your marriage is…is consummated it will be easier to decide."

"I do think our future plans will be a joint decision, yes."

That seemed to satisfy him. I sat back down on the chair I originally chose and Mazdani settled comfortably on the sofa. We didn't wait long before trays were set in front of each of us, possessing a large blue bowl with yellow rice pudding and a small matching cup of tea. A third small table held a tea pot with a large curved handle.

"This is the best rice pudding I've ever tasted!" I exclaimed after taking several spoonfuls. "I wish I could cook like this."

"All it takes is lessons. When you retire, as you suggested, you will have all the time in the world to learn. With your attention to detail you'd be a wonderful chef."

"I didn't say I was retiring," I corrected Mazdani. "I said that was an option."

"Not in so many words, my dear. But you did say you were undecided. To my ear that sounds like a retirement plan. Excuse me if I took a leap of faith."

When I didn't respond, he asked, "Is it true, Jimmy, and you as well I presume, have joined forces with my friend Alterez?"

I hesitated long enough to make him think I was carefully considering my answer, when in truth this part of our conversation had been carefully rehearsed with Fairwell. "And why do you believe Jimmy is doing business with…"

"Come now, Angella, you don't seriously think I haven't a dossier on both of you. Let's be frank with each other, shall we? You are here to convince me that you and your partner can be trusted to deliver valuable wine made from grapes grown in the royal Persian vineyard. Is that not accurate?"

"All accurate," I assured him. "And yes, Jimmy and I are working with Santiago—Alterez—and his people."

"Before we continue, let's be certain we are both on the same field. For reasons you may know, and we certainly may discuss those reasons later if you desire, I must be absolutely convinced you and your partner are being truthful with me. A lie on your part will result in…in let's just say a nasty consequence. Do I make myself clear enough?"

"I don't lie."

"That's not what I asked, my dear. Do you understand the consequences of lying to me?" A curtain of cold steel quickly replaced the earlier soft passion in his eyes: sociopathic eyes.

"That nasty consequences will happen? Yes, I understand that."

"You are spunky, Angella and that's okay. I enjoy spirited women. Honest, spirited women." He studied me with hard set eyes for an uncomfortably long time before saying, "Now, please, in your own words, explain why you and Jimmy are joining with Alterez."

Back on the rails. At least for now.

Over the next hour I told him about the double crosses and other unscrupulous acts on the part of our government, ending with, "the only time we made any decent money was when we worked for Santiago and not against him."

Mazdani sat back and gave me all the rope I required. The cold steel gradually diminished from his eyes, but they were not as soft as they were during dinner. When I finally ran out of talking points, he calmly said, "Nice delivery, my dear. But I have the distinct sense I'm being manipulated. And I don't appreciate being manipulated."

"Manipulated? How so?"

"Your story is perfect. Too perfect. Life doesn't happen the way you just related. You seem to want me to believe you and your partner were in law enforcement all your adult life and then because of a few slights, some miscommunications, maybe a dishonesty or two, you both jumped over the line. In my experience, life doesn't work that way. And especially not when you have just become suddenly very rich. Rich even by your own country's standards. Listen to me, Angella, and listen carefully. I have one goal and one goal only. I will be King of Persia. The wheels are in motion and this wine is the last piece. Well, to be entirely accurate, it's not the wine I care about. It's the ceramic casks the wine comes in. I simply must acquire those casks. They verify who I am."

Really off the rails now!

"Casks?" I was puzzled. We were briefed on barrels, not casks. "I thought the wine was in wooden barrels."

"Whoever told you the wine was in barrels is…is misinformed. I call them casks. Ceramic jars to be exact. Jars with my family crest baked into them. If I am in possession of casks from the royal vineyard, then the Persian people will accept me as their king."

Playing devil's advocate, I replied, "Just having the casks doesn't prove that exactly. Anyone can have…"

"You're not listening to me, Angella. The Persian people are tired of the Revolution and their leaders. They want and need to believe in someone who can lead them back to their past. I am that someone! The wheels are set into motion. When I produce wine casks with the family crest on them then…then the transformation back to the Old Persian way of life will go forward. This is political, not legal, not factual. This is one of those times when the people will rise above logic to achieve something they want to achieve."

Time to close the sale.

"I can produce the wine barrels…casks…if you will trust me to make it happen."

Mazdani's face became very troubled and he spoke softly. "If Supreme Leader Khamenei gets even a sniff of what I'm planning he'll…"

"You can trust Jimmy and me," I responded. "The wine will be yours without question."

"If I allow this to go forward, you hold my life—and the future of Persia—in your hands. Now you understand the consequences of being totally honest with me. If I believe otherwise…no…let's be positive here. I need to know two things. First, can I trust you and your partner? Alterez says I can. And he has never been wrong before."

"As I said, you can trust both of us."

Without commenting on my reply, Mazdani continued, "And two, I need to be certain the wine casks come from the shipwreck of the Pride and from nowhere else."

"Preparations are underway as we speak. On Wednesday I will be there to watch the barrels—casks as you call them—being dug out from under the Gulf where they are buried. I can then personally assure you they are genuine."

"Unfortunately, Angella," he said, his voice soft but firm, "I'm not entirely convinced you are as much of a free agent as you wish me to believe."

Pensive, I sucked in my breath. "So, what will it take to convince you?"

"More than you can give."

"What then?"

"I must be there when the casks are retrieved from under the sea. Witnessing the recovery with my own eyes is the only way forward for me."

"It's dangerous," I protested, even though we planned for this contingency.

"All of life is dangerous. Can you arrange it?"

"I believe so."

"I must look your partner directly in the eye. That is the only way I can be certain of a man's honesty."

"He's being held captive by…by a cartel. He's not available."

"I know where he is. He's remaining alive only on the orders of Alterez himself. I've seen videos. But in my world videos are all too easy to make—and edit. I must have Jimmy directly before me. Look directly into his eyes as I have looked into yours. Nothing else will suffice."

"That is not possible," I said, trying to maintain an outer appearance of calm while agitation churned within. While that mountain cabin video of Jimmy being interrogated hadn't been doctored, Jimmy himself certainly had been. Did Mazdani suspect deception, or was this just caution resulting from years and years of duplicity?

"Everything is possible, my dear lady. Everything. You only must want it to happen."

"What do you propose?"

"Your partner, Mr. Jimmy Redstone, cannot come to me. So, I will go to your partner."

Disaster!

I hadn't given that possibility a single thought. "How would you get there? And do you even know where they're holding him?" Questions flooded my mind faster than I could ask them.

"Details, my dear. Mere details. I'm certain Alterez can provide answers. And what he can't provide, I assure you my people can."

"But that will require," I replied, trying to sound helpful and falling far short, "you traveling up into the mountains yourself, and…and possibly remaining up there a day, possibly two."

"You believe," he said, his eyes more alive than at any time during the evening, "this is me? Look around this room. This is soft, decadent, showy for the western world! I was born on a goat farm in the mountains and that is where I am most comfortable. When you live in a tent, you are part of the land. You are alive! You will see what I am talking about."

"But…but those Mexican mountains are dangerous, maybe even more so than Iran…Persia. Drug dealers, and…" I was going to say sex traffickers but thought better of it. "…very little, if any, law enforcement."

Mazdani again studied me a moment before responding. "As I said, mere details. You up for it or not?"

"Am I going with you?" I stammered, now totally off script, the knot in my stomach couldn't grow any larger.

"Of course, you will be accompanying me. Quite honestly, I haven't yet made up my mind about you. Your eyes are not at peace with your words. That could mean many things: some of them good, and some maybe not so good. We will soon find out which it is."

I didn't know what Mazdani had in mind, but it didn't sound promising. I stood to leave. "If I'm traveling with you in the morning than I better…"

"Not so fast, my dear Angella. As they say, the night is still young. And your eyes are talking to me."

"And just what are my eyes saying?" I asked, challenging my dangerous host.

"In all truth, you are alarmed. Of what, I have yet to determine. But you are clearly frightened. If you are truthful with me, then you have nothing to fear. I can promise you that much. Now, come over to the sofa and sit back down, we have yet to finish here." He patted the area next to where he was sitting.

"I'm being truthful," was all I could manage as I slowly walked across the Persian carpet to where his hand was resting.

"We'll see about that. Now won't we?"

I eased myself onto the sofa, sitting where his hand had been, my leg bumping his as I carefully positioned myself.

"Now, Angella, if we are to be…how do you say it...colleagues?... then you must learn to trust me."

I took a chance. "Trust, as I know you know, goes both ways." Same words I used with Fairwell a few hours ago.

"*Touché,* my dear Angella. And since we will be spending the next several days together, we should both remember that long-standing relationships, no matter what the cost, must be built on trust."

I would have scooted away, but he again grasped my hand and for the second time tonight he raised it to his lips. He again kissed the back of my wrist, this time lingering much longer than before. I was caught off-guard and speechless. In truth, the warmth of his body was comforting in a way that made me feel both excited and guilty at the same time.

Several days together?

"What does that mean? Several days? I thought…"

"I have planned an expedition up into the hills to see for myself what your Jimmy is all about. Only then will I know how to continue."

"Expedition? What exactly do you have in mind?"

"You and I will travel up to where your partner is being held at which point I will talk with him myself. If all is in order, we can proceed to pick up the wine casks. Then, and only then, will I go forward with my plan to liberate Iran from the Revolutionary government."

Facing him and looking deep into his eyes, I said, "You are certain those casks will allow you to claim heritage to past kings. Why such certainty?"

"If they are genuine, yes, I have no doubt," he said with real conviction. "As I have said, the groundwork has been prepared. If I produce an authentic ceramic wine cask with the family crest, then the Persian people will accept me as their king. I'm positive of it."

I held up my wine glass. "Here's to you becoming King of Persia."

Mazdani's glass clinked with mine. "King of Persia."

"Long live the King," I said, and emptied my glass.

"Fancy another glass?" Mazdani suggested, holding the wine bottle in his left hand and taking my glass in his right. Our lower bodies were touching, and I felt the heat from his leg.

"I've had enough. Anymore and I won't…"

Mazdani's sensual eyes deepened. "That's the objective, now isn't it?"

A single knock came from the door, followed by the man calling himself Cav who quickly entered the room. I hadn't noticed earlier, but he bore a close resemblance to his boss. A bit less weight, perhaps, an inch or so taller, but same facial structure. "Sorry to interrupt, General, but all is now in order." He turned to me. "Angella. Please come with me, I will escort you to room..."

"Room Ten," Mazdani said. "Room Ten."

"Room Ten it is," Cav said with what I interpreted as a wink. "Angella, please follow me if you will." He turned on his heel and marched out.

I looked back at the General, but the sofa was empty.

TWENTY-SIX

The sun was directly overhead when I realized we were not going up into the hills but remained on a highway I often traveled. Angella would be in Mexico City and on her way to see Mazdani. That thought again stirred emotions I reluctantly concluded I'm ill-equipped to deal with.

Agitated, I asked the man sitting beside me, whose distinguishing feature was an oversized mustache obscuring much of his face, where we were headed Dark eyes peered at me from above the hair, his lips remaining fixed. I didn't expect an answer. Not one of the three *team members,* as Malcom called them, spoke a word since I was forced to join them. The sound of a vehicle traveling at a hundred kilometers an hour on a badly maintained asphalt road was all I've heard for the past hour. "This isn't the road up to the mountain. Where are you taking me?" I demanded, struggling to control my frustration and fighting a losing battle.

I forced myself to relax and the monotony of the road noise helped. I slept for several hours, awaking only when I sensed our speed dropping. The time was six-thirty-eight and we were passing through the town of Cohoala, the low, western sun throwing deep shadows across the road. At least I now knew where we were. Reclusorio Saltillo Prison was not far away. It took a few more minutes before I put all the pieces together.

But it didn't add up. Prisons, especially Mexican high security prisons, don't typically have nighttime visiting hours. Yet, we were now within ten miles of Santiago's permanent home and heading straight for it. I should have learned by now that with Santiago nothing should be a surprise. That realization didn't prevent me from being puzzled when, at exactly seven, we rolled to a stop at a side gate of the massive prison housing many of Mexico's worst criminals. A guard post stood just ahead. Two uniformed men were posted on either side of the door.

"Fuera!" The driver commanded; the first words spoken by anyone in the car other than me. Mustache man turned his hard-set face in my direction making it clear I would either get out on my own or he'd forcibly throw me out.

There's a time and place for everything. In front of a prison, in the presence of armed guards is certainly not the place to start a commotion. I abandoned all thoughts of overpowering my *companions,* stepped out of the car and walked directly toward the guards.

"Nombre, por favor," the guard closest to me barked when I approached. He was asking my name, but he made it sound as if he was issuing an order.

"Jimmy Redstone," I replied, keeping my hands in plain sight. Mexican officials would not question a prison guard who, after visiting hours were over, shot an American who was dropped off by unknown hombres who immediately sped away.

"Identification, please," the guard demanded, switching to English and adopting a more pleasant tone.

He examined my driver's license, looked up and studied my face. Satisfied, he smiled and said, "We have been informed of your visit, *Señor* Redstone. Please follow me. My name is Rafael and I will be your escort."

This guy was treating me as a VIP. In fact, as we passed the guard house the other guard threw a quick salute. Once inside the prison proper, Rafael said in almost perfect English, "no scanner at this entrance. I must check you myself. Do you have any weapons, blades or anything sharp?"

"No," I answered, smiling as best I could.

"Any cell phones, cameras or electronics must remain with me. You may turn them off if you wish."

I took his advice and turned my cell off before reluctantly handing it to him. "Take good care of my cell please."

"I will have it for you when you leave. I will never be out of your sight, so no worries." He laughed to show me it was okay to trust him. Rafael did an excellent job of patting me down, going so far as to have me remove my shoes so he could check my socks. I couldn't have smuggled a lone blade past him had I wanted to. Satisfied, he pulled out a two-way radio and said something in Spanish that I took to be a code word. The radio remained silent.

He turned to me. "Just a moment. Take a seat over there." He pointed to a cinder block wall where a cork board covered with pinned-on paper notices hung. A single metal fold-up chair was leaning against the wall beneath the board. I walked over, unfolded the chair, and sat. Rafael remained standing ten feet away.

At least fifteen minutes passed before his radio beeped. Holding it to his ear he listened a moment, then said, "Okay, *Señor Abogado,* all is now in order for your meeting. Follow me. And please don't say one word to anyone until you are alone in the room with your *cliente*. Understand?"

Now I'm a lawyer. What next?

I told him I understood. He nodded and proceeded down one corridor and then down another. Cells were on either side, most, but not all, empty. The prisoners I passed were lying in racks that passed for beds. Some were moaning, some threw me hand signals, using their middle fingers. Most remained passive. My assumption was that this was dinner hour and the inmates were off in a mess hall somewhere else in the prison. The ones remaining behind were either too sick to eat or being denied food for some reason.

We went up two flights and along another corridor, passing more empty cells. Rafael signaled me to stop in front of a solid door with a glass window in the center. An armed uniformed guard stood directly in front of the door blocking our way. Through the glass I could make out a man who looked like Santiago, only much thinner than I remembered him.

Rafael said to the guard, *"Toma quince. Lo tengo por ahora."*

"Sí, Capitán." The guard turned and walked off.

Rafael inserted his key which produced a loud pop and the door swung open. "Follow me," he said, leading the way into a small room.

Santiago sat behind a table that took up much of the space. His right ankle was chained to an eye bolt protruding from the concrete floor. There was just enough slack in the chain to allow Santiago to reach the table.

"I will leave you alone with your client," Rafael said. "You have fifteen minutes. I will be out there if you need anything. This room is soundproofed so you must push that button on the wall over there if you need me sooner."

When the door closed behind Rafael, I didn't hear the pop of the lock, so I assumed he left it unlocked.

"Good of you to come see me, Redstone," Santiago began, his voice a shadow of what I remember. "We need to talk."

"You do realize I'm not here of my own free will. Joy issued some rather disturbing options, not in keeping with my understanding of our arrangement."

"My lovely Joy sometimes gets, shall we say, carried away. But you and I will talk. Man, to man."

"We have fifteen minutes, so talk."

"Jimmy, no need to be hostile. After all, I am keeping your double alive am I not?"

"You are," I admitted, wondering how the hell he knew about the double.

"I'm honoring my part of the deal even though your government got you out."

"That's as much for your benefit as it is ours. If there's one thing I know about you, you do what's best for you."

"Does anyone do otherwise? Never mind answering me, we don't have time. Here's the situation. I know Joy told you, but it's important that you and I are together on the same page here."

This wasn't the time to debate Santiago as to whether or not people always put their own self-interest above everyone else's. We'd have no first responders, no soldiers, no volunteers, no charities, if his world view was right. But drug lords didn't see life as I do, and he wasn't about to change now. "Go ahead," I conceded, "Why am I here?"

"As a gesture of good faith, let me first say that the missing gold bar, the one gone from Angella's car, is no longer my concern."

"I never thought it was."

"A little misunderstanding by Joy. That bar was meant to be *stolen* by prison guards. Getting money to them is becoming harder by the day. This is just one of the ways it can't be traced to me. Makes them work for it, so to speak."

"So they knew the bar was in Angella's car."

"Enough of that. This business with Mazdani is...well it's out of control. Way out of control. That's what I get for doing business with a terrorist. But...but who am I to complain. If I were a free man, I could fight back. But that's not where I find myself." He paused, sucked in his breath and added, "This…this terrorist is a master at manipulation. They seem to have bribed everyone. Mazdani set me up, and you as well, by arranging a murder right here in this prison."

"You mean with the shoe and the shank? That was your shoe, not theirs. You saying you didn't commit the murder?"

"It's much more complicated than that, my friend. Much more. Yes, it was my shoe. Yes, I intended to send documents out with Angella. But I never planned on…on them substituting the blade."

"You didn't deny you committed the murder."

"This is a lawyer room. Supposed to be soundproof. But I don't trust anyone. No more talk of murder in here. But I didn't plant that blade on Angella."

"But you used her and now she's wanted for murder. That I can't forget!"

"We don't really have time now, but…but I'm not positive it's really Mazdani behind all this. The stuff with the women…that's not…I've known Mazdani for many years. Never did he treat woman as I'm now led to believe. If he had, I wouldn't…never mind. He's been linked with trafficking only since that Major…Major Cav something…got involved. My sources tell me Cav's using the General…or his name."

"What's this Cav person got to do with me being here?"

"He's booked on a flight to Monterrey later tonight. I'm thinking he's on his way up to their mountain control point."

"The place they had me?"

"They use that for coordination."

"Coordination of what? Drugs?"

"Mostly women."

"If I'm following, you're telling me it's this Cav guy who runs the women."

"That's my best guess. Yes."

"And not the General?"

"That I don't know. Hard to think Cav could pull it off without Mazdani. But...but we go back a long way and Mazdani never said anything about women. If anybody'd know, you'd think I would."

My assessment of Santiago is that he's telling the truth. But I'm also a believer that scorpions are always scorpions. Not to be trusted. "Assume I buy what you're selling. I still don't know why I'm here."

"This whole operation with Mazdani becoming King is off schedule and screwed up. I think Cav's working against it, and I need to know who I can trust. Simple as that. Face to face. Can I trust you? My life hangs with you."

"And Angella's life hangs with you."

"So, we understand each other. That's good."

"That's blackmail."

"Splitting hairs, my friend. Splitting hairs. You have an easy way out. All I need from you is to know I can trust your word."

"What word?"

"In simple terms: your promise to turn over every barrel of wine to Mazdani. Every one of them. The barrels and all the wine casks in those barrels."

"Casks? I thought…"

"You were told barrels. That's more American disinformation."

"For what purpose? Why go to all this trouble and expense and not get it right?"

"Can anyone ever figure out your government? A lot of money's in play. Anything goes. So, are you with me?"

"I'm not sure I buy all you're selling. I don't understand why having every barrel—cask—or whatever, will change the outcome. One cask is enough to prove whatever he thinks he needs to prove."

"If a billion dollars is in the control of Mazdani, then he has a chance of pulling it all off. Without the money, then…then he's at the mercy of others—powerful others."

"For old wine that's been under water for over a hundred years, a billion dollars doesn't seem likely. It's most likely ruined, undrinkable, by now."

"If the value depended only on its taste, you would be correct. But the people who will pay big dollars will never drink it. They want it because…because they can. Like winning a big game. Bragging rights. When you have everything you ever want, you want things you can't have. What can be more exotic than wine that's been under the sea for so long and comes with stories of plunder and intrigue?"

"Who are these people?"

"You know many of their names. Household names. People in power in your government, in many governments."

"They'll pay that much knowing the money's going to prop up a terrorist—a terrorist who just might be behind human trafficking."

"Done all the time, my friend. All the time. A lot of pockets are being lined is all I can say," Santiago took a deep breath, checked his watch, then continued, his face close to mine, his voice low. "Listen to me, Redstone. I need your promise; you and Angella will do nothing to sidetrack Mazdani from taking possession of every cask in that find. You do that and I'll do all in my power to protect you both."

"And what do you gain if we succeed?"

"My freedom."

"I assume you're including Angella's freedom as well."

"Your assumption is correct, my friend. Very much correct."

"And I suppose if we fail, the opposite is also correct."

"I enjoy doing business with smart people."

TWENTY-SEVEN

"You're the last guy in the world I expected to see here," I said to DEA Agent Pickale when guard Captain Rafael opened the door, allowing me to exit the prison. It was night when I walked outside, but with thousands of watts of light flooding down from several towers, the time of day was not obvious. Pickale was leaning against the guard shack talking with someone inside I couldn't see.

He straightened up and said, "Let's get moving. Lots of ground to cover. Plans are changing as we speak." His vehicle, the same one we crossed the border in earlier was parked in a small dirt lot I didn't notice before. For all I knew he had been there when I arrived. We drove in silence for a good ten minutes, neither of us wishing to take the lead. Having the most to lose by remaining silent, I gave in and demanded to know what the hell was going on.

"First thing first. I suspect you haven't eaten all day and neither have I. Nothing good ever happens on an empty stomach. Guard back there told me everything around here rolls up soon." Pickale parked in front of a small, even by

Mexican standards, restaurant. "He suggested this place. Said the ribs are the best there are."

Now Pickale didn't seem to be in much of a hurry and took his time ordering. The ribs, when they finally arrived, were prepared to perfection. Best I've ever eaten. Surveying our table filled with a huge pile of bones and a ton of soiled napkins, I wanted answers. "Now that we ate, it's time to talk. How 'bout beginning with why you abandoned me to Malcom?"

"Orders."

"From?"

"No need to know."

It's a good thing for Dill I didn't have that shank they planted on Angella, because this would be a good time to use it. Jury acquittal for certain. "Could have warned me of the plan change."

"Would you have gone with her?"

"No."

"There's your answer. Look, Jimmy, I'm just the messenger and delivery guy in all this. Your beef is with management. I'm hired help. You've been in my shoes, so cut me a break. I'll tell you what I can, but don't bust my chops. Deal?"

"Deal," I conceded, knowing I needed to gather as much information as I could if this mess was going to have any type of positive ending for Angella and I. "Just be straight with me."

"Do my best. Here's what I know. The original plan was to drive you up to the mountain cabin, substitute you for your double. Idea being that in the event Mazdani wanted to interview you directly you'd be there in person. His reputation is he's hands-on and the profiler believes he'd insist on looking you in the eye, so to speak, before trusting you. Intel has it he's been pressing to have you visit him in Mexico City solely for that purpose. His chief of staff, guy named Major Shirvani, seems to be running the logistics and he keeps changing the plans. Maybe with Mazdani's blessing, maybe on his own. Next best thing then is for him to travel to you."

"Up in the mountains?"

"Don't forget who you're dealing with here. Man's lived in tents, caves, under camels, who the hell knows where else. To the Western world, he's at home with glitter and gold. To his own people he's…he's a goat herder, living summers on a barren hillside with nothing but a shawl—and his ever-present knife—to protect him from the elements."

"So, what changed?"

"Santiago, that's what. He may have told you, but they have him for murder. He's managed to make powerful enemies and his drug lord days are now numbered. And I don't think the numbers go much higher than double digit. Low double digit if I had to guess. He struck a deal with Mazdani for his freedom. Money, big money' involved. My guess, and this is just me putting pieces together, is the money will come from the sale of the buried Pride wine."

"I thought Santiago had unlimited money coming in from drug trafficking. What am I missing here?"

"That source is either drying up or spoken for. You know he went into the art business, stolen and forgeries, and that's doing well."

"But?"

"But the income from the art business is also now being spoken for. Working from prison has become more expensive as time moves on. The other cartels are moving in and his men are getting picked off. Government officials are developing deeper pockets. In short, expenses are out stripping supply, and Santiago is desperate. And we both know desperate men do desperate things."

"Such as?"

"Use the wine money to buy him freedom. He's tying his star to Mazdani."

"He's planning on living in Iran? That's crazy."

"Beats dying in a Mexican prison. Besides, he'll disappear into the Persian hills, or somewhere in Serbia. Hopefully, we'll never hear from him again."

"Let's get back to our timeline. I was to be inserted into the cabin, let's see, it's almost eight-thirty, in about seven hours. We can almost make the time-line if I remember the drive right."

"Couldn't, even if we wanted to. It's a six-hour drive in the best of conditions. At night, that would be suicide going up that windy, dirt path of a road."

"We could get close tonight and at first light go…"

"Plans have changed. Just got word Mazdani's at the airport."

"Going where?"

"Either Matamoros or Monterrey."

"Matamoros! He'd be flying to Monterrey if he was going up to the cabin. Why Matamoros?"

"That's what's so confusing. He's traveling with Shirvani, another woman we don't know and Angella. The tickets have Mazdani and Angella going to Matamoros and the others going to Monterrey."

"You certain? That's backward."

"Nothing's for certain. Best we have. Makes little sense. They're not ready at the tunnel site yet, so they're all panicked up there. Need another day."

"Where's this leading?"

Pickale's jaw set hard, as if he had bad news to deliver and couldn't keep it back any longer. "The latest plan is to reinsert you on the mountain."

"What the hell! Talk about off the rails! You guys always this screwed up? This is pure…"

"I remind you. I'm only the messenger," Pickale said, trying, but failing, to calm me. "My guess; covering all bases because they don't know what else to do."

"That's why you've been slow walking dinner! Waiting—wishing—for the orders to change."

"Just enjoying the meal."

"My ass! You're waiting on orders as to which way to drive: east to Brownsville or west to the mountain."

"You can say that."

"What else could I say?"

"You could ask me what else I'm prepared to tell you."

"So, what else are you prepared to tell me?"

"Angella's with Mazdani."

"You told me that." My agitation with Angella working with Mazdani without backup eased somewhat after it was decided to allow her to wear a camera. Presumably, the camera was working.

"She's listed on the manifest to Matamoros."

Then it hit me. It felt as if I'd been kicked in the stomach. "But she's been Red Noticed! Mexico will never allow her on that plane! Santiago had been right about the operation having gone out of control."

"Precisely the problem. We're on it, I'm told."

"We're on it! What the hell does, 'we're on it,' mean?"

"That's all I know. My assumption is that our government will see to it she's allowed to fly across Mexico and then cross the border. Did it once, don't know why not the second time."

"Let's get on up there. We can drive over in…in five hours or so. We're no use stuck down here."

"Not so fast. Orders are to hold. So, hold we do."

"You planning on sleeping in that heap, or what?"

"Motel will work. I believe there're rooms above this place. Mind staying here?"

"Any port in a storm," I answered, figuring I'd lull the guy into trusting me and at the first opportunity grab the car and go.

Dill called the waiter over and asked about a room. A moment later an old woman, her head permanently bent forward, shuffled over to the table.

"Mil pesos por la noche," she said, her face addressing the table.

Without hesitation, Dill responded, *"Una o dos habita ciones?"*

"Una habitación, dos camas," came the immediate response. Dill turned to me. "Fifty dollars for one room. Good news, she says there are two beds."

"Get two rooms."

Dill exchanged words with the old woman, who shook both her head and her finger.

"Says she only has one," he reported.

"Tell her we'll take it. Better be clean."

Another exchange and Dill said, "Two beds are the extent of the promises." He pulled out his wallet and counted out five tens. When the old woman was satisfied, she dug into her apron pocket and produced a key tied by a leather throng to a small block of grease-stained wood, dropped it on the table and shuffled off.

"Anything further on Angella's flight?" I was only five hundred miles from Mexico City, but it seemed like we were separated by a continent.

"DHS is monitoring the situation is all I know. Now, let's get some shut eye. I suspect tomorrow will be a long day."

The two beds turned out to be a single queen size mattress held off the floor by a piece of plywood and balanced on what appeared to be chicken coops. At least the coops were empty of chickens. The less I knew about the coops the better. A single sink was bolted to the wall and what passed as a head was down the hall.

On my way back from the toilet I heard heavy breathing noises coming from two of the rooms. Should have known these facilities were typically rented by the hour. Whether guests brought their own partners, or enjoyed house supplied entertainment, most likely depended on the guest.

I sat on the edge of the bed too agitated to even pretend I was going to sleep. Dill didn't seem to have that problem. He was lying on his side facing away from me. "I was thinking," I said, "about the money. A billion dollars for old wine. Can't be right."

"Forget about it. Go to sleep. It is what it is."

"I wasn't so much concerned about how billionaires spend their money. The lawman in me…I guess that never goes away…is thinking about the people taking money for this operation. Politicians, others."

"All I can say is the bureau's working it. Can't go into details."

"That's comforting," I said sarcastically. "How far up the line you think it goes?"

"Can't discuss it."

"That Homeland Secretary...I guess she's Deputy Secretary...Diane Sweet I believe her name is. She on the take?"

"Don't believe so. No more of this. Go to sleep."

"Admiral Boyle?"

"Good God, no! That guy's got a rod up his butt, he's so stiff. That's my take on why he's running this operation. Only one they can trust."

"I thought he's running it because he's assigned to this sector."

"When he got kicked upstairs, they assigned him to Key West. He ran the South Padre Island Station for many years and knows this area better than anyone. He's now in charge of everything from Cuba to Playa del Carmen, Mexico. Nothing moves into or out of the Gulf of Mexico without his blessing. But, hey, he's Coast Guard. They could have used Navy—or even the Marines."

"And he's in charge of digging up sunken wine barrels, or caskets, or casks, or whatever, for sale to the highest bidder? That's what an admiral does?"

"He'll do what he's told to do. Admirals follows lawful orders without question. Nothing more. Nothing less. That's what all government agents do—or should do. You get my drift? Now go to sleep. Or just sit there. Either way, I don't care. But turn the sound off. I've had it."

"Sweet dreams," I said.

"Oh, and Jimmy, case you're thinking of hijacking the car and dumping me, forget about it. Car's being monitored and if it leaves without me a drone'll take it out. So, go to sleep or not. But at least shut the hell up."

TWENTY-EIGHT

Room Ten was a suite very similar to mine, only this one had two separate bedrooms, one on either side of the main room.

"Make yourself comfortable," Cav said, the General has business to attend to. Shouldn't take him very long. You'll find a wardrobe of clothes and things in there. Make yourself at home and I suggest you change into something comfy."

I wanted to body slam that guy, but his size made it problematic. I checked the door after Cav left, on the off chance he forgot to lock it. No such luck. I paced the floor several minutes before a plan came to mind. I rushed over to the kitchenette and pulled drawers open searching for a knife. Again, no luck. Not even a fork.

The hall door latch clicked, and the door opened.

Show time!

Catching Mazdani by surprise was my best hope of escaping. But catching him with what? Even if I succeeded, I'd face the hall guards before getting to the elevator. I stepped back and looked toward the window. We were on the twenty-first floor and all thoughts of escaping in that direction were short-lived.

The door opened. I turned back expecting to see the General, but instead it was Rajif, the man *reassigned* after showing me to my room earlier in the evening. He was holding a small envelope. His face a mask of terror as he thrust the envelope toward me. "*Abrelo*!"

Inside, I found a 10,000 tomen note, now worth less than ten dollars. I also pulled out several pictures, and a small piece of paper.

Rajif continued to look furtively back over his shoulder toward the door. "*Leer!*" he commanded.

I slipped the paper from the envelope and saw the words: QUIERO ASILO printed in neat schoolboy fashion. I WANT ASYLUM.

"*Mujer. Nombres.*"

It took me a beat to realize that Rajif was pointing to the photos, trying to tell me they contained names. Female names. I pulled the stack out of the envelope and studied the pictures. There were hundreds, possibly a thousand names neatly printed in some sort of a ledger. Someone, possibly Rajif, had taken these pictures. I carefully passed each picture across the front of my body allowing the button camera to capture the names.

As I proceeded, Rajif's request suddenly made sense. The man was trading the names, and the money, for asylum. Most likely asylum in the United States not in Mexico. I was about to tell him I couldn't help when the door again swung open.

Rajif's face froze with fright, his eyes went wide. Instantly, he ducked under the arms of the person entering the room and was gone. I turned my back to the door while the last few pictures were being captured. I then quickly shoved everything back into the envelope and stuffed the envelope in my purse.

I was expecting Mazdani. Instead, a woman about my height came through the door and stood directly in front of me. We had the same facial structure, except her darker complexion matched her jet-black hair. She was a good thirty years younger than me, but other than that we could have been twins. As it was, we could pass for sisters.

"Do not say one word," she said, her English heavy with a Middle Eastern accent. Cav must not know."

Anything Cav must not know is okay by me.

"My name is Jaleh Moradi. Tonight, we will change places."

I assumed Moradi was one of Mazdani's *women*, and changing places was not on my agenda—and never would be.

The door opened again and another, much shorter woman with graying hair joined us. She wore heavy glasses and was pulling a hard-sided suitcase. "Oh, I see you're both here," the woman said, clearly expecting both of us. "That's very good." She studied Jaleh and me a moment, then commented, "Good match. Let's get to work. Both of you sit over there." She pointed in the direction of two leather chairs facing a plush sofa.

Moradi did as instructed and walked toward one of the chairs. "Wait," I protested, "What's this about? And who are you?"

"Didn't the General tell you? I'm Ziba. I do makeup."

"Makeup?" I repeated, confused.

"Changing places," Jaleh again said, settling into the chair closest to the sofa.

Ziba proceeded across the room, opened the suitcase and poured liquid onto a soft rag. Holding the rag in front of her, she called, "Come on, hurry, not much time."

We're being interchanged! But why?

"Before I consent," I protested, "I need to know why? What's going on?"

"All I know is you're both taking a trip. Flying somewhere I gather. Changing identities. Now hurry. Not much time. When I am finished you will change clothes as well."

This made sense. We had to fly from Mexico City to Monterrey and thanks to Mazdani I couldn't go through security without being stopped. But Jaleh could.

This wasn't going to end well for her.

I sat in front of Ziba allowing her to remove my makeup and proceed to do whatever makeup artists do to transform people.

"Not the best I've ever done," she mumbled a while later, "but it's good enough." Turning to the real Moradi, she said, "Now for you."

In less than fifteen minutes my face appeared on the woman sitting across from me. She brushed something into Moradi's hair to lighten it enough to pass for mine. I assumed she darkened mine when she combed it.

"Now, change clothes. Don't worry about the shoes. Men never look at shoes anyway."

Silently, we did as we were told. Ziba produced hats for each of us to mask her work. She then stepped back, shook her head up and down several times, and exclaimed, "All ready to travel. Cav is unaware of the makeup. Speak as little as possible. I can't do anything with voices." She checked her watch and with one final glance in our direction, said, "Handbags must be exchanged. You're changing identities, so leave everything. Ready? Show time!" She opened the door to the hallway and the three of us left together. Strength in numbers it seems.

"Everything you will require for the trip," Ziba said as we walked down the hall toward the elevator, "is in the van. All that's missing are the two of you. Let's go join them, shall we?"

The guards were not in the hallway, nor were they in the lobby when we stepped out of the elevator. They were, however, standing just outside the front door, a black van idling between them. One of the guards held the door to the second row open for us. Cav was sitting in the far back. I climbed in first and resisted the temptation to say hello to him. Ziba slid in after me and Moradi came in last.

No one spoke until General Mazdani, sitting in the front passenger seat, turned to face us. "It promises to be a long night. I plan to nap on the way to the airport. So, no talking from anyone." His tone was pleasant, but his words were clearly an order.

Whether he actually napped, I couldn't determine. But nonetheless, the only noise inside the van was the tires whooshing on the roadway. As we approached the airport, Cav leaned forward and called to the driver, "You can drop Jaleh and me off over there." He pointed toward the first gate.

The van slowed and the driver carefully maneuvered to an empty area. "Change in plans," Mazdani announced. "Major, you're accompanying Angella over to Matamoros."

"That's not..." Cav struggled for words. "...not the plan...not what we...we agreed to. I'm booked on a flight to Monterrey. Jaleh and I are on that flight. That's the way our tickets are booked."

"As I said, plans have changed. Do I make myself clear, Major?"

This was the first time I heard Mazdani's command voice. The concealed menace was unmistakable. What he had not said was far more important than what he had said.

"But, sir, I need to be up on the moun...I need to be there."

"Would you please care to tell me what is so important I can't do it myself? It is essential I visit with Mr. Redstone, and he's up on the mountain."

"I know, but..."

"I've issued you a direct order, Major. Are you disobeying that order?"

"No," Cav mumbled, adding, "Sir," as an afterthought.

"It pleases me to know you will carry out my orders flawlessly," Mazdani replied.

"It is dangerous up on the mountain, Sir," Shirvani said, continuing to plead his case. "Please allow me to go in your place as originally planned."

"That was *your* plan, not mine. You are now bordering on insurrection! I will not have any more of it!"

Piecing this conversation together, it appeared the new plan was for Cav and Jaleh to pose as the General and me and together they would fly to Matamoros. That would leave Mazdani and me to travel to Monterrey masquerading as Cav and Jaleh. Unfortunately for Jaleh, she's on track for a very unpleasant surprise when I'm—she's—arrested going through security.

Mazdani stepped out of the van and came around to my side, opened the door and extended his hand. "Madam Moradi, may I?" His eyes were again alive, but his face had been transformed into that of Shirvani's. Had the real Shirvani not been in the back seat, I would have been fooled.

Using Mazdani's arm for balance, I stepped down. "Thank you," I said pulling my hand back.

Mazdani leaned in close as if he was about to kiss me on the cheek. "Until we are free of the airport in Monterrey," he cautioned, "you are to remain close to me and address me as Major."

Thinking of my now Persian-looking Jaleh Moradi face, I replied, "Only thing missing is the burka." I laughed.

His eyes went dead flat. "My customs are not a joking matter! In my country you would indeed have your face covered. But in your country it causes problems I prefer to avoid."

Pulling away and shocked at the rudeness from my host, I shot back, "We are not in my country! And neither are we in yours!" From the look on his face I had stepped in it big time. "Sorry, Major," I said, trying to repair the damage, "I apologize for being insensitive. You're right, of course."

"Apology accepted." Mazdani quickly responded, taking my hand in his. "Continue smiling. Pretend we are going on a nice vacation together. We'll get on that plane without incident and have plenty of time to discuss all of our differences later tonight." He turned to the driver. "Take them around again and park somewhere out of sight. Their flight isn't until two. That'll give Señora Ziba time to make him into me. I want him on that plane to Matamoros without incident."

This was one of those times I wanted to throw a Jimmy salute but controlled myself. This promised to be a long night and Mazdani with me was a whole lot better than Mazdani against me.

The airport was surprisingly busy for midnight. Mazdani kept me in his sight the whole time we were in the terminal, the only exception being when I went to the ladies' room. Several times he answered to Major Shirvani without hesitation. Interchanging identities with Cav didn't seem to be a one-time occurrence.

I didn't know whether Jaleh Moradi was new to Mazdani's entourage because of me, or whether she was just a happy accident. It was likely I'd never know that answer. It was also likely I'd never really know how many camp followers he really had.

I learned from what little the General would share that we were scheduled to land at two-twenty and would be met by, in his words, 'our guides'. In answer to my questions about clothes and equipment, he would only say it had all been arranged and not to worry.

But worry I did. Not so much about what I would be wearing, but where I'd be sleeping and under what conditions. He spoke about living in a tent. I had the distinct feeling that's where we were heading, a tent somewhere in the mountains of Mexico.

Once on the plane I tried to sleep, but my mind was busy recalling what I knew about Rayones, Mexico which is south of Monterrey. I didn't know much about that area, except a foggy memory from a DHS briefing back when Jimmy and I were agents. Hilly, even mountainous, terrain had been a favorite rock-climbing location back before the Pilón River Valley became too dangerous for tourists. The cartels now controlled the roads leading up from Highway Eighty-Five and the number of women and children who crossed the border under cartel control from that area alone was over five thousand a month. That translated into a large number of women and children being hidden in and around the area we were going to. That certainly could explain why Mazdani had insisted on going up to the mountain.

Then it dawned on me. Mazdani wasn't here at the pleasure of the Mexican government as much as he was here at the pleasure of the cartels, the drug lords. That meant he was more than a money man. He was part of the supply chain of enslaved women to be exact! Was my double, Jaleh Moradi, a victim, or God forbid, a boss?

Needless to say, I didn't sleep a moment on the plane. Thankfully, Mazdani was busy with his cell phone and remained silent until we were parked at the gate. "Come on, my dear," he said, resuming his 'we're lovers' tone, "our crew is waiting."

Indeed, they were. Two well-built Mexicans, one sporting a full beard that hadn't been trimmed in years and the other limiting himself to a neatly clipped goatee, were sitting in the front seat of a deep green Chevrolet Silverado pickup. Both men got out, making it easier for Mazdani and me to climb into the back seat. No introductions were made.

As I anticipated, we eventually turned onto Highway Eight-Five. In the daytime, the trip would take under two hours. But night was another story. There was almost no traffic going south. But northbound trucks appeared out of the darkness every few minutes. They seemed to enjoy the center of the two-lane road, which meant the Silverado would bump off the crushed stone roadbed onto the rocky berm. Not a pleasant ride to say the least.

We passed through Allende at three-forty, and not surprisingly, nothing was open. At four-fifteen the driver suddenly braked hard, pulled onto the bumpy rock infested berm, and instead of coming back onto the road, he turned the Silverado into a stand of trees. The low branches hit the windshield and thankfully parted without doing any real damage. Once through the trees, we gained speed as the headlights led us onto two narrow ruts through the rocks. We followed the ruts a good mile before the primitive terrain widened into a roadbed.

Soon, the ground sloped upward, and my focus switched from trees and brush to a massive rocky hill ahead of us. I didn't know how far up the mountain Mazdani intended to go, but unless switchbacks had been cut into the rock face, this truck would be of limited help, even if it had four-wheel drive.

"Faster," the General commanded, leaning forward so the driver could hear him. "We must be camped before first light."

The bearded driver answered in a language I didn't understand, causing me to rethink his nationality. As if in answer to my unasked question, Mazdani switched languages, I assume to Farsi. The truck then sped up. The General continued to monitor his watch, finally barking, "Okay, over there! Get us set up and this truck covered. Fast! Now!"

The Silverado bounced to a stop and the goateed passenger bolted out and began hauling equipment from the truck bed over to a clump of small trees. When the truck was empty, he covered it with a tarp. Meanwhile, the bearded man, with help from Mazdani, set up two tents, moving several crates into each of them.

"Angella, I don't know how much camping you've done or how much training you received from Homeland Security but listen to me carefully. Heat sensing drones are used up here and can spot just about anything alive. These tents are designed to send back a cool heat signature. That way, our presence will not be detected. Because of that, you and I will remain inside that tent from now until sundown. The tent has no facilities, so take a roll of toilet paper and go inside the truck tarp right now. Sorry, but that's the best I can offer you."

I started to protest, but Mazdani quickly cut me off. "No time for that. In ten minutes time we will be locked up tight for the next twelve hours. Go or don't go. That's up to you. What's not up to you is where you spend the rest of the day. And while you're at it, change into fatigues. There is a pair in the tent that will fit you. And hurry."

I took his advice, found the toilet paper and the fatigues which were in an orange nylon carry-all bag along with several other items of clothing. I grabbed what I needed and started across the rocky hillside toward the truck.

"Don't make the tragic mistake, my dear," Mazdani called, "of running off. There are bad people out here, unmistakably bad people. If they don't find you, the heat sensors will. And...," he paused to emphasize the seriousness of what he was saying, "...and I won't be in a position to offer you protection."

I hurried to the truck without responding. Taking care of business and changing my clothes under the filmy tarp wasn't the best situation. At least it was private.

What will I do when I'm locked inside the tent with this womanizing terrorist for twelve hours? And unless I'm mistaken, there's only a single mattress!

Emerging from under the tarp I realized it was close to dawn as its pale colors filled the morning sky. A faint droning sound, just barely audible, was rising from the riverbed. I quickly ran into the tent, pulling the flaps closed behind me. Mazdani was kneeling, his head touching a small carpet between his knees and spoke softly in a language I didn't understand. I stood quiet until he finished.

"*Salat al-fajr*," he said when he realized I was behind him. "Dawn prayers. They must be completed before sunrise."

"I'm sorry to have disturbed you. I didn't..."

"It is alright. We will be spending many prayer sessions together in the next few days. We will both become accustomed to it—and to a lot of other things as well."

"Such as?"

"Such as living together in cramped quarters." Mazdani pointed toward a corner. "I hung a blanket over there. There are several plastic bins behind it. Use them as necessary and slide the used ones out from under the tent flap. I'll have to trust the heat sensors are not that good."

"What happens if we're detected? What will happen?"

"Good question. Depends on who does the detection. The Mexican authorities will notify the local police, who will eventually drive up to investigate." He made a sly face, akin to a smirk. "Nothing to fear there. However, if a rival cartel detects us, then all bets are off. They might investigate or they may just shoot us from a helicopter—or drone."

"What are the cartels looking for?"

"They move a lot of...let us just say merchandise along this river. If anyone up here poses a threat to their supply chain, they kill them. It's that simple." He smiled to lighten the mood. "Now, Mademoiselle, I plan to eat some lavash bread. We talked about its origins earlier in the evening. It's similar to fajita. Care to join me before we tuck ourselves in?"

"I know," Mazdani said, seeing my hesitation, "the temptation is to not eat because...Well, trust me. That would be a mistake. Some lavash, a little water, and off we go. And, oh, don't even think about sleeping on the ground. Those rocks are razor sharp. They will rip your beautiful face open. Even if you sleep on a pad, they'll slice right through. You're safe right here beside me." He patted the mattress. "I promise you that much."

Choosing between being cut to pieces and sleeping on a bed with Mazdani, I opted for the bed, all the while reviewing the moves I learned in survival class. I was prepared to break his neck if he so much as accidentally bumped me.

TWENTY-NINE

Dill's phone began buzzing at exactly seven. I was finally in a deep sleep, having stayed awake until well after two-thirty. I was worried about Angella knowing that the only way she could pass through Mexican security without being detained was if Mazdani greased the skids. But the question that plagued me was how he knew she was wanted for questioning about the prison murder?

The last thing I remember before I fell asleep was my conversation with Santiago. Mazdani was the one who set Angella up and not Santiago. At least that explained why Mazdani knew about Angella's travel restrictions. So, either Angella was now in custody, or security was looking the other way.

I headed down the hall to the john and returned in time to see Dill throw his phone on the bed. "Here, Jimmy, take a look for yourself. I'm about to burst."

Apparently, Dill's messages were blocked all night because the timestamp on the first one was soon after he fell asleep.

Tues 1:20am: Mexico City International Airport (MEX) Angella M. detained for questioning.

I was wrong about Mazdani arranging safe passage. Or possibly Mexico City security hadn't received the stand-down message in time.

Tues 2:04am: MEX Mazdani cleared for travel to MAM. Angella M is being held.

Tues 2:34am: MEX Mazdani on flight to MAM.

Tues 2:55am: MEX Woman believed to be AngellaM is Iranian National female named Jaleh Moradi..

Tues 3:05am: Monterrey Airport (MTY) Person named Jaleh Moradi landed 2:28. Left airport with male identified as Major Caveh Shirvani, (Iranian passport) in private vehicle-green Silverado. License plate NA

Tues 3:06am: MEX Papers found on the person of Jaleh Moradi (Iranian passport) claims asylum. Papers contain photos of names of women thought to be held in trafficking operation. Pictures are of pages of a ledger. Jaleh M claims el Bandito as head of trafficking. Bureau database lists Gen. Bijan Mazdani Iranian passport) as el Bandito

Tues 6:46am: Matamoros International Airport (MAM) Mazdani detained upon landing

Tues 6:52am: MAM Mazdani's fingerprints match Maj Caveh Shirvani and not Mazdani.

Tues 6:59 am: MEX One of the pictures in the possession of JM shows a map of staging areas along the Pilón River. 800 women are believed to be staged in the valley for delivery into US within 24 hours.

Tues 7:03 am: Handwriting confirms the ledger was created by Caveh S. New thinking is el Bandito is Caveh S, not Bijan M.

I was still holding Dill's phone digesting what I just read when its ring tone startled me. *Answer or not?* Sometimes the easiest questions are the hardest to deal with. I decided to answer and hit ACCEPT. The receiver was almost to my ear when Dill reappeared. "Heard it from the hall," he whispered, apparently not wanting the caller to know he abandoned his communication device. "Oh," he exclaimed, "Madam Secretary…Of course this is a good time…"

Turning to me, he mouthed the word 'Sweet'. Turning his attention back to the phone, he listened quietly for a good five minutes. Then said, "I understand the operation, Madam Secretary. Do I have your permission to brief Redstone? He's here with me now."

"Thank you, Madam Secretary. We will do all that we can to ensure we don't interfere. Good day."

The line went dead and Dill turned his attention to me. "Been another slight change of plans as I'm sure you gathered from that text thread. Secretary Sweet's been briefed about the women's names found in that ledger. She's ordered the Mexican government—well, perhaps not ordered, exactly, let's say coerced them—to free them all. Our Mazdani operation is on pause until that is accomplished."

"Just how's she expect that to occur? That supply line crosses several countries and borders."

"She's only talking about the women in the Pilón River Valley right now. Not the entire supply chain. That will be dealt with later. The women are only moved at night. Her plan is to strike the smugglers the instant they begin moving them."

"Women are moved every night. Why would the Mexican Government agree to help them tonight and not on other nights?"

"From what Sweet said, she has a list of the women's names. The found photocopies of the same names in Jaleh Moradi's purse, which turns out to be Angella's purse. Perhaps Sweet now having actual names gives her leverage with the Mexicans. Maybe the operation's been on the books a while and the names give her clout with Admiral Boyle. We'll never really know why the timing is what it is."

"Won't rounding up the women put them—and the children—in jeopardy of being killed by the traffickers?"

"They're valuable cargo. The cartels will do anything to keep them alive. Especially with rumors of *el Bandito* being in the area, they'll hold their tempers, thinking it'll blow over. Thinking even more money will change hands. For them, it's business as usual."

My hands clenched. "Makes me sick to even think of it!"

"Be glad you got out when you did, my friend. This stuff can easily break your spirit." Dill looked away a moment then turned back. "The long and short of it is we're delayed for several hours."

"Makes sense. That shack's in the hills above the river. Santiago claims it's a control point for trafficking.

That's where *el Bandito*—now thought to be Major Shirvani—was heading. What time are we now scheduled to be up there?"

"Zero-fifteen."

"Just after midnight. Isn't that too late? If Mazdani's going up there, we figure him arriving around twenty-one hundred at the latest. We can't be going in after he gets there."

"That timing was predicated on their drive time from Monterrey. That would get him to the river valley a few hours ago, around daybreak. Our assumption was he'll hole up for the day and resume after dark. It's roughly a three-hour trip."

"That's where our original timeline came from."

"Sweet believes he's connected well enough to be briefed on the roundup. He's crafty enough to stay put under a heat-shield tarp an extra four hours."

I thought about what Dill just said. All very logical. But terrorists don't always follow logic. What happens if no one tips him off?"

"Man with aspirations of becoming the King of Persia is tied in everywhere. Money talks. And the larger the amount, the louder and clearer the language is. He'll get more than one call."

"Could ignore and go up anyway."

"And risk being killed or captured in Mexico during a military roundup of trafficked women? Even in his country that wouldn't play well."

The message alert on Dill's phone sounded. It took him a while to digest what he received. Satisfied that he thoroughly understood the message, he offered me his phone, stopping just short of where I could reach it. "I shouldn't show you this, but I did promise I'd keep you informed. Now I require a promise from you. I let you see this, you'll continue the operation as planned with no deviation. Agreed?"

I tried to snatch his phone, but he anticipated my reaction and deftly moved it out of my reach. "Must be something to do with Angella," I said. "What the hell's wrong? Is she…is she okay?"

"Not in the mood for twenty-questions. Either promise it or forget it."

Knowledge is power, I thought. Without it, even the best plans are hopelessly inadequate. Promises are easy to make; keeping this one is entirely in my control.

"Let me see what you have there. I'll stay on mission."

Dill handed me the phone.

CONFIDENTIAL: TO NAMED RECIPIENT ONLY

Maj Caveh Shirvani (CAV) being detained at MAM. Transcript of call between CAV and Asesino (AKA Cutthroat) follows: (English translation from Farsi)

Call Start: Tues 09:12

A: Hello?

C: This is *Shirvani*. Is this *Asesino*?

A: *Shirvani*?

C: It's *El Bandito*. Listen to me. I'm being detained. Mexico knows about the...about the Pilón merchandise. Where are you?"

A: With the wom...merchandise."

C: Good. Move it out tonight.

A: All of them? That will be hard to do.

C: All of them! And...and do you know where the General is now located? He was going up to the mountain."

A: He's in a tent a few miles from where I am. Has his own *chica* with him. Looks like one of ours."

C: The information on the...the merchandise came from...from that *chica*. Name's Moradi. Kill her!

A: But the General is...

C: You take my money! You do what I say!

A: I want no trouble with the General.

C: He won't care. She's just another *chica* to him. I keep him well supplied. Got a special one up in the mountain place. Moradi must be eliminated! Understand?

A: This will cost double.

C: Double, plus a bonus if all the...the merchandise is delivered across the border.

A: That will be hard. Payments will be very high. I can't promise the condition.

C: We're under contract for head count. No guarantee of condition.

A: Do my best.

C: Make it happen! All of it! *Chica* and everything!

CALL END Tues 09:17.

THIRTY

I have to say this about Mazdani. He's a quiet sleeper. Maybe stillness comes from years of living in tents with enemies all around, maybe for other reasons. I can also say he never once touched me, not even so much as an accidental brushing.

My eyes opened; the tent still seemed bright. My watch displayed five-thirty. Two and a half hours until full night fall when it's safe to continue up the mountain. I tried to fall back to sleep, but thoughts, mostly random, flooded in. I lay as still as I could for as long as my bed partner remained sleeping. I dozed off several times before coming fully awake again, aware of the unmistakable sound of a helicopter not far off. Helicopter, following Mazdani's logic, means it's still daylight.

I sat upright, my legs swinging over the side of the mattress in preparation for standing. In that same instant, Mazdani came fully awake and sprung to his feet as if catapulted upward. A Glock appeared in his hand. From where I don't know.

His eyes focused on the tent opening which he carefully had stitched closed using a long cord. The sound I was concentrating on moved slowly away until it became a faint buzz. Then nothing.

We remained silent for several more minutes listening. Other than a few frogs ribbiting, and an occasional bird chirping, I heard nothing of interest.

"Okay, who goes first?" Mazdani asked.

I started to ask what he was talking about but refrained when I realized he was looking toward the screened off area.

"I prefer the truck," I said.

"We're still a good hour away from going out, I'm afraid. If you're not going to..."

"Okay," I said, suddenly realizing my bladder was about to explode, "I'll go first."

When I emerged from behind the screen Mazdani was studying his phone. "You're turn," I called.

Without a word he slipped the phone into his pocket and ducked into the make-shift head. Coming out, he snapped on a small battery-powered light, then announced, "There's been a slight change of plans. A government operation is scheduled to take place near here beginning very soon. We must. remain under the heat shield for several additional hours."

"What do you propose?" I wasn't certain he was playing straight with me and I resolved to remain on high alert.

"We fix ourselves a nice breakfast and relax until it is completed. Waiting might not be easy for you, but for me it comes with the territory. I have spent much of my life waiting, so what is a few moments longer?" Mazdani opened a box and produced more bread, a small wheel of what appeared to be Gouda cheese, and two bottles of water. "I prefer coffee," he said, but heat signatures prevent that I'm afraid. We'll have to settle for plain water and save anything heated until later into the night after I interview your partner. I arranged for the cartel to release your partner and bring him to us. Apparently Major Shirvani had other ideas. One of the men up there is carrying a…how do you say it...a grudge against your partner. We would be forced to deal with that man if Jimmy…if Jimmy comes down here."

"Santiago promised to protect him until Tuesday," I said, suddenly realizing it was sundown Tuesday afternoon. "Time may have already run out."

"He has until tomorrow morning, sunup. Unfortunately, as things go, your friend, Santiago, no longer holds the power he once had. I have arranged to extend Jimmy's time by a day. You have a phrase for it. I forgot how it goes. Something about a sheriff."

"New sheriff in town?"

"That's it. I'm not exactly a sheriff, but I do ride horses, if that means anything." A large smile softened his face and excitement returned to his eyes. He handed me one of the lavash breads and pointed me to the cheese. 'Cut whatever amount you want. We have plenty more in the other tent."

I decided to eat as light as I could, but after the first bite I realized how hungry I was. I managed two of the breads and half the cheese. Mazdani did the same, commenting, "Fresh air works up an appetite, I am certain you agree with me."

"I'm certainly hungry," I admitted. "That's obvious."

"It makes me happy you ate. This will be a long night and who knows where or when we will be able to next eat."

"Aren't your…your team going up with us?"

"No, Angella. Only the two of us will be allowed in that hut with them."

"I thought…" I didn't know what I thought. "I was thinking your folks, the two men in the other tent would help overcome the Zetas and free Jimmy. I guess I was…"

"They would never agree to three soldiers approaching the cabin. The arrangement I worked out allows for just me and you, and neither of us armed. I interview your partner and we leave."

"And Jimmy?" This was not sounding good. If this guy with all his money and influence couldn't free Jimmy, then how was that going to happen?

"You'll have to trust me. He is critical to proving the crest on those wine casks is genuine. I can't allow him to remain behind."

"But just…"

Alarmed, Mazdani's hand suddenly shot up in the universal *be silent* signal. When he was certain I understood—and would comply—he raised the Glock and motioned me to crouch as low as I could and move behind the mattress. Kneeling on the ragged stones was hazardous so I dug a shirt out of the orange bag to cushion my knees.

Extinguishing the light, he pointed to my cell and then to the blanket. I followed his lead and slipped both of our phones under the cover. Satisfied no light would escape, he quietly moved toward the door flap and peered through a small opening. After a moment, he crept across the rocky floor to the head area, pulled the blanket down and used it to pad the floor. Kneeling and using a small camping shovel, he began digging a trench under the tent being careful not to touch the tent sides as he worked.

Something put the General on high alert and I still didn't know what it was. Jimmy would have signaled me what was bothering him because of our mutual trust. Protecting each other was a way of life for us. Working apart was no longer an option.

Enough nostalgia, Angella. Pay attention!

Focusing on the situation at hand, there was more reason for Mazdani to trust me than there was for me to trust him. Lying flat, he pressed his cheek hard against the blanket and forced his fingers under the nylon, or whatever tents are made from these days. The material folded upward just enough so he could see out. It was now fully dark and if it hadn't been for this last-minute operational hold we would already be on our way up the mountain.

Mazdani sprang to his feet, moving much faster than I expected. He knelt beside me and leaned close. "They're gone!" he whispered. "Tent and all. Gone!"

"Without telling you?"

Mazdani retrieved his cell phone, covered it with his shirt, and checked for messages. "Nothing," he quietly announced. "Those two traitors, gone without a word."

"What's that mean?" I asked, matching my voice level to his.

"Someone's coming for one or both of us. They've been warned away."

"Aren't they your…your team out there? Where'd they go?"

"Everything and everybody's got a price. I live eight thousand miles away. Someone much closer, someone they fear more, has given them an order." He went back to the front flap and peered out. "Can't see the truck. Maybe's it's too dark. I believe it's gone also."

"Was that what you heard before?" I asked, trying to come to grips with how we would manage to get up to Jimmy by daylight.

"Yes, an engine being started, but the sound was further away."

"They could have pushed it down the hill before it started."

"Quite possibly, yes," Mazdani answered, flipping the light back on.

"What are you doing?" My voice was louder than I had planned, but he said nothing. "Aren't you worried they'll see us?"

"Whoever it is, they know we're both in here. However, they don't know we know the team is gone. That provides an advantage for us. We do not know which one of us they are coming for. That provides an advantage for them."

"What if we're both targets?"

"Then, my dear woman, we would both already be dead. No, one of us is destined to live for another day. My job is to be certain we both do."

"With this light on they can see shadows," I protested. "They can shoot right through."

"Not if we remain near the center. One of us must be too valuable to take a chance on killing. No, they'll wait for us to open the tent. Pick off the one they're after. It's now just a waiting game. These people are good at that."

"Did you see anyone out there?"

"They would not remain alive very long if they were that sloppy. They are good, but you have my word I am better."

"So, we wait?"

Mazdani's seen this movie before.

Ever the General, I can almost see the wheels turning. But if he has a plan, he isn't sharing it. I was working on my own. So far, I'd drawn a blank.

"Time for prayers," Mazdani announced. "This time you should get down low. Pull that blanket over and sit. I will only be five minutes. Then we can finish our little meal and after that we move on with our lives."

"You're sure calm about all this," I commented, digging my fingers into my palms. "One false move and one of us will die. Doesn't that…"

Mazdani's right hand went up. "People have been stalking and shooting at me all my life. Allah has protected me. I have faith. Now please allow me to tend to my prayers."

We both went down on our knees, he on his small prayer pad and me on the blanket. Mazdani's prayers came as a stream of sounds. Mine, well my prayers came in my mind, with no guarantee they were even heard. I added one for Jimmy just in case.

THIRTY-ONE

It's always a surprise how long a day seems when you're waiting for something positive to occur, and how fast that same time frame flies by when a dreaded event is on the schedule. This was one of the longest days I can remember in a long time, bringing back memories of another long day; the day of my twenty-second birthday. I was a newly minted Army Ranger scheduled to parachute into Iran with my teammate, Roger Soxly, in advance of a planned Kurdish rebellion against the newly formed Iranian Revolution. The two of us were going in to evaluate the tactical strength of the Revolutionary forces. Our information was to be used for determining the magnitude of the resistance the Kurdish forces would encounter.

I was junior behind Sox and was assigned to jump second. I couldn't wait to get into action. We were given eight hours advance notice and each minute of that day seemed like an hour. Sox yelled, "See you on the ground, Redstone!" and was gone. I moved into position by the open door, reached up to unhook my safety belt when the abort horn sounded. I later learned a navigation glitch had occurred. Instead of Sox landing two miles from the Iranian encampment, he came down less than a hundred yards away. An Iranian who happened to be using the latrine put a round through him before his feet even touched the earth. This was all captured on tape and haunts me to this day.

"Ok, Jimmy, show time," Dill called. He'd been focused on his cell for over an hour and I hesitated to guess what all he was following. "Latest plan," he announced, "I'm to drop you at a small private field forty minutes out from here. Flight time down the river's twenty-eight minutes. Waste time, thirty minutes. That puts you in the river valley at," he checked his watch, "at twenty-three, forth-five. Fifteen minutes up to the cabin. You're back on schedule."

"What the hell's waste time? Never heard the term."

"Time between tasks. Walking to the car, getting the engine started, loading your gear, forgetting something, taking a wiz, that sort of thing."

"Those times are already built into the operation."

"Only if you use computer simulation, or an actual run through. Maybe someone else did it for this, don't know. Call it the fudge factor. Anything you want. Get off your butt, it's time to go. If all goes well, you'll be reunited with Angella in about four hours."

"I take it you haven't heard anything further on her."

"You'd be the first to know."

"How's the roundup operation going? You've been briefed, I assume."

"As a matter of fact, I have. And it's going surprisingly well. So far, they've freed five-hundred eighty women and two-hundred-thirty children. Freed is the wrong word. Separated from the traffickers and in government custody is more accurate."

"Which government"

"Which one would you prefer?"

"I'd say U.S. but…but knowing the politics of it, I'm not certain."

"If it makes you feel better, Sweet is working closely with the Mexican government. I have a good feeling about this one. That woman has her head on straight."

"Any casualties?"

"As I said, went surprisingly well. The women and children were out in the open and when the government copters came in, all the traffickers scattered."

"Probably because they expect their charges to be returned to them by daybreak. They're thinking it's only a shakedown."

"Between you and me, Redstone," Dill said, his voice lowering a notch, "I'm pretty certain this roundup operation was preplanned. Went off too well. I wouldn't be surprised to learn Sweet and Boyle are working the same operation."

"You thinking some of the billion dollars from the wine's going to grease some pockets down here?

"I'm hard put to think otherwise. All too convenient. Check that," Dill said as his cell buzzed. He listened a moment, then said, "Two people were just found dead on the road leading up from the river. No further details."

"Were they hostages or…cartel, or what?"

"No further details. My guess, for what it's worth, cartel."

I agreed with Dill. Two dead bodies reduced the chance that one of them was Angella. Assuming, of course, that *Asesino* had paid attention to orders to only kill the *chica*. I couldn't decide what was worse, knowing for certain or not knowing. I opted for not knowing. Going along with him, I said, "Exchanging eight hundred and some women and children for only two dead could be considered a small price to pay."

"That's certainly one way to look at it."

"Is there another?"

"No one dies," Dill compassionately said

"Optimist."

"That's why I do what I do."

I studied Dill a moment to see if he was serious, or just busting me. "A few more years and you'll change your tune."

"That's when I quit."

"That's what I said."

"You did quit."

"Took me almost forty years."

"Some people are just slow learners." Dill smiled, the first time all day. "What can I say?"

I envisioned an airport with a dirt strip where crop-dusting planes land for refueling. Wrong. This place is essentially a wide patch of dirt at the side of the road, not even large enough for a petrol station. There were no lights, no signs, no flags, nothing. Also no trees or large bushes, no stones of any size, and no one to monitor comings and goings. Most important, there was no helicopter either.

Dill stopped the car on the edge of the opening. The moment my feet hit the ground I heard a faint humming and a bird appeared with no lights and very little sound. As soon as the door opened, I jumped in, landing on my butt, feet hanging out, just as my Ranger survival training taught.

I don't know how much *waste* time Dill built in for the transfer, but this pilot hadn't been part of his calculation. As soon as my bottom hit the deck we were moving upward, even before I could haul in my legs and pull the door closed. It was almost as if he prided himself on not touching ground. Or maybe he was worried about plausible deniability. "No, Congressman, I never landed in Mexico." As Clinton taught us, lying is mostly definitional.

Two other passengers were on board, one beside me and one in the front seat. I assumed these were the folks who would administer the knockout drugs and retrieve Jimmy2. I wondered if this was the same crew who had extracted me. Training required that I not ask.

"Lotta birds out tonight," the guy sitting beside me shouted. The noise inside seemed much louder than outside. He pointed to a set of earphones hanging in front of me. I put them on. "Know what's go'n on?" he asked.

"I'm told the government's freeing women and children from traffickers."

The man's facial expression didn't change. At first, I thought he hadn't heard me, but then he said, "I'd say it's about time! Makes me sick to the stomach seeing it and know'n I can't do nothing!"

"Close to nine hundred so far. Operation's over for the night."

"That why we're delayed then?"

"Be my guess."

"Hey, how's that knee of yours come'n along? Almost forgot about it. You look spry enough."

So, this guy was involved in my extraction. "On antibiotics. Pain's mostly gone. Healing as well as can be expected."

"Guessed that from the way you jumped aboard. You couldn't have done that last week. Personally, thought you'd be lucky to keep the leg."

"You a doctor?"

"Health Service Technician. Same as a Navy corpsman. Only for the Coast Guard. Margaret up there's the same."

"And your name?"

"Horse. Just call me Horse."

"Jimmy," I responded, sticking my hand out in greeting. He reluctantly shook it, as if by doing so he was breaking some rule. That was the end of our conversation until we reached the Pilón River, just south of the town of Rayones. It was dark in the valley, the only lights coming from a few cars on what I determined to be Highway Eight-Five.

"Bird," Horse called out a moment later. "At three o'clock."

I bent in front of him and peered through the side window. A helicopter was less than a mile away, heading in our direction. I held up my hand and mentally took an angle reading between my thumb and the nose of the approaching copter.

Ten seconds later I took a second reading and the angle hadn't changed, but the distance had shortened. To me that meant we were on a collision course. I couldn't determine with any degree of accuracy if we were at the same altitude. It seemed so, our pilot continuing to talk into his microphone as if he hadn't a care in the world.

The angle between us hadn't changed at twenty seconds and the distance was down to less than a half-mile. We were clearly at the same altitude. Unless one of us changed course, altitude, or speed in the next several seconds, we'd all be dead.

Margaret turned to look back, fear written across her flushed face, her lips moving. At first, I thought she was talking to me without her microphone being on. Then I realized she was praying. Horse just continued to stare forward, as if by not seeing what was about to happen nothing bad would occur. Ostrichitis I had called it in my Ranger days. It won't hurt you if you don't see it.

Wrong!

Ten seconds until impact and the angle was closing fast. None of the parameters had changed. I could now clearly see the pilot of the approaching copter, and for a brief irrational moment I tried to figure out what was going through his mind. Then suddenly and without warning, we veered to port and slowed dramatically. I immediately lost sight of the other copter, my impression is it also took action, except turning starboard and gaining speed.

The internal speaker buzzed alive and a shaky voice demanded, "What the hell's that about?" Horse was still in his ostrich imitation. So, by process of elimination, it had to be Margaret seeking answers, her prayers having been answered.

"Blew our cover, that's what that was!" The pilot was more angry than frightened. "Damn cowboy demanded we set this puppy down. They love to play chicken. Picked the wrong man's all."

This wasn't the time or the place to engage in testosterone wars. I hit the mic switch, but instead of following my instinct and complaining, I said, "It's a temporary maneuver. He'll circle back and follow us up the mountain." I kept my voice calm despite wanting to chew him out for putting the operation in jeopardy.

"Not if he's assigned another objective. Admiral's working on that now. We'll take a little detour until he breaks off."

"So, he *is* following us?" I said, quietly patting myself on the back for correctly assessing the situation.

"Directly beneath us," the pilot said, turning the bird back toward the river. "They have a couple of dead bodies down there. He'll be assigned pickup detail. Shouldn't be more than a few minutes."

As had been scripted, three minutes later the other bird suddenly popped up directly in front of us causing me to jump and Margaret to resume her prayer chant. This time Horse watched the action, a what-me-worry expression plastered to his face.

Our pilot cooperated in avoiding a collision by both slowing and moving off to port. The other copter followed suit, forcing us to slow even further. "We can't sustain this slow speed much longer," our pilot announced. "The mountains churn the air, and this isn't safe. I'm taking her down."

"Your call," I replied, even though I had nothing to say in the matter. This was his show all the way.

The copter tipped slightly to starboard and we began losing altitude. Just below tree top level the pilot said, "Okay. He's been called off. We're back on mission. Looks like I'll get you up there on time. That is, assuming no more interruptions."

Landing time on the mountain was previously set for 00:15. We were now on target for a 00:21 drop-off. I hit the talk switch and said, "I was looking for a vehicle coming up the mountain. Didn't see it. Any of you?"

Horse was first to answer. "Negative."

The pilot confirmed with, "Likewise. Nothing."

Margaret then said, "Maybe. Something might have been moving, but no lights. Can't be sure if it was a vehicle or…or my imagination playing tricks. Never got a good look."

The pilot added, "Our mission plan is to come up the far side of the mountain to avoid being seen. It's unlikely Margaret saw what she thinks she saw. No roads down that way. I'll put us down behind the house in case someone comes out."

The pilot was both right and wrong. When Dill and I discussed the human trafficking situation, he produced a map of the mountain. He then pointed to several structures in this area, such as the one we were now approaching. "They use those shacks to *train* the women," he explained, his lips twitching. "God only knows what they do to those poor girls."

That meant paths of one sort or another existed all through these hills. And with the operations going on in the valley, there's no telling what or who would be roaming around up here armed to the teeth. I wouldn't expect Angella and Mazdani to be anywhere near those shacks, except with Mazdani anything could be possible.

I turned to Horse. "When I was here there were three men guarding me. Something you said earlier makes me think there's only two now."

"Roger that. Our briefing says only two."

"Who left? And why?"

"Don't know either answer."

"Go! Go! Go!" interrupted the pilot, and all three of us jumped to the ground in unison. My task was to keep low and wait for Jimmy2 to be brought out. Margaret ran to the front of the shack, pulled the top off a small glass vial, opened the door a crack and rolled the vial inside. She then closed the door and found a place to conceal herself.

"Now we wait exactly five minutes," Horse said, tapping his watch. "Then, in you go. Margaret will administer the serum and I'll bring your double out. Keep in mind their memories will be hazy, so play along. Yours should be as well. The worst part for you will be putting on his filthy clothes. I can't imagine what the make-up on his knee looks like now. So, don't let anyone get too close or they'll know something's wrong."

Nerves talking. I had gone over all this with Dill. Horse had to know I had been briefed.

I concentrated on the inside of the cabin; shack would be a better description, wondering which two of the three remained inside. I also wondered why I wasn't briefed on who to expect. I visualized *el Carnicero*, the Sinaloa butcher along with the small, wiry, Zeta cousin known as Fasthands. And then the big guy, *Encarnizado*, Cutthroat.

"Three and counting," Horse announced. "By the way, who's Angella?"

"Angella?" I was puzzled. This guy shouldn't have been given this much information. "What are you talking about?"

"'Angella, I love you.' That's what you said just before that copter pulled away back there. When it looked like we were going down."

"We're enga..."

"Shit!" Margaret interrupted, her voice hanging in the air, her body nowhere to be seen.

Shit what?

Those are the last words I ever want to hear on an operation.

"Guy walking," Margaret's now muted voice said. "Coming this way. Big guy. Coming down the hill."

I studied the terrain for several seconds before picking out the form of *Señor* Cutthroat. *Encarnizado.*

"Can't allow him inside," Horse said, dropping his backpack and reaching inside for a small spray bottle.

Encarnizado paused in front of the cabin as if he sensed, or smelled, a problem. The copter engine turned off the instant we touched down, but the large rotor was still slowly rotating. I couldn't hear anything, but this guy survived by paying close attention to his senses. Twice he reached for the door and twice he yanked his hand back. Something had set him on edge.

Finally deciding, he turned and walked around the cabin, passing between the rock I was crouching behind and the shack's windowless wall structure. Two more steps and the copter would be in plain sight.

Horse slipped out of the shadows, a spray bottle in his right hand. Coming up behind *Encarnizado,* Horse reached around him and discharged several sprays directly into the big guy's face.

"Que demonios?" Encarnizado yelled, recovering from being momentarily blinded, his hand reaching for his ever-present knife. During the time he held me captive I often marveled at how fast he could produce that lethal weapon.

Horse turned away from *Encarnizado* to look for Margaret. At that instant, the big man charged, knife at the ready. I was up and moving, determined to interrupt *Encarnizado* before he sliced Horse's throat from ear to ear. I had to accomplish this without causing injury to Horse—or to myself. Simply landing on the ragged rock ground would be enough to inflict severe trauma on either of us.

My shoulder slammed into his hip causing the knife blade's trajectory to change enough to miss Horse's neck. However, it did catch his flak jacket, slicing the cover open from neck to waist.

In order to minimize damage to *Encarnizado* I wrapped both my arms around his torso with the intention of landing on my own body parts and not his. My plan worked, but it now prevented me from securing the knife. He took advantage of the situation by bringing the blade up over my back. My body tensed, helpless to stop him from plunging the blade into my neck.

A blow hit my upper back just below my head, knocking my face deeper into *Encarnizado's* side. At first, I thought he hit me with the knife shank, but the area of impact was too large and the pressure from the blow didn't ease. The continued downward force pinned me against the big man, preventing any movement. The force on my body pushed out what little air I had remaining in my lungs. I gasped for oxygen to no avail, all the while fighting to release myself from the pressure. Nothing moved. I was pinned. My lungs screamed for relief.

Calm yourself down Jimmy. Conserve what little air you have for as long as you can.

Good advice, assuming something was going to change before I lost consciousness. One last time. Angella, I love you. I really love you. I can't go another…

Suddenly, the pressure on my back eased and air rushed in, filling my lungs. Cool mountain air. A second breath. A third. My strength slowly returned, allowing me to turn my head. A leather boot was between my shoulder blades, a knife buried in the arch. The boot lifted, allowing blood to flow freely from the sole.

I tried to stand but was pulled back down by *Encarnizado* who was also struggling to stand. I gathered myself in anticipation of making a sudden surge to break free. It was unnecessary because *Encarnizado* suddenly went limp.

"Thought that spray'd never work!" Horse said, helping me stand while ignoring the knife imbedded in his foot.

"Thanks for sav…"

"Repaying the favor. Nicked a couple a bones is all. Nothing we can't fix up."

"At least pull the knife out."

"It'll bleed all the more. I'd leave it in until we get back to base, but the knife must stay with this hombre. He won't remember shit if we do this right. Need to haul him inside. The others are gone by now."

Margaret took the head, Horse the feet carrying him inside, Horse ignoring the knife sticking out of his boot. Jimmy2 was lying on his side on the same mattress I had been on. His clothes were worse than disgusting and it appeared he hadn't been allowed to wash in days.

The Zeta, cousin of the man I killed, was the other guard in the shack. Apparently, *el Carnicero,* the Butcher, the man who had been tasked to save my life, was now gone.

Margaret undressed Jimmy2 and did her best to preserve the filth on the shirt and pants as she found it. Then she dug in her backpack for makeup and smeared me with a combination of stuff, taking care to cover the scratches and small lacerations I received when I tackled *Encarnizado.* She rubbed something into my beard in an attempt to imitate Jimmy2's. "There, that's the best I can do. Didn't train as a Hollywood makeup artist. But it'll have to do. Put his clothes on and we're outta here."

"Hey," I said after they put Jimmy2 on the copter and she came back for one last inspection, "better clean up that blood." I pointed to the bloody tracks Horse made around the room. He had been right. When Margaret pulled out the knife, blood splattered everywhere, stopping only when she tied a shirt around his foot.

"Meant to do that," Margaret replied, digging a rag from her pack and pouring liquid on it. "Horse's lost more than he thinks. Having a hard time stopping the flow now the knife's out. Doesn't look good. Got a tourniquet on it. It'll be touch and go. As soon as we're in the air I'll alert base doctors. Those folks perform miracles."

I didn't know if she was giving me a pep talk or was consoling herself. Probably both.

Margaret finished cleaning and gave one last look around. Satisfied, she injected both of my captors with the antidote to the knockout drug. "This one'll be awake in a few minutes and shouldn't remember anything. The big one got a full blast so it might take more time. Not to worry. He'll come around. He won't know what hit him." She saluted. "Thanks for saving Horse. Safe mission." The door closed behind her. A moment later I heard the soft whine of their bird lifting off the mountain.

I was again alone with my captors, only now without my protector.

THIRTY-TWO

Plans had changed so many times I no longer knew how Angella and the General would arrive—or when. By helicopter? By car? Alone? With others? Would these two thugs allow them in or cut their throats? And when did *el Carnicero,* leave? And why? There were far too many moving parts to expect a positive outcome to this operation. Right now, I was concentrating on keeping myself—and Angella—alive.

"When the hell he come back?" a drowsy *Manosrápidas* asked, nodding toward the still sleeping form of *Encarnizado.* "Didn't hear him enter."

"Don't know. I was sleeping."

"I wasn't sleeping. I was sitting here playing cards. How'd he get past me?"

"Don't know," I repeated. "Maybe you dozed off."

The small man frowned, then started to laugh. "Look at that big guy sleeping like a baby. He was up at *la puntas. Chicas* wore him out. No wonder he looks like he's been in a fight." Thankfully, *Manosrápidas* picked up his cards and resumed his game.

If only that's repeated when Cutthroat wakes up, we'll be halfway to our goal. Then all we require is Angella and Mazdani to arrive and the mission will be back on track.

A half-hour later the big man was still not awake. I could hear him breathing. Shallow, but steady. There was nothing I could do if he stopped breathing, so why worry. But worry I did. Not so much for Cutthroat, but for Angella. What was taking so long? Again, when I wanted the hours to pass quickly, they dragged on second by second.

"I don't remember coming inside!" a voice I didn't immediately recognize barked. "What the hell happened?"

"*La puntas*! Got the best of you. Been sleeping it off."

"Hey, I remember walking down the hill. Hearing a noise and then…then nothing."

"You been sleeping," *Manosrápidas* said. "Like a baby."

The big guy slowly sat up. "Hey, that hurts." He moved his arm back and forth several times. "Hurts. Like I fell on it. Hey, look, I'm cut on my arm."

Manosrápidas turned in his chair to face the big guy. "What the hell you expect, you spending all that time up there. They musta thrown you out. You drink'n?"

"Little. Not so much. Hey, walked out myself. What ya talk'n 'bout?"

"Learn to enjoy. Is all I'm say'n."

"Can't tonight. Something's going on. *Chica*'s gone. Mostly men there. Government's gone crazy."

"You're making no sense! Been *Chicas* up there for years. Only the very best. For the big bosses. The best ones."

"Gone now, I tell you."

"Be back, bet on it. Hey, gotta pee. Your turn with him." The little man threw his cards on the table and walked outside, not waiting for acknowledgment. It wasn't entirely clear which of these two was in charge. If I were a betting man, my money'd be on the little guy, the Zeta cousin.

Silence again. Strain as hard as I could, I heard no vehicle coming up the mountain. I didn't expect them for another hour, yet my agitation rose by the minute.

Two dead bodies!

The thought stuck terror and made it virtually impossible for me to think clearly. I had no plan to get myself down off this mountain in the event Angella and Mazdani didn't show up. Worse, I couldn't process clearly enough to make one.

"Hey, you must be dying over there," the little guy said after returning from his *bathroom* break. "You haven't been out since early afternoon. Now don't go mess'n in your drawers 'cause you the one gotta live with it. That leg really troubling you, you don't wanna go take a piss. Bad news for you, well, in a way might be good news, this your last day up here—alive. Deal is to keep you alive until daybreak."

"*El Carnicero* won't be happy you do anything to me."

"You see him here? You think he's hiding in the corner?" The little guy laughed at his own humor. "Santiago's not in charge. *el Bandito's* paying us now. Tough hombre. Paid us double. Had an option for extra day. Didn't hear from him. Option time's over. You got less than four hours. Then I can revenge my cousin and get off this stink'n mountain. You wanna go piss or what?"

"Don't go jump'n the gun," the big guy called from his corner. "Keep him alive 'til time's up. I need the money."

"He get outta line, he go visit my cousin. You understand?"

"Here's what I understand," *Asesino's*, shot back, the shotgun that had been propped against the wall now in his hand.

Before the big guy's outburst, I slowly began swinging my legs over the side of the mattress in preparation of standing.

"Hey," *Asesino* called out, swinging the gun in my direction, "where the hell you going?"

"It's okay," Fasthands said. "He's just go'n to piss. With that bad leg he couldn't get ten feet before I put a knife through his back. He makes a break for it; we earned our money. That'd make my day."

"He gotta be outside when we shoot him, we want paid."

"Put that gun down," Fasthands repeated, "I got this."

Asesino took a moment to contemplate his next move. He turned the gun back on his partner. "Don't go do'n nothing foolish."

"I said, I got this! Put that thing down! These hills are dirty with Federales. You shoot that thing; they'll be on us faster than flies on shit."

As the Zeta cousin spoke, *Asesino* sank backward into his chair. "What the hell's...wrong...with me?" His voice was garbled and barely audible. "I feel...like...sh...t." His chin fell against his chest and he slumped forward, the shotgun falling at his feet.

"Too much *Chicha*s. That's your problem. Too much. You're too old for that."

Asesino's head popped up and his eyes went wide. He bent forward for the shotgun, lost his balance and slumped heavily to the floor. *Señor* Fasthands howled with laughter. He then turned to see if I was enjoying the show. Instantly, his laughing ended as he jumped to his feet. "What the hell?"

I stood up. Not knowing what was troubling this guy, I froze.

"Your leg! You been playing me! It's straight!"

His knife was already out and in a second he'd be on me. "Been work'n it all day." I stalled, hoping he'd remember his deal with *el Bandito*. Money speaks louder than hurt feelings with these mercenaries.

Not this time. His knife flashed and he was on me before I could raise my arms in defense, the blade coming directly for my neck.

I fell slightly backward, though not nearly enough to escape the arc of his hand. Three disconnected factors saved my life. First, and foremost, the drugs were still in his system causing his balance to be slightly off, affecting his aim. The tip of the blade nicked the side of my neck.

Second, *Asesino,* now sitting on the floor, the shotgun in his hands, said to Fasthands, his voice barely loud enough to be heard, "Back off or I shoot you. I want my full money."

Third, the door off to the side and essentially behind me flew open. A booming British male voice commanded, "Drop that knife or you're a dead man! You, on the floor, drop that shotgun!"

Asesino's reflexes were so slow that even I could get to him before he could react. He did nothing, sitting there confused, the gun slowly lowering to his lap.

For my part, I moved out of Fasthands' reach by sitting back down on the bed. I could see by his determined look he was assessing the situation. The little guy was still in this fight, only he now had a new adversary.

The voice behind me repeated. "Drop the knife! Now!"

Fasthands began slowly moving his hands downward as if he was in the process of complying. But his eyes told another story.

I opened my mouth to scream a warning. Unfortunately, I was too late. Fasthands had been waiting for his new challenger to make another sound so he could accurately judge location and range. The instant he heard what he had anticipated, his body rotated left and the knife was gone, all in one gracefully smooth motion.

A single shot rang out. Fasthands' body fell at my feet, half his head missing, dead before what remained of his skull hit the floor. I turned in the direction of the gun blast, only to find the person behind the voice not where I expected. Rather Iranian General Bijan Mazdani was several feet to the side, his gun now pointed at the big guy. Fasthands' knife was embedded in the wall to the right of the General. My eyes went to the door in search of Angella. I saw nothing.

"What's the matter with that one," the General demanded, "too much alcohol?"

"Drugs," I said, pulling myself up from the uncomfortable mattress. "From the extraction. We had a slight problem and he was overdosed. Take a while. He should come around soon."

"Please remove the weapon. And check him for knives while you're at it. These guys act before they think."

I satisfied myself all was in order, then turned to my visitor. "I'm Jimmy Redstone. I'm an American being held captive by these...these cartel people. I demand to see someone at the American Embassy." I was now back on script.

"And I'm Bijan Mazdani. I'm from Iran and come here at the bequest of Roberto Alterez Santiago. You can call me Bryan if you wish. Please allow me to assure you that you are in no immediate danger."

I wanted to ask where Angella was and to have assurance she was safe, but I couldn't ask without tipping him off I knew about this visit. "Santiago?" I responded. "He's currently in jail here in Mexico."

"We don't have time for games, Mr. Redstone. You and Alterez are…shall we say…business partners, are you not?"

"Depends upon the definition of business partner."

"Let's just say you and he recently had a successful business relationship pertaining to several pieces of artwork. Is that not true?"

I took my time before agreeing what he had just said was true.

"Now we're making progress, Mr. Redstone."

"Please call me Jimmy."

"Ok, Jimmy. Just so you understand, I am aware of your…your partner, Angella's recent visit to the jail to see Alterez. And, so that you don't continue to waste time, understand that I also know she is wanted by the Mexican government for questioning in a murder that occurred while that visit was in progress. Do I now have your attention?"

"You most certainly do. Please tell me how Angella is. Is she okay?"

"That, my dear friend, depends upon your definition of okay."

THIRTY-THREE

I've been in Mazdani's presence for over thirty hours and not once has he been anything other than a gentleman. The dossier on Mazdani in this respect was accurate. However, on the subject of regard for human life, it fell far short. In my mind, the General is a cold-blooded killer without an ounce of remorse. I base this conclusion on snippets of insight taken from various stories he told me on our ride up the mountain. "You drive, Angella," he said when we confiscated the would-be killer's truck. "I need to concentrate on keeping us safe from human predators."

Me driving is okay with him. Allowing me to help with physical work is not. This morning when he needed to dig a trench from under the tent, he refused all offers to help. Using a small camping shovel, he strenuously dug the trench, cutting through stone and rock. It was slow going. His knuckles bled, but he declined my several attempts to clean his wounds, instructing me to remain low to the ground and stay in the center of the tent. He disappeared into the hole several times, each time coming out feet first dragging a bucket of debris with him. The pile of broken stones, rock and dirt grew inside the tent as he painstakingly widened the trench to fit his body.

When the opening was finally large enough for him to fit through, he came over to where I was crouched, and said simply, "Stay down until I return."

"What happens if you...don't return?"

"Not a valid question."

"Good luck, then."

"Not a question of luck, my dear woman. These are learned skills. Those two will be dead within the hour. Give me a password. You can cut the tent open when I say the word, and not a moment before. Above all, remain low."

"Jimmy."

"Jimmy, it is." Mazdani shoved his gun into a small bag and carefully tied the bag around his ankle. He crawled over to the trench and went in headfirst.

As soon as his feet cleared the tent, I moved over to the front and began working the binding loose enough to see out. Problem was there was not enough light to see more than a foot in front of the tent. Almost an hour later the clouds gave way enough so that I could see vegetation perhaps a hundred feet away by moonlight. Nothing moved.

The clouds came back and again my visibility dropped to zero. I thought lying on the ground would keep shadows from forming on the tent. Without light behind me there could be no shadows, so my precautions were useless. Realizing this, I opened view holes farther up the entrance flap. In retrospect, I was wrong. It hadn't been light shadows Mazdani was worried about, rather heat images being picked up by infrared detectors.

The clouds came and went, even viewing from a higher elevation I saw nothing. I worked the top loops open just enough to see out and stood to position my eyes level with the opening.

Two heads suddenly appeared from behind a large rock outcropping, silhouetted perfectly in the moonlight. I should have immediately dropped to the ground, but I didn't. I froze as an amateur would, even as two assault rifles leveled their sights at the tent.

Two shots rang out in quick succession. The heads disappeared.

A moment later a shadow approached from behind the rock moving toward where the heads had been. Moonlight transformed the shadow into the person of General Bijan Mazdani.

I dropped to the ground.

A moment later, Mazdani, standing just outside the tent, said, "Jimmy."

I opened the tent.

Mazdani then added, "Why am I using the pass code when you watched me walk toward you in direct violation of my orders? You should be dead young lady. Hurry, open the tent. We have an aggressive schedule to keep."

Later in the truck I tried to redeem myself. "They couldn't see me. There was no light behind me."

"There was body heat," Mazdani patiently said, patting the object sitting on the seat between us. "Heat binoculars. The second you stood they had you in their sights. Lucky for you they held up for some unknown reason, or you'd be reuniting with your dead relatives this very night."

Mazdani studied his cell phone as we wound our way up the mountain. At first glance I thought he was following a Waze navigational map which didn't make a lot of sense given there was only one narrow road and no other vehicles going in either direction. From time to time he instructed me to stop and if the headlights were on, which they were only for certain portions of the road, he'd insist I turn them off. Sometimes he had me pull off the road and turn the truck off. On those occasions he'd jump out and position the heat shield blanket over the hood and up over the cab. Usually, within minutes, a low flying surveillance plane, or once a helicopter, would pass overhead. Sometimes nothing would happen. After a while he'd remove the blanket and we'd be on our way, with him controlling the speed.

Almost three hours into our trek, when we were stopped under the heat shield again, I asked, "You obtaining that information from Google Maps? Must be a special subscription."

Not appreciating my humor, Mazdani turned to face me, his eyes now cold and deadly serious. "There is a great deal you do not know about your southern neighbor. There are two governments operating here. The one you know who for the most part are good men trying to keep their people safe. The other are the cartels that control the drug and trafficking trade. The first government spends about four billion a year fighting the cartels. The cartels spend over five billion in counter measures. For every measure the government takes, the cartels take two counter measures. This app is but one example."

"I knew the cartels were big, but not that flush."

"Mexico is the gateway to America. Every government in the world wants in on the action, whether they admit it or not. There is no limit to the money flow."

Even discounting for his bias, I believed there was more than a grain of truth to what he was saying.

"And remember, my friend, where there is money flow there is influence. That's precisely why your business partner, Alterez, is allowed to remain alive. He has powerful friends and…" his eyes were again playful, "…and not all of them are outside of your country."

I wasn't as shocked about that piece of information as Mazdani thought I would be. Over the years there were rumors of Santiago's close ties to various senators and other government officials. "That's a troubling statement. Do you know the names of any U.S. government people tied to Santiago?"

"If I did, my dear lady, you certainly would not be privy to them. Knowledge is power as they say." He studied his screen a long while, then slid out of the cab, retrieved the blanket, threw it in the bed, and climbed back in. "That's the last of them. Up we go. You can drive as fast as the road allows now. Use your lights if that helps."

"What's changed?"

"No more reports of surveillance, and…and perhaps of even more importance to you, my deal with *Manosrápidas*…"

"Who?"

"*Manosrápidas,* that means..."

"Fasthands."

"So, you know Spanish. Okay. My deal with *Manosrápidas,* he's a relative of the man Jimmy shot and killed, is to keep Jimmy alive until sunup today. I instructed Major Shirvani to extend it by one day. That order, unfortunately, was not carried out."

"Sunup! That's only about three, maybe four hours from now!" My foot went down hard on the accelerator and the truck shot forward.

"Take it easy on these curves. No guard rail."

I eased up a little, but only a token. I didn't know how far up the mountain we still had to go. What I did know was that arriving a minute late was forever.

"You're going to kill us both," Mazdani shouted, "Slow down!"

I ignored him until the front tire caught a rock and slid off the solid dirt roadbed causing the hood to dip to the right. There was nothing out there but empty space. I twisted the wheel to the left, and for a brief instant the truck hung in the balance, the two right wheels spinning while the left ones tried to maintain traction.

The left won and we shot back onto the hardpack. I slowed a little and Mazdani said, "I'm fresh out of prayers. We have time. Don't do that again."

Short of shooting me, Mazdani was now my captive. And killing me would doom him as well. If I stopped, he'd take over driving. So, we continued up the hill, faster than his comfort level and a tick slower than disaster.

"Lights out," he instructed an hour later causing me to slow down to less than 30 KPH.

I half expected him to jump out, but he simply said, "We're close enough for them to see our lights."

"I thought they were expecting us?"

"Better to be safe than sorry. Plans have changed many times tonight. Major Shirvani has been making calls. This could well be a trap."

My curiosity was at a boiling point. I stopped the truck. "I need to know what's going to happen before I take you any closer to Jimmy."

Mazdani took his time answering. Most likely going over his options. "Drive. Keep the lights off. I'll tell you what I know."

I slipped the truck back into gear and pulled back onto the road. I need to trust him. Jimmy's life depends on it.

"As you know, tonight has not gone according to plan. Major Shirvani was detained at the airport."

"But he was traveling as you, just as you're traveling as him."

"That's not why he was detained. It's because of that...that woman Moradi, who, I might add, was traveling as you. Papers were found on her. Papers linking female slavery to someone called *el Bandito*." Mazdani had been studying my face as he spoke. "Oh, so you know about the papers? They were found in your purse at that airport."

"They were given to me by…"

"Not important now. What is important is that the names in the ledger were handwritten by Major Shirvani. That explains a lot of what's gone wrong tonight."

"You're telling me you're not this *el Bandito.* The man behind sex trafficking." I was relieved to learn this, but not ready to fully believe.

"It would appear Shirvani is *el Bandito.* Keep in mind where I come from, appearances can be deceiving."

Where I come from as well, it seems.

"Am I being deceived?"

"Not by me, Angella. Is that what you were told?"

"Yes," I confessed, "the dossier on you says that."

"What else does this dossier have to say for itself?"

"That *el Bandito* is a mastermind behind human smuggling into the U.S."

"Yet, you are still here to help me regain my rightful place in Persia."

"Because Santiago asked me to do so. You said yourself he's our business partner. Jimmy and I do business with him—and with his contacts—so, yes, I'm willing to turn a blind eye. That is until…until I know for certain."

"I assure you with all I stand for, I'm not *el Bandito.* Not now. Not ever! I have better things to do than smuggle women into your country. I have a war to fight. And hopefully, a country to run. That is, if we are successful in obtaining those casks."

"If you're not *el Bandito* then why allow him to use your office?"

"I only became aware of these facts in the last few days. Apparently, he has for years been using my status to protect his trafficking operation. Using my cover, he's been transporting women and children from our part of the world. Iraq mostly. I had no idea. I now believe it was you who he ordered killed tonight thinking you turned him in." Mazdani's cell buzzed. He studied it a moment, then commanded, "Stop here!"

"For what now?"

"We will walk the rest of the way. I do not wish them to hear us coming."

"How long a walk? I'm concerned for the time."

"Not far. Walk fast. We're not driving any further." Mazdani grabbed the keys from the ignition and a backpack from the truck bed. Ten feet away he turned back to face me. "Come with me or stay with the truck. Those are your only choices."

I had another option. Coasting down the mountain to find help before it was too late to save Jimmy was an attractive plan worth considering.

THIRTY-FOUR

"I'll get right to the point," Mazdani went on even while I continued to process his statement about Angella being okay.

"Hold up a moment," I protested. "Exactly, what're you saying? I mean about Angella. Is she okay or not?

"I do not exactly know. We drove up here together. Stopped about two kilometers down the mountain and I walked up. I gave her the choice of waiting in the truck or coming with me. She chose to remain with the truck. I can't vouch for her after that."

That was unlike Angella. Intentionally separating herself from him. Why? Something serious, or she wouldn't be freelancing an operation, especially not at its critical stage.

Did he take liberties with her? Stay calm, Jimmy. Focus!

Perhaps he's lying about her being okay. She could be lying dead for all I know. I fought an almost overpowering urge to grab this guy, jam him against the wall and shake the truth from him. But he was the one holding the weapon. He owned the room—for now. "Did something go wrong on the way up?" I asked, commanding my voice to remain calm, a tinge of worry still seeped through.

"Everything about this night's gone wrong. Now the sooner you settle yourself and answer a few questions the sooner we can resolve everything that is troubling both of us. If it is any consolation to you, two men arrived earlier with orders to kill your partner. Both of them are now on a journey with this one." Mazdani pointed to a very dead Fasthands.

At least the number of dead bodies coincide.

"I'm listening. What do you need from me?"

"Tell me about your relationship with Alterez. Leave nothing out. I want to know your thoughts on working with the cartels, everything."

We were now back on script. Too bad my performance would never make it to the big screen because I planned on making it worthy of an Academy Award. As we progressed, I sensed him buying into what I was selling. His questioning went a little off the rehearsed script, not far enough to cause any real problems. The truth is this guy firmly believes that if the casks are genuine, then he'll become the next King of Persia. End of story for him. Tough as he is, hardened by a lifetime of treachery, deceit, murder, and God only knows what else, he wants to believe. A rookie con artist can fool a person desperate to believe. Barnum built an empire on it. It's just the way it is.

"That's all the questions I have for you," Mazdani finally said, getting up from the corner where he settled and stretching the stiffness from his legs. "I'm satisfied I can trust you to be honest about producing the casks. Though, I do have one requirement. It shouldn't be..."

"Watch out!" I shouted, pointing toward the big guy who hadn't moved the entire time we were talking, who now was coiled to dive at Mazdani.

Mazdani twisted around to face his attacker, his hands empty, the gun on the floor beside his foot. *Asesino* was more awake than I first thought and must have been planning his attack for several minutes. His shoulder drove into Mazdani's midsection with a sickening thud.

Asesino's sheer size would make it no contest and I could visualize how this would end. He will lift the General and throw him to the floor headfirst, snapping Mazdani's neck. *Asesino* would then proceed to kick in his ribs, adding a few extra kicks to the groin for good measure.

Except it didn't exactly work out that way. The door flew open. Angella grabbed the knife from the frame and lunged toward *Asesino* before he could right himself from the initial attack. The blade entered his body just above the right kidney sending blood spraying everywhere. *Asesino* immediately released Mazdani and grabbed for the knife. Mazdani slid to the floor.

I dove forward intending to pull Angella off Mazdani and out from under *Asesino* who now held the slippery knife. He was bleeding profusely but was focused solely on cutting Mazdani's throat rather than tending to his own wound. Moving Angella away from the line of action was my prime concern but her arm was wedged between *Asesino's* knee and Mazdani's leg. I could only move her upper body a few inches which was not nearly far enough to get her head and neck out of *Asesino's* range. He now had a choice of driving the knife into Angella's throat or doing the same to Mazdani. He couldn't accomplish both fast enough to escape me.

With Mazdani already down, if I were *Asesino* I'd go for Angella. This in mind, I threw my arms up to cover Angella, intending to take the knife blade in my arm. *Asesino* saw my arm moving, and halfway through the arc his target changed. Instead of aiming for Angella he came directly for me. I was too far committed and entirely vulnerable. An easy target for someone with the killing skills this guy honed over a lifetime.

This time when I said, "I love you Angella," she heard me.

But the knife didn't end up where *Asesino* intended. Not because of bad aim and certainly not because of lack of resolve, but because the front of his head was blown away.

Mazdani had located his gun and without hesitation fired one shot from point blank range into the big guy's brain. Blood, bone, brains, and skin fragments splattered all four of us.

I rolled away, allowing Angella to spring to her feet. She reached down to help me up, mouthing words I couldn't hear. Mazdani shook her off, preferring to remain on the floor, his back against the wall. He also was saying something I couldn't hear.

"Angella," I began, "where did..."

I can't hear myself!

Angella's lips moved again and still no sound.

I was dizzy and slumped down against the wall opposite Mazdani. Angella, using pantomime, asked if she should call for the copter. I gave her a thumbs up.

Mazdani said something. Angella answered and the two of them became embroiled in a heated conversation lasting several minutes. When it ended, Angella turned to me and tried to explain what the situation was.

I shook my head indicating I couldn't understand what she was trying to say. She tried pantomime, a skill neither of us performs very well. After much laboring to understand her I put my thumb up to end her frustration. My takeaway was that Mazdani was going into the tunnel with us. My assumption was he still didn't trust us enough to be sure the wine casks were really coming from an underwater buried treasure site. He was determined to see it for himself. I don't blame him. I would've insisted on the same thing. If anything was strange, it was this trek up the mountain to see me. That's what seemed over the top and not something I would've scripted. This was more of a cartel operation than a regime change scenario. In a complicated world you learn to live with strange bedfellows, each with grossly mismatched expectations.

While we waited for the bird to arrive, Angella busied herself cleaning away the blood and other human debris as best she could. I tried to help, but she insisted I remain seated. Several minutes later she tapped me on the shoulder and pointed straight up, her finger making a circle.

Helicopter. If our bird was here already, then it's the same one that brought me here. Most likely it never left the mountain. Horse was still aboard, knife wound in the foot and all.

Mazdani and I followed Angella out of the cabin and around to the back. Indeed, it was the same machine, with Margaret holding the door open, her hand stretched out to help a still woozy Mazdani up onto the platform. I went next. Margaret said something and I answered by shaking my head. Angella spoke to her as she climbed in last. I think she explained my hearing loss because Margaret then repeated something into her mic. I didn't immediately see Horse and it wasn't until Margaret pointed to the small cargo area behind our row of seats. He was sitting against the bulkhead wrapped in a blanket, his bandaged foot out in front of him. His mouth was moving, and I believe he was speaking to me. I threw a salute.

Margaret said something and Horse gave me a thumbs up. Angella pulled the door closed and we were off the ground just as the sun peeked over the far horizon. Out of habit, I pulled the headphones over my ears. The good news, with background noise being blocked by the headset, I was able to faintly hear Angella, who was sitting to my left, ask, "How long until we can get medical help for Jimmy's ears?"

Margaret answered, "It's called threshold shift and, frankly, there's not much to be done. It's either temporary or permanent damage that occurred when the gun went off. There's no medical reversal that I know so we'll know the extent of the damage within an hour."

"Why didn't you take Horse back to base?" I asked, letting them know I could hear them, and curious about what was going on.

"Hey, welcome aboard. Glad you can hear," Margaret said.

"Left ear. Only still faint," I answered.

"That's a good start," Margaret replied. "In answer to your question, we managed to stop the bleeding. Have enough plasma on board to shore him up. Orders were to set her down on the mountain. Too much activity below to chance going out and back."

"Where are we headed?" I asked.

"Orders are to drop the passenger in Brownsville along Highway Forty-Esight. Car's been arranged for him. You two are headed for Coast Guard Station South Padre Island."

"Check that," Angella injected. "All three of us are going to SPI."

"Negative," replied a voice I identified as belonging to the pilot. "Not our orders."

"Please get command on the line. Better yet, get Admiral Boyle. Tell him Angella says it's mission critical urgent."

"I can't…"

"You can—and you will!" Angella demanded, her voice hard with authority.

Mazdani, who had been quiet up to this point, came alive. "This is General Mazdani speaking. I am your passenger and I demand to speak with Admiral Boyle. That is a direct order."

The earphones went silent. The pilot must have switched to an external communication channel. Hopefully, a highly secure external channel.

It took several minutes before the pilot said, "Angella, Admiral Boyle on the horn for you. Go ahead."

"Admiral. This is Angella."

"Go ahead with your traffic."

"Our passenger has requested being present when we first uncover the…the…merchandise. He insists on personally observing its removal from the site and verifying for himself the authenticity of the crest."

"Put him on. I must speak directly to him."

"He is listening."

"Please state your name."

"General Bijan Mazdani."

"Standby for voice identification. One moment."

The line seemed to go dead, causing Angella to throw me a puzzled look. I held my finger in the air signaling for her to give it a few minutes.

The silence continued far longer than it should take to verify his voice print. My assumption was they were working other logistics.

"Sorry to take so long, General," Boyle finally said. "Go ahead, state your request."

"Admiral Boyle, it is my desire to personally inspect the recovery site and observe in person as the first cask is uncovered. That would mean a great deal to me."

"General, what you request comes with a high risk? Do you accept the consequences of such a risk?"

"I have been at risk my entire life, Admiral. A life is only worth what one is ready to risk it for. I am ready."

"Your voice has been verified. We will honor your request. New flight instructions will be delivered momentarily. Have a good flight." The headphones again went silent.

Two good things came from that conversation. The first was that Boyle cooperated with minimal fussing. The second was that the hearing in my left ear came back almost entirely and I could now hear faintly from my right.

THIRTY-FIVE

I removed my headphones and leaned close to Jimmy's left ear and whispered, "I love you." He immediately pulled me close. We sat that way for several minutes with my head against his shoulder. I wanted to tell him everything that had happened, but I knew it would have to wait until this operation was over.

I dwelled on what happened in the last six hours. Four dead men, three of whom I witnessed having their heads blown open. My stomach retched at the horror of it and I hoped I'd never become immune to that horror. My resolve to retire strengthened. Do it, I told myself over and over. Just do it.

SPI? Not Brownsville?

The original plan was to land at Brownsville and from there quickly drive over to Boca Chica Beach, go up the beach a distance and head down into the tunnel. All straightforward and exactly the way we rehearsed it on Sunday. A lifetime seems to have passed in those few days. My headset back on, I hit the talk switch. "Anyone know why SPI and not Brownsville?"

Margaret answered immediately, "SpaceX launch day. Road's closed. Camera's everywhere."

"What's changed? We've known about the launch all along."

"Over my pay grade. Sorry. Just following orders."

"New plan is?"

"We drop you at Coast Guard Station South Padre Island. From there they'll land you wherever you're going."

The SPI Coast Guard station is a major search and rescue facility near the southern end of the island. Admiral Boyle was in command before his promotion, so he knew the area well. My guess is he's arranged to approach Boca Chica Beach from the Gulf using some form of landing craft. "ETA?" I asked.

"Barring any unforeseen…eh…turbulence…we should touch down at thirteen-thirty-five," the pilot immediately responded.

By turbulence I assume he meant Mexican air patrols. For all I knew the cartels might have their own air patrol. This is a world changing by the hour, and one I barely understand anymore. I said a silent prayer for all the women victims released last night and another prayer for all the women still held captive. I added a third prayer, giving thanks I wasn't one of them.

I forced my thoughts back to our operation. If we landed on SPI at one thirty and immediately transferred to a watercraft, we could possibly be on Boca Chica by, let's see, say, two-forty-five, give or take. Knowing Boyle, there wouldn't be any big delay in the transfer from air to sea, so my calculation shouldn't be far off. I again leaned close to Jimmy and signaled for him to remove his headset. When he did so, I asked, "Do you happen to recall what time the SpaceX launch is scheduled for today?"

He didn't immediately respond, and I thought he hadn't heard. I started to ask again.

He held up his hand. "I'm trying to recall. I think there are two, possibly three, twelve-minute windows. First possibility, I believe, opens at two-twelve. The preferred window opens at three-eighteen. I don't recall the third window."

"Why would they pick one window over another?"

"Weather, primarily. Could be something else, though. Electronics. Some tracking device. Some glitch downrange. Who knows what?"

"You think they have the tunnel repaired and the rest of it ready for us?"

"We wouldn't be going to SPI if they weren't ready. I'm guessing the tunnel was repaired within hours after we left. These folks do this all the time. I saw their faces. No one was overly concerned. All in a day's work."

"I want this over, Jimmy. Over and done with. Behind us for good."

I sensed Jimmy wanted to ask or tell me something, but he held back. When Jimmy acts this way it's usually something serious. I silently agreed with him, this wasn't a good time to work through important decisions.

Glancing over at Mazdani, I saw he was busy on his phone doing God knows what. Maybe directing an attack on

Bagdad or bombing one of our embassies. I knew. He could be supervising the capture of more woman and children to fill the now depleted supply chain. He worked hard to convince me he was one of the good ones, a gentleman. There's no denying he's a sociopath through and through. A dangerous sociopath. The thought of him becoming King of Persia sent chills down my spine.

"Better of two evils," I'd been told by Dill when I voiced that concern earlier in the week. I didn't believe it then, and I certainly don't believe it now. I thought about the guys who dropped atom bombs on Hiroshima and Nagasaki and how they learned to live with the aftermath. At least for them they hadn't known ahead of time what was in store. I can't say the same for me.

Jimmy nudged me. "You're agitated. Suggest you get some shuteye. We'll need everything we got to bring this home. Love you."

"Love you as well," I said, laying my head on his shoulder and forcing my eyes closed.

"Five minutes to touchdown," the pilot announced four hours later. I blinked my eyes open and searched the ground for clues as to where we were. That proved rather easy. We were passing low over the Brownsville shipyard where several offshore derricks were in various stages of repair.

The pilot followed the ship channel out to the bay. The SpaceX launch pad was off to our right and the view was blocked by both Jimmy and Mazdani's bodies. Dolphins were ping just beneath us in the bay, leaping and having fun while chasing their dinner. The sun was bright as it most often is, and the bay was calm. A good sign if we were going to amphibiously land on Boca Chica Beach.

I had a thought and clicked on the mic button. "Any chance of rotating this puppy so I can see the rocket getting ready for launch?"

"Negative. Our flight path is being tightly controlled for security reasons and I can't deviate." The earphones clicked off, then came back on. "But…but here's what I can do. When we're over the pad I can rotate in place. Give you a good view. That won't concern them one bit."

"Much appreciated," I said.

The landing pad appeared directly below, and off to its side an ambulance was parked, its red lights flashing. I assumed that was for the guy, Horse, in the back. The pilot, true to his word, turned the copter 180 degrees allowing an unobstructed view of the majestic rocket tethered to the launch pad, smoke billowing up from its base.

"What a view," I said into the mic. "Thanks."

We then went straight down, the door opening almost before the wheels touched. To my surprise, the person standing just outside the door was Deputy Homeland Secretary Diane Sweet. "Welcome to America, General Mazdani," she said. "You are hereby granted a diplomatic waiver for this day only. When your business is concluded on Boca Chica, you will be escorted back into Mexico. Is that clearly understood and agreed upon?"

"It is, Madam Secretary. I very much appreciate your kind offer of assistance. My appreciation extends to your President as well."

"So, there is no misunderstanding, there is no record of you being here. If all goes according to your plan and you are accepted as King of Iran..."

"King of Persia," Mazdani corrected her.

"...King of Persia, then you will be welcome to come visit us officially. Is this your understanding?"

"It most certainly is, Madam Secretary. It most certainly is. And I thank you for this opportunity for me to prove my heritage and claim my rightful position. I will be forever grateful to your country."

"You do understand going out to where the merchandise was found can be extremely dangerous. We built a tunnel under the water, but even so it can..."

"What is life without its risks? If I am unwilling to take the risk, why then should anyone do so for me?"

"I understand Jimmy Redstone and Angella Martinez will be your guides in the tunnel. Is that also your wish?"

"Indeed, it is so. I have the utmost trust and faith in these two fine people. I am pleased to call them friends."

"Then I wish you every success and I hope it all works to your satisfaction."

Secretary Sweet then helped Jimmy down from the copter and said a few words in his ear. I started down to the ground behind Jimmy and she took my hand, holding it longer than necessary, "Thank you, Angella, for what you have gone through. Getting a lead on those poor women and children was an unexpected positive outcome from this operation. And I can't thank you enough. Tomorrow, you and Jimmy will be debriefed in Washington. I've set aside time on my calendar for you so we can have a little private chat. And, how about tomorrow night you and Jimmy be my guest for drinks and dinner at the restaurant of your choice?"

"I don't know…"

"I'll see you tomorrow. Now go, bring this all home."

Sweet stepped back and a uniformed Coast Guard officer directed the three of us to follow him to the water side of the building. A relatively small skiff compared to the massive ocean-going cutter towering over us, idled at the dock. We boarded and proceeded slowly, clearing the other vessels in the small artificial harbor. Soon, the engine revved and we skimmed over the water, seemingly airborne.

We passed dolphins frolicking at the southern tip of the island and headed southeast through the long channel known as the Brazos Pass. The craft slowed when three-foot waves sprayed over the skiff drenching us. In the warm sun it felt refreshing.

The Starship rocket grew larger as we progressed south, its bottom half now totally engulfed in smoke. I searched for the derrick over the tunnel but couldn't see it.

Fifty minutes after leaving the Coast Guard station the skiff turned west, heading for the sandy beach. The only evidence of activity on this part of the beach was the port-a-potty sitting in the dunes. The beach was closed for the launch and was deserted of cars and people. The time was two-fifty.

The captain skillfully maneuvered the skiff through the small breakers, allowing the waves to wash it up onto the sand where it came to a rolling stop. "Carry your shoes. You'll be more comfortable that way," he suggested "Hurry, though. You've only a half hour before the three-twenty launch time. I believe it's still on schedule. Enter through that Jonny up there. Code's two, one, four. They'll do one more sweep of the beach at three. Gives you ten minutes. Go!"

All three of us went over the side, our shoes held high, running through the surf and across the shell-free sand like kids on vacation. I arrived at the potty first and quickly entered the code. Brushing the sand from my feet, I slipped on my shoes, swung onto the ladder, and descended into the darkness. Jimmy, and I presume Mazdani, not far behind.

THIRTY-SIX

Angella went down the ladder first. I sent Mazdani ahead of me and was half-way down when I realized we had no equipment. That meant no light. Cell phones, perhaps. How long would they last if we used them for flashlights? There was no turning back. I visualized the area inside the potty-shed, trying to determine if we overlooked a stockpile. I remembered nothing. I thought that since Angella was a few minutes ahead of us she would have found lanterns by now and turned them on. Yet, no light was visible from below.

I went down ten more rungs and a circular shutter-type mechanism unexpectedly opened around me. Shadows were visible through the opening. Two more rungs and I heard Angella's voice.

When I finally touched the bottom, Mazdani, who had been mostly passive since we left the cabin, except for his brief exchange with Boyle, was animated. "Jimmy, this is great work. I know tunnels very well and this is certainly first rate. Come along. We have work to do."

I followed him into the main tunnel, where the flat work truck we rode on before was replaced by a teacup appearing car with space enough for two people. Angella was already in the car. "This wasn't designed for three, but we can make it work if we stand instead of sit," Angella suggested.

"Not enough height in the tunnel," Mazdani said, taking command. "Jimmy, you and I sit. Angella, you sit on Jimmy's lap, put your feet in mine."

I didn't like that arrangement, but he was right. There was no other way. "Worth a try," I said. "I doubt if Angella can get her legs in."

It took several iterations before we could make it work, with the exception that Angella's leg now covered the control panel. Mazdani leaned as far to his right as he could and extended his arm to its limit so that his fingers just slid under Angella's calf.

"Off we go," he called.

The car lurched forward into the dark tunnel. Lights came on as we entered the dark area and they went off behind us. This continued as we progressed down the track, retracing the path where Angella and I took our trial run.

"Hold on," Mazdani called, "I can push this even harder."

The teacup gathered speed, seemingly flying down the track. At this speed the car would certainly come off the rails when we rounded the bend and headed out under the Gulf. "Slow it down. There's a curve coming up," I said to Mazdani who was grinning like a schoolboy at Disney World.

My warning was of no avail, coming a moment too late. The cup, on its own, slowed almost to a stop, rounded the bend and again gathered speed. These engineers sure love their automation; that much was for certain. I assumed it would stop near the end before crashing into the raw earth where the barrels were buried.

"How will we know how far to go?" Mazdani asked a moment later.

"To the end of the track," Angella said. "That's where the wine is. That's where we're going."

"I mean, how will we know we are there? So, I can stop this thing."

"Good question," I said. "The lights are automatic. They sense where we are. It slowed for the curve. Can't imagine it won't stop at the end."

"One way or another," Angella quipped, "it'll stop at the end. Promise."

We didn't have much longer to wait. The car began to slow. "You doing that?" I asked.

"Haven't moved my hand," Mazdani replied.

"Seems we're at the end of the line," I said, stating the obvious. "All out."

Angella, of course, went first, untangling her legs and awkwardly maneuvering to stand. I motioned to Mazdani to follow her out of the car, but he declined. "I'll sit for a moment. I want to pray. You go."

"Tools are over here," Angella called from several feet in front of the car.

I followed her lead and found the tools, as well as an orange circle sprayed on the dirt wall directly in front of us. The end of the tunnel structure butted up against the dirt face. Any digging we did would be in an unprotected environment and subject to cave-ins and slides. I hoped we wouldn't be digging into the dirt wall too far.

Mazdani's prayer session was shorter than I expected and a moment later he stood beside me. "Should I assume the wine casks are within that orange circle?" he asked.

"That's what I assume," I answered. "Angella, you have any other take on this?"

"Can't think what it would be. My understanding from Steve Hathcock is that the wine was in barrels. That's what the historians believe. The General, on the other hand, believes that only if it's in casks would it be genuine. That's why he's down here with us. To see for himself."

"The family crest is definitely on casks," Mazdani insisted. "I know there are stories of the crest being on the barrels, that's of no importance to me."

"Okay, let's get at it," I said, anxious for this to be over with. "There's two shovels and two pickaxes. I'll take an axe."

"I'll do the same," Mazdani said.

"I'll follow you with the shovel," Angella said. "I say we start at the top of the circle and work downward."

Angella called out three-twenty-two as our start time, coinciding almost exactly with the rocket launch. How's that for a coincidence? Going up into space to find treasure of one kind and going down under the sea to find treasure of another.

The hole grew from top to bottom and side to side. It was slow going, but an hour later it had grown to a full two feet deep and three feet in diameter.

"Nothing, yet!" Mazdani announced, a trace of dejection creeping into his tone.

"Should we call it quits," I asked, knowing what his response would be.

"No! No! No! It's in there. All good things take patience. We will keep digging." Mazdani insisted,

"Another go at it then," I said. "It's getting too deep for good leverage."

"We are close," Mazdani insisted. "I can feel it!"

"Stand on this dirt pile then if you need to," I said, "it'll give you better leverage.

Mazdani did as instructed and proceeded to swing his axe with the authority of a twenty-year-old.

He and I, standing on either side of the hole, synchronized our strokes so that either his axe or mine hit every two seconds. The hole was going deeper and getting wider by the minute. Water began seeping in. At first it was welcomed as a way to soften the dirt. But soon the dirt turned to mud, and the ground became dangerously slippery.

"How about you two taking a break," Angella called. "I'll clean the mud out of that hole while you rest a moment.

By the way, they rigged cell reception down here. Launch was delayed until next window."

I gladly stepped away. I don't know about Mazdani, but my back throbbed, as did my arms and legs. I climbed into the cup to rest.

A few minutes later, Angella announced, "Hit something! Something hard."

"Probably a rock," I said, too sore to move.

"Bigger than a rock."

Mazdani grabbed a shovel and moved Angella aside. "I'll do it." His strokes were fast, but shallow. "Something's here all right. A big something." He threw the shovel into the mud and leaned into the hole, using only his fingers.

I called to him. "You can't get far with only your…"

"A barrel!" Mazdani shouted. "A barrel! I believe more than one! Two! Possibly, even three!" He pointed to two humps, before resuming his attack on the wall, working even faster than before.

Mazdani's fingertips were raw and coated with red mud, but he continued to pull pieces of earth away from the barrels. Angella, using a small pointed shovel, was busy freeing the second of two barrels from the dirt.

It took several minutes before the fronts of two barrels were essentially free of dirt and mud. Fastened to the fronts of each barrel was a coat-of-arms with what appeared to be five black lions on a once yellow background. I jumped out of the cup, grabbed my axe, and called to the General, who was frantically scraping dirt from around one of the barrels. "Take a break, General. This pick will work faster."

To my surprise, Mazdani stepped back allowing me to lean into the hole and begin chipping the dirt and rock away from the barrel. The dripping water was now a steady stream and a real threat to collapse the hole.

"It's moving!" shouted Mazdani from over my shoulder. "Got to get those two out before this all slides in!"

I dropped the axe and started using my own fingers to clear away what was now essentially mud. I wiggled the first barrel toward me. Its movement caused a mini dirt slide behind it, which served to free the second barrel. I couldn't lift either barrel, but they slid rather easily on the now slippery surface. No liquid sounds came from inside either barrel. I feared for the worst.

"Help me lift this one down," Mazdani directed. "We'll get the bung out and see what we have." When the barrel was safely on the ground, he expertly loosened the bung. For a man who didn't drink I had to wonder.

For Mazdani, the moment of truth had arrived. For me, I just wanted this over—one way or the other.

"Mademoiselle," Mazdani said to Angella, slightly bowing, "Please do me the honor of opening that barrel."

Angella stepped forward and pulled the loosened bung out with a single tug. Mazdani leaned over the barrel, peered in, frowned, then pressed his nose to the hole. He stood with a slight half-smile on his face. "I smell nothing," he pronounced joyfully.

Why the lack of smell pleased him was a puzzle, as were so many other things with this *would be*-King.

"Jimmy," he called, "please hand me your axe."

I did so, fully expecting him to slam the axe head into the wooden slats. Instead, he lifted the axe over the top of the barrel and twisted it until the pick was positioned directly over the bung hole. He then carefully lowered the point of the pick into the barrel. The pick slid in a little more than halfway and stopped. He tapped lightly a few times, his smile growing broader with each tap. "Solid as I thought! I think we found it!" He threw the axe on the ground and called, "Hurry, lay this on its side."

When the barrel was down, Mazdani again took the axe only this time he used it to strike the metal barrel hoop. It moved slightly. He then hit the bottom hoop. Same result. Six more hoops to go. One by one they moved. It was slow going, but Mazdani worked as a man possessed. Finally, the last hoop slipped off and the barrel staves fell away leaving behind a pile of ceramic casks. On the floor under the pile I saw two gold coins.

At least Steve would get his payday.

"See!" Mazdani shouted with elation. "I've found my heritage!" Angella take a picture!"

While Angella retrieved her phone, Mazdani carefully rotated the casks so that the baked in imprint of each one could easily be seen. To my eye the imprint was a collection of hieroglyphic symbols. Mazdani translated, saying, "Shiraz, Persia," as he pointed to one set of symbols; and "Qajar Dynasty," while pointing to another set. What wasn't in question was the coat of arms fired into the clay on each cask just below the symbols: Three black lions leaping from a vivid, yellow background, just as Mazdani had envisioned it. I trusted the powers that be were capturing this historical turning point on video.

"Allahu Akbar!" Mazdani shouted, planting a kiss on Angella's cheek. "When I am crowned King of all Persia you must come to celebrate with me. You will be an honored guest!"

"What about the wine?" the practical side of me asked. "I thought it was worth a lot of money."

"Enough to finance my succession, yes." He then carefully pulled the seal from a cask, smelled the fragrance again, and smiled. "It has not turned. It is still good!" He tasted it and handed it to Angella. "Here, my lady, be the first after me to taste my ancestor's handcrafted wine, from the royal Persian vineyard."

Angella took a sip, smiled and passed it to me. I'm by no means a wine expert, but this stuff tasted okay to me.

"We must get that third barrel out," Mazdani said. "See it back there? We will dig that one out."

"That's not possible," I told him. "This entire wall could collapse and bring down the tunnel with it."

Mazdani studied the muddy hole, water still pouring in, before conceding. "Then you and I will remain here," he said decisively. "I must keep watch to assure the integrity of this find. Angella will go back and bring workers."

"All this water coming in. It's not safe," I replied. "Come out with us and we will all come back with the right equipment."

"This is the future of Persia! I cannot leave anything to chance. Hurry, Angella. Call back and tell them to prepare."

"Come with us," I insisted. "We can…"

"I issued an order," Mazdani barked, his back ramrod straight, his jaw clenched. "I expect that order to be obeyed. Now go!"

This had been one of the scenarios the team had rehearsed. After an appropriate amount of fussing, Angella *reluctantly* agreed. Saying her "goodbyes," and "be-carefuls," she kissed me lightly, climbed into the waiting car and started back toward the front. She hadn't gone more than twenty feet when the walls, the floor, the barrels still in the hole, everything around us, began to rumble. The noise continued to increase, and the rumbling turned to shaking. At first the shaking was slight, a few seconds later it increased dramatically.

"It's not safe down here," I called to Mazdani. "Even if this doesn't collapse, we could drown! Come out with me. We'll come back when it's safe." I turned to leave, hoping to catch up to Angella. Remembering how explosives had been set to collapse one tunnel section to save the others. I wanted to at least move into the next section.

"I'm not leaving!" the General proclaimed. "This is entirely too valuable to the future of Persia. It must not be forgotten; it is worth a fortune!"

Was it kingship he was seeking—or wealth?

Angella stopped the car and I could see her checking her phone. Then the teacup started back toward me, stopping a few feet away.

"Jimmy," she shouted, "This should pass in a moment." Her voice was barely audible over the din. "Rocket launch. Five…four…three…two…one. Blast off!"

The ground stopped shaking almost the instant Angella announced 'blast off'.

"Go!" I said to Angella. The sooner you get them down here the sooner we can get out of here. There's too much water already. Love you. Now go!"

The teacup shot back down the track and I turned my attention to Mazdani. He was standing ankle deep in what is best described as a thick rock and shell infused, sand-laden muck. Leaning far into the hole, he continued chipping away at the now almost fully exposed third barrel. The only good news, the water had slowed to a trickle.

THIRTY-SEVEN

The further I move away from Jimmy the higher my guilt level increases. The violent rumbling and shaking thankfully stopped and the water from the walls and ceiling had slowed to a dribble. Going for help felt better than remaining and arguing. Still, I couldn't quell the sinking feeling building within me. When my cell buzzed and I reflexively reached for it, my finger slid off the control button. I was fascinated watching my cell phone screen as the rocket slowly lifted off its pad, trailing fire and smoke in its wake. Starship was going straight upward, slowly at first, then quickly gaining speed. Down here it was deathly quiet, but up there I could only imagine the noise.

Without warning, the rocket wobbled, the fire spewing from its bottom stopped. Instead of continuing straight upwards, or tipping slightly east, its trajectory went flat. Starship was now heading out into the Gulf of Mexico on a direct trajectory to Florida.

The fire reignited at the same time as the rocket's nose rotated downward toward the water. Seconds later the rocket, seemingly under full power, impacted the water. The screen went blank.

"OH MY GOD!" I screamed when the tunnel again began shaking, only this time even more violently. I threw the gear into reverse, racing back to Jimmy. The car slowed on its own before the tunnel end and rolled a short distance before it came to a complete stop. I was still a good distance away from where I last saw Jimmy. The only sound I heard was that of dirt chunks, shells, sand, maybe water, hitting the top of the tunnel section, which was beginning to sag under the weight.

Jimmy suddenly appeared not far ahead waving for me to go back. Without waiting for my reply, he swung back toward Mazdani who was working a few feet behind him, almost lost in the haze of falling dirt and water.

Mazdani appeared oblivious to the impending disaster and continued to knock the rings off the second barrel. Thrusting two casks into Jimmy's hands, he motioned Jimmy to get them out of the tunnel. Jimmy grabbed his arm, but Mazdani pushed him away and picked up two more casks.

The end of the tunnel above Jimmy's head separated from the dirt wall and was bending inward showing signs it was about to collapse. Positive that if we didn't get out in the next few seconds the whole tunnel would collapse and we never would, I screamed, "Jimmy! Get out!" Even if his hearing hadn't been impaired, he couldn't hear me over the rumbling of the shaking earth.

We're directly under that rocket!

"Jimmy," I again screamed, "run!"

I can't imagine he heard me over the noise, but he swiftly sprinted toward me, both casks held tight against his chest. Horrified, I watched the tunnel begin to collapse as the far top corner rolled up behind him rapidly progressing toward me. If Jimmy could outrun the collapse, it was going to be close.

Dropping one of the casks, he picked up speed and was now thirty feet, ten yards, a first down length, away. Something was wrong! His gait was off! His knee! It must have split open because the tunnel was now clearly rolling up faster than he was moving.

Pointing to the cord over my head, he gave the universal tug sign. Oh My God! He wants me to set off the explosives in his tunnel to save my tunnel—and my life.

Pulling that cord would kill him. I couldn't! I just couldn't! "I love you!" I yelled, knowing he was unable to hear me, but I had to say it.

Suddenly, he gained ground and I was sure he was going to make it out of his tunnel section in time. I reached for the cord, planning to pull it the instant he crossed the line into my tunnel.

"Five…four…three," I called, encouraging him to run faster.

Remembering the problem on Sunday I was ready to pull that cord with everything I had.

"Two," Jimmy was less than five feet away.

"Boom! Boom! Boom!"

The explosive devices around Jimmy's tunnel section went off on their own a second before I was ready to pull my cord. Tons of dirt, rocks, shells, fell from the top and collapsed from the sides. Jimmy was caught in full stride and his body tossed forward. We were only a few feet apart when a stream of sand laden water slammed into my chest sending me sprawling backward.

Knocked out of breath, I lay on the wet tunnel bottom struggling for air, covered in sand listening for any sound coming from where I last saw Jimmy. All I heard was water dripping and an occasional chunk of dirt hitting the tunnel. Then the earth ceased shaking. A moment later my lungs recovered and I began digging myself out from under the sand and crushed shell-laden dirt.

Soon I was able to take a couple of wobbly steps before my body kicked into full motion. Standing at the top of the heap of rocks and sand where Jimmy had fallen, I frantically tore into the mound determined to find and free my lover.

"Leave it, Angella," Dill's familiar voice ordered through a speaker mounted somewhere close by. "Team's on their way. They'll dig him out."

I wasn't going to leave it. I couldn't. Jimmy was under here somewhere and I had to free him. I desperately clawed at the muck, pushing rocks and shells to the side, ignoring my raw and ripped fingers and totally unaware that blood flowed freely from a deep cut on my arm. I heard a muffled sound and stopped digging for a moment horrified that the dirt mound might be collapsing.

The sound came again. From almost directly below me. I dropped to my knees and frantically dug toward the source.

There he was! Lying face down, covered in wet sand, his left hand, the one still holding an unbroken cask, outstretched. A ton of dead weight lay on top of him crushing him against the tunnel floor.

My heart pounding wildly, I frantically cleared his head and face and pressed my cheek against the tunnel floor. His eyes were closed and his lips blue from lack of oxygen. If he was breathing, it was shallow at best. I squeezed his hand letting him know I was there with him. "I love you, my darling Jimmy. I love you," I whispered, my lips pressed against his ear. "Hang on. Help's coming."

It felt like an eternity passed before I sensed—or imagined—a return squeeze.

Other Books by David Harry

Jimmy Redstone / Angella Martinez Series

the Padre Puzzle

the Padre Predator

the Padre Paranoia

the Padre Pandemic

the Padre Poison

the Padre Phantom

the Padre Phony

the Padre Pirate

General Fiction

[Under the name of David Harry Tannenbaum]

Standard Deviation

Out Of The Depths]

Adventures In The Law

Acknowledgement

The idea for a Jimmy Redstone/Angella Martinez venture into sunken treasures came over lunch one day at one of SPI's many watering holes. I sat listening while my good friend, Steve Hathcock, spun tales of shipwrecks, hidden doubloons and buried treasure. His stories are fascinating, as are his theories of where valuable items are most likely to be found.

Steve has researched the sailing ships *Pride* (and its alter ego, the Arrow Gance), and the *Queen of The Sea* and he has studied the Union Navy's blockade of the Rio Grande during the Civil War. That blockade alone, one can imagine, raised havoc among the pirate trade and many a shipment of wine surely found its way to the bottom of the Gulf of Mexico. Steve's accounts of the Peacock Thrown and how it relates to Iran and of pirates banished from Texas to Matamoros, as well as what all's buried in the SPI dunes are fascinating to say the least. You can follow Steve's adventures at Steve@southpadretv.tv

Thank You

A great big Thank You goes out to my co-editors, Charles Hamilton Kappauf, Jr. and Brenda Goldberg Tannenbaum. They both went far far beyond the call of duty in their quest to correct my grammar, punctuation and seemingly endless spelling "typos".

Longtime fans will realize that Tiny has changed from using the slang word *Kapish* to the proper form *Capisci* at both Chuck and Brenda's urging.

Special thanks to Ginger Wakem, a fellow member of the Dead or Alive Mystery Writers Forum, for her painstakingly detailed plot comments and editing. Thanks also to Rick Pullen, also a member of the Dead or Alive Mystery Writers Forum, who provided valuable comments on an early draft.

Thank you also to Suzie MacKensie and Susie Morehouse, two great neighbors who took the time to read and comment on the first proofs.

My deepest appreciation, as always, goes to my wonderful wife Mary who spread her orange marker over the manuscript—and made it better in the process.

About The Author

David Harry and his wife, Mary, have a home on South Padre Island, Texas. When he isn't writing, David enjoys biking, traveling, and model train building. If David is off the island, he, Mary, and their dog, Franco, can usually be found enjoying their old stomping grounds of Pittsburgh, Pennsylvania, and more recently, Miromar Lakes, Florida.

Communications

David Harry can be reached at Authordavidtannenbaum@gmail.com. You can follow David Harry on Facebook: davidharry (or patentguy) and on twitter: david1harry.

www.ingramcontent.com/pod-product-compliance
Lightning Source LLC
Chambersburg PA
CBHW032142010726
47494CB00002B/317
* 9 7 8 0 9 9 6 3 6 5 0 7 9 *